Out of Stone

by john g rees

BLACK WATER BOOKS, 2013

Cover Design by Mohamed Sadath
Interior Layout: Danil Mullagaliev

Printed in the United States
ISBN: 978-0-983-19207-7

*For all of us
who struggle with demons.*

Out of Stone

PART ONE

Sechra hid in the cab of the small forklift. With the salvage barge suddenly abuzz, the little girl was forgotten about, for the moment. Usually she would hide away and read, oblivious to what the adults were about. This time it was different. Instead of running, they were making a stand. Sechra was not about to miss it.

She gathered her little bag of toys. Dolls and teacups. If she became bored, at least there would be something to do. On the way to her hideout, Sechra stopped by the galley and smuggled some fresh Danish, napkins and some flatware to finish up the table settings. Last night was Chinese night in the dining hall and all of the utensils had not been put away. A tray of chopsticks sat with the forks and knives. She grabbed a handful, determined to finally find out how to work them. Once in the cab, her breath steamed up the windows and in her mind, she was invisible. Mittens on, Sechra would wipe a small circle on the glass to be able to watch what was happening.

With the barge deck pitching from side to side, the young charge of Karuna Danesti strapped herself into the operator's chair to keep from being tossed about as she watched four people dressed in funny clothes put on a play. The audience stood in the sleet and blowing rain while Riana Danesti stood before a lectern like a priest in church. She could not hear what Riana was orating, but the whole atmosphere became serious, the way adults get when it's important to them. Sechra screamed when one of the men in the play stabbed Riana in the leg with his spear. *It was only a play*, she told herself, in an effort to deal with the shocking realism. The blood and look of despair in Riana's eyes triggered within the little girl a series of horrible memories. In her short life, she had seen despair far too often in the eyes of the men and women of her tribe. Blood always came with it. The anger, hatred, anguish and wretchedness she witnessed through the cracks in the boards of the outhouse molded her innocence into something that would ruin the child in her.

Sechra's memory:

The gypsy encampment in the mountains had swelled in recent weeks. Armed forces were rounding the people up and taking them away. The gypsies came to Sechra's camp for safety, but found only death and enslavement. The camp normally held around thirty people and children. It had grown to more than 150. With only two outhouses, there was always a line. Sechra accepted this, as did the other gypsies from the camp. The people that came were refugees, fleeing bondage. It could easily have been themselves that were forced to hide from merciless forces with no more than could be carried by hand. It was a terrible situation that made a hard life harder. But this was how the gypsies survived. They were a very loose, tight-knit group.

When the soldiers came, there was nowhere to run. They had encircled the camp like a noose and closed in. Helicopters strafed, mothers held babies and children. Did I mention there was no mercy? Sechra's grandfather grabbed the child and made for the outhouse. He pried the seat up just far enough for both of them to squeeze in. Easing Sechra into the sludge, he followed, resecuring the seat, then huddled with the girl in the farthest corner away from the drop zone.

The air was thick, making both of them choke and gag for the first few minutes as water streamed from their eyes. Thick ammonia fumes left them convulsed in agony. Through her pain, she only dimly heard the screams of her family and tribe. Herded like cattle, the captured Roma were given a lesson in obedience they would never forget. Some of the head men were crucified, their bellies split and entrails hung in the open air. They died slowly before a hundred pairs of eyes. Others were impaled. Whips and the butts of guns were used to force the bystanders into participating in the ritual. Beaten until they could take no more, a skinned pole was placed in their hands and the orders given to skewer one of the leaders. Stripped and shamed, they begged for mercy, but there was none. Most died before the tip of the pole exited their mouths. Those that didn't bore grave witness to the extremes of the demented mind.

Sechra viewed the horrors within the mire beneath the outhouse. Her grandfather was a little too tall to take advantage of Sechra's perspective. Otherwise, he would have wrapped her in his coat to keep her from viewing the unspeakable. She watched in shock, unable to voice her feelings at the terror she was witnessing. Sechra choked on the inhuman desecration she was being forced to learn. You could say she was too young to see such things, and she was. The innocence of youth was washed away in a tide of blood and excrement. The hatred that was being nurtured by the madness within her would not let Sechra look away. Her fear was subdued by accepting the law of darkness. Darkness lives at the expense of light.

Sechra was pulled from her macabre trance by her grandfather. Someone had entered the outhouse. A gun was set down, followed by the unclasping of buckles and zipper. Light shone for a moment as the lid was raised and was just as quickly closed as an ass took its place. They froze in fear. Grandfather held her close, his back to the hole in an attempt to shield Sechra from the splatter.

After the exhibition killings, the soldiers went to ransacking the camp. Forcing the slaves, as the gypsies now were, to gather their tools, food, and clothing, they loaded them into the wagons for a trip deep into the mountains. It took two days and the outhouse was in continuous use until the wagons, people and military left for hell on earth.

The heavy clouds that hung over the glen where the gypsies camped mimicked the pall of doom that arrived with the soldiers. Even with the cloud cover, their eyes stung painfully from the glare as grandfather and granddaughter climbed from the shit-filled hole in the ground. Dray set the child down once they were out in the open. He could no longer carry her. For two days and more they stood in the knee-deep filth, unable to sit. When Sechra's legs failed her, Dray held her in his arms. They both collapsed. The lack of food and water left them spent. They slept the afternoon into dawn the next day.

Sechra was up before the old man. She hobbled through the encampment in search of water. If it were lighter, perhaps she could see better. If the tears would stop pouring from her eyes, that would help, too.

She stood before the cross on which her father had been hung. She thought of the Christ staring at her world. Guts dangled from the gash across her father's stomach. Sechra stood on her tippy toes to touch what was left. Glands and intestine hung limp and semi-dry, around which buzzed black flies. She wobbled on her toes and grasped the innards in a futile attempt to keep from falling. Sechra hit the ground before the cross, into the mud created by Dad's bodily fluids. A sloppy mass of organs and entrails cascaded down upon her, burying her face. She screamed, but when she attempted to inhale found herself suffocating. She choked in silence.

Dray limped as fast as his crippled legs could carry him towards the cry of the child. She thrashed and flailed amidst the crucified in the center of the camp. God, it was a horrible sight. He stumbled and fell next to Sechra. Dray immediately began wiping the ugcch from her face. Pulling smaller glands from her nose he sat her up, slapping her flatly on the upper back. It failed to eject whatever had gone into her mouth. Grabbing Sechra from behind, he performed the Heimlich maneuver. On the third attempt, a section of lower intestine erupted. She coughed and gagged while Dray soothed her.

From behind a cluster of destroyed yurts, the mobile homes of some, came a clank, followed by steps. Dray forced Sechra back into the filth at the base of the cross.

"Do not move, little one," Dray whispered, hoping whoever it was would assume they were dead. The two gypsies sure looked the part, covered in shit, guts and flies.

The noise became louder and moved into the open area around the pikes. It was slow in its inspection of the grounds as two sets of steps came closer. Dray was able to hear the heavy breathing, like that of a large animal. Sechra remained perfectly still while the old man forced himself to keep from trembling. The nightmares of childhood were becoming all too vivid in his aging mind. The breathing was now right on top of them. He could feel the heated air being exhaled onto his neck. Dray cringed, fearing the worst as it brushed the back of his neck. Then, without warning, the wet lick of a large tongue was felt tasting the sweat on his neck. The smell of the creature somehow came through the odor of feces and rotting flesh.

"Sasha, where did you come from?" Dray sat up and petted his mule's nose. "Sechra look! Sasha is here." He knelt and picked up the little girl who was now frozen in panic. Dray limped around Sasha to the wagon, placing Sechra down in the bed. Someone in his camp had hidden Dray's wagon from the soldiers and left some supplies. He walked Sasha to the stream and unhitched her from the wagon so she could feed and drink. The supplies held some clean clothes, potable water and a handful of potatoes.

Downstream from where the mule was drinking, Dray carried Sechra to a still pool and undressed them both. He treated the little girl most delicately. As delicately as a stonemason could anyway. Her skin was blistered and rashed from continuous contact with bodily waste. Dray scrubbed her gently with grasses and fragrant weeds. Once the smell and filth were far downstream, Dray was able to get her to smile and laugh a little while playing in the water. It lightened her melancholia, but did not abate the darkness that occluded her young eyes. To be certain, they had seen too much. And it wasn't over yet.

The next week was spent burying the dead. Sechra wanted to help. It tore at Dray to allow it, but she was all he had. So he let her dig the graves. Dray would do the nasty work of bringing down the crucified and impaled. Her soft little hands began to scratch at the ground. It wasn't long before they were blistered and bleeding. A fierce determination gripped her. She hid her hands when Dray would come to help. He would stop her digging if he knew. By the end of the week, Sechra's hands were scabbed over, beginning to callous. She decided that from now on, there would always be some difficult task and to keep her hands hard as a constant reminder of survival and its cost. If you were to look past her hands and into her heart and soul, you would find a similar ossification to these otherwise tender areas. Sechra's hate and anger would inure her, nurturing a darkness usually reserved for the damned.

Sechra wiped clear the little circle on the fogged windshield just in time to see a man shoot Riana in the shoulder. Sechra screamed within the confines of the cab once more. It began with the firing of the gun and seeing Riana recoil as the bullet hit her in the shoulder. The wailing continued as a monster rose up from the deck of the barge in front of Riana. It was hideous and soon Sechra was whimpering for she recognized the monster. It was akin to what she nurtured in her heart.

Riana's words now echoed across the work platform, pounding the beast into submission. Sechra was frightened as the words drubbed into her.

She grabbed her bag and opened the door to the cab, just as the beast was being exorcised. She saw the wisp of smoke—it was all that was left of the monster—and ran across the deck to a stairway below. Every time she looked back it was there, getting ever closer. Sechra became lost amidst the maze of containers. The door was ajar on one of the big boxes. She ducked in and hid amongst the storage. The phantom wisp of black smoke curled around the door. Sechra screamed and backed up against the wall of the container. The smoke roiled towards her, engulfing her, forcing little Sechra to breathe it in.

***

The Present

It was her first exhibition. Well maybe not the first, but it was her first big one. The Bucharest Metropolitan Museum held 'New Artist' symposiums twice a year. 'New Artists' generally meant those who were still living, mostly aged sculptors and painters who led prolific lives but were never world renown. Sechra was the youngest sculptor ever to grace the halls of this elite institution.

Thora Wozniak stalked the open spaces where Sechra's work would be displayed. She was tall and thin, with close-cropped red hair, simple business suit and black flats. She moved smoothly around the Cneajna wing of the museum, effortlessly, like she was at home.

Her speech was clean and businesslike, but could warm to the occasion when necessary.

"I still don't understand why she won't give us pictures of the works, instead of just the dimensions. This is highly irregular. Without knowing what they look like, how will we create a flow to the space?" she said speaking to Sechra's manager, Frederick Cezar.

Cezar replied, "I am aware of this, Thora. It is the way she has always worked. You get to see one piece of the installation. She gets away with it because of the exceptional nature of her work."

Thora ran her hands through her hair. "She gets away with it because of who she is. Don't get me wrong, Frederick. The museum board still can't get over the restoration paid for by her stepfather. It cost millions and we are very thankful. It's just that I spend a good deal of my time planning these installations and feel a little out of the loop on this one."

"When it comes to her art, everyone is a bit out of the loop," Frederick replied in commiseration. "Here is the layout," he said, pulling a file from his briefcase. "It's pretty normal for her. Sechra drew the floor plan for you." He handed the plan to Thora.

She looked the print over along with a page of instructions. Thora shook her head.

"The lighting will be awfully low for a gallery showing," she remarked, more to herself than Frederick.

He heard her just the same in the large empty hall. "Sechra's work leans toward the macabre. In her words, 'the darkness enables the viewer to better see themselves.' Don't ask me. I am just a liaison between her and the outer world." Frederick laughed a little uncertain. He had been managing Sechra for years. The work was difficult, but rewarding. Bringing an obscure artist to the forefront is never easy. She was, however, very prolific, which is one of the reasons she avoided the limelight. Carving granite, marble and basalt took up her time. All of it.

Sechra's craftsmanship set her apart from her contemporaries. When compared to Balzac or Giger, she would blush for her sculptures were not imitating either, yet seemed to have a blend of both. The grit of realism morphing with the bizarre captured the onlooker in an extremely disturbing moment in time. Even the most rigid and experienced art experts came away unsettled, shaken to the core and looking like they needed to go to the bathroom. Were the sculptures grotesque? Some. Were they utterly fantastic forms from a wild imagination? No, they were far too realistic. To say they came from a dark and morbid mind would be right and wrong. Talking with Sechra was always a pleasant affair. But then you never knew what was going on just behind the eyes.

One of the challenges in trying to show her work was the nature of it. The human forms were carved with meticulous detail. One could almost see sweat and tears pouring from straining muscles and pleading eyes. It was the detail that gripped you, keeping you from looking away and compelling you to look closer. In some cases, a patron of the arts would be carried away from the mutilations of human nature turned in upon itself. Whether it was scenes of torture and humiliation of the damned or the look on the face of the torturer - one saw oneself: the crucifier and the crucified.

Polite society avoided it. Her name, however, opened doors and closed others. Kcirb. It was an old Romanian name. By itself, it would have left Sechra to be another starving artist, even though her grandfather, Dray Kcirb, had written the constitution of the New Republic. It was Sechra's relationship with the Danesti-Cneajna's that gave her a leg up. She was too young at the time to be any real help, but she had been there when the now Prime Minister, Vlad Cneajna and his wife, Riana Danesti, stood against the dark forces and prevailed. The result was a free Romania.

At the time of the election, tradition was kept to satisfy those who remembered, but was altered to be pragmatic in a modern world. Instead of just the Boyars, or wealthy landowners, deciding the outcome, now all landowners had a voice. Those who did not own land could also be heard, but their voice was smaller. The new constitution was ratified without contention. Just giving the people basic human rights would have been enough; they had been so long without any. The constitution mimicked the old U.S. constitution, with a spin to accommodate the gypsy peoples.

***

The old smallish beach house and barn had been fashionable two hundred years ago. Now it was derelict, a victim of war and sea air. The Black Sea pounded the empty, rock-strewn shoreline. Just beneath the roar of the surf one could hear the steady 'tink, tink, tink,' of a mallet tapping a chisel against stone.

The home may have been a wastrel amongst the beach houses, but was by no means empty. The signs of life were few enough, a motorcycle in the carport, smoke from the chimney and the 'tink, tink, tink,' of a hammer. It was the metronome of a madness hidden behind sparkling eyes, a hard body and brilliant smile. For the last five years, Cezar had driven to the seaside estate between Eforie Nord and Eforie Sud to plan exhibitions and keep an eye on his artist. Every time he arrived, Sechra was hard at it. Never once had he seen her relax. His other clients needed to be driven to produce. Frederick was forever dangling money in front of them for incentive. Not so with Sechra. He always felt as if he were intruding. As far as Sechra was concerned, he was. Frederick Cezar, like all middlemen, was a necessary evil.

Shafts of light pierced the night through gaps in the roofing and blankets over broken windows. Within the cavernous barn, lights on a string lit works in progress. Grim shadows darkened the walls, which were covered with the drawings from which Sechra carved. The sketches were life size as were the sculptures. Eleven monoliths stood in the open area. Some complete and some still needing work—all of them a gruesome reminder of the past. A few depicted atrocities more than a thousand years before and some far more recent. Patrons of the arts could rarely distinguish between the older scenes and the newer. Man's inhumanity to his fellow man and the nightmares that ruin our lives are timeless.

A black face juts from a huge chunk of basalt. The muscles and veins of the neck are stretched and taut. The cheeks are pushed back as the mouth, with lips curled in terror, screams in silence. The tongue is missing. In its place something pointed is protruding from the esophagus. The eyes bulge in agony as a hand pulls on the hair.

Hammer blows are busy creating the shoulders and torso. Chips fly from the rock surface into the light and escape into darkness. A cloud of dark dust is suspended by the warmth of a floodlight. Squatting on a makeshift scaffold, clad in a jumpsuit and dust mask, Sechra hammers away at all the bits of rock that don't belong. Removing the excess to reveal that which lies just beneath the surface. Her hands are calloused from years of handling the rock and the steel tools that shape them.

Sechra was short like all the Kcirbs. Her body was sinewy and strong from hard work. From time immemorial the family Kcirb had been stonemasons. One could say it was in her blood. Shaping stone came naturally to her. But it was not easy. It was not often that she would break from the grueling effort. When she did, there was no sleep. If it wasn't the relentless imagery that assaulted her mind, it was the ache of cramped hands and arms that kept her from slumber. Each time she finished a piece, the memory of it would disappear. This was one of the reasons Sechra worked so maniacally, to rid herself of the scenes of death and torture. Day and night she went at it until she would collapse, unable to hold onto the mallet or chisel any longer. More than once Frederick Cezar would come on his regular visits only to find Sechra unconscious on her work platform. This time was no different.

Salt spray was already drying on the hood of Cezar's four-wheel drive. The waves were big this summer, blown by steady trade winds across the vetch of Black Sea. The BMW motorcycle was in its carport protected from the elements. With no sound of a sculptor's mallet, Frederick knocked on the door to the beach house and waited patiently. After ten minutes and hurting his hand pounding on the door, he followed the trail around back to the barn.

The barn had been built back in the dark ages as an insane asylum. Chains still hung from the rock walls and a few instruments of torture rotted underground in a cellar. There is no history or legends of the asylum, for who would want to remember what horrors took place in this little piece of hell where the sick of mind were treated by the Inquisition. More recently, it had been used as a barn to stable horses used by tourists to ride the beach in summertime. The enterprise failed after two seasons. Some say it was the brackish water, others that the darkness had come again. Either way, the horses slowly lost their minds. Out on a late summer's ride, a pair of honeymooners rode at sunset when a cold wind out of the north chilled the coast. With the onset of the wind, the guide had them change course to return to the stable. Hoofs kicked up the sand in an effort to beat the weather. Nearing the trail that would lead them home, the horses became disturbed, refusing to go any farther. When the guide, Torx, spurred his ride to go up the path, the horse bucked wildly, sending the unprepared rider to the ground. Torx got up and took the reigns, pulling on the crazed animal. At this the other two horses reared up and began to stomp Torx with the bride and groom still astride. The couple began screaming as all three horses crushed the life from Torx, finally shattering his skull. In panic the wife fell from her mount. Immediately the horses were on her, breaking little limbs and spine.

After sunset a search was organized to look for the missing party. It didn't take long to find them. At the edge of the tall grass that borders the high side of the beach, the three people were found. Torx's corpse was a few feet from where the husband futilely tried to protect his dying wife. The ponies returned to the stable late that night, but would not allow themselves to be handled or groomed. The stable boy was scared. He had seen the bodies. The image of a shod hoofprint stomped into the woman's face was still etched in his memory. The last thing he wanted was that mark on his face. The gate to the pen was open and the lead mare was being more than stubborn. He went to slap her bottom. His hand barely brushing the fur when a rear hoof came at blinding speed and connected with his forehead, peeling the skin back and dislodging a large section of his skull. He wobbled as the world began to swim around him. Now the other horses were kicking their gates open and began to finish what the mare had started.

By dawn all the horses had been put down. A backhoe was brought in and a mass grave dug.

Then the barn sat empty for nearly twenty years before being stumbled upon by Sechra during one of her long, solitary walks up the beach from the family estate. In her early years, while learning to sculpt, she had the time for such walks. She was an orphan. Though adopted, she would always consider herself one. Her parents/guardians were gone much of the time, dealing with 'matters of state' as they would say. She was raised by the estate staff and a small army of tutors. But it was Aunty Karuna who first noticed her desire to shape stone. As a child, Sechra had her share of toys to help her forget the past. Instead she played on the beach, finding hard rocks to chips way at softer ones. She chiseled away at one for days. Karuna had to come and get her for dinner. The poor child had passed out from sunstroke. Karuna rushed her to hospital in the big Mercedes. Two days later, they were able to bring her home. During that time Karuna went back to the beach to see what had so absorbed the little girl. What she found should have disturbed the woman. There were full face and profile carvings out of rounded beach stones. Karuna mistook the crude and hideous cuts for talent without training and took immediate measures to have an art teacher included in the home schooling. Of course this proved slightly more difficult than she originally perceived. One look at the little macabre carvings and the artist would refuse to teach the child. What was it about them that caused this reaction? Let us say love is blind. For Karuna truly did love Sechra.

Eventually a young stonecutter saw potential in the little girl's work. To make ends meet, Igor carved tombstones. In the evenings, he cut stone for himself. Igor was smart and had been to college. He was also the only one who offered to teach Sechra.

"Perhaps it is my heritage that draws me to teach the young one. My family goes a long way back in time with the Kcirbs. We had been indentured with the Draculs then. The Kcirbs were brought in to build their fortresses. We were the laborers and the Kcirbs worked us hard, for there was no other way than hard. But they also raised us up with education. Wherever they went to work, education came with them.

But quietly, for they would have been put to the pike if it were known that they taught the serfs to read and write. But mostly I would like the position out of respect for Dray. He died before our people saw freedom, but he led the way," Igor finished, with no small amount of national pride.

"Yes I know," replied Karuna quietly, remembering the old man and his wagon and mule. "They were inseparable," she said absent-mindedly.

"Did I miss something?" questioned Igor.

"No, no. Just an old woman musing."

"If it's any consolation..." began Igor.

"Yes I know. I look fabulous," Karuna laughed.

"How did you? Well, you do!" Igor laughed as well, being fool enough in the pleasant banter without worrying about social barriers. It was one of the gifts a hard life had given him. Igor was able to look at any man squarely and see his equal, be they Voivode or broom pusher. On the other hand, Igor was no fool. He knew whom he was talking to.

He had been a young cutter when revolution and terror cut a bloody swath across Romania. Fresh out of college, he was keen on the current events. The internet provided ample graphic coverage, but little of the inside details. His computer courses were as vital to his schooling as art classes. He just wanted to know what was going on and became an accomplished 'closet hacker' in the process. Igor knew of some of the adventures of Karuna Talian, now Voivode Danesti, and her daughter. They had been integral in aiding the Roma in their fight for freedom. There were gaps though in the history and Igor hoped to fill some of them in while training the gifted young girl.

'I must have had the right answers,' Igor said to himself as Karuna led him through the museum of a house to Sechra's room. Sechra was examining some different stones when Karuna knocked. She hardly acknowledged the two adults when they entered and selected one rock from the pile; a piece of black volcanic glass.

Sechra walked across the room, eyes locked on the ebony sheen. She looked up when she was toe to toe with Igor. "Good morning, Karuna," her big black eyes turned to Igor, "Good morning, Igor, can you teach me to carve this?" Sechra asked smiling.

"Let me see your hands," he replied.

Sechra carefully set down the stone and looked at her worn and beaten callouses. She turned back to Igor, slightly embarrassed and a little proud. Sechra glanced at Karuna, who nodded affirmatively. She turned her palms up and lifted her arms.

Igor held the little hands delicately as one would a Hummel. He looked closely; rubbing her callouses with his thumb and forefinger. Sechra didn't fidget. Instead she was amazed at Igor's hands, thrilled with what a life of working with stone would do to them. The scars and misshaped digits were like medals of honor. When he was through, he gave Sechra her hands back.

"You have beautiful hands," he said, meaning it.

"Can you teach me?" Sechra asked hopefully as she had just found some one who understood beauty.

"No."

Her heart sank through the floor. Sechra lowered her head, but did not cry.

"I was hoping that perhaps you could teach me?" Igor said smiling and lifting Sechra's chin.

"Do you really think my hands are beautiful?"

"Yes, I do," Igor responded.

***

The Cneajna-Danesti estate, which housed the mysterious mosaic tiles, had been turned into a museum after the revolution. The mosaics still captured one's attention if not awe, for they still had the effect of hypnotizing the viewer. The tile though no longer drew the spectator into the drama. Instead, it thrilled the eye with exquisite graphic detail. Archaeologists still came to spend their summer vacations studying them. The mosaic tilings were the most accurate source for understanding life in the fifteenth century. The battle scenes were the most popular. Here the graphic details were the most satisfying and repulsive. The mundane images away from the fight, however, were equally as full of life, death and detail. Merchants, sailors, tradesmen, women and children all had their lives told in little pieces of broken ceramic.

A long, sleek and deadly looking black boat rested at the private mooring in the estate. The vessel satisfied those who came to the museum with less than an avid interest in history. Like the mosaic tile work in the house, the boat was one of a kind. Karuna had it brought back from storage in Istanbul. To her, it was fitting that the boat be moored here as it played an important role in the liberation of Romania. Few knew of the vessel's history except the immediate family, and Karuna kept it that way. Too many unanswerable questions could arise from knowledge of ownership. Mostly, she had it brought to remind her of Jake and Giovanni.

***

Karuna had visited the two a few years after uniting the Roma. She spent a year with them at the little hideaway on a beach in Baja, just north of Todos Santos. Learned to surf and tried her best to 'kick back'. Her relationship with Jake grew and blossomed like she never thought possible. The passion that was held in check for years was finally able to release itself, free of the dark past and worries of a nation.

"This is a side of you that I have never known," Karuna said as they walked the beach at night. "It suits you Jake."

"I'm still trying to get to know the new me, too. Learning to deal with more time on your hands than you're used to isn't as easy as it sounds."

"You have a handle on it, Jake. The palapas probably never looked so good," Karuna laughed lightly making Jake smile.

"That laugh is pure magic. It suits you well too."

"There was never much time for it, or reason."

"I'm glad there is now," Jake replied. After a moment, his smile slid off his face. He could always tell when there was something going on in Karuna's head. "What is it?"

"I have to leave, Jake." Karuna was solemn.

"I know, when?" Jake asked.

"Tomorrow. I made arrangements last week."

"Is there something I should know about?" Jake's query was dark. He was not worried about their relationship, although he would miss her desperately.

"No Jake. It's Sechra. Riana and Vlad are busy with their child and the business of running the country. They just don't have the time the little girl needs."

"The kid's been through a lot, that's for sure. I'll miss you." Jake stopped and took off his backpack and unfurled a beach towel. They made love till dawn under the light of a full moon.

***

Karuna lived at the estate. Vlad and Riana would come whenever the chance to get away presented itself. When the family gathered, the museum would be closed to the public to allow them some privacy. Vlad, as Prime Minister, rarely had a moment out of the public eye. His knowledge of Romania and its history—he had lived so much of it—made him an ideal candidate. Dray Kcirb, before he died, had written a letter to the governing committee endorsing Vlad Cneajna, as long as the Voivode pass a simple blood test. Which of course he did. This pseudo nomination was seconded by several other members of the committee, one of which had walked in Cneajna's shoes for a while. Bela was one of Cneajna's staunchest supporters.

Since then it was all work. Putting the infrastructure of a nation back together was nothing compared to trying to erase the devastation wrought by Tepes. The minds of the men and women that had seen horrors beyond imagination are much more difficult to repair. The psychologists had their hands full, but Vlad knew what men needed. And that was work. There was plenty of it. The Romanians didn't quibble about putting their backs into the effort. Cneajna had learned from the Americans circa 2010. When their country started coming apart at the seams and the people needed work, there was none to be had. Community projects, such as those in the 1930s, smacked of communism. And that would not do. But it was the people themselves that opened the door to Megacorp. They didn't want to work anymore, preferring a monthly government check. The thought of actually having to work for the money didn't fly. Needless to say, a few years of this bullshit made Megacorp's takeover that much easier.

Several years before, Romania experienced what would be termed an aggressive takeover in business terms. It was. The fact that it was bloody beyond compare was the only difference. Megacorp had purchased a cash-strapped Romania for the land, to run an energy pipeline across it. Once the line was in place, Megacorp wanted to flip the country, which had no other resources to capitalize on as far as the huge corporation was concerned. Through a twisted turn of events, they found a buyer. One of the former ruling families, the Draculs, was willing to strike a business deal with Megacorp for taking over the land. The only stipulation was that the Draculs keep the energy pipeline free of harm.

When the darkness returned to Romania, it bled the land and its people. Contractual agreement allowed Vlad Tepes the II to rule as he pleased. And he did. An iron fist reached out to crush the soul of a people.

Then there were those like Karuna Danesti, her daughter Riana, and Vlad Cneajna who desired a free country. Life under corporate rule was a yoke to wear. You were worn to death slowly and unnoticeably. Of course life under Tepes' rule was death. Neither was considered an option.

Shortly after Tepes' return, there was a revolution. Thousands upon thousands died horribly. In the end, a few patriots were able to wrest control from the new ruler. Now the Cneajna-Danestis were trying to rebuild their county's heart and soul.

After returning from Baja, Karuna eased into her position. It was only natural she keep a low profile and out of the public eye. Were she not of native blood, Karuna would not have been allowed to return. She acted as curator for the estate and filled in when the regular staff was gone, giving tours and lectures. She knew the art better than anyone, except perhaps Vlad Cneajna, and those lucky enough to have her as a docent came away with an experience they would not soon forget. She used her position to explain not only the distant past as depicted by the mosaic panels, but also how the recent revolution mimicked the ancient battle. She did this to get it across to her audience to 'never forget', or let it happen again. Igor was always in the groups that Karuna led. He also came away with understanding more of Karuna and her role in the recent past.

"And here you see the slave under the load saving those it would have crushed" Karuna explained to a group of students. 'Oohs' and 'ahhs' rolled through those in the tour, including Igor. "We believe this a recent addition to the mosaics."

"But how could it have been changed?" Igor asked the unvoiced question in the students' minds.

"An excellent question Igor. Does anyone have an idea of how that could be?" she asked the group. Silence was her answer. About half the older students had become hypnotized by they tiles, the other half were simply mesmerized.

"Okay! Okay! Snap out of it everyone!" The sharp claps of her hands along with her raised voice brought the kids back into the here and now.

When the chatter settled down, "Did you all see how you were drawn into the image?" There was scattered agreement among the young adults. All were a little embarrassed at how easily they had been duped. "Don't worry kids. It happens to all of us, but it does help to explain how the change in this particular piece may have occurred."

"I don't understand, Dr. Danesti," one student piped in.

"Trust me," Karuna looked over her darkened glasses to read the girl's nametag, "Charna, you are not alone. The artist who created the mosaics used a most ingenious technique to capture the viewer's attention. As you all just witnessed."

"Way better than four-d, doc," shot the group's smartass.

"You are correct, young man. Now take the idea a step further. Modern video arcade games do the same thing. They pull you into the action and you become part of it. Your decisions affect the way the game goes, at least to some degree. The difference is that with virtual, it is just a game. Nothing really happens. With the mosaics it was different. There was a time that not only did they capture your attention, you became part of the action as well, physically. Only, in theses scenes you could die by becoming part of it." This last statement was accompanied by guffaws from the student body. But they clammed up when they saw the serious look Karuna was giving them.

"The man you see supporting the load had entered the image by focusing on one of the slaves and 'became' him. He was nearly killed for saving his fellow slaves, and for beating the whip master. If you look closely you can see the whip master being tended to. He glares at the slave." Only a few of the students concentrated on the tile images. Most held back, not wanting to be drawn in. Igor was among the close lookers.

"We have no proof that the image was changed. It is now in a digital format. Fortunately the tiles no longer have the added dimension of reality. Look around all you want. There are refreshments in the gazebo. Please remember the boat is only for looking at. Please do not board it." There is always someone in the crowd that has to sit in the captain's chair and pretend to be racing across the sea.

Karuna bowed politely to the students, slipping to the side and disappearing into her office. She started coffee. By the time the French press was ready to deliver, there was light knock at her door.

"Come in," Karuna said getting another cup. "Have a seat, Igor. I assume you came for the coffee."

"It was one of my motives. This is perhaps the best coffee I have ever had."

"It is an old family roast with beans grown in Turkey. How is Sechra doing?"

"Quite well," said Igor sitting and sipping his coffee. "Her talent with stone is undeniable. Teaching her to draw however was difficult, but it has added dimension to her work."

"Why was it difficult to teach this?" Karuna sipped her brew.

"All she wants to do is carve," he said with a shrug. "It wasn't until I proved it could aid in her creations that she took it seriously."

"Go on," Karuna prodded.

"You haven't been to the studio in a while so you will notice the dramatic change in her work. Up until we started sketching, her work was two-dimensional. Simple reliefs. A little dark for a kid perhaps, but excellent random renderings nonetheless. Now I fear I have opened a Pandora's Box by adding another dimension to her work." Igor swallowed hard. He had a casual relationship with the Voivode Danesti and enjoyed it, but didn't want to step over the line by saying something negative about her granddaughter.

"What do you mean, Igor? You have always been open to me. It is a trait I value highly. So tell me. I have witnessed much worse things than Sechra's taste in the macabre."

"If half the tales I have been told are true, there is no doubt that you have. Sechra's work has become increasingly disturbing now that she is able to grasp her ideas and pencil them out during the moment of inspiration. Who is the man in the mosaics that almost died?" Igor had not intended to ask. It just sort of slipped out after running around inside his head.

"It sounds like I should come down to the studio. Would tomorrow morning be all right?"

"I would like to show you when Sechra is not there. Tonight would good. Say three AM? I know it is a little early, but Sechra is driven by the devil himself and it is the only time I could be sure she is not working."

"I will be there. The hour is not an issue as my concern is only for Sechra. She has had a difficult life, not that you could tell now. But it does come out in her art. So if you are wondering where her inspiration comes from, it comes from her experience. The man in the mosaics is an old friend who gave his life so that we might be free."

***

Sechra hammered away into the night, like she did every night. Instead of running and playing like other kids her age, she spent her time trying to relieve herself of the memories that taunted her, driving her in a maddened frenzy to turn them to stone before they turned her to dust. Of course she hid this manic mental turmoil with a smile, long black wavy hair and a blossoming womanhood. She learned long ago to hide the darkness that crept into her soul. The only release of this nature that anyone would ever see would be the sculptures. Everything else was but a masquerade.

At the age of eleven, Igor had taught her to draw. It was appropriate, for when her blood began to flow her dreams became all too vivid. Sechra was now able to capture the moment in pencil and paper when she would wake from sweat and bloodstained sheets. The crude drawings would be refined over the next few days. When her blood stopped, she was ready to carve. Using the techniques Igor had taught her, to draw to scale and in perspective, unleashed her creativity to levels she had only dreamed of.

Late in the night she would remover her dust mask and safety glasses to review the work. Sechra would run her leathery and cracked hands over basalt surface, marveling at the sense of touch. She saw as much with her fingers as her eyes. Sechra felt for the life, her life that she hammered into the basalt.

Covered in black grit and dust Sechra would climb down from her work platform, tired and sore but hesitant to leave the work for only a few hours. And hoping that during the respite she would not be haunted by that particular image. There were so many.

***

Thora Wozniak walked the empty hall where Sechra Kcirb's sculptures would be displayed. Masking tape marked locations on the floor, like so many police victim's outlines, designated the location for each piece. Of which Thora had only seen one. It was the centerpiece of the exhibition. An outhouse. The detail of the structure was complete down to the nail heads in the wood. The door was ajar, propped open by a machine gun. A soldier sat, his pants down around his ankles as he leaned forward with his arms braced against the door jam. His face is distorted in the spasms of a brutal discharge.

The viewer, in looking over the sculpture, not only feels a rumbling in his or her intestines, but searches for the point in the piece. Most witnesses to the display miss it on the first look over. It wasn't until you bent low, fearing you might shit your pants because of the position and the loose feeling in your bowels, that you saw a split in the boards beneath the seating. A knothole in the wood at the split reveals the eye of a young child staring desperately out at you. You go back and look at the soldier, then back to the split in the wood. At this point there is usually a distinguished dash for the loo. Some never made it in time.

Thora had made a career working at the museum. She started as a docent in college, then hung around after getting a degree in medieval art until there was an opening in the staff. This came after the revolution when Cneajna poured money into saving the nation's cultural heritage. Her first assignment was to oversee the restoration of the castle/museum originally built sometime around 1100 A.D. by the Draculesti during the Crusades. At that time, the ruling family bonded to the Church of Rome for protection. They paid a hefty fealty to the church to keep from being obliterated by the Christian army. Gold gave the Draculs what they wanted. A Papal writ giving them the authority to form an army to help secure the Black Sea ports and trade routes across the country. And most importantly, to rid the land of the infidels of Islam. The Papal writ also gave the 'Order of the Dragon', as the army was known, the same rights as other crusaders. And that was to pillage and destroy anything they saw unfit in the eyes of God.

By the 1600s, the castle sat empty, abandoned and left to rot while the city of Bucharest grew up around it. In 1917, it became a shelter for the gypsies displaced by WW1. Ditto for WW2. Except this time, it was a prison for gypsies captured by Nazi invaders. The castle was a holding pen before the prisoners were sent to Auschwitz or Dachau. After the war, the castle was bought by Vlad Cneajna. There it stood for centuries, a defunct museum. The mammoth gothic structure waited to be reborn as a tribute to the Roma people.

Thora was proud of what had been accomplished. Craftsmen from all over the country had come to aid in the work of restoring the old castle. The task had been formidable. Many of the building practices of the original Goths had been forgotten and needed to be relearned. Thora burnt the candle at both ends to supply the architects with the information they needed to keep to the original design. She loved her work, but did not know at the time that she would end up the director of the museum.

Now that she was the director, Thora was glad she worked her way up. She knew the place by heart. Every gallery, stairway, closet, secret passages, all had been lost to time. The castle had revealed her secrets to Thora. Thora kept them safe.

The Kcirb Exhibition would be the largest show the museum had ever put on by a single artist. Eleven life-size pieces would be brought in by semi-trailers. Thora had done the engineering calculations to be sure the floor would sustain the weight of several tons per piece. She wasn't concerned about damaging the huge slabs of granite that composed the main floor. They had survived much worse during their life. It was the hidden vaults and chambers carved into the earth beneath the floor that raised her concern about the load bearing capabilities. This is also why she had done the math. The knowledge of the passages were hers alone.

Thora closed the door behind her. The unadorned, unremarkable, alcove was like a large walk-in closet. She used it to hold the museum's safe. Thora leaned against the black steel box. It rolled silently and easily on well-oiled casters. The space created was just like the one that was covered up by the safe, empty. She pulled a long screwdriver from her pocket and swept the debris away that camouflaged a small hole at the base of the wall. Inserting the tip of the screwdriver into the hole, Thora dropped to her knees, putting all her weight on the tool jamming it to the hilt into the switch. This triggered a counterbalance inside the wall. A muffled continuous scraping could be heard as the floor began to slowly drop away taking Thora with it.

This was certainly not the first time Thora had used the passage. On the ride down, she tied her hair into a bun and put on a hardhat. The ancient elevator stopped silently in a pocket of sawdust. Suddenly the darkness was swept away by the glare of a powerful flashlight. The soft glow of a GPS display screen showed the complete underground passages that Thora had so far discovered. She tapped at the keys; zooming in closer till she could see where she was and where she wanted to go. Long legs took confident steps in a southerly direction, following a corridor that would take her to a room directly beneath the auditorium where Sechra's works would be displayed.

Thora put on a respirator. The smell of the rotting flesh of several laborers that had discovered the passages had not quite dissipated. She had covered their bodies with a blue tarp. She should bury them, but what with the rock floor and all... Instead she pulled a tape measure and calculator. Rats scurried from the bright light as she measured the support columns, spacing, logging all the information into the calculator. Later she would punch the numbers and grind out the relative load ratings for the different locations. The GPS was invaluable for this work. Especially since she did it alone. With the last of her entries logged, there was still time to explore and map more passages.

Cold and damp from centuries of being unexposed to air, Thora stepped around puddles and parted curtains of cobwebs and tree roots that feebly attempted to clog the route. As she was discovering, all the tunnels led to somewhere. One lead to a freshwater spring where the water was cold, clean and potable. Another to a grotto amphitheater with seats carved into the walls. A torture chamber, a bathroom, a kitchen. The tall thin museum director could only guess at some of the various functions the rooms could have provided. Of actual artifacts, she had found none. There were holes that once held chains, but no chains. The kitchen had no cutting boards or utensils. All that was left were a couple of carved depressions in the rock, used for grinding or washing, and the wood-fired oven. Thora wondered why everything had been taken. No clothes, rags, broken tools or torches. With the exception of the murdered workmen, the place was empty. Passing the 'bathroom' she took advantage of the facilities. When she was through, the tape measure came out again. With it came the dimensions of the openings into the cesspool. Two things came immediately to mind. One was practical, the other rather a disgusting idea. Thora aimed the light into one of the holes. She had to do a double take. There was a ladder descending into the depths.

The safe rolled noiselessly back into place. The hardhat was removed and put away with the flashlight. She dusted herself off, opened the door and headed back to her office.

***

The setting full moon lit the way across the courtyard to the art studio. Karuna admired the way the moonlight dappled the structure and came through the many windows. The silvery illumination helped to capture the essence of Sechra's work. 'Almost bringing it to life', she whispered to herself. The little girl had yet to produce the large works she would become infamous for. The smaller sculptures held, however, in no less a degree, the same disturbing depth of the depraved mind. Karuna knew that Sechra was not insane. To her the girl just had a lot to work out. One piece, her largest to date, was being hewn out of a boulder she found on the neighboring property. Karuna remembered the heavy equipment that arrived to relocate the stone from the beach to the studio. She did not know that Sechra had already begun carving it. Just before the moon slipped behind the foothills in the west, Karuna was able to get a look at the preliminary drawings of what the boulder was destined to be, taped to the wall.

She gasped, stepping blindly away from the renderings and twisting her ankle. Karuna fell into a pile of rock chips and clutter. She turned just enough to let her arms and hands take the impact. Shards of rock cut through the soft fleshy parts of the palm flaying the skin back to the bone. Karuna was just getting to her knees when the lights came on.

"I'm over here, Igor," Karuna said quietly.

Igor shuffled around the tables and easels to find the older Voivode rising to her feet, dark ochre blood running from both hands, looking as if crimson ribbons dangled to the floor. With no rags in sight, Igor ripped his shirt off and tore it in two. He sat Karuna on a bench and wrapped her hands after laying the skin back in place.

"We should get you to the hospital!" Now that the blood had stopped flowing, he could get excited.

"That won't be necessary, Igor. It looks worse than it is."

"Karuna, I saw bone under the flap of skin," Igor said, exasperated at her response.

Karuna knew the wounds were serious. She also knew that she would heal without the aid of a physician. But Igor did not know this and she was temporarily at a loss as how to explain this to the younger man.

Karuna should have known Sechra would show. Since they first met, the girl always had her back. The entry door to the studio slammed open hard enough to shatter the window glass. There stood Sechra in blue jeans and t-shirt, hair tied back without being combed and a nine-millimeter semi-automatic pistol in her hands. She shot one round through the roof. "Who is in here?" she screamed.

Igor stood in front of Karuna protectively. "It's me, Sechra, with Karuna. Now put that gun down." Igor did his best to put all of his authoritative ability into the last sentence. It sort of worked. Sechra pushed the little lever on the side of the gun to release the magazine. It dropped silently into her hand. Setting the clip down she racked the slide back, ejecting the bullet in the chamber, catching it on the fly in a practiced maneuver. The empty gun went in her back pocket, the bullet got installed back in the clip and when it went in her other pocket, she asked, "Just what is going on here?"

"I wanted to see your work. Igor said you were..." Karuna was interrupted by Sechra.

"Don't lie to me, Karuna. If you wanted to see my work, all you had to do was come by."

"All right." Karuna was used to the strong-willed Sechra and wasn't surprised Sechra saw through the whitish lie. "I wanted to talk to Igor about your sculpting, without you here. Where did you get that gun?" Karuna didn't have a problem being equally frank to Sechra.

"Thank you, Karuna," Sechra began, acknowledging the truth. "I've had it for years. I think it was one of uncle Jake's."

"It looks like he taught you how to use it, too."

"He showed me how before he left and told me to practice. So I do. Well?"

"Well what?" Karuna and Igor said at the same time.

"What do you think of my work?" Sechra picked up one of here early busts and looked it over. The eyes were clenched in pain. Lips curled back exposing the partially open mouth that had just begun to scream. Sweat gathered in the wrinkles of the forehead, puddled and ran down the side of the face merging with the rivers of tears.

"I hadn't really had a chance to look," Karuna raised her bandaged hands, "I tripped over something. Igor was just in time to help me."

Sechra raised the sculpture she had been holding and smashed it to the floor, shattering it in a thousand pieces. "That's okay, the old stuff is all shit. Now let's get you in the house and redress those hands."

Karuna looked at Igor and not allowing the youth's rash actions to confound her, smiled and shrugged, "We'd better listen, she has a gun," Karuna laughed. "Can you lend me a shoulder, Igor?" Karuna's ankle was swollen and black and blue.

"If you don't mind?" Igor easily lifted Karuna into his powerful arms. "Sechra, can you get the door and kill the lights?"

On the way to the main house Igor asked, "Is Jake the man from the mosaics?"

"Yes he is. How did you know?"

"Just a guess really. I thought you said he gave his life for the revolution. Sechra sounded as if he is still alive." Igor was pushing it.

"He is. It was a metaphor."

"Oh." Igor sensed that was all he was going to get this evening just as Sechra came running to get the door for them.

He set Karuna on the couch and asked, once again if he should call a doctor. Karuna smiled benignly and declined as Sechra lugged a big white medical box into the living room. "I think I can handle it from here," Sechra said taking the gun and clip from her pockets and setting them on a coffee table.

"My father told me to never argue with a gun," Igor grinned a little nervously.

"Thank you, Igor. Your father sounds like a wise man."

"He was. Good night. I will come and check on you in the morning." Igor bowed his head and left the two women.

Sechra unwrapped Karuna's left hand and sponged it clean. "You have already begun to heal. This is going to hurt." With a small pair of forceps Sechra began removing tiny chips rock, like splinters, from the palm and fingers.

Karuna winced a few times. She knew what pain was and this little surgery was not it. She got to thinking about what Igor said before he left. "Why did Igor use his father's name in the past tense?" she asked Sechra.

"Aturo, his father's name was Aturo, was taken by the black guard before the revolution to work in the mountains. He was never heard from again," Sechra replied.

"How do you know? Did Igor tell you? I have had long talks with him and he has never mentioned his family."

"His whole family was taken. He doesn't talk about it because he is ashamed for not being able to save them. His vengeance runs deep."

"How did you find this out?" Karuna was now wondering more about the girl's own vengeance. She would never speak of it to anyone, even when melancholia would overtake the young mind and weaken her resolve. Karuna would use the times of despondency to try and get Sechra to open up about her feelings. Never once was she able to penetrate the barriers that held back visions of unknown horrors.

"I just know. He did not have to tell me. I can see it in his eyes," Sechra explained.

"What else can you see, Sechra?"

Sechra remained quiet and focused on Karuna's other hand. When she was through, both hands were neatly gauzed and taped. Dark red spots leaked through the cotton but the wounds had otherwise stopped bleeding. Sechra put the big box away and returned with a plastic bag full of ice. After securing it around Karuna's swollen ankle she said, "Don't forget to rewrap your hands tomorrow so that Igor does not get suspicious."

"Thanks for the reminder and your help. Just..." Karuna let the thought drop.

"He wishes for the chance to kill all that remains of the Draculesti family."

***

It was summer in the foothills of the Transylvanian Alps. The alpine meadows of pine and black walnut covered the rolling hillsides in a blanket of dense green. A road had been cut through the forest years before. It ended in a small valley where waterfalls fed a turquoise lake. Brightly colored tents clustered near the shore, shelter for the group that had taken holiday. Fishermen plied the water in little boats while children played at the shoreline. It was a Hallmark moment.

"IGGY!" his mother called from the cook fire. She was busy making borscht for lunch, her fingers tinged purple from the roots.

Igor came running from the beach when he heard the call. He was red from the sun and wet from the cold mountain water. "Yeah Mom. What can I do to help?" He really didn't want to help and one eye was watching the shore where the rest of the kids were preparing for a sand war!

"Go find your brother. He went to gather some more firewood."

"Aw Mom. The guys are..." Igor whined.

"Just get Tomas. It's almost time for lunch. You will have all afternoon to play. Now SCOOT," she said seriously with a smile for her youngest.

Without hesitation, the lightning fast reflexes of youth sped him off in the direction of the nearest trees. If he found Tomas quick enough, he could still get back in time for the war. He had already made an arsenal of sandballs and hoped they wouldn't be found until he got back. Then he could charge in and let fly, saving his comrades from a most embarrassing attack by the girls. Igor's imagination was as quick as his feet.

Soon he was deep in the canopied forest. The shadows were thick and cold, chilling his wet skin. The forest floor was thick with soft humus under a carpet of undulating moss. Igor imagined he was walking across green clouds when a deep roar began to creep through the trees. Igor spooked.

"TOMAS," he called out. The yell was stifled by a hand that quickly clamped over the young boy's mouth. "Shhhh, Igor," Tomas said under his breath. Igor froze in his brother's arms. The noise was getting louder. It was the sound of machinery crunching through the undergrowth.

Without warning the tall pine forest began toppling around them as the tracks of heavy equipment smashed through the trees. Tomas grabbed the smaller Igor and ran for a huge black walnut he remembered on his hike in. The mossy floor slowed his progress but not the tanks.

"Faster, Tomas! I can see them!" Igor yelled into his brother's ear then closed his eyes.

Tomas saw the tree. It was at least a meter and a half in diameter. On the far side of the walnut, Tomas lifted Igor to one of the lower limbs. "Climb Igor, CLIMB!" And up he went into the green and out of sight. There was no time. Tomas turned to see the personnel carrier less than thirty meters away. They saw him! Tomas spun and ran towards the lake. The treeline was near. He could see the hard line of shadow and bright sunlight.

Igor climbed fast and high. His brother's command had spurred him and fear kept him going. He found a cluster of branches at a spot where a storm had broken off the main branch. The grouping of young suckers that grew from the break would shield him from view and keep him from falling. The height was dizzying. In the bush below he could see Tomas busting through the ground cover. A little farther and he could break into an open run across the valley to the camp. Looking back he could see the machine was having no difficulty gaining on Tomas.

Igor wanted to scream to Tomas to hurry. But he knew he couldn't. The big green machine was now beneath him, belching black diesel smoke high into the tree, making Igor cough and tear. The men riding on the vehicle were dressed in black. A sigil or crest was emblazoned on their caps and shirts. Igor could not make out what it was. He was craning his head out of the nest to see better.

An explosion of gunfire erupted from the carrier in a deafening staccato. Igor watched as the weapon fired bullets that cut down the trees in search of Tomas. When they found him, Tomas was just leaping into the sunlight. His strong body, in a full downhill charge, suddenly exploded in a burst of red and limbs. The torso had disintegrated in a splatter that turned the grass crimson. Before Igor could pull himself back into the branches, he lost his balance and slid through the little saplings. One could say Igor was lucky to have worked with his father the gargoyle sculptor for his strong hands. He grasped for anything as his body succumbed to gravity. A branch slid by and he got hold. The fresh wood bent, but held without breaking. He was facing the lake in a desperate situation as more men and machinery passed beneath. There was nothing he could do as the vehicles ground his brother into the soil.

When the armored carriers and tanks rolled into the open field, helicopters leapt the hills on the opposite side and began to coral the people before they could run. Igor watched, he could not help himself, as his family and friends were rounded up. Everyone was forced into the freezing water of the lake; splashes of gunfire on the water kept them huddling in a group. The men were separated from the women and moved into deeper water. To the relief of the group, the women were allowed out. The relief was less than momentary. Distance kept Igor from witnessing the details of the crime. His youth kept him from understanding. The women were forced to take their clothes off. What Igor saw then would be etched in his memory forever. He could not remember when he closed his eyes, or if he ever did. Nor the fall when his hands could no longer grip. How long he had been embedded in the foamy moss is a good question too.

Igor woke covered with a sheen of sweat. His head ached like he had been kicked. It was always this way. He dreamed the dream of his generation. It was like ancestral memory only current, personal and horrible. Forest rangers followed the path of destruction left by the mercenaries of the Order of the Dragon. They found Igor wandering the shoreline and ruins of the campground, alone, crying, cradling a broken arm and clutching the cap of one of the enemy soldiers in his good hand. The crest, though smeared with blood and gore, bore the image of a dragon.

Igor knocked at the open door of the beach estate house waiting patiently to be invited in. The smell of fresh coffee almost overrode his civility.

"Come in, Igor. When coffee is on there is no reason to be polite. You are always welcome to make yourself at home," Karuna said returning to the kitchen.

Igor was stunned to see her up and about with a rosy glow in her cheeks. "I thought you might be sleeping in today after the injuries last night."

Karuna raised her freshly bandaged hands, "They seem to be doing quite well. Of course Sechra is an old hand when it comes to first aid," she said passing Igor a fresh cup followed with a pantomime of 'the old soft shoe'.

"Thank you," he said watching her hands and noticing she didn't favor them at all.

Karuna noticed Igor notice and chose to change the subject. "The boat mechanic is here this morning to service the Dracul. He'll be taking it for a spin, so if you want to go and blow the cobwebs out, you better get down to the dock. Here." Karuna filled a travel mug for Igor as the still morning was shattered by the roar of twelve cylinders coming to life. "You better get going!" Karuna smiled. There is nothing like a big engine for distraction.

Dino, the wrench, was just closing the engine compartment when Igor, mug of coffee in hand arrived.

"Ms. Danesti said I might have a passenger this morning. Personally I was hoping for the young artist." Dino saw his candor lost on the stone carver. "Did you ever see the engine before? Ferrari, twelve-cylinder boxer. You will never see another one in this life."

Igor was into rocks, but he couldn't help being impressed by the massive motor. Like the rest of the boat it was in impeccable condition.

"You want to get the bow line?" Dino was loosening the stern mooring line.

"Sure." Igor took his shoes off, untied the line and stepped onto the bow. Stowing the line he noticed a deep gash in the Kevlar on the port side. It looked old and the damage was in stark contrast to rest of the vessel. He followed the non-skid walkway to the cockpit, sat in the passenger seat and began to buckle up.

Dino idled out of the breakwater before strapping himself in. He visually inspected Igor's safety harness before saying, "You ready?" Igor nodded. "Hold on here we go!" Dino smoothly and swiftly pushed the throttle wide open.

The two were crushed into their seats as the Dracul accelerated across the flat expanse of sea. Skimming the surface at 180 kilometers an hour, Dino cranked the steering wheel hard to port then to starboard, putting the 72 feet of Kevlar through some radical maneuvers before shutting her down. The coast was a fuzzy dark arc on the horizon by the time they came to a halt, rocking gently on the water.

Dino left the engine idling while he slid a long screwdriver from a leather scabbard. "Touché," he pronounced with a flair of the slender driver. "Going to adjust the carbs and see if we can get a little more punch out of her. He raised the engine compartment lid like a surgeon opening a chest. With a vacuum meter in one hand, he capped one of the carburetor venturis and made minute adjustments to the fuel-air mixture. Igor sipped his coffee and admired the low-tech instrumentation. 'So twentieth century' he thought stepping up onto the forward deck to take in the view. From this point of view, the panorama hadn't changed in thousands of years as he gazed out to the horizon.

On his knees, Igor ran his fingers along the gash in the bow. His calloused digits snagged slivers of fiberglass and resin. The boat rocked while he was absorbed in removing the little shards.

"She won't let me fix it." Dino commented.

"Huh?" Igor looked up rubbing his thumb over his fingers, searching for any more splinters.

"Ms. Danesti. That big cut. She says to leave it as a reminder."

"A reminder? Of what?" Igor replied satisfied his fingers were free of debris.

"Haven't a clue. Come on." Dino and Igor shuffled to the cockpit. The idling engine sounded like the breathing of a sleeping monster that you didn't want to rouse. Dino didn't mind waking it and seeing just how fast it could come to life.

Freighters from all over the world jostled for space along the coast of the Black Sea. Dino used them as pylons for an insane high-speed slalom race. In that moment, the man was in his element. The tight turns and g-forces generated were however a whole new experience for Igor. They idled up to the fuel dock in Varna. Dino was used to the spotlight of attention that came with the Dracul in public. In a seaport that has been in operation for thousands of years, the eyes have seen every type of boat ever built. The Dracul, however, was unique from hull design to the power plant. And it was ungodly loud.

While Dino was busy showing off the boat, Igor went for a refill at a coffee kiosk on the dock. Upon returning he saw a portly older man squatting near the bow, examining the gash. His hand jerked away when his soft fingers were stabbed.

"You got to watch out. It's still a little pointy," Igor cautioned.

"Yes, even after all these years," the man said dusting off his suit as he stood. "I heard the Dracul come in and was wondering if it was Jake. It is a folly of mine. Besides if it was Jake, he certainly wouldn't be here in the middle of the day."

"Jake?"

"Yes, the man who built her. I don't believe we have been introduced. I am Boris and you?"

"I work for Karuna Danesti teaching Sechra to sculpt. My name is Igor."

"I have heard about you. How can you teach a child to carve such hideous figures?"

"I teach her how to use the tools and the techniques necessary. The ideas are hers alone. How have you seen them? She has shown very few."

"I guess I am one of the few." Boris lifted a briefcase that Igor had not noticed before. "If you would be so kind." He handed Igor a small heavy package from the case. "It is for our young artist."

"What..." Igor began.

Boris brought the index finger of his right hand to his lips. "Ahh," he paused. "It was a pleasure to meet you, Igor. Give my regards to Voivode Danesti and thank you for delivering my gift." Boris turned and headed back up the dock. Igor watched until he blended with the crowds and disappeared into the warehouse district.

The gawkers had thinned and Dino was paying the fuel bill. Dino cruised the Dracul to the open area of the harbor before putting on the safety harness. Igor did likewise and asked, "Do you know that man Boris? He came to the boat, but wasn't part of the crowd."

"He always comes. Sometimes he has a parcel to deliver. Ahh, I see you were given one. Who is it for?" Dino was casual in his response, not seeing anything strange in the occurrence.

"It is for Sechra. But who is he?"

"Listen Igor, I don't know what world you come from, but there are some people you just don't want to know about. And he is he of them. If you want to start digging for answers about Boris you should dig your own grave while you are at it. You're not from around here are you?"

"Bucharest," Igor replied.

"Ahh." Dino revved the engine a few times. The ride back to the estate was deafeningly quiet. The roar of the twelve cylinders, however, could not drown out the questions forming in Igor's mind.

***

Karuna and Sechra were having a late lunch when the Dracul returned. Dino set about cleaning and prepping the boat to sit and wait until he came again next month. Igor wobbled along the dock, through the wall and across the lawn regaining his land legs. After a brief but needed stop at the bathroom, he went to the estate to let Karuna know he was back.

"Did you have a blast? Dino lets me drive sometimes!" Sechra glanced to see how Karuna took the disclosure.

Karuna smiled. "I've seen you at the helm." She nodded to a spotting scope.

"Busted, Sechra," Igor laughed lightly. "It was fun. Thank you for the opportunity. You are lucky to have found someone with the abilities and love for the Dracul in Dino. A friend of yours stopped by the dock while we were refueling."

"Really! Who?" Sechra piped with the eagerness of youth.

"Boris. He sends his regards to both of you."

A flash of concern crossed Karuna's face. 'As it should' thought Igor especially after what Dino had told him. Sechra on the other hand kept her excitement and anticipation in check.

"I wonder why he was there?" she asked.

"Dino says he always comes when he hears the Dracul enter the harbor. I should go."

"You're welcome to stay and eat," Karuna added.

"It will be a while before my stomach settles. Thank you again. I will be at the studio."

After Igor left Karuna said to Sechra, "I wasn't aware that you knew Boris."

"We met, like Igor said, at the fuel dock in Varna. He has always been very kind," Sechra said in his and her defense.

"I am sure he has, but there is another side to his personality."

"No doubt there, Karuna. Dino explained that he is an arms dealer and a murderer. And that I should keep my distance and be very discreet. I suppose there are worse things."

"There are, dear. Thanks for being open with me about Boris."

"I love you, Karuna. Without you..." Sechra's eyes welled up but did not spill. Karuna reached across the table and held the hard little hands.

"I love you too, honey."

After lunch Sechra returned to the studio in a knot of anxiety. She had been lying to Karuna for years and the guilt tore at her.

Karuna sat at the dining table trying to digest what she just heard. Sechra was not the sort of person, for she was now an adult and no longer the little girl Karuna had first met, who was of a deceitful nature. Sechra was paranoid to a certain degree, but then who wouldn't be after living her young life on the run. Otherwise she was an upfront, in your face sort. And even though she carved for twelve hours a day, her education continued. It was part of the agreement Karuna had made with Sechra and her stepparents. The schooling came first. Everything Sechra came second.

The girl was quick. She always had been. At the tender age of seven she was already a compulsive reader in an effort to escape, if but for a moment, the disaster life had become for those of gypsy descent. That was all in the past now. Life for the Roma peoples had changed significantly and for the better. This was also true for Sechra, though she had to live through hell to get there.

'She must have been aware years ago when we planned and battled against the odds. Listening behind her books to all we said. How else would she have known of Boris?' Karuna had not thought of him in more than a decade. Sechra said the pistol she had the other night was Jake's. Now she wondered at what had seemed normal before. Sechra's casual manner with the gun had disarmed Karuna. The older woman did not miss the fact that the younger knew exactly what she was doing. Someone had trained her.

When Sechra got to the studio, Igor was busy sharpening chisels. He had also retaped the handle of her mallet. The feel had been gouged by a miss hit and was cutting cruelly into the girl's hand. She hefted the hammer. "Thank you Igor. Sorry I ruined the feel."

"Tell your hand you're sorry. You'll have to redo the tape every once in while. How is your hand healing?" Igor asked.

Sechra had taken a bad swing with the mallet and caught the handle on a sharp edge of stone. "That will teach you pay attention!" Igor had said. The stone had peeled away the skin over her knuckles as well as creating a gnarly rough spot on the handle. Sechra continued to use it the rest of the day and the rough spot wore a bloody blister into the heel of her hand.

"Let me have a look," insisted Igor.

Sechra rolled up her sleeve and took off a cotton glove. "You should wear those more often," he recommended looking under the bandages. "No infection, a little swelling, you're good to go, but I have to insist on the glove until the wounds close." Igor lifted a rag, exposing Boris' package and wiped his hands. "That's for you, from Boris."

"Oh man! I didn't think it would be here so soon," exclaimed Sechra. She caught herself and clammed up.

Igor could tell she knew what it was by the size and weight. "That's the second time today. You're slipping, girl. I've warned you this shit would catch up with you."

"You're right, I'm wrong, I'm sorry." Sechra lowered her head, ashamed.

"You should be. That woman thinks the world of you. But hey, you're an adult and still going through a lot of your own stuff. There are worse things. Well?" Igor asked.

"That's the second time today someone has said that. Well what?"

"It's the sound of someone caring for you. What's in the box?"

Sechra hesitated, laughing derisively at herself for her lack of discretion and began tearing at the tape.

Igor was nobody's fool. He would have been one if he had opened the package to take a look. He had a good idea of what it was. Math had never been one of his shortcomings. Which made the surprise, shock, and thrill of coming face to face with a Heckler and Koch submachine gun all that more spontaneous. It was the most compact, devastatingly functional tool of death Igor could think of. And the first thing out of his mouth was not concern or fear, but a guy thing. "Can we go shoot it?"

Igor started the generator that powered the air compressor for background noise. Then the two headed north along the beach for a few hundred meters. They came to a rock outcropping that stretched from the high side of the beach out into the water for 100 meters or so.

"This is where I come to practice. Dino pointed it out during a test run with the Dracul."

"Is he the one who taught you to shoot?" Igor was going to get as much information as he could during this bonding session.

"Here, load this magazine." She handed him a banana clip and a box of nine-millimeter bullets. Igor knew what he was doing; still he wanted to stretch the moment. Sechra caught him inserting the rounds the wrong way. "Pull those out if you can. See the picture on the side of the clip."

"Duh," was the appropriate response by Igor.

"Dino mostly," she said inserting a loaded magazine. "Out on the boat you know. But that's not very often."

Sechra racked the slide back and from the hip squeezed the trigger and chewed the sand in front of them before drawing a line out in to the water.

Igor was dumbstruck. There is something about seeing a babe shooting full auto that – well, it's a guy thing. She dropped the clip and opened the chamber.

"Boris tried to teach me, but he gets distracted."

"Distracted by what," Igor inquired innocently.

Sechra looked over her sunglasses at Igor and rolled her eyes.

"Oh, and duh again. A little old for you, ya think?"

"Yes, but he is harmless enough."

"Not from what I hear," inserted Igor.

"Fear is an excellent deterrent."

"That may be so but I 'fear' you have it backwards."

"No," she deadpanned. "He is afraid of what would happen to him if his desire went beyond his imagination."

"I know I would want to kill him. With this too!" He held up the gun.

"It is not death he fears. There are worse things." Sechra laughed and loaded the gun for Igor. She handed it back to him with the safety on. "Just keep it pointed at the water."

Igor held tight and squeezed. Nothing happened.

"Flip the safety off," Sechra instructed, "Geez—where were you during the revolution?"

"In a mental hospital." Igor let fly, trying to kill the memories Sechra's remark invoked.

A few seconds later, a grin stretched across Igor's face from ear to ear. "Now that's therapy." Sechra missed the joke but knew it was a good thing.

On the way back to the studio, Igor asked, "Just how did you meet Boris?"

"Like you did. He comes down to the dock. Usually to talk to Dino, but he always has an eye on me."

"Yes, you explained that."

"No. Not like that. More like he is keeping tabs on Karuna and I. Asking how we've been and what we have been doing. Discreetly you know."

They arrived at the studio. Igor opened the door saying, "Wha..."

"This is your last question for the day, make it a good one."

"Well you got me there, young lady. Thanks for putting up with it. Who built her?" Igor said referring to the Dracul.

Sechra thought for a moment, "Jake built it after the original was destroyed, he had the name and registration transferred."

"There was another one?"

"That's all for today folks. Thanks for coming by."

Igor wouldn't be getting much sleep tonight.

***

Thora was eating in the bistro at the museum. Green salad, turnip dressing, and bread sticks. She was reviewing the museum's monthly newsletter when Frederick Cezar strolled through.

"Good afternoon, Thora. Your secretary said you would be here. May I?" Frederick motioned to the empty chair.

Thora nodded saying, "Coffee?"

"Thank you, please," replied Frederick sitting and turning a cup over.

Thora poured. "I suppose you're wondering why I asked you to come in today," she said setting the carafe down.

"I assume it has something to do with the Kcirb installation,"

Frederick replied, realizing the meeting would have nothing to do with his assumption.

Thora pushed her plate to the side and sipped her coffee. "I have always considered you a friend, Cezar. And now I can use one."

Thora always called him Cezar. He liked it. He had always hoped the relationship would move to the next level, but the tone in her voice was more conspiratorial than romantic.

"What's up? Are you okay?"

Thora looked around at the busy restaurant. "We should walk and talk." She stood and waved to the maitre'd, picked up her coffee and left, arm in arm.

"I have been here at the museum since before the restoration."

"You know the place better than anyone I guess."

"Yes and that's also the problem. I found something, Cezar." He glanced around quickly to see if there was anyone close. "What is it, Thora? You're getting me paranoid."

"I suppose there is no reason for it. You see, years ago, after the revolution when the work here began, I found a hidden stairway to rooms beneath the museum. I had sort of forgotten about them. It wasn't until the Kcirb exhibition, and the weight of her pieces, jogged my memory. I went down there to calculate the floor load. Oh Jesus, Cezar."

"What? What is it?"

"Someone else must know about the passage. When I was taking measurements, I found two dead bodies."

"Oh my God! What did you do?"

"Nothing. I don't know what to do." Thora knew she was pushing her luck. She needed help to dump the bodies into the loo. But before that she wanted to climb into the cesspool to see what might be down there. And for that she needed a safety. Someone who knew where she was if she got into trouble.

"I guess you should call the cops."

"NO," barked Thora a little too loudly, turning heads in the area. "I mean, well, you know how the police are. At the very least they would close the museum until their investigation was through. The wrong kind of publicity, and with the Kcirb display in two weeks." Thora feigned confusion and frustration, hoping that Cezar was buying it.

"Who were they?" Cezar asked, bending close to Thora and placing his hand reassuringly on her shoulder.

Thora put her hand over his. "I don't know. But it seems that whoever they are, no one is very much interested in their disappearance. I have been watching the newspaper since discovering them. It was horrible, Cezar."

"I'm sure it was. What do you want to do about it? Remember, I am an art agent, not James Bond."

"I have been so shocked by the whole thing that I really haven't given it much thought. There is something else though." Frederick nodded thoughtfully, indicating she should continue. "While I was down there I came across a cave I want to look into. When I discovered the bodies, well, I realized I was in over my head and could use some help. Would you?"

"I'm not really all that big on enclosed spaces. The thought of going into one to get in another one..." He wasn't joking. A trail of cold sweat ran down the center of his back.

"I'll go into the cave, I just need you there in case I get into trouble or the murderers show."

Frederick's shoulders slumped. 'She needs a watchdog,' he thought to himself. Then again one thing may lead to another. "If you need me, Thora, I will be there. When would you like to do it?"

"This Saturday. I come in often on my days off so it won't look suspicious." She didn't miss his disappointment in the way things were going. After making sure they were reasonably alone, she took his hands. "Thank you, Cezar. I had always hoped something would bring us together." Before he could say anything, Thora wrapped her arms around him and kissed him passionately. He resisted at first. But like all men soon succumbed to the warm embrace and moist lips.

***

After the shooting lesson, Igor spent the rest of the night on his computer. What he was looking for didn't require any amazing hacker skills or state of the art equipment. All it took was knowing it existed. Of course there wasn't much in the way of chronological history, just bits and scraps of information that he would try and put together.

There was an article about a swamped schooner salvaged some thirty years ago. It was discovered adrift in the waters off Varna. Salvage divers patched her up and had the Dracul towed to the harbor at Constanta. Old grainy photographs showed the derelict vessel being pushed into place by a tugboat. An older man is directing the tug while another somewhat younger man stands by, watching. Igor zoomed in on the picture to get a look at the men's faces. The younger man is pale and has his arm in a sling. Curious Igor made a copy of the photo and the blow up. 'I wonder who that guy is?'

The next image, a copy of a detailed woodcut, showed the Dracul, beached and lying on its side. Six pallbearers carry a casket away from the wreck. A seventh follows reading from a book.

Another picture was of the harbor in Varna circa 1895. The docks were full of sailing vessels. It took a while to visually separate the ships from one another. The Dracul was dwarfed by the bigger hulls but stood out the way a racecar would at a truck stop. 'Funny,' Igor thought, 'but there were no onlookers taking advantage of the opportunity to view such a thing.' Looking closely he spied an individual standing in the stern. He held what appeared to be a bottle of wine. Igor zoomed in again and took out a magnifying glass. The man on the fantail was captured in profile. A large beak of a nose reached out from the rest of his face, underneath which rode a black mustache that stretched across his cheeks to the ear. Unquenchable anger flared up inside Igor. There was the man whose order destroyed his family. Igor drew his arm back without thinking and drove his fist through the computer monitor.

***

Thora arrived at six AM on Saturday morning. The pieces for the Kcirb exhibition began arriving earlier in the week. All of them were covered with a heavy nylon fabric that locked around the base so they could not be removed. She growled at the veils. Even she would not get to see them until opening night.

Thora looked over the sample sculpture of the outhouse for the thousandth time. It was so real you could almost hear the soldier grunting and smell the rot. The realism was so disturbing that when she caught the eye of the child peering out, she had to control her urge to puke. Of all the times she looked at the piece, this was the first physical reaction. The eye seemed to be looking right at her. The child knew what Thora had done in the catacombs. Her mind screamed 'That's impossible!' Her guilt was playing tricks on her. Still she couldn't look away from the riveting stare. Thora saw past the eye and head of the child into the depths of the pit.

Sweat broke out in beads on her forehead. Was it the light? Thora's rational mind was being pushed aside. Movement! There was something moving behind the child! There was someone else trapped in there. It moved towards the girl, towards the light, grabbing frantically to get to the little opening. The child would not budge as the other began to scream for help to Thora. Thora staggered back, stumbling over a stack of shipping pallets. So did the woman in the cesspool, stumble backwards and fall into the filth, her scream swallowed by the black water. In a flash before the woman fell from sight, Thora recognized the voice along with a flash of red hair. It was her own.

The night watchman was finishing his rounds. The morning shift would be arriving soon. He entered the unfinished exhibit expecting everything to be as it was the hour before. It was – with one exception. Thora Wozniac was lying on the floor. She had met with Walter, the security guard, when she arrived. They had coffee with conversation consisting of Walter's uneventful evening. He liked his job and enjoyed being around the art. His relationship with the director was purely professional. They had come to like each other as friends and Walter always looked forward to the little conversations with coffee.

When he saw her on the floor, his heart skipped a beat before he broke into a sprint. He stopped when he got next to her, taking a moment to look the scene over before disturbing it. As far as he knew, the building was empty but for the two of them. On his knees, Walter placed his hand on her shoulder and shook firmly, "Ms. Wozniac, are you okay?" He shook her again.

In her nightmare, Thora was running, but there was nowhere to go. Her eyes fluttered. Walter's face came into focus.

"Oh, thank God. Can you see me? What's my name?"

"I can see you Walter." Thora smiled weakly, "What happened?" She couldn't tell him so she played dumb. Which is harder than you think.

"We'll get to that. Right now we check for injuries."

"Oh come on, Walter," Thora said in a lame effort at resisting.

"It will only take a few minutes. How many fingers am I holding up?"

"You're sure you don't want me to take you to the clinic," Walter asked from the door to Thora's office.

"No thank you, Walter. I don't see how a doctor could be any more thorough than you."

"Just the same, director..."

"Go home and have a nice weekend. I'll be fine. It was really quite kind of you. Thank you again   Walter. Oh, let's not make an issue of this. Just between you and me – okay?"

"Unless it happens again," he said sternly.

"That's a deal." The phone rang.

***

Frederick arrived with three semi-truck flatbeds. The rigs held the remaining pieces of the Kcirb exhibit. Thora was at the loading dock when they pulled in. Frederick, a file in one hand and a small pack over his shoulder, dressed in casual business attire, was taking a look at the load when Thora came up and smiled.

"You always come with the deliveries?"

"Only when it is important," handing her the file. "It will take the boys a few hours before they're ready to move the sculptures inside." He looked around to make sure no one was close. "We could do that thing now if you would like."

Thora nodded while inspecting the shipping invoices. "Everything here seems in order. You bring a change of clothes?" Cezar held up his pack and waved to the truckers. They slipped away in plain sight.

Thora closed the door to the storeroom and flipped the deadbolt. Frederick looked around. The room was big enough, but it only took a few seconds before the walls started closing in. He squeezed his eyes shut to shake the vision. When he opened them, the walls were in place, but he knew they wanted to move. There were no other doors or openings. "I thought you said there were stairs?"

Thora went to the far side of the safe and leaned against it. By the time he thought to lend a hand, she had it moved. He still didn't see anything that would verify her statement.

"Why don't you change your clothes while I figure this out?" Frederick wasn't a prude and he knew he would have to change somewhere, he just didn't think it would be in the same space. His imagination took over while unbuttoning his shirt. Thora would have to change here, too.

He slipped into a jumpsuit and was pulling the zipper closed when the sound of stone scraping over stone broke the silence. He jerked his head in panic as he tried to look at all four walls at once. He was sure at that moment he would die before long, crushed to death, slowly by the granite slabs. He froze.

Frederick came out of it with a sharp slap across his face. It left a stinging hot spot on his cheek and before he opened his eyes, he thought another on the other side would balance the sensation. Thora stood before him in jeans and work jacket staring intently at him.

She was taking a big enough chance just bringing him in on this. Having Cezar change while she keyed the trap door, kept him from knowing exactly how it was done. Thora poured some coffee from a thermos. "Here this will help calm you down. What happened to you, Cezar?"

"When I heard the stone grinding, I thought the walls were closing in. I'm okay now, sort of. I'm sure you hoped I was braver than that." His ego took the hit.

"I needed someone I could trust. If it were a real emergency, you would have stepped up. Besides, nothing is going to happen. We are just looking around and the walls down there haven't moved in thousands of years." Thora checked her watch. "Give it go?"

Frederick took a deep breath and put on a hardhat with a built-in flashlight.

*** *

Igor took the next week off for several reasons. First his hand needed to heal. His hands were his life and he had been stupid to unleash his emotions in such a way. The machine gun on the other hand would have been a much better way to deal with them. The way he was feeling, however, had him afraid he even knew about it for fear he might use it for more than therapy.

Somehow his employers were in league with those responsible for the death of his family. The boat was a visible sign of the connection, but it also served as a distraction. The estate was after all an historic monument because of its age and, more importantly, the mosaics. The last few years working for Karuna Danesti had kept him busy: too busy to spend any real time studying the panorama in tile. The tours he had taken were more of a tourist thing, marginally informative and very entertaining. He wanted to study them now more than ever. His nemesis is a key figure in the mosaics and he knew there was more to learn if he could find the time, alone. Karuna would become suspicious, he thought, if he began spending long hours immersed in the many images.

A slow burn ignited within Igor. The kind and lovely Karuna Danesti, her daughter Riana and the Prime Minister Vlad Cneajna were not the saviors of Romania, but a sham to fool everyone that the evil had been put to rest. Was not Karuna a lover of Tepes, even to the point of bearing his child who now sits at the most powerful position in the land? The mockery of the three families united smoldered with plenty of fuel deep within Igor. He would have to watch himself and hide this knowledge. If they knew he knew...the paranoid mind knows all the tricks.

***

Frederick was barely able to overcome the urge to race back up the stairs. Thora took his hand saying, "It's this way, Cezar," in an effort to take his mind off the stairs. 'Why had she told?' she scolded herself mercilessly. Instead of being helpful, he had become a burden. 'If he doesn't hold up, he'll end up like the laborers.' Killing the two men had been easier than she imagined it would be.

'Once you get them thinking with their dicks...'

She wouldn't kill Cezar today unless she had to. They had already been seen together and the truckers would wonder why he had abandoned his ride home. With her hand, she squeezed the small nine- millimeter handgun she had used to kill the workmen. If it was a sense of false security that the gun gave, 'It sure feels like the real thing' she thought.

"How are you doing, Cezar?"

"Hanging in there. The open space is bigger than I thought it would be. It's comforting, as long I don't look at the ceiling."

"Keep your eyes on the floor."

"What's that smell?"

"The murdered workmen."

Cezar felt his breakfast head in reverse and swallowed hard to keep it down.

They had been walking for about ten minutes when Thora said, "We're here."

"Where exactly would here be?" He was completely lost.

"Directly beneath the Kcirb exhibit."

Cezar looked around at the columns supporting the floor above them.

"It will hold," Thora said, seeing the man tense up. "Here is our objective." She pointed to a little room cut into the wall.

"I'd rather not go in there just yet. One step at a time you know." He was trying really hard to keep it together.

"That's okay. I just need you here in case."

"In case what?"

"Take it easy, Cesar. Everything is going to be fine. We've made it this far," she finished reassuringly, putting on a pair of gloves. "Wait here, I'll call if I need anything."

"Be careful, Thora."

Thora eased herself through the opening to the loo careful to get her feet firmly on the ladder. There was still water at the bottom and she had no desire to become part of it. The rungs were corroded but held solid. At six meters down was the surface of the pit. Thora had expected, well, she didn't know what she expected, but at least it wasn't full of shit. Her light shone on the surface of the water, creating a reflection that made her wince. The light was waterproof. She made a face dipping the light into the liquid. Thora was shocked by what she saw. Suddenly the steel rung she was holding onto began to bend. Dropping the light Thora grabbed wildly for something to hold onto.

"Cesar!" she screamed when the rung snapped and she fell into the pool.

Frederick heard her scrambling, his stomach beginning to fall. When she yelled for help, he knew he had to do something. His feet were stuck to the ground, frozen with fear. A cold sweat began.

'MOVE GODAMNIT!' he yelled at himself. The space around him began to grow smaller. One foot moved forward. He was breathing heavy, fighting the fear. The other leg followed. He was moving! The next step was a little easier bringing him closer to the pit. Thora had stopped screaming. Now Frederick was moving. He only looked to verify the location of the ladder. He was no longer thinking.

Frederick Cezar, for the first time in his life, was doing something. Thora held on with one hand, flailing with the other and choking on the water. Her wet clothes and heavy boots were pulling her under. Cezar was almost to the bottom rung when her head went below the water. Her hand clutched the broken rung with a final spasm before releasing and following the rest of Thora's body.

Frederick reached out and grabbed Thora's hand just as it went under. It took all he had to haul her out with one hand and climb the ladder.

One step at a time, while muscles unused to such treatment rebelled. The powerful surge of adrenalin in his system filled in when all else was failing. On the floor, he frantically went through the motions of CPR. He had never done it before outside of a few class rehearsals. He knew he was doing something wrong but there was no time to critique his lack of skills. Rescue breaths then chest compressions. Over and over again. He was trying to remember the proper ratio of breaths to compressions when Thora began to convulse. Yellow fluid was expelled from her lungs, spewing from her mouth. A ragged intake of breath, more puking.

Frederick sat next to her. He was spent. There was nothing more he could do. Her breathing came in halting gasps as the spasms subsided. Frederick waited for her to wrap her arms around him and smother him in kisses for saving her life.

Thora staggered to her feet. "We have to go back in there!" She stumbled towards the loo before falling face first in the dirt. Frederick crawled over and rolled her on her back.

"Come on, Thora! We have to get out of here!"

"No! There is something down there!"

"Not today, Thora." He stood and put out his hand to her. What had gotten into her?

Thora resisted until her sense was restored. She knew better than throw a fit. Cezar may have saved her life, but he was now a liability that she would have to deal with. One step at a time.

For once Thora was thankful that the Kcirb exhibition was out of her hands, the physical aspects of it anyway. In the week before the show, there was more than enough to keep her busy with the administrative aspects of directing the museum. Even with the last minute frenzy that these things always turn out to be, she was not able, not for one minute, to forget about what she had seen in the pit. Thora wasn't even sure of what it was, other than she had to have it. Amongst the other detritus in the hole, the one item sparkled bright calling out to her. To be certain, her destiny demanded she have it, whatever it was.

It was Thursday. The show opening was tomorrow night. Thora neglected to return the calls made by Cezar. He had been in and out all week under the guise of checking on the exhibit. It was Thora he was keeping an eye on. Normally she was an all business 'chatty Cathy', it was part of her position. After the incident in the catacombs, she was subdued and pensive. Always somewhere else when she was talking and he didn't like where that somewhere else led to.

During lunch, she went to a sporting goods store. Thora bought a length of climbing rope, a snorkeling mask and another underwater flashlight. When she got back, Cezar was waiting for her in the office.

"I'm worried about you, Thora. You haven't returned my calls. You've been avoiding me. Thora, you almost died the other day!"

"Thanks to you I am still here. I've just been swamped with the show and all. To be honest, I have haven't had a chance to really think about it." The last thing Thora was being was honest.

"You said you saw something down there. Any idea what it was?"

"I fear it was my imagination."

"You seemed certain about it then. Hell – you wanted to go right back down there!"

"Easy now, Cezar. Now that I look back on it, the whole escapade was an Indiana Jones moment and I got caught up in it. Cezar, if you had not been there..."

"It was rather adventurous. Quite thrilling. I'm jut glad that business is now over. It is, isn't it?"

"Yes. Maybe after the show we will call the police and straighten the whole thing out."

"Now it sounds like you're back on track. Dinner tonight?"

"I'm sorry there is no way I can get out of here. Let's have drinks tomorrow after the opening when I can take a breath."

"That's a date, no rainchecks."

Thora took Frederick by the hands. "Thank you for all the help. I look forward to tomorrow night." She leaned into him and planted a warm kiss that hinted there was more to come.

***

Sechra sat back from putting the finishing touches on 'Enlightenment'. It was another blatant vision of horror. A half-dozen men were being tortured in different ways. One was being flayed; the skin on half of his body had been peeled back from head to toe. Another was being forced to eat excrement. The suppliers of this particular element were busy having the shit whipped out of them. Still yet another was staked to the ground and forced to watch his family being crucified. You get the idea.

Each sculpture exhibited a desperate realism. Combine the refinement of Michelangelo's 'David' with the dark witness of Munch's 'The Scream' and you have the disturbing essence of her work.

Tears began to make wet trails in the dust down her cheeks. She stood, looked deeply into the hate-filled eyes of one of the torturers, began sobbing and hugged the figure. Her tears spilt onto the stone, which absorbed Sechra's pain and anguish. She went to each of the figures in the piece, be they the damned or the damnable, holding each as if she knew them.

The fact was she did know them. The dead and dying were her family and friends. If someone had a scrapbook with pictures of the gypsy life, you would see the faces of a nation before and during the nightmare. A hard life created a hard people. Sechra captured the moment in the wrinkles of wind-burned skin, cracked lips and gnarled hands. Honest eyes beheld horrors no man was meant to view. Some lived to remember it, but none spoke of it. Those of gypsy heritage would be allowed free entry to the exhibit. They already paid the cost of admission. All of them would weep upon seeing the sculptures, for only the Roma could understand the works. The effect was similar to victims of the Holocaust returning to 'their' nightmare.

It was still early. The trucks wouldn't be coming until later in the day. She jumped in the shower, wondering where Igor was off to. He would surely be here tonight to supervise the loading. But she wished he were here now. Her young body wanted him. After Sechra had turned sixteen, she pressured him to teach her more than sculpting. She was old enough and he was single. He was a patient and fulfilling teacher. Sechra was a willing and demanding student.

Surprisingly, they did not become a couple. Sechra had no desire for a relationship and Igor seemed incapable of one. After a year of instruction, Igor drifted away, physically. He was increasingly preoccupied and would not discuss it.

With sculpting and school taking up her time she did not have the desire to pursue pointless relationships with kids her own age in the little town of Eforie Sud. Instead, she would snare college students or their professors when they came to study the mosaics. They provided Sechra with what she needed without the entanglements of more traditional relationships.

She rode south on the main road to Eforie Sud. Her hair tucked into the helmet as she hugged the BMW trying to break her own speed record. It was exhilarating. The brisk fall weather made her wish she had dried her hair before heading out. Sechra checked the clock when she pulled into the hair salon. It wasn't a record-breaking run, but she had still made good time. Just as she sat to get her hair trimmed, Sechra's cell phone went off. She checked the number. It was Karuna.

"Did you get back from Bucharest?"

"I did and I need you here, NOW," Karuna said urgently.

"I just sat down to get my hair cut. Can't it wai..."

"Sechra, it's Igor. Something horrible has happened. Please!"

"I'm on my way."

Sechra got out of the seat, pulling on her leather one-piece Aerostitch Roadcrafter.

The ride into town was nothing compared to the ride back. The 1200 c.c. motor was running at the red line doing 240 K.P.H. weaving through traffic at an insane blur. A roostertail of sand and gravel sprayed from the rear tire as she sped up the drive to the estate. A cloud of dust enveloped her coming to a stop next to the ambulance. Karuna met her at the front door.

"What happened?" Sechra surged towards the door.

"Let's wait a minute. The medtechs are just getting him on a gurney."

Sechra stepped around Karuna into the living room. A trail of blood led from the mosaics to where Igor was now being lifted onto the stretcher. Igor was unconscious and deathly pale. His hands were bundled in balls of gauze. It must have been her perspective, but the limbs seemed foreshortened. He was alive! The medtechs were trying to hit a vein to start an I.V. when Karuna came up behind her putting her hands on Sechra's shoulders. When she saw the techs struggling to find the nearly collapsed veins on Igor's arm, she stepped in to help. At this point, the medtechs were thankful when help was offered. Karuna knelt by Igor and felt the inside of his arms. Her eyes were closed, she was seeing with another sense. Smoothly and with all the care of a mother, Karuna eased the tip of the needle though the skin until she felt the resistance of the vein. Years of experience controlled the little push to puncture the collapsed tube without going through the other side. A weak stream of sanguine fluid backbled into the catheter.

"Thank you, ma'am, we'll take it from here," said one of the techs.

Karuna stood and stretched her back. She heard a sharp short scream from the hall. Glancing about she saw Sechra was gone. One of the medtechs chinned at the trail of blood. "We didn't pick them up yet. Figured the cops would want to see them." He was talking to thin air. Sechra was staring at the mosaics and back to the floor when Karuna got to her. 'They should have laid a towel over them,' she thought.

"Have you seen Igor lately?"

"Not for the last few days. When did this happen?"

"We don't know. I found him when the cab dropped me."

"How could this have happened?"

Karuna looked down to Igor's hands lying on the floor, then to the tile work. "There are no signs of a fight." Karuna struggled with the words. "I think it happened in there." Karuna chinned at the wall.

While the older woman went to the linen closet to get a towel, Sechra knelt next to her teacher's hands. She picked one up, holding it carefully, studying the scars and calluses she knew so well. Her gaze drifted to the mosaics. There, a scene was being played out that filled in the blanks for Sechra that her imagination could not. The location was the beach in front of her cottage and studio/barn. The studio had yet to be built. The barn however was as it was originally meant to be, an insane asylum. Crazies hung out the windows yelling to the world of their misery. Others, who could be trusted, roamed the beachfront. Those who couldn't be trusted were tied to poles or each other to keep them from getting free. A mock court was being held on the beach. One of the inmates had stolen a guard's weapon. Back in the day, punishment for stealing was as cruel as it gets. A man knelt in the sand with his arms stretched out before him on a block of wood. The wide-bladed axe had just come down severing the hands. Blood shot from the stumps. The face of the dismembered was blank. Expressionless except for the eyes, which saw the future of a handless man.

Karuna lifted the hand from Sechra's grasp and placed it in the towel before shaking the girl out of trance. A medtech rounded the corner with a cooler. "We just got notified to bring the hands. There's a small chance, but they may be able to reattach them. Could you put that in here?" he said opening the cooler. He settled both into the ice and turned to Karuna. "I know some people who clean up these kinds of messes."

"That's alright. We can handle it. Thank you for getting here so quickly."

"It's what we do. You know you're pretty handy with a needle. You ever need a job..." The ambulance's horn honked. "Good luck."

Sechra had barely noticed the techs departure, as she couldn't take her eyes off the tile. "Karuna look!" Sechra pointed to the particular image. "It looks like Igor, the way it looks like Jake. Could it really have happened here?"

"We know that 'was' possible, but nothing like this has happened since... Let's go to the computer and pull up the digitals."

"Will they really be able to put his hands back on?"

"I don't know. If it happened a few hours ago, maybe. This may have happened right after I left for Bucharest to see Riana. In that case..."

Sechra didn't buy it that it happened a few days ago. She had been to the estate a few times in Karuna's absence and there wasn't blood all over the place then. But she had finished the final sculpture for the show a few hours ago. She remembered how she felt when it was done. The emotional release was incredible. But then it was always that way when she would say goodbye to one of the nightmares that life had bequeathed her. Why had she wanted to be with Igor immediately after completing the work? One of 'Enlightenment's' scenes portrays the grisly punishment that was meted out on Igor. Sechra tried to shake the weird feelings of synchronicity.

"Let's have some coffee and clean this up before we get into the pictures," Sechra offered.

"I suppose we should," Karuna said heading to the kitchen. "And then to the hospital. Igor has no family."

***

It was midnight by the time Thora Wozniak was able to call the museum her own. It had been an exhaustive day preparing for the show. The pieces of the exhibit were now in place. The museum had to be ready. When the staff wearily left for the evening, Thora went to her office and made a pot of coffee. A long night brewed ahead of her.

When Walter, the security guard, began his regular rounds, Thora slipped from her office to the storage room. She changed into a clean jumpsuit, this time wearing a pair of sneakers instead of workboots. The water would be cold, but she didn't plan on spending too much time in it, just enough to get a look at the bottom and grab. Thora rammed the screwdriver into the tiny hole releasing the mechanism that held the slab of flooring. While it was rasping into the recess, she shouldered the pack with the gear and grabbed a thermos of coffee, checking her watch before going down the hand-hewn stairs.

Thora wondered why she was doing this as she weaved through the passages. With the opening tomorrow night, the rational part of her mind screamed, 'What are you doing?' Of course there wasn't much of her rational mind left. She had felt it slipping away upon discovering the ancient passage. When she killed the two laborers, a line was crossed. But when she saw what glistened at the bottom of the pit, all that was left was an insane desire to have it. None of the staff at the museum picked up on it, except maybe Cezar – and his worries were dissolved with a kiss. In her new mind, Thora sensed she had fooled them all and the task ahead of her was justified. After all, she had thought it out.

The stench of the bodies indicated she was close to the loo. When she was through, the bodies would be thrown into the pit and the whole affair put in the past. At least that is what she told herself. Now at the pit, she poured a cup from the thermos to shake the chill. It seemed colder than it was before. Thora laughed a little crazed, 'it's because I have nothing on under the suit'. The coffee warmed her as she pulled the rope out and tied it to the nearest pillar. The rest she uncoiled and dropped into the loo until she heard it splash. She spit into the mask, rubbing it around the lens like the salesman at the sporting goods store told her and put it on. She downed the last of her coffee, climbed up onto the seating and stepped into the loo.

The rungs on the ladder were solid. Just to be on the safe side Thora wrapped the rope around one of her arms letting it snake along in case another step broke. She stopped when her feet went under the water. She pushed her mask up on her forehead and took a look. The big dive light lit the pit like day. Scanning the water Thora ignored the coils of rope floating on the surface. Her excitement didn't allow her to see the danger they posed. Aside from the ladder rung that broke, the steps kept going down into the water. Thora followed until she was chest deep and breathing hard to cope with the cold.

Steeling herself for the plunge, a 'moment of clarity', as alcoholics call it, infused her. She saw the murder of the two men. Her hand trembling when the explosion ripped through the underground lair. The gun glinting in the darkness as smoke roiled from the barrel. The second shot was sure and steady. Thora gulped in shame, realizing for the first time she had killed them in cold blood to keep her secret. The flashlight lit on the prize at the bottom as the frigid waters hardened her heart. The moment passed as insanity reveled in victory. She slid the mask over her face, took a deep breath and let go.

The icy water shocked like nothing she had ever felt before. She screamed and scrambled for the surface, her arms tangling in the loops of rope. Giant breaths followed, purging the fear and calming the body. She steadied herself bringing what was left of her wits back into the moment. Her body was already aching from the cold and precious seconds went by before she was ready to go for it.

Having grown up in Bucharest, Thora had little experience with exposure issues. Sure, she had to bundle up in the winter like everyone else, but never really understood what cold will do. Especially ice cold water. Water steals the body's heat 70 times faster than air. This one little fact might have altered Thora's approach to her current predicament. Of course considering her state of mind, maybe not. It only takes a very few minutes for the unprotected body to succumb to hypothermia. But Thora didn't know this.

She was shivering by the time she went under again. The cold made her forget about the lines around her arms and as she swam down the rope wrapped her legs. She didn't know this either as her legs had gone numb. At the bottom, with the mask, she could clearly see what had caught her attention before. Thora reached for it at the same moment her internal signal went off for air. She pushed off the bottom reaching up for the surface. The rope kept her from swimming freely and had snagged on some of the bottom's debris. Her lungs began to burn for a breath and panic was kicking in. She could touch the surface with her fingers but could not get her head above water. Bubbles were trailing from her parted lips when a calm settled over her racing conscious. She smiled as the struggling ceased and she drifted back to the bottom. The dive light still shone brightly on her quest. As she reached for the golden handle the illumination seemed to dim until all she could see was her hand clutching the prize. The light went out.

***

Karuna sat alone in the waiting room at the hospital. Sechra needed to be at the art studio for the loading of her pieces. With Igor still in surgery she pulled out her phone and dialed Riana's number. "Oh Mom, I'm so glad you called. How is the exhibit going?"

Riana's life path had diverged from Karuna's after the revolution. It was a reality that both of them had accepted. Hard as it was, Karuna needed to stay out of the limelight that Riana and Vlad lived with. Vlad, with his personal knowledge of Romanian history, and of man in general, made him an excellent choice for prime minister. He was not a dictator or a puppet, just a man with an uncommon amount of common sense. Vlad could separate himself from the issues of a new nation to see the many sides of an argument clearly without his personal shit interfering. So many leaders could not do this and their countries suffered for it. Vlad, however, made but simple suggestions to the parliament. He would come down hard only when special interests threatened the nation's stability.

Riana stood beside her husband, supporting his ideas and healing that which politics could not. With the blood of the Dracul and Danesti running through her veins, she could reach a broader demographic of the Roma peoples. And with a child that has the blood of three Voivode, the touch extended further. With the culmination of the ritual that bound the Roma, Riana had achieved that which no one had before her. Though she was Voivode, she was also a peasant and accepted wherever she went.

This one aspect went far to dispel the influence of Megacorp and give the people a sense of unity. It extended as deep into the mountains as it did the depths of the inner city. What did she have that influenced so many people? Surely it wasn't just the blood thing, but that was a big part of it. Nor was it the ability to transcend the different layers of social fabric. Simple as it was, words scarcely do it justice. A basic combination of unconditional love and education was what it took. It was love and the righteousness of a people that allowed her to overcome her moments of desperation when confronted with a millennium of evil. When it was all over, she was driven to share it. Her position as wife of the P.M. served most effectively for this purpose.

There was no political campaign or state mandates to make it happen. Without fanfare or massive advertising, Riana instigated a slow reawakening for those who had been put to sleep by Megacorp. Generations had been manipulated by the internet. When it began, no one really knows. Sometime after the 'information on demand' was initiated, subtle changes began taking place. These changes were innocuous. Only the ones who programmed them into cyberspace knew. Like a leaky faucet, one drop at a time fills the tub to overflowing, thus were the mind-numbing alterations. Riana's methods were equally as subtle. It was her message that made all the difference. Like drug addicts, the population needed to be weaned from the net. She knew firsthand what cold turkey did to people. The tub was still full. Her work was far from over.

"Sechra is dealing with the shippers right now." Her voice shifted a few octaves lower and the words were clipped. "It's Igor. When I was visiting you, he took the time to enter the mosaics."

Riana immediately picked up on Karuna's lack of ease. Everything had been going so well, she missed the obvious. "Thank God there is nothing to be concerned with any more, besides a little trance."

"I'm in the hospital waiting for Igor to get out of surgery."

"What! What happened?" Riana asked in shock. She couldn't believe what her mind was hinting at.

"He went into an image and came out without his hands." There was a silence after the statement. Karuna could hear what her daughter was thinking.

"There was no sign of a struggle and the picture he was viewing would verify the results."

"Have you checked the digital reproduction?"

"Not yet. They're trying to reattach his hands and I wanted to be here."

"Do you think...?" Riana began.

"They do not know how long he was without them."

"I'll catch the first flight out tomorrow morning. Can you pick me up at the airport?"

"Of course, darling. Talk to Vlad about this. He knows the mosaics better than anyone."

"I will. Is there anything you need?"

"Just you. See you in the morning. Give a hug and kisses to Miruna." Karuna hung up, as the doors to the O.R. swung wide. A doctor, his blues splattered and smeared with blood, came through. Karuna rose from the chair.

"Ms. Danesti?" The doctor bowed briefly from the waist. "Doctor Koroloff. We have just finished with the surgery. He will be in recovery for the next few hours. You should be able to see him tomorrow morning."

"Were you able to put them back on?"

"Da. Were you there when this happened?"

"No. I found him like that," Karuna responded.

"The medtechs said the hands were lying on a marble floor. It is possible the coolness of the stone preserved them better than say... carpet. We reassembled them as best we could. Blood flows. Now only time will tell. I suggest you take him to a specialist in Bucharest after he can be moved."

"Thank you, Dr. Koroloff, we will. Igor has been with us for so long he is like family."

"All the better for him. I will be with him through the night to be sure there are no complications. If I may, there is one question I have to ask." Karuna nodded. "How did this happen?"

"I am asking myself the same question. Thank you again for your help."

Koroloff bowed again at he waist, turned and went back into the O.R. Karuna knew better than to involve the good doctor any further until she knew more. Hopefully there wasn't anymore but she knew better than that as well.

Karuna drove the Mercedes back to the estate that night, slowly. Her mind was thousands of miles away and she didn't want her inattentiveness to cause an accident. Instead she came upon one that had just occurred. A loaded pickup truck had run head on into a sedan. Karuna hit the brakes, pulling over to the side of the road and flipped on the emergency flashers. She was out the door dialing the emergency number as she ran to the car. There was a family inside. Without thinking and using strength uncommon in a woman her age, anyone at any age for that matter, she ripped the rear door from its hinges and flung it aside. Three children broken, bleeding and crying writhed in a pile on the floor. When she reached in for the first child the smell of gasoline burned into her sinuses. The child screamed, pulling away. Karuna asserted herself before losing her grasp.

Karuna had never relied on the abilities that came with the life Jake had given her. During her time in Baja with Jake and Giovanni, she did more than just learn to surf and kick back. Both men had been diligent teachers on what she should and should not do as well as what she could and could not do. Their teaching styles were at opposite ends of the spectrum. Giovanni would plan his lectures with graphs and pies. Simple chemistry experiments explained what hours of excruciating experience had taught him. Karuna took his word for it, having no desire to put the observations to the test. Jake, on the other hand, taught what he considered the fun stuff. Strength, speed, agility, improved sense of smell, sight and touch, how to use them and when. And what the side effects were. He taught her to feed when there was nothing else available, how to survive when there was nothing at all. Giovanni taught her discretion at all of the above, while Jake stressed a 'get-r-done' mentality. It was an extreme balancing act and Karuna was the fulcrum. For her it was a bag of tricks that remained closed. Except...

She sent a wave of calm surging into the back seat. The children quieted. They were still hurt and crying, but the nightmare was over for the moment. First the biggest one then the other two at once were carried behind the Mercedes and set in the tall grass of the drainage ditch. She could tell the injuries were non-life threatening and quickly returned for the parents. A fire had started at the truck and the fuel was draining towards it! She removed the driver's door the same as the rear. The steering wheel had crushed into the man's chest, pinning him to the seat. He was unconscious. So was the wife. Her head impacted the windshield. Blood pulsed from a gash on the man's neck. His life was ebbing away. There was nothing that could be done to save him. Karuna looked over at the unconscious woman and said, "I am sorry, there is nothing that can be done for him." Tears ran down her cheeks in an attempt to forgive herself for what she was about to do. She leaned into the car and began to drink from the pulsating crimson fountain.

Minutes passed as the man's heart slowed. Karuna remembered to stop before the heart's beat ceased. She lifted her head from the neck, her mouth a smear of red like a mad clown. The wife awoke to see Karuna finish the fiendish act and began screaming. Karuna berated herself as she rushed to the passenger side and opened the door. The woman recoiled and fought back from Karuna's attempts at rescuing her. Karuna tried to calm her, but the frenzy had gone too far and Karuna was out of practice. Just then the stream of fuel reached the burning truck! In a whoosh the fire raced back to the car and engulfed the rear end in flames. Seeing no other alternative Karuna made a fist and hit the woman in the cheek with a right jab. Karuna took hold of the woman who was now out cold again, dragging her to where the children were. In the distance, she could hear the sounds of the ambulance well before the lights came into view. Tears of shame now coursed down her face. When the car exploded, she hardly budged so entrenched in the horror she had just committed. Karuna mentally entered the minds of the four damaged people and tried to impress upon them to forget what had happened. She left a flashlight turned on to signal where they lay and a bottle of water in the woman's hand. Hardly able to control herself, she sped away from the scene moments before the lights of the emergency vehicle lit the site.

This was Karuna's first 'call of the wild.' Along with the rush, came the knowledge of the man she had just aided, mercifully, on his way. The fear in the forefront of the man's mind moments before the crash left Karuna shaken. 'A truck ahead, unavoidable collision imminent,' yet his thoughts were of his family in those last seconds. Love poured from him as he swerved to take the hit on the driver's door. His family would never know. Karuna, however, now knew him to be an honorable man along with the sacrifice he had given to save the ones he loved. This instant knowledge thing was new to her. Bagged blood no longer retained the essence of the living soul. And it was good, too good. She would have to learn to control herself, lest she go on a thousand year binge. She already had enough bad habits without adding another.

***

Frederick Cezar had wound himself up in a knot. Between his desire for Thora and the fix they found themselves in, he was out of his league of experience. His true love was art. It was easy to love. Even the works of Sechra Kcirb evoke a certain level of it. The skill and vision put to stone, no matter the subject matter, stirred his emotions, as they should. People skills he had. They came with the territory. Without them you withered and died in the verbose nature of the artist and the arts. But here in the sea of human emotion, he was a fish out of water.

When she didn't return his calls on Friday morning he tried not to be thrashed by it, knowing she was busy with the last minute details. 'It always happens before a show,' he thought, trying to calm himself. Frederick was at his office taking care of details himself. Since saving her life last week, to say that it was difficult to concentrate would be a gross understatement. Since he couldn't talk to anyone about it made matters worse. That whole night just spun around in his head. What was he doing there? Chasing pussy? Hell – there were two dead guys down there! Frederick didn't personally look under the tarp to confirm this. The smell was enough. It had gone from a semi-romantic escapade to a life and death struggle in a matter of minutes. If they had only gotten together afterwards, the next day, or the day after the next day. But Thora made like work and Frederick knew she took her work seriously. If they were a couple, she would be the alpha. Frederick in turn tried to keep a lid on his feelings and be manly about it. Of course he failed on a personal level. Having saved her life, however, did something to him. Frederick Cezar now knew he had a pair of balls.

***

Before Thora Wozniac blacked out, she had grasped what she believed to be a gilded handle. When in fact she grabbed the knob that opened the door to her own personal hell. The price we pay when we kill someone is different for each murderer. The only thing that is the same is that you will never be able to afford it.

Thora was enveloped in a soundless black void. She was neither conscious nor unconscious in what she felt was a dream state. Slowly a sense of self returned. In remembering who she was, a wave of relief washed over her. She was safe and alive. She wondered if Cezar had saved her again. Her clouded mind wandered over the current events, eventually focusing on the Kcirb exhibit. If she could have avoided this one thought, perhaps Thora would have remained in that emptiness and avoided the consequences of reality. To her everlasting regret, it was not to be.

A sharp pain in her back greeted Thora when she opened her eyes. She shifted on the hospital bed away from the rock that dug into her spine. 'A rock,' she thought? Then she realized she was blind. A darkness so black she could not see her hands before her face. She yelped as her arms flailed about. Her hands found nothing but a crumbling wall of dirt. There was no hospital bed! Thora looked around in panic. She didn't feel blind. There! There! A few feet away, a thin crack of light. She stumbled towards it over the uneven surface and fell into the muck that covered the floor. The stench of shit and piss overwhelmed her.

'Where am I?' she screamed, crawling towards the light! Getting closer to the shaft of light she saw a figure peering out the gap. Thora clawed her way to a little girl who was frozen at the fissure in the wood. She tried to pry her away from the opening but the girl wouldn't budge. It wasn't until Thora squeezed her head around the child to peer out the hole that a blood curdling scream climbed rapidly from her gut and burst from her mouth. It echoed deafeningly in the confining space. A primal fear gripped her; the screams became maddened as she tore at the wood to get out.

The realization of her predicament surfaced in the boiling cauldron that had once been her mind. There was no doubt in her that she had gone to hell. When Thora glimpsed what existed through the gap, the last threads of sanity parted. Of course what she saw would have snapped anyone. Outside the filthy pit was the auditorium of the museum. Before another round of screaming began a fetid squirt of diarrhea shot down upon her. The little girl appeared to turn and 'shhhed' Thora.

***

Sechra pulled up the digital reproduction of the mosaics while waiting for the delivery trucks to arrive. She scrolled from the beginning until the end, rapidly assessing each panel. On the third try, she found the particular mosaic renderings. A chill ran down her spine as she recognized Igor. At least she thought it was him. Sechra would know soon enough. She scrutinized the image while the printer was active making copies. It took a minute before she realized what she was looking at. The insane asylum in the background was her art studio, less the cottage. Igor was dressed as one of the inmates. Sechra remembered the day they went shooting and she had asked where he was during the revolution. His reply was a mental institution.

A digital bell sounded. The copier was done. Her hands were trembling as she lifted the prints. Sechra riffled through the images until she found a close-up of the trial on the beach. In the original, a lunatic was on his knees arms stretched out before him on a wooden block. The person in the original bore no likeness to Igor and still had his hands. The executioner stood at the ready, axe held high.

The way the tiles were now was frighteningly different. She gasped dropping the pictures when the doorbell rang.

Sechra took a moment to compose herself before answering the door. Only one of the five semi-trucks came down the drive to get Sechra. She hopped on her motorcycle and slowly led the way up the road to the studio. After that, all she had to do was turn the floodlights on and worry. Unfortunately, there was more to worry about than the shippers dropping one of her pieces.

It was a few hours before dawn by the time the truckers were finished. Sechra had the good sense to have the covers on the pieces when they arrived. That alone probably saved a few hours of explanations. Once all the paperwork had been signed and the trucks on the road to Bucharest, Sechra killed the lights, went to the cottage and crashed. She was beat. The last twenty-four hours had been brutal. So tired that her personal walls came down for a moment. Thoughts of Igor and the implications of the mosaics come to life again poured in. Quietly, so quietly that it couldn't be heard above the sound of the surf, tears of sorrow fell from her eyes for what she had done. The scenes of decrepit evil she created were but the beginning of a nightmare she had breathed as a child.

✳✳✳

Karuna crept the big Mercedes down the drive to the estate. Her hands were trembling as she tried to deal with the rush of what she had done. Why had she done it? Her teachers had explained that something like this might happen. 'Even with a steady supply in the fridge, you can be overwhelmed in the moment,' Giovanni had once said. 'Shit happens,' was the way Jake put it. She tried to pool all their schooling in order to rationalize it to herself and failed. Karuna had to deal with it. 'In the moment,' it had seemed the right thing to do. Hastening what would have been an agonizing demise. It was the good that evil can do, that is until his wife woke and began screaming at the monster who was eating her husband. Then the dream crashed down upon Karuna's heart and soul as she witnessed herself doing the foul deed. No one would ever understand that her actions were done for all the right reasons. A part of her now understood the way Jake felt when he consumed the essence of evil so long ago.

It wasn't that Karuna regretted taking a life. If anything she revered it more now than ever. There was something different this time. The incident did involve a matter of life and death; however it was not a kill or be killed situation as had been her previous experiences. So if death was not the issue that was bothering her, what was? Karuna was no fool and the answer was as plain as the blood on her hands.

She had never had to really face what she had become. The blood that she occasionally required was always taken care of and taken with care. Currently Boris and Chief Tobias Kuchta of Deep Salvage were and have been her suppliers for more than twenty years. Jake and Giovanni had taken care of her when she lived in Baja. Karuna had never heard 'the call of the wild' that Jake heard. That is until tonight. And even that meal was supplied. There was no wet work involved, no reach out and take what you think is yours...Would she do it again? Her heart screamed 'NO' but her mind knew better. A part of her liked it. I mean really liked it. I mean like it so much you'd kill for it.

Karuna wept until dawn.

***

In the weeks before Igor lost his hands, he had been awash in thoughts of bitterness and revenge. The family that destroyed his family had to be destroyed in a manner no less horrendous than the torture and vicious slavery his had suffered. Igor had regressed to what he considered his natural state, a seething vengeful anger of a nine-year-old boy.

When Igor had been discovered amidst the devastation that had been the family reunion campground, he was coated in filth and catatonic. Seated at the waters edge, he was staring at the emblem of the invaders. It was the sigil of a dragon, wings spread, talons ready to strike. When the rescuers tried to move him, he became a violent thrashing animal of a child, harmless but uncontrollable. When the hat that bore the sigil was taken from him, he began to scream like you were tearing his arm off. With no doctor on site, the rescue team tied him to a stretcher to keep him from hurting himself. They returned the hat to his possession. Eventually, he was taken to Bucharest and spent the next ten years learning to hide his vehemence.

It was at the asylum that he learned to carve. At first he was found in the yard smashing rocks to dispel his anger. Igor put all of his effort into the work. To him, the rocks were dragons. One of the social workers noticed this and approached the resident shrink. They teamed him up with an older obsessive-compulsive stonemason that, like Igor, had escaped the slave camps only to lose his mind.

In the beginning his carvings were crude dragons that he smashed upon completion. Falco, the stonemason, always busy hammering away at all hours, would stop briefly to look at the fragments of Igor's work, then hustle over to a pile of stones. There he would dig around and find a stone suitable for Igor, then return to his work. All the while, the social worker observed and took notes on his progress. After six months, it was decided to stop the little experiment, as Igor did not seem to be progressing. His skill level had improved, but it was the anger and acting out that came when he finished a sculpture that cancelled the program.

Once again, little Igor was dragged from his rock meditations kicking and screaming. Only this time, he was sedated rather than tied. Falco appeared not to notice, but after several days he stopped his hammering when the social worker checked up on him. When the sound of the mallet and chisel ceased, the worker stopped dead in her tracks. Falco never stopped for anyone.

"What is it, Falco?" Delores, the social worker, asked taking control of the situation and not taking her eyes off the hand that still held a potentially deadly hammer.

"The boy. Where is the boy?" he demanded, gripping the hammer tighter but making no threatening moves.

"He has been moved. The doctor thought it best." Delores reached to her back pocket and slid a can of mace into her hand.

"NO," yelled Falco, suddenly standing with a menacing body language.

Delores had never seen him upright before. He was huge and towered over her. She thumbed the protective cap off the mace and brought it up taking aim at his face. Lightening quick reflexes snatched the little can from her grasp, hardy touching her skin. Delores staggered back, bringing her hands in front of her face. She started to fall backwards over a stack of stones. She didn't see Falco's look of madness change to concern or his hand drop the hammer, as he reached out and kept her from taking a nasty tumble. Delores struggled futilely in the big man's hold. Her life passed before her eyes by the time his grip eased. He held out the can in an open palm while lowering his gaze to the floor.

Delores almost pressed the panic button. It would send an alarm blaring all over the facility. When she saw Falco motionless, her thumb slid off the button. To the best of her knowledge, no one had ever seen him completely still. Studying him from head to toe to make sure he calmed down, she noticed the sweat beading on his forehead, dripping down his face like tears. Wait...there were tears, too. Standing still was taking all Falco's effort. 100 percent. Delores lifted the can from his hand, recapped it and put it back in her pocket. Then she took his hard calloused hands in hers. "I will see what I can do. Can you get him to stop smashing his work?"

"I will try. Thank you, he reminds me of my son."

Two hours later, after Delores had explained the situation, Igor was returned to the crafts room. He was still heavily sedated and sat listless in front of the stone he had been working on. 'That will change after the drugs wear off,' Delores hoped. She had to take full responsibility. The doctor in charge was not going to take the fall. By the end of the day, Falco, instead of choosing a stone for Igor, began to teach Igor to find a suitable piece for himself. But only a little at a time. After all, he was just a kid.

The next morning he began to relieve the stone of its excess material. Delores created a mini-office in the crafts room so she could better monitor the two. Falco and Igor hardly noticed as Delores was a typical overworked social worker. She didn't have time to just sit there and watch them. There were other patients. The first thing she noticed was that Falco had now taken Igor under his wing. Before he was merely sharing the space. The unease that Falco went through when he stopped hammering to teach the boy bothered Delores. That it was difficult for the man to cease his habitual motion was apparent, but she had to let this play out. She did not listen to their lessons. Though it was hard for Falco, it was also good. In time, the lack of comfort would lessen and fathering would come through.

Falco watched as Delores became a more permanent fixture in their lives. He paid her scant visible attention, but was otherwise completely aware of her presence. Teaching the boy made him feel worthwhile, but he knew better than to focus on it or he'd get all O.C.D. over it. 'Play it cool,' he thought. Two or three days after Igor had been returned, he began instructing. It was a casual bargain he had struck with Delores and Falco had every intention of keeping up his end of the agreement. He had his own selfish reasons to help the young Igor. Falco wanted out.

Four days after Igor was released from the fog of barbiturates, he finished his first dragon. Delores had left earlier to do her rounds of the other patients. Falco had been watching Igor with one eye and could tell he was finishing up. Igor lifted the piece, by far his best rendering yet, and examined it closely. Falco viewed 'his' work, Igor, just as intensely. He saw the boy's anger and hatred rise inside the young body as its language changed to something darker. He set the stone down reaching for a heavier steel mall to smash the atrocity into oblivion. As he raised the sledge high adjusting his grip for a mighty swing, Falco scooted over and placed his big hand atop the carving. Igor was just about to deliver a crippling blow to the hand. He stopped in mid-swing, his own hands shaking. Falco reached up and took the hammer from the little trembling hands. Igor began to sob uncontrollably. The older man took him in his arms and held him close. There were no words, only the unspoken language of love and purpose.

When the snot quit running and tear ducts closed, Falco released him, saying, "You must not smash any more of your art. We are here to work out our problems you and I. Do you want to stay here the rest of your life?"

Igor shook his head no, using his sleeve to wipe his nose and eyes. "But it feels so good," he squeaked.

"So does jacking off, but it does no good," Falco replied knowing his remark went over the child's head.

Igor didn't quite get it. He had seen the men doing the jerk in private and they did seem to be enjoying themselves. But once he got caught trying to imitate the men and his mom nearly took the skin off his butt with a whipping. So in his young mind, he agreed with Falco that no good comes from it.

"Delores must see that you are growing. And no more dragons."

"But what else is there?"

Falco went to his workbench and removed a stone from one of the drawers. A design had already been sketched and a chisel had begun to chip away what didn't belong. "This was started by a young apprentice I once had the honor of working with. I would like you to finish it." Falco did not mention that the apprentice was his son.

Igor held the stone to the light. "What is it?"

"Nothing yet. That is for you to decide. I have shaded the areas that need to be removed. Do that and you will see." The older man returned to his work at his normal frenzied pace.

Igor stared at the rock for the next hour, turning it and viewing from a variety of perspectives to see what it was. "How am I supposed to carve it if I don't know what it is?"

The repetitious hammering paused briefly. "Once you remove the shaded parts, the stone will tell you."

Igor picked up his hammer and chose an appropriate sized chisel and took a few tentative swings when Delores returned. Igor stopped and glanced at Falco. The man looked him in the eye and after a moment nodded. Igor set his hammer down and picked up the dragon that Falco had stopped him from destroying. Standing with it, he walked over to Delores' desk.

"Miss Delores, I have something for you," Igor said innocently.

"What is it, Igor?"

He brought his hands around in front of him and held out the finished carving. "I would like you to have it."

"Are you sure, Igor?" Delores looked over to Falco who sat with folded hands. He smiled and nodded to her.

"Why thank you, Igor. It is beautiful. I will keep it on my desk. Why did you not destroy it?"

"I want to get out of here," he replied, again with a childlike innocence.

The response caught Delores by surprise. Whatever his reasons, it was progress. She didn't notice Falco cringe, just a little, at the words.

The next few years were like a dream for young Igor. The works of the two men littered the grounds of the institution. Igor carved gargoyles for the exterior of the building. Smaller works adorned the halls and public areas. At the age of eighteen, he was released. It was contingent on his going to college and working at a local burial monument business. Here Igor earned himself an education and reputation as a diligent, exacting craftsman. He hid his past behind slabs of granite and marble until one day when Karuna Danesti entered the shop.

Falco was never released from the sanitarium. One hot summer it happened. It was one of those sticky irritable days when everyone it seemed was just about to blow their tops. There was no air conditioning. For those that lived in it, the muggy weather was merely unbearable. For those not used to it, the clock was ticking. Falco hammered away as usual. The effort no longer had the manic energy that used to come along with it. He slowed down. Often he would stop work to help another patient struggling with their projects. He had grown old. Igor had left several years before and Falco went through a period of depression at the loss. Instead of working like a madman, he did nothing and to him this was completely normal. He had lost someone close. Falco was in mourning. He came out of it, dispelling all the theories that suggested he 'lost it'. 'Quite the opposite,' thought Falco. He had found it. For the first time in more years than he could remember, he was sane. He worked, became socially active and in general was more help than a burden. Even that summer's heat didn't break him like so many others that crumbled beneath it. That is until the family of one of the inmates came to visit.

Once a month family members were allowed to spend time with the loved ones, who for one reason or another found themselves unable to cope with reality. Henri was 85. He was not so much crazy, but a victim of one of the many Alzheimer-like degenerations of the brain. He was here like many who had no business being in an insane asylum. There were just too many old and not enough places to put them. When his daughter came, she brought her husband and two children of a rambunctious age. She was wilting under the heat but maintained. The husband was a heartbeat away from snapping while the two kids raised hell in the crafts room. Henri was busy doing a portrait on canvas. Whether a profile or front view they were all the same. The sad clown. Over and over again. He had hundreds of them, each sadder than one before it, no matter how you shuffled them. The current painting tore your heart out with the irony. Of course no one really noticed the difference anymore other than Henri and sometimes Falco.

The kids were harmlessly harassing the nuts. The nuts on their part feigned a crazy anger that was expected, but otherwise relished the attention. It happened every month. And on visitor's day, the crafts room was full to capacity with anxious nuts. Today, the weight of the air pressed down on you with claustrophobia. Even breathing was hard. The children came by pulling on his rags and making dust clouds by ruffling his hair. Falco produced two little bas-relief carvings, each one a pony. When you set them next to each other they either faced each other or assed each other, like bookends. The boys were thrilled and their shrieks resounded in the room. When they moved on, Falco went back to his work hammering away. He was unaware that the sound was chipping away at the husband's eggshell-thin temper.

Heated words were flying at the wife regularly and more randomly at the kids when all at once he turned and stomped to Falco. "Do you have to keep up that incessant pounding? My head is about to explode!" he cried.

Falco looked up in a quiet manner. "I apologize. I was not aware it bothered you so. I will stop until you are done. Henri is happy you are here."

"Like he could tell. The old bastard doesn't even know it's his daughter," scoffed the husband.

"He knows. Henri just cannot express himself anymore. He worries for her."

"He worries for her. That's priceless. If he worries so much, why doesn't he cough up her inheritance? What are you in here for?" He didn't wait for an answer.

Since he was at it, "Hey you little bastards get over here before one of them decides to plug your buttholes." The kids stretched their moment, but knew better than bug dad when in one of his moods. Falco saw this as he pretended to sort some stones. When the boys got back to the sad clown, they started a push-pull match that stressed dad's temper. They were kids, they couldn't help themselves. At one point, push had come to shove and the younger tumbled into the easel tipping it and falling into grandpa at the same time, sending them all to the floor.

Dad snapped. The older boy caught a backhand across the face that sent him sprawling and bawling across the floor. He grabbed the younger by the scruff of his neck, lifting him until his feet were dangling. "I told you to quit playing around. Now look what you've done!" Dad raised his free hand to strike the crying youth. It was caught by Falco before finding its mark.

"The boy has done no harm. Henri is fine," he said calmly.

"Get your hands off me, you crazy old shit!" Dad went to jerk his arm away, but was bested by superior strength.

"I am not crazy. But if you hit that boy, I may decide to be."

"Call the guar..." Falco let go.

All the while, the wife had been attending to Henri, missing the altercation. The older boy had crawled back and was pleading to his father to put his brother down. "It was my fault," he cried. "Hit me!"

He kicked the older boy back to the ground and belted the younger a cruel right jab that split his lip and broke his heart. It was the last thing Dad ever did. When the blood from the boy's lip splattered Falco in the face, he decided. Falco picked up his heaviest mall and clocked dad before he could strike the boy again. He knew what kind of man this was. He would never stop beating his kids and wife and so Falco went to work. By the time security pulled the blood soaked mason away from the body, it was too late, Falco had gone total O.C.D. In fact, all that was left was the body. The head had been smashed to pulp, even the bone.

The boys cheered Falco on while mom grabbed them and ran for help. Henri sat on the floor watching him do what he could not do himself. A smile spread across his face and he said the first intelligible words Falco had ever heard him say, "Thank you." Henri never painted another sad clown. There is a small house in suburban Bucharest where a widow lives with her two sons and aging father. Happy clowns cover the walls.

Igor was never quite sure why he visited the estate in Karuna's absence. He wasn't driven to it and was, so far, above snooping through drawers. Yet he was compelled, not exactly against his will, but not with it either. As if there was something to be learned in an uninterrupted viewing.

As Karuna told the mysterious tale to a group of students, most blew it off as just that – a tale, with no basis in reality other than to inspire interest, Igor listened and remembered. A part of him had hoped to be drawn into the scenes. To go the step farther than the mesmerizing effect that captured anyone who gazed for too long. Fueled on Karuna's coffee, he sat all night long. It wasn't until dawn hinted at itself on the eastern horizon that he tasted the humid salt air dusted with drying fish and sweat. Hot sand burned the soles of his feet. He had done it!

As dusk turned to night Igor wandered the hallways alone viewing the menagerie. The light of a full moon cast a monochrome glow over the colorful mosaics. He stopped when he recognized the stone walled barn set back from the beach. The asylum was alive on a summer's day. The crazies were busy being themselves while the staff was frantically trying to keep them in a herd. Studying the grounds around the building, he spied a hammer and chisel lying on the grass next to a stool next to a boulder. The stone was partially carved. A hand wielding a short sword was frozen in a moment in time as it jutted from the rock. Igor felt himself having an out-of-body experience. The next thing he knew he was being manhandled, his body was being dragged through the sand. He struggled against the rough hands receiving a hard blow to the head for his efforts. Igor was dumped on the ground before a tent that provided shade for those inside. A man dressed in the clothes of the aristocracy sat on a dais and was being fanned by one of the obsessive-compulsive inmates. They were perfect for this kind of duty. The man looked down on Igor with pity and disgust. He did not understand the insane, but the nut before him had broken the law and was subject to it. There was no such thing as an insanity plea.

The man had a weak voice. Try as he might Igor could not understand what he was saying. The language sounded like his own, but gibberish instead of words. There was no mistaking the gravity of his tonality. When he finished, there was a pause wherein Igor seemed to be given a chance to speak. When he did, the man seated in the shade shook his head, barked an order, and waved his hand. Next.

Igor was dragged to the side of the tent, not knowing what was going to happen to him or why. He was clubbed hard on the back of his shoulders, bringing Igor to his knees. His arms were taken hold of and stretched out before him and place on a stump. The terror of the situation ramped up when a big man with an axe stepped into view. Igor closed his eyes when the tool whistled through the air as it came down. In his minds eye, before the bolt of blinding white pain, he saw the judge. Dressed in red and black, the cruel face with its broad mustache peered down on him, damning Igor with eyes darker than the pits of hell.

If there was a next frame to the mosaics, it would show Igor's blood draining into the sand as he was pulled back into the sanitarium. It was in that moment of pain and agony that disengaged him from the hypnotic reality of the images. Igor crawled away from the tiles in his last conscious effort, laying on the floor and waiting to die.

Igor woke to the glare of fluorescent. The smell of isopropyl alcohol assaulted his sense of smell while a tube jabbed painfully into his nostril. There was a hum of little machines and the sound of voices just beyond a closed door. He had never noticed how many shades of white there were as he took in the hospital room. The I.V. had a morphine drip. Igor went to press the little button that would give him more when he was shocked out of dream into reality. He raised his other hand. Thick layers of gauze wrapped his hands and wrists, which were held immobile by metal braces. The heavy ache that came from beneath the bandaging made him try again to hit the button, successfully this time.

There was no big 'where am I?' going through his head. He remembered everything clearly and was amazed he was not dead. Who taught him to use the morphine dripper was another question. His short- term memory was shot. The drugs he decided, when the door opened and Karuna and Riana entered. As usual, she looked fabulous for a woman her age, but even through his haze he could see worry and anxiety. He figured it was for him. Riana on the other hand was angry, veiled thinly with concern.

"We came by earlier. You woke up this morning," Karuna was smooth.

"I don't remember. Where is Sechra?"

The two women replied simultaneously. "She is on her way to Bucharest for the opening. What do you remember?"

"Good. It is important she is there," replied Igor.

"You were to be there with her, remember?" Riana shot back.

"Yes I do." Igor was ashamed for his neglect of Sechra. But he was not about to apologize for it to these women. "I remember everything and will satisfy your curiosity if you will be patient. Would you be so kind as to answer a few questions for me first?"

"Of course, Igor. It must have been a horrible experience," consoled Karuna. Riana assented by her silence.

"Who found me?"

"I did, upon returning from Bucharest."

"Why did you not let me die?"

"Of all the things to say. After all we have done for you!"

"Riana, that is enough," snapped Karuna. "Igor, why would I have? You have always been a fine teacher and a friend, I hope."

"And if I was your enemy?"

Riana was out of her chair slapping Igor hard across the face. He sat there. Not stunned but accepting like a servant after being struck by his master.

"I suppose I deserved that. It must be the drugs." He seethed beneath a placid exterior. "If you will be seated." Igor began his story, omitting nothing. With the exception that he discovered what he was searching for. "...I was carving a stone at the asylum. Having been there for some time I began to take certain liberties. For this sculpture I needed a sword and took one from a sleeping guard. You see it was important to have to get the musculature right when being fiercely gripped. My theft was discovered, for I made no attempt to hide it. When I explained why, they laughed at me saying I should have used a hammer. In my mind, it was a sword I desired and I had to have it. After all I was crazy then. My plea went to the magistrate, a Dracul. This was his judgment." Igor raised his clenched fists. Fresh blood saturated the gauze and began dripping on the sheets.

Karuna went to the door and hailed a passing nurse. In a very short order, Karuna and Riana were asked to leave.

***

K aruna drove back to the estate with a furious Riana in the passenger seat.

"Just who does he think he is?"

"Come on Riana, let it go. He is confused, doped, and may have lost his hands for Christ's sake. We know nothing about his youth and what he may have gone through. We know how bad it got. Maybe he does, too."

"We'll know soon enough," replied Riana pulling a file from her handbag. "Rank has its privileges. When we get home we'll find out all about our stonecutter. I'll tell you this. He has it in for the Draculs."

Karuna stepped harder on the accelerator.

With coffee brewing, Karuna went to her room for a few minutes, returning a little less dour. Riana had left a laptop on the dining room table tabbed to the sequences they wanted to look at.

"Mom, did you just..." asked Riana.

"It's been a rough few days." Karuna really felt no reason to explain her actions.

"Haven't you had enough?" Riana slipped a newspaper out of the file, folded open to the second page.

"I was wondering if it was going to hit the papers." Now she had to defend herself. "It just happened. I stopped to save them."

"Not all of them." Riana took a big swallow of coffee.

"He would not have survived."

"That's not the way the paper sees it. One of the survivors says, and I quote, 'It stole my children and ate my husband before my eyes!' The article goes on to say how the vehicle exploded into flames destroying any evidence that would corroborate the woman's story. The local news is eating it up and the national is just getting a taste of it."

"How do you know all this?" Karuna asked, suddenly very nervous.

"It's my business to know."

"Should I leave the country?"

"Vlad says no. Not yet. The media can only take it so far. If there is no evidence to warrant an investigation, the story will dissolve for lack of sensation. He also wanted to ask if you have had any visions, intuitions or are aware of any synchronistic events."

"Other than that," Karuna pointed at the paper, "no. But there may be activities of which I am unaware." Giovanni and Jake agreed on one thing without exception; never apologize. Karuna wanted to most desperately, but held tough. To apologize would indicate guilt, of which Karuna really didn't feel any. It would also imply that it wouldn't happen again. Karuna was not so sure about that either.

"Of course now there is Igor, so yes, there are at least two events."

They sat and began reviewing the tabbed items. As suspected, the mosaics did change and the handless man certainly looked like Igor. Upon closer examination, the one who appeared to be the judge was not Vlad Tepes III. Perhaps a brother or close relative. The crest of the dragon was emblazoned on the cloak. Karuna picked up a magnifying glass.

"We can blow it up, Mom. What do you want to see?"

"The magistrate. Bring it in close, a bust," Karuna indicated.

Riana tapped the keys and the screen jumped four times in progressively closer images. "That's as big as we can make it without it pixelating on us."

The magnifying glass came up. After a minute that had Riana tapping her fingers on the table, "Oh my God. I just don't understand," Karuna said more to herself than Riana. She handed the glass to Riana. After a moment there was a sharp intake of breath.

"What are you doing in there?"

"I don't know. But I intend on finding out. Come on!" Karuna got up and led the way to where she found Igor's hands and the mosaic image in question. "I'm going in and would like you to stand by."

"We have to shower and dress. The flight back to Bucharest is in a few hours. Sechra's opening, remember?"

"Yes dear," Karuna began pulling up a stool to sit on. "This, I think, is more important at the moment. She will understand if we are not there. All I am planning is a little look."

"I've heard that before. Your call. What do you want me to do?"

"Pull me out if I start bleeding."

A searing wind flapped the side of the beach tent. It was the end of the month and the lord of the county was there to pass judgment on those who had broken the law during the last twenty-eight days. Her own curse flowed red at this time, too, and the redress for those was always ruthless as she took her spite out on them. The first, today, was a witless fool from the asylum. Dracine sipped from a cup of cool water before reading the charges to the condemned. She enjoyed watching them as they drank with their eyes the fluid that she allowed to dribble from the corners of her wet mouth.

"You have been accused of thievery. The penalty for this crime is the loss of your right hand. But, and today is a lucky day," she smiled with sinister pleasure, "since you happened to take the weapon of the Boyar's guard, you will lose the other hand as well. We should kill you now as I'm sure you wish for it. But then the lesson would be lost, would it not?" It was a rhetorical question. "You may now state your case." Dracine sat back and smoked from a hookah. She was already forgetting about the man who stood before her pleading for his life. Within the cloud of smoke, she began to shake violently.

Karuna came out of the trance in a coughing fit. The smell of hashish and tobacco was pungent. In the distance she could hear someone calling to her. The sound came closer and closer.

"Mom! Mom! Wake up!" Riana took her hands From Karuna's shoulders as the older woman's eyes opened. "What happened, Karuna? I know you said to wake if you started to bleed. You were smoking!"

"That is how Dracine coped with condemning the peasants," Karuna rasped, her throat still irritated.

"Who is Dracine?"

"The magistrate. I had to know and now I do. It was the judge's features and the way the cloak folded around her. You can barely see the outlines of breasts. Karuna pointed at the computer monitor. "The face was too soft when compared to the men standing about."

"But she is dressed like a man," Riana replied looking closer.

"During those times, women were not allowed to hold positions of rank and power. She is, however, a Dracul. Tepes' sister or perhaps a cousin. I wasn't there long enough to find out."

"What else?"

"She enjoyed her work. I guess it runs in the family. We should call the hospital and see how Igor is doing." Karuna stood and stretched her back, heading to the kitchen and more coffee.

"This is Doctor Koroloff," came from the phone.

"Good afternoon doctor, Karuna Danesti. How is Igor?"

"As well as can be expected, considering...Can you tell me what caused him to throw such a fit?" asked Koroloff.

"No. Why?" Karuna was being cautious.

"If it happens again he 'will' lose both hands for good. We plan on keeping him sedated for as long as we can."

"Should we call in a psychiatrist? He has a history."

"Yes I know. I have a good man on staff, but Igor has no insurance."

"I will pay," she said. "Whatever he needs."

"Have you read the news about the collision on the main highway?" Koroloff asked, changing the subject.

"Only what was in the paper. Why do you ask?"

"I was wondering if you saw it. You left the hospital around the time it happened and the accident was not far from your home. You know, Ms. Danesti, I have read your history, too."

A threat is a threat no matter how you phrase it. Karuna took immediate dislike to the implications, regardless of their accuracy. "It is a matter of public record. Riana and I have been fully vetted. Everyone has access to our life history."

"Not all of it."

"If you have something to say doctor, say it."

"I am just curious. Perhaps when you come to visit Igor, we can schedule a talk."

"Curiosity is overrated. Remember the cat?"

"I said I am curious, not a fool. Good night, Ms. Danesti."

Karuna was staring at the receiver, when Riana interrupted her reverie.

They stopped by the hospital on the way to the airport. Igor was out of it and Dr. Koroloff was gone for the day. Karuna left a flower arrangement she knew would be gone when they returned. Her mood darkened as the sun dipped below the horizon, the jet chasing it on its way to Bucharest. Karuna kept Dr. Koroloff and what he said out of the conversation...

"...in all your research never came across the name Dracine?"

"There is no Dracine on record. She seemed about the same age as Miruna...how is my granddaughter?"

"Still the same. Ever since that incident when she got her first period, we have had to keep her in an asylum. She has decided to continue with her education, so we hope." Riana pushed back her emotions. "Wait till you see at Christmas? She is blossoming into quite a woman."

Karuna inserted a memory chip into her laptop. It contained a reproduction of the Tepes diaries. She skimmed through the files looking for the entries written after his return from Turkey at the age of fifteen. She had never read the entire work. If anything Tepes was prolific, 56,000 thousand pages in all. Setting the computer to continue the search, she put the tool away in preparation for landing in Bucharest.

A stretched black limousine was waiting for them at the baggage claim. "One of the perks," Riana glibbed, concerning her lifestyle.

The sky was white with glare from spotlights strategically placed around the Museum. The structure, built by the Goths in the eleventh century, was now used by lighting artists around the world. Pinnacled chapels, coppiced walls, arched windows and flying buttresses all waited for light and shadow to bring them to life. Tonight the façade was lit to capture its torturous past. It prepared the guests for what lay beyond the doorway. The rich and famous stepped from luxurious cars only to be harassed by paparazzi and flashing bulbs until they reached the massive oak doors of the entrance. There, security stopped everyone that was not allowed inside, much to the relief of the guests. The foyer and lobby were devoid of any adornments, refreshments, appetizers, or explanations. The artist had consented to let them use the front door to keep up their appearances, but it was around back that the real celebration was being held.

Wagons with mules, beater trucks, and every other form of non-traditional transportation that you could think of, were parked back there. The people traveled from all parts of Romania to witness the exhibition. Sechra Kcirb said 'it was for them'. Roast lamb and pig on spits, kegs of beer and cases of spirits and more, fed the gypsies. These were the people that made the country strong. They were also the ones that paid the dreadful price of their independence.

The limousine that carried Riana and Karuna cruised the main entrance, but did not stop. Taking a left around the corner then another, they came to a blockade of gypsy vehicles. Men with dark faces and black wool suits patrolled the access to the loading docks. The driver rolled his window down.

"You must turn around. You belong up front," said one of the guards brandishing a machine gun and pointing with its barrel.

Riana placed her hand on the driver's shoulder, "I'll take care of it, Ahmed." She pressed the little button and the back window slid silently down halfway. The guard immediately noticed his disappearing reflection.

"I told your driver, now get out of here! You do not belong."

"Young man. Do you know who I am?" Riana asked politely in the guard's dialect.

"Just another rich wannabe by the looks. Now do as you're told." He raised the gun.

Ahmed dropped the car in reverse, catching the guard's attention. He did not see Karuna slip out the passenger side door. Not that he would have, but distractions are always nice. She reached around the guard while he was trying to assess what had just happened and yanked the gun from his grasp while she kicked him in the back of his knees, dropping him the ground.

Karuna was dressed in a shimmering black pantsuit, pearls, and her salt and pepper hair pulled back tight in a ponytail. Elegant and austere at the same time. Her right foot stood on the guard's hand. She held the barrel of the gun to the back of his head.

"This is a fine weapon you have, young man. I see it is stamped New Romanian Acquisitions. Boris really should have more discretion." The guard jerked at her statement. She leaned harder on her foot and pressed on the barrel. He relaxed.

"The woman you were pointing this thing at is my daughter. That alone is reason enough for me to splatter your brains all over the ground." Karuna inhaled deeply. "However you are of the blood and this is your night."

A group of men were on their way to see what the holdup was. They were still a few moments away. "Now young man. I hope you have not soiled yourself as your boss is coming to check on you. When you stand I will hand your gun back and you will greet Riana Danesti respectfully and pass the car through."

"Lon! What are you doing there?" came a voice from behind. Lon, the guard, with his gun suddenly back in his hands turned to the voices. His face began to turn red as the warm stain in his pants began to cool.

He pivoted again, remembering his instructions.

"Good evening, Riana Danesti. We have been waiting for you. Please enter."

A barricade was moved. Ahmed put the car in drive and began to ease through the opening.

"Thank you, Lon," Riana waved from the window. "We are lucky to have such brave young men." Lon's embarrassment couldn't have been worse.

As the car disappeared in to the mélange of vehicles, the other guards caught up.

"Hey man, do you know who that was?"

"Riana Danesti," Lon said proudly.

The sniffing began to get obnoxiously loud. "Jesus, Lon, get a little nervous seeing celebrities?"

"You don't know the half of it," Lon said less embarrassed. "Can I go clean up?"

"Geez, Mom, just where did you learn that?" Riana asked, exasperated at Karuna's display of stealth.

"Jake and Giovanni taught me more than how to surf and consume tequila to excess."

"Yeah but did you have to scare the piss out of him?"

"Well... he did point a gun at you."

A wave of hands and faces converged on the limo. "Come on, Mom, out of the pan and into the fire." Ahmed got out of the car, opening the door for Riana. She wore a conservative black wool skirt and jacket. The difference was the cut, style and quality of the wool. The color was all the same. Two older women pushed through the crowd. They offered Riana a traditional babushka, an abundance of color in the otherwise fuscous attire. When she tied it on, Riana was transformed into one of the family and once she blended with the crowd it was impossible to pick her out. The gathering surged with Riana away from the car. Now that he could, Ahmed went around to the other side and got Karuna's door. There were a few stragglers waiting for the next of the biggies to arrive. Ahmed reached in and took the cool hand reassuringly. Karuna took it, noticing several guns beneath Ahmed's jacket. She smiled and stepped out into the night.

"Thank you, Ahmed. It would seem we are on our own. Would you like to come into the exhibit with me?"

"I have not been invited."

"I just did. Besides I will not know anyone here and I will feel more comfortable with you and those guns around."

"I really don't think 'you' need my protection," Ahmed said respectfully. He watched the incident happen and was still unsure how she did it.

"Please?" Karuna put on her best smile. Her charm overwhelmed him.

Arm in arm they meandered through the party. Riana was invisible, but wherever the crowd pulsed is where she would be. Smiles and laughter rolled around the gala. Sparkling bright eyes lit the night. It wasn't the collage of happy faces that caught Karuna's attention. Interspersed in the action were freeze frames of bitter, piercing, glares. No sooner did she see them than they would dissolve back into the crowd. She began to grow paranoid. Did it show? Had she been seen the other night? Dark eyes lanced into her, cutting deeply. 'My God, what have I done?'

"Ahmed, let us go inside. I feel a chill."

"I, too, feel the cold, but I fear it has nothing to do with the weather." He looked down on her with dark knowing eyes and nodded his head in understanding. Karuna replied in kind.

Their eyes adjusted to the gloom inside the museum. Spotlights lit the sculptures but shared little of that light with the surrounding areas. Since the pieces were life-size, it was sometimes difficult to separate the silhouetted patrons of the arts from the art itself. 'Oohhs and Ahhs' of tuxedos and gowns mingled with the tears and weeping of babushka'd women. Here we had two groups of Roma. One had viewed the revolution on vid screens from the safety of fortified estates in foreign countries. Their status gave them inside information they could have used to help their brothers and sisters in the mountains and urban areas. Instead they used it to save their own skins and pitied those left behind. The ones who stayed were of the other group. Though all had witnessed the horrendous events that led to revolution, there is a difference in watching it from an easy chair with a cold scotch, and living it, forced to witness loved ones butchered and fed to the masses.

Standing next to the exhibit of the impaling process, Ahmed said quietly, "Riana has shown me photos of the work, but they do not capture the essence." He blessed himself in Arabic. "Are these really scenes from her childhood?"

"Yes. When Sechra came under our care, I fear it was too late. These images were carved into her young mind. Consider this. She was one of the lucky ones." Her words summoned a scream from the crowd.

"Katrina!"

Security was on the move. Without creating a stir, they worked the exhibit auditorium locking doors then herding all the kids and their families to one side of the room. Tempers began to flair amongst the stiff collars and gold for the interruption. Everyone had been mingling without problem. The sculptures had them ensorcelled. Now the tide of economics began to divide the room into the primary groups. For the sake of understanding, the rich and the poor. Riana consoled her way out of the ranks of the poor to take a stand on the Maginot line that separated them. She raised her hands.

"Please, please. I would like your attention." Respect swept the room quiet. "A little girl has been lost. We need to come together to find her. She can't have gone far. Word is being passed outside the building, but she probably didn't get that far. When we find her, we can witness the final unveiling for the night. Let's all assist security. Please people!"

'What the hell was the matter with everyone? So quick to make assumptions and take sides,' Riana thought scanning for her mother. Another scream broke the white sounds of the crowds murmur. This one was less descriptive, but just as terrible. Then the specifics came.

"YOU," yelled a well-dressed woman who had fallen on the floor in a pool of red gunk while a couple of young boys ran through the adults tossing a ketchup squirt bottle. The woman was not yelling at the boys, but at Karuna who was victim of the prank, too. It was going to get ugly. Karuna looked down the front of her outfit. A heavy blast from the ketchup bottle painted a gush of crimson down her chin and across her chest. The woman had slipped in the puddle and by now smeared it all over herself. She began to rave and the situation started to get that out of control feeling. Men in tuxedos stepped forward reaching for their cummerbunds. Ahmed took hold of Karuna's arm backing her into the crowd of gypsies. They parted like the Red Sea for Moses and closed in afterwards. Several coarse black overcoats absorbed the first few bullets, crumpling to the ground. Flashes and the pops of handguns being used in close quarters echoed around the hall, stirring the corralled and nervous group into a stampede that wouldn't end until half of them were dead.

Ahmed guided Karuna to a service door. "Through here. Follow the hallway to the exit! I must stay and take care of Riana. Run!" he yelled, tossing her one of his guns. The door slammed shut behind her followed by a rapid series of shots being fired. She raced down the hall taking the first left she came to. It ended at the employees' lounge. Karuna spun on her heels, bolting back the way she came, but then stopped dead in her tracks. She heard something from the lounge. Disregarding Ahmeds's advice, she backed down the hall, cautiously peering through the door. A refrigerator door was opened. There sat a little girl eating ice cream at the table. Karuna slid the handgun into her back pocket.

"Sure looks good. Can I have some?"

"I guess so," the girl said tentatively. Seeing Karuna's smile she added, "There is a lot more."

Karuna retrieved a spoon and dipped into the common bowl. "MMM, you're right it is good. What's your name?"

"Katrina," piped Katrina.

"Do your parents know where you are?"

"I don't know. I was hungry."

"You think we should go find them and let them know you are okay?"

"I suppose. They're busy doing adult stuff."

"I bet they are worried. Come on. You can bring your ice cream."

"Oh no. I'm not suppose to have ice cream. You're not gonna tell them are you?"

"It will be our little secret," Karuna replied wiping a drip from Katrina's chin.

Karuna pulled her phone dialing Riana's number. She cancelled it and dialed Ahmed's instead. Riana would be dealing with the riotous crowd.

"Hello," came the harsh voice.

"Ahmed, it's Karuna. I have found the little girl."

"Hold on."

"Karuna, where are you?" Ahmed gave the phone to Riana.

"I don't know. Have Ahmed meet me at the door. He'll know."

Karuna closed the line and took Katrina's hand and headed to the exhibition hall. They waited at the door. There were no more shots being fired. The door handle turned opening just enough for Ahmed to squeeze his head in.

"Give me the girl." He reached one hand in through the opening. Katrina pulled back hiding behind the older woman.

"Katrina? He is going to take you to your parents. Take his hand." Karuna reached behind her pulling Katrina around.

"Noooo!" Katrina squirmed trying to break Karuna's hold. Ahmed opened the door farther. From behind him a man yelled, "There she is!"

He wasn't hollering about the little girl. Several guns fired splintering the door and jam. Ahmed's body jerked as his knees buckled. He grabbed Katrina and made a protective ball of his body round her. "Run!"

A posse began clambering over Ahmed and Katrina. Karuna had a head start and rounded a corner to the right this time before bullets slammed into the end wall. The exit sign was ahead. When she got to the door it was locked. She pulled Ahmed's gun, emptying the magazine into the locking mechanism. Karuna threw herself into the door, crumpling to the floor when it didn't give. She crawled back away stood and put all she had into another charge. She crashed into the door as a hail of bullets careened down the hall. Karuna took two in the midsection before bursting through the door.

Lon was smoking a cigarette waiting for his pants to dry when bullets hammered the exit door. He brought his gun to bear when Karuna came tumbling into the driveway.

"Help me," she cried, clutching her side.

Lon dropped to his knees beside her. "What can I do?"

"Get me out of here!" They both heard men charging down the hall. "Hurry!" Lon may have been new to the game, but he was big and had one hell of a survival instinct. He lifted Karuna over his shoulder and ran into the maze of parked vehicles. Bullets pinged off steel and shattered window glass as he zigzagged to the far side of the lot. Returning fire would just pin them out. He leaned Karuna against a car.

"Can you stand?"

"Yes."

"Do you think you can ride?" Lon was busy fishing the keys to his motorcycle out of his pocket as a spray of lead splattered through the chain-link fence.

Karuna was on the back of the cycle before he was.

"Keep your legs and arms tucked in real tight."

The engine started with a roar that didn't subside. Lon dropped it into first, let out the clutch, spinning the rear tire as he smoked the bike down the narrow lanes between cars. He blasted into the exit lane, shifting gears as fast as he could. "Hold ON!" They smashed through a barricade, leaned hard in a left hand turn and vanished down the darkened streets of Bucharest.

***

'Life goes on,' thought Sechra as she helped the truckers secure the last of the sculptures to the truckbeds. The drivers did not know Igor and carried on the way men do around a pretty young girl, all 'haw haw' and crude innuendo. She played on it; otherwise she was liable to burst into tears at any moment. Somehow she rose above and persevered against her emotions. They never served anyway, always being a distraction to keep you from dealing with reality. Then there was the fact that there just wasn't any time for it. She had to follow the trucks to be there to unload. She and Igor were going to share in the responsibility. Sechra already called Frederick Cezar half a dozen times to see if he could handle the Bucharest end of things. He had not returned the calls. She figured the museum was a madhouse preparing for the big night and didn't hold it against him. But at fifteen percent of the take, the least he could do was return her calls. Sometimes you just have to take it as it comes and this was one of them. Sechra hastily loaded clothes and toiletries into the panniers on the BMW. Pulling on the leather riding suit, she lifted the headboard to her bed to get the handgun. Underneath a silk scarf were the gun boxes. One held the pistol – the other, WAS GONE! The machine gun had been stolen! 'Ah fuck,' she said to herself. Taking a quick inventory, not only was the gun gone but two mags and all her ammunition. Her jewelry and items of personal value were left alone. 'God damn it!' Sechra didn't care about the gun, but the thought that it could get into the wrong hands terrified her. Oddly, thankful the pistol was loaded, she slipped it into an inside pocket of her suit and locked the house.

The five-hour ride to Bucharest was barely long enough to clear her head. She passed the delivery trucks a few hours after leaving the studio. She waved, they honked, she rocked back on the throttle and left them in the dust.

The establishment was a Russian-era block tenement purported to be a five-star hotel. Sechra doubted if it rated two stars, but it had secure parking and was only a couple blocks from the museum. She checked in, then showered away the last two days of sweat, worry and road grit. The missing gun rattled her to the core. No one knew she had it, except Igor, and he was in no position to be using it. Could he have taken it? But why?

After a bite to eat at the hotel's diner, which dropped the rating to one star, she headed out to get some clothes. Typical artist attire, black on black on black seemed best. At five PM, Sechra met with Frederick at the loading dock of the museum. She walked up to him, palms up before her in a 'what the fuck happened to you?' display.

"I thought Igor was going to show."

"He's had an accident. I rode in an hour ago. Why haven't you returned my calls?" she asked non-accusatorially.

"Guilty as charged," he replied. "I have some personal issues and would rather not get into it. But don't worry, Thora has been working hard and I've been pitching in. This end of things is under control. What's with Igor?"

"Are your personal issues about Thora? You jump her bones yet?" Sechra still hadn't shaken hanging out with the truckers.

"No."

"Ah ha. There's the problem."

"I wish it were that easy," Frederick began before being saved by the air horn of a semi as it pulled up to the loading dock. They both looked up. Sechra waved, the horn sounded in reply.

"You think this area will be big enough for the party?" Sechra pointed to the parking area.

"Twenty-five thousand square meters, I hope so."

"Me too. People from all over the country are coming and some have arrived already."

"Security is already dealing with them," responded Frederick.

"What!" she shouted.

"They have been turning them away at the gate."

"I was specific with Thora about letting the people in. Not all can afford hotel rooms and this show is for all of Romania."

"Yeah...about that," Frederick said slowly. "We think it's a bad idea."

"Now you tell me?"

"You have been kind of unapproachable on the subject. You're trying to mix water and oil, using gas to put out a fire. It doesn't matter how you phrase it. The Boyars do not readily blend with those who live close to the earth."

"Just say it, Cezar, they're poor and the fucking Boyars are just going to have to live with it."

Frederick knew he was on thin ice. He was saved again by the truckers backing into place. "Stay here Frederick. I'm going to talk with Thora."

A half-hour later, a plethora of mobile dwellings rolled into the lot. Sechra had not been able to find Thora Wozniak, so she went to the head of security and laid down the law. Let the gypsies and the poor in.

***

A motorcade and SWAT van pulled into the front of the museum. The SWAT van continued around back. The riot was over, but Vlad Cneajna wasn't taking any chances.

"Stop that van," Cneajna ordered. It wasn't the gypsy's that began the shooting. "Have the van at the front steps. Any guest with a gun is to be taken into custody. No exceptions." The order was radioed throughout the motorcade. It wasn't long before a line of tuxedos led to the waiting van.

Vlad had seen this day coming. He'd only hoped...it didn't matter what he hoped. The reality was that it struck close to home. The last decade saw a growing division begin to separate the people. The wealthy, traditionally the Boyars, were colluding with Megacorp to do something about the current state of affairs. Not all the Romanians were for or pleased with the outcome of the revolution. Many were left with nothing once Megacorp pulled its presence from the country. How quickly they had forgotten, as Cneajna knew they would, within a generation, that Megacorp had relieved itself of the responsibility of a nation that couldn't produce and gave it to a madman. Megacorp had used the people and the land: when they were done with it, they couldn't care less.

A tight circle of heavily armed guards absorbed Cneajna as he stepped from the stretch. He eyed the faces glaring at him from the line. Their hands cuffed behind them couldn't hide the body language. If it were not for the restraints, they would have leapt on him and torn Cneajna to pieces. Some of the faces were familiar and turned in shame for being caught up in the madness. 'Good men or not, they made their choice.'

Vlad knew better than to assume Riana would be waiting for him. At a signal, one of his guards broke rank to search for her. Vlad eyed the scene. The mob was spent, yet it was still easy to see what had happened. The young Katrina wandered away, not interested in the affairs of adults and followed her cravings. When her curiosity led her from the crowd and her parents panicked, the shit began to fly. Old prejudices reared their ugly heads and warped reality into a nightmare. The Boyars immediately began accusing the gypsies of stealing the child, and other children, for generations.

The question surfaced, 'Why had they been so well armed?' This was a social affair meant to bring the groups together. Was it just fear or was it a set up? Sure, the wealthy were outnumbered ten-to-one, but Vlad felt no compulsion to ramp up security against the gypsies. Instead Riana had spoken with the heads of the clans asking them to come with open hands. They agreed and there was no reason to suspect otherwise. If his intel was correct, most of the injuries were bullet wounds, a few knife wounds, and collateral scuffle damage. His common sense kicked in and Vlad had a wry laugh to himself. 'If the gypsies had brought guns there would have been a hell of a lot more people killed.'

Riana arrived with Ahmed leaning on her shoulder and a security guard. She asked the guard to help, but he replied that his job was to protect her and if he was helping Ahmed he couldn't very well do that. There was no use arguing with the mindset.

"Thank you, Ahmed. Riana said you went above the call and it looks like you did. If you hadn't saved the kid...well let's not go there. Can you drive?" Cneajna asked.

"Yes, it is nothing a few stitches won't cure. But you should thank Karuna. Have you heard from her?" Ahmed was suddenly concerned as his memory recounted the events. "She gave me the child." He choked with emotion. "I am sorry, Prime Minister. I have failed you."

"Karuna is quite a capable woman, Ahmed." Vlad sensed the man's guilt and gave him the means to clear his conscience. "Since you feel this way, then you must find her."

"Thank you." Ahmed snapped his heels, bowed at the waist and wasted no time returning to the doorway where he last saw Karuna.

"He's already tracking her, isn't he?"

"That's why he was hired, dear."

***

Frederick Cezar paced Thora's office. It was the morning of the opening and she was nowhere to be found. After a thorough search of the museum, he wound up in the midst of the Kcirb exhibition. A shiver ran down his spine. For years he watched Sechra create them, but given the right moment and lighting, the sculptures still gave him the weirds. This was one of those times. The auditorium was silent for the moment. Frederick listened. He could almost hear the screams of the tortured all around him when he thought he heard Thora's voice amongst them. There it was again. The same cries as the victims of the sculptures, but her voice. HELP! MERCY! He ran back to her office where he now stood deciding whether he had the balls to do what he felt he had to.

He waited outside the storeroom door for staff traffic to stop and allow him unnoticed access. When the moment came, his hand reached for the doorknob, he turned and pushed. The deadbolt was locked. 'Damn, damn, damn,' he thought when Thora's secretary came up to him. "Do you need to get in?"

Frederick was so wound up he jumped, passing gas at the sudden fright. "Uh yes, I do. Some files Thora was suppose to get for me. Have you seen her?" he asked with a huge amount of trepidation.

"Whoa Frederick! What did you have for lunch?" Thora's secretary took another whiff, keyed the lock and backed away. "Bad glumki, ya?"

Frederick was embarrassed, his face turning appropriate shades of red. "I guess. Thanks for the door."

"You're welcome. Heck of a day not to come in or call. Maybe it's her mom." She turned heading to wherever she was going.

Frederick turned the knob again, glancing up and down the hall before going inside. The safe was pushed over to one side giving access to the secret door. The stone slab was back in place, mating seamlessly with the stones around it. Frederick stood there scratching his head. 'How did she do it?' he cursed himself for not being more attentive.

Angie, the secretary, stuck her head into the storage room. "You find what you wanted?"

For the second time today, Fredrick's bowels loosened. He was afraid to fart for fear he might shit himself. "Yes," he said picking up some files. "One slipped under the safe."

"That happened to me before. You know there is a secret doorway where you're standing." Angie reached over picking up the long screwdriver. "We used to sneak down there and get high in the old days."

"No kidding?" not having to fake his astonishment.

"We were young, then I forgot about it till now." Angie inserted the driver leaning on it to release the mechanism. "Unhh, that ought to do it."

Frederick watched in amazement. "You mean you've been down there?"

"Lotsa times. But not recently, you know." The odor of the corpses below wafted up through the open door. "Ooh, man. That reminds me.

Here you go." Angie handed him a bottle of something to ease his stomach problems. "I'd do a double dose right now if I were you."

"Thanks, I guess." He unscrewed the cap downing a good swig. "Find anything?"

"No, the place is empty. Somebody really cleaned it out." She left the screwdriver in the hole. "That will keep it from closing on you."

"I'm not going down there."

"You will, Frederick, once your imagination gets a hold of you. If you get lost just scream, I'll hear you. The sound really travels through those halls." She smiled conspiratorially and laughing, "See you later, some of us still have work to do."

"Uh, yeah right." Now he was really confused. If Thora was down there screaming, why hadn't Angie heard her? Then it hit him. The doorway was closed. But why had he heard it?

***

Lon rode Karuna all the way to the coast. She was afraid, injured and who knows why she was being chased. Karuna invited him into the estate for coffee and something to eat. After the ride, they were both starving, each in their own way.

"Shouldn't we get you to the hospital?" Lon asked more than a little concerned.

"I'll be fine, Lon. The bleeding made it appear worse than it is." Karuna made a mental push for him to drop the subject.

"Mmmm, good sandwich. Why were those men chasing you?"

"They thought I had something to do with the missing girl."

"Did you?" Lon asked.

"No, Lon," Karuna eyed him over her glasses. "I found her. They misunderstood."

"Heck of a misunderstanding."

"The men were afraid. I don't hold it against them."

"I would," Lon said protectively

Karuna leaned into him, "Thank you, Lon."

She knew what he really wanted and gave it to him.

Shortly after dawn Lon left for Bucharest more of a man than he had ever been. Karuna packed her bags, cooler and laptop, loading it into the Mercedes. She was torn. Something was happening that was out of her control. The 'call of the wild' the other night was part of something larger. She was afraid. Not only for her daughter and Sechra, but also for the peoples of Romania. Yet it was herself that she was most afraid of and what she might do. Riana and Vlad would not need the added distraction of Karuna's uncontrollable nature with a nation dividing. She changed the voicemail message at the estate saying it would be closed until further notice while she penned a note to Riana.

'Dear Riana, I have gone. I don't know where I am going or when I will return. My presence would further complicate matters for you. Sechra has been taken care of. Use her if you can. She understands more about what is going on than you or I ever will. I love you, Karuna.'

She wanted to say more, to pour her heart out to her daughter. To talk to someone about the madness that was going on in her mind. Karuna knew it was not to be. At the end of the driveway, she looked up and down the highway. Winter was coming. She took a left heading south.

***

When the shooting started in the auditorium, security guards grabbed Sechra taking her to a safe room. The sculptures were more than controversial. She received hundreds of threatening letters and emails. Sechra didn't take them all that seriously. Thora Wozniak did, Cezar concurred. She didn't argue. Her previous shows had drawn a few nuts, but she had never been assaulted. It was one of the reasons she packed a gun when traveling alone. The other was the way she was raised, hardcore, forever on the run. Tonight her attire wouldn't allow her to have the bulges. She told her guards this before the show. They were just being hyper-protective. It was their job. All she had to do was be patient. The guards made poor liaisons as regarded the situation beyond the closed doors. Normally, Frederick Cezar served this purpose. 'Where was he?' Sechra wondered. This was her biggest showing to date. He should have been all over it like, well...He not. She couldn't get hung up about it. The riot had a way of keeping things in perspective for Sechra. 'He was lucky he missed it,' she got up and stretched.

Sechra fought against the guards when they took her to safety. Upon seeing the mass of people going mob, she submitted physically. Once they got her into the room, they wouldn't let her out regardless of her ranting. Only after the SWAT team cleared the museum, locking it up, was she released. Everyone was gone. Two hours ago the sounds of a thousand conversations filled the hall. Now – emptiness. Even less than empty. People had been killed in a mad rush of panic leaving a void, a vacuum in space that could only be filled with life. 'Tomorrow maybe or the next day, but not tonight,' Sechra thought as she wandered the vacant hall. Debris and splotches of blood littered the floor. Masking taped outlines marked the locations of those who fell to the madness. She lost count, 'just too many.'

Unlike most artists Sechra had not once asked about her sculptures and whether any had been damaged. The lives were what mattered. She had seen too many die for a young person, or anyone for that matter. Her imagination was too vivid as she pictured the riot at its peak. Sechra lowered her head as tears filled her eyes, splashing onto the floor. Chips of stone sat near where the droplets fell.

She was standing next to her piece portraying the impaling process. Five men held the end of a pole while a sixth applied lard to the pointed end. Examining the sculpture to find where the chips came from, she found a bullet hole punched into the head of the man being impaled. Sechra laughed a little darkly, 'somebody did him a favor.' She froze, her heart began racing. From her position, Sechra had only glanced at the men holding the pole when looking for the bullet hole. She gulped and reached for where her gun would have been. Not that it would have been any help. There were now six men clutching the pole. The last in the torn rags of a tuxedo. Face and eyes twisted in terror. She had not carved it. It was impossible! The work was crude and faceted, the details blunt yet striking. How could this be?

Sechra began checking each of the sculptures now. Not for damage but additions. Some of the changes were small, a face or an altered position. Others, like the first one she found, had a new figure in the groupings. Indeed every piece of her display had been altered. That is with the exception of the outhouse. This, the centerpiece of the exhibit, appeared untouched. She scrutinized it closer than the others for this very reason. Nothing. But that nothing bothered her more than the rest. Something had changed. Sechra just couldn't see it.

Consumed with the examination, Sechra did not notice a figure skirting the edges of the shadows at the perimeter of the exhibit, getting closer. When he did step into the light, Sechra jumped at the sight of a filthy, haggard, Frederick Cezar.

***

'There was still plenty of time,' Cezar thought, closing himself in the storage room and locking the door. 'The opening isn't until tonight, plenty of time.' He left the screwdriver in place. If he had to get out in a hurry, he didn't want anything stopping him. Both the flashlights worked. He didn't have a chance to get new batteries, but they were still plenty bright. Already he was getting nervous. He drank some water and started down the stairs. His brain was drawing a blank. At the base of the stairs, he was already lost. His hands were shaking. Cezar followed his nose. If he could find the bodies, the loo was close by. Rats scurried away from the lights. It was foolish to use both of them, but he couldn't help himself. The smell was getting quite heady, boosting his confidence. He turned one of the lights out. As soon as he spotted the blue tarp covering the bodies, the second light came back on. Rats were feasting. Undoubtedly interrupted by the intruder, the vermin holding on to whatever they could carry in their mouths, scrambled passed Cezar who danced out of the way. He shivered as one brushed his pantleg, dropping its dinner of a partially desiccated eye with all the trimmings on his shoe. He quickly dropped to his knees, barfing up his lunch. He was losing it. The strain of puking activated his loose bowels, pouring a stream of diarrhea into his jockey shorts. He couldn't help himself. Only when he was wiping his mouth off with his sleeve did he comprehend the warm mass in his pants. "Aw Jesus Christ!" Cezar carefully took off his shoes and peeled his pants and underwear off. 'I can rinse them in the water at the bottom of the loo.' His confidence once again boosted him to get on his feet and get it over with. There were several passages within the area of the bodies. One of them was what he was looking for. He saw the line tied to one of the supports. He ran up to it, letting it lead him to where he was going.

One of the rungs broke the last time. Thora must have brought the rope in case another went. There went his confidence. Why didn't she ask him? All week she had pretended to forget about it, he now realized, feeling stupid for not seeing it sooner. He shined both lights into the cavity of the loo. Before, clean water was flowing through the pool at the bottom. Now a brown sludge stagnated on the surface. Frederick pulled up the rope until the once floating coils of line were in his hand. The smell of the filth close up made him gag again. There was no more to regurgitate as he struggled against the dry heaves. Part of him had hoped Thora was at the end of the line. Mystery solved, his tribulations would be over. He still had to clean himself. Dropping the rope back in stirred the surface sludge. Cleaner waters lied beneath it. How clean was a good question. Anything was cleaner than the paste irritating his ass. Dropping his pants and shorts first, he followed cautiously down the ladder. With one light in hand, the other in his shirt pocket; he stirred the mire with his foot, pushing it away from where he intended to get in. Frederick eased himself into the water, hanging from the rung just above the water level. He washed vigorously in the freezing water, continually fanning away the encroaching sludge. His own waste only added to the fetid stench. He changed hands on the rung. The one was cramping painfully from the exertion. Frederick was out of shape. A clumsy effort got the pants clean enough. He couldn't stand the cold any more.

His conscience stepped in, 'Come on, Freddy, you got to take a look down there or you will have wasted the reason why you came.' He didn't have the chance to ponder this, as the rung snapped from years of corrosion. He surfaced, gasping and swallowing some of the water. He just couldn't help it. The light he held flickered once and died. "Shit!" He automatically began to push the sludge away. 'The light in my pocket is supposed to be waterproof.' It was, but the batteries were getting low, the bulb giving off the dim yellow glow of flashlight death. "Oh Jesus, what am I going to do?" He took a breath, diving to the bottom, panning the light. There was stuff, but nothing that would indicate Thora was down there. A bright piece of crumpled foil gave off a jaundiced glint before the light began to fail. Faster and faster the little bulb went dim, the filament deep orange. It winked out.

Frederick found the rungs. Something had happened inside him. He didn't care about the lights, figuring he could find his way without them. The anxiousness bordering on panic was gone. Somehow, he remembered his pants. This was all very unlike Frederick Cezar.

'What would have caused the water to change so drastically?' Frederick wondered as he climbed up. He pulled his pants on. They would have to do. At least he'd gotten his butt clean. He began walking in the direction he thought was to the exit/entrance. Conking his head on a low ceiling, Frederick started crawling. He didn't remember a low overhead. It wasn't long before he had no idea where he was. Sitting down his wet ass on the cold floor, the worry and fear returned. He began to cry. Now this is very Cezar.

***

Ahmed arrived at the estate on the coast at midday. Karuna was long gone, the trail cold, dead. It didn't take long to surmise she was exiling herself. From what and why? These questions bothered him more than where his quarry was. Karuna Danesti was quite a capable woman.

Ahmed searched the big house for more clues. He found scant few. Karuna had been careful to cover her tracks, at least on where she was going. The bedroom was still in disarray. It was obvious two people had slept in the bed. Who? Surely it had to be someone from Bucharest. One of the gypsies perhaps?

Motorcycle tracks weaved in and out under the overlay of the Mercedes tire prints and his own. These tracks did not match Sechra's tire treads. At the highway, the bike tires took a right. The big car, a left. 'The rider might know where she is going,' thought Ahmed. In the garbage were several used hemoglobin bags like the ones used at a hospital. He remembered Karuna talking about Igor and his injury. That must be it, a transfusion. But four liters seemed a little excessive considering they rushed him to the closest emergency room in Eforie Sud. Taking note of the serial numbers on the bags Ahmed took photos of the tire tracks before following the motorcycle north into the mountains. A single rider at this time of year should be easy enough to track.

A call to an associate in Bucharest traced the bags to a hospital in Varna. They were part of a shipment that was stolen from the loading dock when the institution was taking in supplies. Ahmed felt Karuna wouldn't be stopping for any length of time in Eforie Sud. From there the roads spoked out from the coast to points south, west, and north. She could have taken any of the roads or highways. The motorcycle was his best bet. Ahmed headed north after the biker for information. The trail was hot, easy to follow and when he would lose it, somebody in the vicinity would have seen it. Once he got into the mountains however, things changed. He crossed the imaginary boundary into gypsy country. No one saw or heard anything. Gas attendants went stupid. Even bribery wouldn't open the mouths. The trail was cold as ice. Ahmed turned around heading to the coast again. What would have made him choose such an obviously bad route? It had seemed like his idea at the time, but now he wondered. His normal instincts would have been to chase after the Mercedes and not worry about some limp dick and his conquest. Karuna wouldn't have told him anything. Ahmed stepped on the gas, kicking himself for being duped. 'Karuna must have done it. But how?'

∗∗∗

Four hours before the opening, Angie, now acting director, was working with Walter securing the building. Administrative offices, maintenance facilities, separate wings and storage areas, all needed to be locked up, prior to the front and back doors being opened. With Thora missing and Frederick gone, Angie wanted to have the job done. She was juggling enough projects as it was. They worked together as there were many doors and it would be easy to miss one or two. Walter caught several doors that Angie missed in her rush.

When they came to the storage room that held the stairway, Walter was a few steps ahead. The door was locked. He keyed it, stepping in to find the stairs exposed.

"Angie, who opened the hatchway?"

"I showed Frederick earlier. He had to move the safe for something or other.'

"Remember when we used to go down there and..." Walter began.

"How could I forget, Walter? Those were good times and the weed was pretty stony."

They both laughed, remembering the old days.

"Ahh, to be young again," Walter sighed, digging around in his breast pocket.

"What do you mean, Walter? We're not that old!"

"I suppose we'll find out." He fished a joint out of his pocket. Angie's eyes went wide.

"Geez Walter! Where'd you get that?"

"I never quit." A lighter came out of his pocket.

"It would be a lot of fun Walter, but we are kind of busy."

"Come on, you haven't grown up yet have you? It only takes a couple hits. Now come on down these stairs, just like old times. Look girl, you're wired and strung out from running the show. Relax, Madame Director." Walter laughed and waved the joint, stepping down into the darkness.

Angie was giggling before she even had a hit. The smoke was sweet, the flavor of bubble gum. She held the first hit, trying to remember how it was done before bursting into a coughing fit.

"Good one," he laughed taking a hit.

"Jesus, Walter, this is way better than what we used to smoke."

Walter exhaled a billowing cloud of smoke. "Yeah, here, take another then back to work," he said laughing like he meant it. Angie went through another coughing fit as Walter lifted the lighter and joint from her hand and set them on the stairs. He steadied Angie. "You'll be all right. I'm with you for the next hour and will keep an eye on you."

"Walter," she giggled, "I'm bonkers."

"Just be cool, Angie. Remember, you're the boss." Their laughter resounded in the subterranean corridor. Climbing the stairs, Walter pulled the screwdriver out engaging the floor mechanism. "Wouldn't want anyone going down there tonight."

"God no. Thank you, Walter."

"You're welcome, anytime. Now let's finish up with these doors."

✷✷✷

Frederick curled up and went to sleep after his bout of feeling sorry for himself. 'Maybe when I wake up this will all have been a bad dream.' When he did wake, it was to the sound of distant coughing and laughter. In the darkness of the catacombs, "am I awake?" he said out loud to no one. He was confused and pinched himself. Getting the appropriate pain response, he listened harder into the blackness. 'Where had the sound come from? Was it that way? Or that way? Was there any noise at all,' he thought hopelessly. There it was again. Coughing and laughter. 'Which way! Which way!' Silence again. He chose a direction walking straight into a wall, clobbering his forehead again.

Frederick went back to crawling, always staying to the left. Why left? He had to start somewhere. Hours passed. Twice he came close to the corpses. The odor drawing and repelling him at the same time. But no stairs. Frederick crawled to what he hoped was the opposite wall following along to the right this time. This way was farther and the going slow. His right hand sank into the rotting body of one of the murdered men. The tarpaulin parted. Frederick could not see what happened. The smell however seemed to follow him and though he brushed his hand clean, his skin still crawled. In the dark, it was impossible to clean all the maggots off, even if you did know they were on you. Ignorance is bliss. He knew he was on a new passage because of running into the dead men. A little excitement. A little adrenalin. Frederick took the first right turn he came to. The smell of burnt reefer hung in the air. His thought processes began working better, bringing on a positive attitude. Or was it the other way around. He didn't care. Someone had been here recently. The coughing, ganja. Frederick let out a resounding 'Hurray' when his hands found the stairs. He went up on all fours, his hand just missing the lighter and joint stub. A grin went from ear to ear, relief surged thru him and he was busy thanking god when the stairway disappeared into the ceiling.

"Goddamnit," he screamed. Tears rolled down his face. "Be positive, Fred. They came down here. They will be back. Don't lose it now boy!"

To be honest, Frederick was losing it, just a little. He scuttled back to the bottom of the stairs to wait. This time he caught the lighter. Shortly thereafter the joint stub. And shortly after that Frederick was stoned for the first time in years. He settled into the nirvana of being lost and found at the same time. 'They will be back.' He relaxed with this thought, got comfortable, wishing he had some tunes and a candy bar.

Dim, far away as if in a dream, something told Frederick this was real. Pock, Pock, Pock. Distant screaming. More pocks randomly, some strung together like gunfire!

Somewhere something was going horribly wrong. Thumbing the lighter, Frederick checked his watch. 'Shit.' He was down there for hours. Too many, the show was already in full swing. But what was with the gunfire and screaming? As quickly as the quiet had been ruined by the sounds of death it returned. It had been brief. Using the lighter to give off a candle–like illumination, his eyes searched the walls and stairs for a way to open the hatch again. When the lighter became too hot, Frederick felt the surfaces with his palms and fingers, searching for some deviation. Near the floor he felt a big nail with square sides and exaggerated smooth head. He got all the information he could get with his fingers. Strike. Strike! Strike! A flame, weak, blue, and small barely lit the scene before winking out.

He kept the rising panic in check. He made it this far blind. Surely he could find a way out. Frederick knelt, feeling for the metal pin again... When it was in his hand, he wiggled it. The pin wobbled in the hole but would not pull out so he pushed on it leaning hard into it as Angie had done. The steel resisted at first. With continuous pressure it penetrated the rock until the head was seated. He sat back and waited for the door to open. It didn't.

On his knees again, hands searched the walls and stairs for another pin, anything at all. In the dark, most everything is a little more difficult to find. But when you have no idea what you are looking for, the process is doubly hard. There were bas relief carvings on some of the flat surfaces. Frederick's fingers could not see what the images portrayed. This was to his benefit, though he didn't realize it at the time. Digits probed eyes, nostrils, a vagina or two and assholes for the mechanism that would unlock the door. Some of the orifices felt quite real. In fact, Frederick would sniff his fingers from time to time after particularly deep penetrations.

He had gotten sidetracked by the carvings with a morbid and deeply perverse curiosity. His hand reached back up to the reliefs, wanting to feel more. Fredrick Cezar fought the sick cravings that he didn't even know he had, summoned as they were by the orgy in stone. With his left, Cezar pulled his right hand down to the ground. Here was another spike in what he felt was the same location only on the opposite side of the stairway. It wiggled too. He leaned on this spike with all he had until it penetrated the stone to the nail's head. Nothing happened. Pushing the spike into the hole interrupted Cezar's thoughts with a Freudian implication. A rock-hard erection stretched the crotch of his pants. This was very Cezar too.

He became absorbed in the bas and deep reliefs. The erotic carving seemed to feel Cezar, too. A cleft where a pair of legs joined beckoned his manhood. He undid his pants till they were on the floor around his ankles. He started to fuck the stone. Pain and pleasure mixed bringing him quickly to climax. Then the pain took over as a mechanical blade activated. Cezar screamed in agony, stumbling in the booby trap of pants, wound up on the ground clutching his crotch. His whimpering turned into a full on wail as his fingers, now attuned to a higher sense of touch felt the stub that had once been his dick.

While what was left of his penis dripped blood, Frederick Cezar collapsed, spent from the wound and shock. His clothes were too filthy to consider using them as bandages. He pulled some threads from a shirttail to make a little tourniquet. He had yet to realize that he was seeing what he was doing. Not very well at any rate. When he did he skooched over into a better lit spot on the floor. Cezar was now able to see it. There wasn't enough left to tourniquet.

He had been looking down for so long, looking up hurt. Straining against the kink in his neck, Cezar finally saw the stairway was clear. Whatever it was he did, opened the portal. A grating sound interrupted the silence again. The 'window' of light was growing smaller. The hatchway was automatically closing. He scrambled up the stairs. Hunched over and moving quickly, Cezar squeezed through the opening in the nick of time. Unlocking the storage room door, he stole a look down the hall in both directions. No one and the place was dead quiet. He searched for some clean clothes. Finding none but a roll of duct tape, he made a cautious painful run to the nearest bathroom.

He washed his hands three times before he could deal with what was left of his penis. Tears streamed down his eyes as a red swirl of blood chased them down the drain. Cezar packed the stub with paper towels, securing them in place with the tape.

Cezar was coming down from his nightmare. The bathroom lights shone brilliant his personal catastrophe. He was a mess. Covered in shit, maggots and God knows what else, he wandered the empty museum. He was thankful for its vacancy, yet wondered why the party was not still going on. At the very least, clean up crews would be hard at work preparing for the next day. No, the place was quiet as a crypt.

When he came to the Kcirb exhibit, Cezar froze in his tracks. Someone was here, at the far side of the auditorium and seemed to be examining the sculptures. Staying within the shadows Cezar crept through the room to get a closer look at whom it was. As recognition took place, Sechra looked up from her sculpture to see Frederick Cezar.

"Good God, Frederick! The mob got you too?" Sechra stood up straight stretching her back. "You look awful, Frederick. What happened?"

Frederick couldn't tell her exactly what happened. This much he knew, but beyond that he was entirely ignorant of the evening. He took the hint. "I guess so. It all happened so fast. I woke about an hour ago and have been looking for someone."

"You found me, Frederick, I'll take care of you."

"I am afraid not, Sechra. The mob did something to me," Cezar lied.

She rushed to his side. Her nose told her the mob shit on him and she was just about to laugh out loud about it when she saw the pain in Cezar's eyes. He didn't look beaten. He was a wreck. Cezar's forehead had a few contusions but his face had not been hit. He held the front of his pants protectively as his knees buckled. Sechra could not catch him in time as Cezar hit the stone floor with a resounding whack from his head. Sechra dropped to her knees to cradle him. There was no bleeding but he was unconscious. His arms splayed out revealing his crotch. The zipper was down, button undone, with silver tape sticking out his fly.

Sechra could not help herself. He was bleeding and it had to be stopped. Pulling his pants down she also removed the crude bandage. Sechra gasped, running as fast as she could to get something to clean and wrap it. She returned with a bucket of hot water and towels from the staff kitchen. Cezar was sitting up and made no attempt to cover himself when she came near.

"Frederick, I need to clean it and rebandage it before we can take you to the hospital. Emergency crews and all the hospitals are doing double time to keep up with the injured from the riot. I'll do the best I can. It's possible there is no room for you." Cezar was so out of it he simply laid back weeping. Sechra went through towel after towel scrubbing through the layers of filth. How could this have happened? From what she garnered from the guards that protected her, the riot had been pretty straightforward. Tempers flared, people chose sides then they started fighting. Guns kept the duration of the mayhem shorter than what would be considered normal. The fighters tired quickly, then it was over. It didn't seem enough time elapsed for what had been done to Cezar or the logic.

During the course of her life, Sechra witnessed countless forms of torture and extermination. Her art spells this out pretty clearly. There was also always a logic behind the insanity of Tepes' forces. There were none of the society left and Cezar's injuries, though not life-threatening, would not have come from the mob mentality.

"Do you have, uh, the end?" Sechra asked.

Cezar shook his head no.

"Then where did it happen? We can go look for it!"

"I couldn't tell you where it happened, Sechra."

She knew he was lying. The smell of his cum underlied the feces. Cezar winced and groaned as Sechra wiped his severed dick. "Tell me about the riot. It will help to keep my mind occupied," Cezar asked.

She swabbed the sweat from his forehead.

"I kind of missed it, too. Security rushed me to safety. Apparently a little girl..." Sechra wound her tale as best she could from what she had been told. Cezar held tough.

Beyond his trauma, Cezar hoped the story would kill his urge for an erection. Sechra's cleaning was perfunctory, but guys will be guys, not that Cezar was much of one anymore, and he began to bleed profusely from the wound as the stub swelled. Sechra wadded gauze and covered him. With her other hand, she reached behind one of his knees fingering a pressure point. This little trick is known to masseuses and used across the battlefields of the world. Activating the pressure point would not kill a man's desire, merely dissolving ability for a while. She used the trick many times in her early years when the battle was brought to her family's doorstep. Even though Sechra was a child at the time, she was required to perform the fieldwork like everyone else who was too young or old to do the killing. When there was time, the older women would pull her away from the vision of horror.

Diodora was ancient in the eyes of the young girl. Yet somehow they always found themselves on the frontline, working desperately to save men who were now better off dead. Most of the injured wouldn't survive a week. Someone had to do it. Separated by the overwhelming demand for their service, Sechra found herself applying tourniquets to a commander who lost his hands and feet in an explosion. His clothes were torn and burnt from him in the blast that shredded his torso. The battle also cost him his mind. As the girl shut down the pulsing fountains of blood, the extra pressure in his veins flooded his groin. He pushed her to the ground, rolling on top of her, supported by stumped forearms. The commander struggled futilely with his predicament. He knew he was dying and some despicable primal urge was forcing him to express himself one more time. Sechra, screaming and flailing, was silenced by an explosion. The commander's head burst in thousands of crimson droplets before being carried away by the blast. Diodora stood nearby with a smoking hand cannon. Tears rolled down her face as she stuffed the gun in her pack and excavated Sechra from beneath the corpse.

"Are you all right, child? Did he?"

Diodora spread Sechra's legs and saw that the girl's pants were still in place under the dress. Sechra pulled away in shame and fright. "No! No! What did I do? I would never touch him there!" She burst into tears falling into Diodora's arms.

"There now, Sechra, cry, it is good." Diodora looked at her watch then to the corpse. A single tear welled in each eye. They dripped in sorrow, but no more followed. She glanced again at her watch. The minute was up. For both of them. "Come Sechra there are still many men who need our attention. We must shoulder our sorrow and help them. It is best this way." Diodora stood, bringing Sechra up with her. "We must stay busy comforting them and fight to protect them if we have to. But first I will show you three things you are never to forget." Diodora looked back to the man she had killed. Her son would not have survived his wounds, both physical and mental. 'It was better this way,' she said to herself taking Sechra's hand.

Kneeling next to a man who would survive the day, Diodora began looking him over. Pulling a pair of shears from her pack, Diodora cut the pant leg from the man's trousers and raised the knee in a bent position. She took Sechra's hand again, pulling it to touch the inside of the knee. The young girl pulled back. The old woman was stronger.

"Feel that? If you push here a man will lose his erection. "Do it," Diodora commanded.

Sechra followed orders and after a few attempts was able to locate the pressure point and use it. They applied compresses to bullet wounds and splint limbs, made him comfortable and moved on to the next. On the way, Diodora removed the side arm from a dead soldier. Nine millimeter semi-automatic as most handguns were, that is with exception of Diodora's gun. It was much too big for the young girl.

"Hold it like this," Diodora explained, handing the gun to Sechra. She adjusted the girl's grip, "Pull the slide back."

Little fingers slipped the first time. Diodora grabbed her fingers, squeezing them hard to the metal and pulling. A bullet popped out of the chamber as another went in. "Do it again. Her hands were strong from a young life at hard labor. Still it took considerable effort to rack the slide. A burnt out hulk of a military vehicle provided a target.

"Aim at the window, shoot when you're ready." The gun went off knocking Sechra back a few paces. It scared her, but she wanted to do it again. She strained against the slide, getting it to do its magic again.

Diodora didn't know much about shooting with all the proper stances, breathing, and the gentle squeeze. All of hers had been in a panic, on the run without time for stuff like that. The gun went off again. This time the passenger window exploded in a zillion fragments. Sechra squeezed again and again until all the windows and bullets were gone. Diodora took the weapon and showed Sechra how to load a magazine and then load the gun. Sechra mimicked the movements then handed the gun back.

"You keep it. Here is an extra magazine and some bullets. You can always find ammunition on the battlefield."

Sechra wrapped it, stuffing it in the bottom of her bag, only aware of the weight but unaware of the tonnage of responsibility that came with it.

The next man they came upon also supplied the third lesson. Even a child could see there was no chance. It was a stomach wound that went clean through the body, taking away the spine in the process. Diodora had Sechra help him into a more comfortable position if that was possible. Then a syringe was loaded with an overdose of a morphine-based solution. A vein suitable for puncture was found at the neck. The drug worked quickly. The heavy moans subsided and Diodora and Sechra were able to continue with others.

Sechra leaned into the pressure point. Then, as quickly as she could, secured a bandage before the stub disappeared. Beyond the obvious injury, Cezar was unharmed. If the mob had attacked him surely he would be beaten to a pulp from head to toe before the cruel surgery. This one thought gave Sechra some peace of mind. Not having all the details of what went down, she had begun to put together the story with what she did have. 'A frenzied mob had gotten a hold of the man they felt responsible for the little girl's disappearance. The scent of his manhood, a missing girl.' Sechra hardly knew Frederick beyond what he did for her. They were friendly, but were they friends? She was wondering if she was doing the right thing, if that were truly the scenario. Who knows what goes on in a man's head when something like this occurs, but Sechra knew what happened to their bodies. And Frederick didn't have many of the trademarks of an encounter with insanity, aside from the missing appendage. He was filthy and dehydrated. Sechra refilled the bucket and gathered some fresh towels. "Here, clean yourself up. I'm going to see if I can get you some real help."

"Don't leave me!" Frederick screamed and reached out to her receding silhouette.

"You're safe, Frederick. Now just suck it up and deal. People were killed tonight. Although I feel sorry for you, you will live."

"I am sorry, Sechra," Frederick brightened in the face. Excitement and insanity are similar that way. "Do you have any idea what this means for your art?"

"Right now I could care less about it. So should you!" Sechra stormed away before unleashing on him. 'We all cope with stress differently,' Karuna once told her. 'God I hope so,' thought Sechra. She had at least surmised the situation of emergency care. There was none available. They would just have to wait the night. Care would come with the police in the morning. Frederick would survive.

***

Ahmed pressed the accelerator and his luck on his way south. Karuna would not have stopped in Eforie Sud. Although she existed at the edge of society, Karuna was still well known. Her presence in the increasingly volatile sociopolitical climate that Romania was entering would inevitably trigger alarms. Then again, his gut feelings failed him, sending Ahmed on a wild goose chase into the mountains where intruders, especially foreigners from the south, were highly distrusted. Normally, he would have been able to transcend the social boundaries, he had a way with people, a certain savoir faire, but with peoples' heightened awareness that came with living on the edge, he could not blend their differences. Ahmed did not come away from the detour empty-handed. The mountain roads followed the rivers, flowing through the deep valleys. The air near the normally fast running water was foul to breathe. For centuries trout fishermen waded into the currents to catch the breeders heading upstream to the spawning grounds. The relative calm of the grounds was ideal for nurturing the eggs to hatch, sending the striplings downstream into the effluence that is the river. He took a few samples of the copralitic water and the life that lived within. Ahmed was not all that concerned with the environment. What bothered him was that he had not heard about it. To be certain, pollution at this level would be catastrophic.

Ahmed stopped at Sechra's art studio to see if she returned yet. She had, but was no longer at home. He drove to the estate, sure that she was there. Well, maybe not all that sure, but pretty sure. Her motorcycle sat outside the closed garage doors. She was inside nursing a cup of coffee. She looked up to see him enter. "Hi Ahmed. A cup of coffee?" Sechra asked getting out of her chair.

"No. No, well okay. You have not slept, yes?" he asked.

"Yes, looks that bad, huh?"

"Hard work becomes you," replied Ahmed.

"Thanks, I guess. Did they find the man who abducted the child?"

"There was no kidnapping. The little girl wandered away in search of ice cream. When her disappearance was noted, everyone sort of lost it."

"Lost it! Ahmed, are you making a joke? Lost it?" Sechra laughed a disturbed little chuckle.

"No Sechra, I made no joke. There is nothing to joke about in death."

"Perhaps, but in life there is always something."

Ahmed looked at Sechra. 'Losing it' seemed all the rage these days and he wondered if Sechra had become infected. She noticed him notice.

"Did you hear of the rioters capturing a man and cutting off his penis?" Sechra asked cautiously.

"No. Many were beaten severely, but no mutilations that I know of. But I did not see all of what went on. Only my part in it."

"What would that be?" Sechra asked. Ahmed looked at her queerly, not understanding the question. "Your part in it," she filled in. Then a light was turned on in his head.

Ahmed smiled, but you saw no teeth. "Lost it. I get it now. Poor fucker."

"Come on, Ahmed," Sechra chided. Ahmed had been the family driver for the Cneajna's since the revolution. They didn't know each other extremely well, as far as time spent together goes, but as part of a family where you have no real part, they were well acquainted. This unspoken, unrealized bond kept Ahmed candid over the years. Sechra's youth and good looks made her easy to talk to. He also trusted her.

"Your father, rrrr," Ahmed growled at his faux pas. "Prime Minister Cneajna, as usual, allowed me the discretion to serve where best I thought was needed. He has his personal guards for himself and the family. It was they who pulled you from the teeth and claws of madness." Ahmed paused, gathering his thoughts.

"I figured they were Vlad's men, but they wore plain clothes and of course were trained to keep their mouths shut."

"Highly capable men one and all, which was why I felt comfortable leaving his side."

"Have you seen Karuna?" Sechra asked, jumping ahead of the conversation.

"I was just getting to that. Karuna sensed I was free for the evening and asked me to be a chaperone."

"She really doesn't need a guard, as you know, and I was looking forward to listening to her. She really speaks beautifully. The story will get a little confusing at this point as I must speak of two things at once."

"I will bear with you, Ahmed. More café?"

"Yes please. Karuna and I were having a pleasant evening. The exhibit opened and it seemed you were on the verge of creating your vision. Then the girl, Katrina, went missing. I stayed with Karuna who was feeling the need to get out of there. Who wouldn't, but the museum went into a lockdown. I knew a way she could flee undetected and led her to it. There was something in her demeanor that went beyond being afraid of the crowd. She was afraid of herself. Of what she might do. You see, there was an accident a few nights ago on the highway near the estate." Ahmed stumbled mentally trying to make sense of it.

"What has this to do with anything?" Sechra was becoming frustrated with Ahmed.

He could hear it in her voice. "Everything. Karuna was at the accident. She did not cause it. Two men died at the scene and Karuna may have been involved in the death of one of them. One of the survivors told of a succubus that sucked the life from her husband. This is one of the reasons why Karuna was so scared, she thought she might be recognized."

Sechra's powerful hand slapped Ahmed hard across the face. "Just what do you mean, Ahmed?!"

His face turned red, but not out of shame. Sechra's did. She knew what Karuna was and also that the woman had the utmost discretion. Karuna would not have exposed herself unless something had happened. So much had occurred in the last few days Sechra could hardly keep up with it, yet she knew it began with the finishing of her sculptures for the exhibit.

"I mean something must have happened for her to lose control. After getting Karuna through a doorway, I closed the door and made sure that no one followed. You see, my loyalty lies with Vlad Cneajna, I could not leave. Minutes afterwards came a hard pounding from the other side of the door. When I cracked to door ajar there was Karuna with the child. Unfortunately there were others that saw her, too. Karuna shoved the child into my arms. I fought to keep the door closed but was soon overwhelmed. The mob stomped us into the floor in their mad rush after Karuna. It was the last I saw of her." Ahmed paused again making sure he hadn't left out anything important. "Did you know the rivers coming out of the mountains are polluted?"

"They have been polluted since the Communist occupation during the 1900s. What does that have to do with Karuna?"

"It's true the rivers were spoiled, but men still fished them. Now it is as if the world's sewage is being dumped into the high mountains. Vlad needs to send a team up there to find out what is happening."

"Why are you telling me?"

"Because I must follow Karuna's trail."

"Sure, I'll pass the word along. Which way are you headed?"

"South, into Bulgaria. Beyond that I do not know." He stood and finished his coffee. "I must be going. Here is my personal number. If you hear from Karuna call me. Be careful and watch out for yourself. Whatever is happening has just begun. It will get worse before it gets worse."

Sechra stepped up, giving Ahmed a hug before he left. "Where are you from?" Sechra asked as they came apart.

He headed out the door on the way to his car. "Persia," he yelled from the driver's seat.

It must have been the way the light was coming through the clouds catching his angular face lines that spelled out his lineage. The eyes spoke of a branch in the family tree. One would naturally assume he was Middle Eastern, dark skin and chiseled features. But the windows to his soul were European. For the first time, Sechra realized he was of mixed decent. The more she held on to the image, the more familiar it became. The face was older than the one she remembered, as of course it would be. She topped her coffee and made a beeline to the mosaics where Sechra hooked a u-turn heading back to the dining room. There was no one else here. She would be a fool to enter them without a tender to pull her out. Her laptop at the studio held a complete viewing of the mosaics in the estate. She donned her leather and went to the motorcycle. The battery was dead. It had been giving her trouble the last few weeks, but she had been too busy to deal with it. After locking the estate Sechra headed to the shoreline for the long walk up the beach. The wind was biting cold and the water flat as ice. She did a double take on the Dracul and thought, 'What the fuck?'

Half a tank of gas later, she nudged the boat into the sand in front of the studio. Securing a line to a stout beach tree, Sechra hustled into the cottage and cranked up the heat. After drinking more coffee than was prudent for anyone and studying the images on her laptop, the figure she sought in the mosaics still eluded her. One of the cottage's quaint features was less than desirable in the moment. The outhouse was fifty meters away. Sechra dashed from the warmth through the tall grass that held the sands in place to the little shed with a crescent moon. She yanked the door open, jumped inside, and closed the door to keep the wind out. After a few moments, Sechra stretched a foot out to hold the door open. Her backhouse had never smelled like this. It was horrible, too horrible to use. With pants half on, she took care of nature in the grass. Hustling back to the cottage, Sechra washed her hands vigorously then rolled a cigarette to cleanse her lungs of the filth. Normally she only smoked when she worked, which is to say all the time. Nicotine, along with copious amounts of caffeine, produced the mental acuity she needed for her art.

Reeling from the first smoke of the day, she began scrolling quickly through tile images. Not focusing on anything brought what she had been looking for into view. There! Amidst the crucified on the beach fronting Eforie Sud. Again! Swimming in stormy waters that were sinking the Persian fleet. His features were similar to the panic stricken sailors. The only difference was in the eyes. Then again in the marketplace, a blind beggar, starving amidst mountains of food. There was no mistaking it.

Sechra closed her eyes, leaning back in her chair. The recognition took her back to her early childhood. Ahmed suddenly appeared on the scene 20 years ago after the revolution, staying on with the family ever since. Sechra's revelation answered fewer questions than she had hoped for and brought up even more. She was stunned. Part of her wanted to step out, have another smoke and go for an epiphany. But not tonight. Hearing a helicopter off in the distance helped to pull her into the present. Part of the reason she came was to get a battery charger so the bike would be ready in the morning. Sechra wasn't sure what she was going to do, but sitting around wasn't one of them. Putting the charger and laptop in a shoulder bag, she headed back to the Dracul.

During the last few hours, the tide had gone out. "Shit!" Sechra tossed the bag onto the deck and began rocking the boat while pushing it into the sea. She put her back into the effort, which was a lot harder than she thought it would be. If the boat didn't come free this time…

The Dracul idled through the breakwater. As soon as the boat touched the dock, floodlights raked a wicked, brilliant glare across the pier. Sechra was effectively blinded momentarily. Squatting still, next to the Dracul, she kept it from bumping into the pier while her eyes recovered. Footsteps and weapons being engaged broke the uncomfortable silence. Looping the mid-ship line to a cleat, she dropped her hand into her coat pocket gripping her pistol. Although she had every right to be here, reality was changing again.

Drawing up all the sarcasm she could muster, "Thank you for the light. A little bright, ya think? Could one of you brave men help me tie her up? I know you have those big guns and everything, but I could sure use a hand."

Light footsteps came down the steps onto the floating dock. "Enjoy taking her out on a spin?" Riana's sarcasm was unmistakable as well.

"The bike's battery died. The Mercedes is gone. What's a girl to do?"

"You could have called. Since the other night…"

"Yeah I know. Could we go inside? The boat doesn't have any heaters."

"Already been. Since when do we keep shit on the kitchen counters?"

"About that…" Sechra led the way past the helicopter in the yard and into the house.

"… is all I know. Your guards kept me in the dark, you can trust those guys. The rest I got from snooping around, talking with Ahmed."

"Is your agent going to be…?"

"He will heal. I have certainly seen worse. The psych damage though, something really strange is going on. Not just with Cezar and Igor but all over the place." Sechra reached over picking up one of the sample jars Ahmed had given her, scrutinizing the contents. "Ahmed wanted me to give these to you. The 'shit on the counter' are water samples from the mountains. He said you should get some people up there."

"I agree. This is disgusting. But we have been busy with the chain reaction of events set off by your exhibition."

Sechra felt no stab of blame. It was just a statement of fact. "He said it was important. If you can't spare anyone I can go. It has been years." Sechra wasn't in the mood to play politics.

"Your choice. You know the area better than anyone I guess. But what about the exhibition?" Riana eyed Sechra carefully. "And what's behind the sudden urge to return to the homeland?"

"Frederick and Igor can figure it out. It will give them something to work on. Frederick actually had the gall to say the riot would boost me into the ranks of notoriety."

"It's what he does, Sechra. About heading into the country," Riana paused, "Stay in touch. Call once in a while. Speaking of, if you take the Dracul out again you 'have' to let somebody know. Alarms start sounding."

"Turn them off. Nobody messes with this place. Scares the crap out of everyone. Besides, you have to know how to start the thing. How is Igor doing? I've had my hands full lately." Sechra couldn't help herself. She was still pissed he stole her gun.

"Jesus, Sechra, he almost lost his hands!"

"So they were able to put them back on?"

"From what I've heard, yes. Karuna was dealing with it. I have to fly out shortly, so it would be a good idea if you could stop by and see him before you leave. He's welcome to stay on at the estate once he is released. That is as long as he leaves the mosaics alone."

"Bit of a Pandora's box, that one," Sechra replied.

"It's his choice. My guess is that if he enters the pictures again, he won't be coming out." What Riana meant was very clear.

"Why would he have chosen for his focus to be on a condemned man? I mean there are so many other fantastic scenes. The one he got caught up in is mundane by comparison," Sechra was fishing.

"By comparison maybe, but the details are as excruciatingly executed as the more dramatic vistas. Vlad says people tend to be drawn to the ones that most exemplify their nature. The convict was in an asylum. He was a sculptor. The question is, "What did he steal?""

"My machine gun," Sechra said into her coffee.

"Your what?"

"I have a few. When I was packing for Bucharest, I discovered it was gone."

"How do you know it was him?"

"I don't, really. He built the place where I stash them. I meant to ask him about it but then well, everything started coming apart."

"It fits in with the scenario. Are you sure he didn't take it to use as a model for one of his pieces?"

Sechra thought for a moment. "Could've, but why take the magazines and all my ammo?"

"It's not my problem, but I have a feeling it will be. Now you 'have' to talk to him."

The helicopter rose from the courtyard, leaving Sechra behind in the silence with only the crashing waves for her to confide in. She went to the phone dialing Dino's number.

"Yeah, Dino here," he growled coming out of a deep sleep.

"Hi Dino, it's Sechra. Can you have a new Beemer battery ready for me in the morning?"

"I'll bring it out with me. Riana beat you to the phone. Did the Dracul run okay?"

"Sure did. See you around dawn?"

"Arrgh. Anything else?" There was a pause, "Later." Dino hung up and got out of bed.

Sechra paced the halls of the estate, her footsteps echoing loudly as the sound bounced off the mosaics. 'Why would Igor have taken my gun? Why and how had Cezar really been injured? The riot? Karuna's sudden disappearance? Why did it seem like everything was coming apart?'

Because it was.

**

Karuna headed to Eforie Sud, stopping only long enough to draw a considerable sum of money and fill the fuel tank. So far her 'mental push' was working or Ahmed would have caught up by now. Karuna knew him to be a fine man, but right now she couldn't trust anyone for fear of involving them in she knew not what. Karuna knew she had to dump the Mercedes. Too big and remarkable. Of all the directions she could take, south was the one chosen, to Varna. It was not out of trust that she headed to Boris' office, but for his discretion.

She navigated the 6.9 Mercedes through the narrow, darkened alleyways. Even though it was in the middle of the day, the warehouses blocked the sunlight to a comfortable level. Karuna pulled beside a steel roll up door, locked the car, weaving her way through broken crates and dunnage to the single door. She knocked once and waited. After a few minutes of being scrutinized by video cameras, the door snapped and banged from the inside as locks were being disengaged.

Boris' stocky form and balding head stood in the shadow of the open door. He clicked his heels, bowing curtly from the waist, "Voivode Danesti, what a pleasant surprise. What brings you to the pearl of the Bulgarian coast?" He laughed through yellowed teeth, putting on his best smile. The muscles of his face rebelled at the expression for lack of ever being used.

"I need help, Boris," Karuna said without emotion.

"So I have heard. What is it you require? Perhaps I can be of some humble assistance. Please, come inside." They passed through the waiting room to the inner office. "Please be seated. A drink, perhaps?" Boris' glass was already out. He pulled a clean one from a cabinet into which he poured vodka. Karuna downed her shot after clicking glasses with the gun dealer. Boris waited for her to gag the shot. When she didn't, his serious face came to the front.

"You need to get out of the country?"

"Yes."

The smile returned, but this time there was little kindness in it. "This is a serious business, you know."

"I have enough money." It always came down to money.

"It is not that. These things are very difficult to arrange…" Boris started sputtering as Karuna's hand closed around his windpipe.

In a split second, Karuna was out of her chair and squeezing hard. "I don't have time for this! Blink if you want to live."

Boris did, as if his life depended on it. Karuna's grip relaxed ever so slightly. He wheezed a few breaths.

"Anything! Anything!"

Karuna let go. Boris slumped back in his seat, rubbing his throat. "I need a boat to get me to Istanbul." She withdrew a large bundle of cash, peeled off a fair portion of it, dropping it on his desk. "This should cover it."

Boris eyed the money while his right hand moved toward the edge of his desk. Karuna was way ahead of him when he made his move. A big metal nut of a paperweight came down hard on his hand, shattering the bones of his palm.

"Why Boris, were you going to pull your gun? Lie to me and your other hand will…" She grabbed his left hand, pinning it to the desk and raised the weight.

"There are people who don't want you to leave," he sniveled as the smell of fresh urine wafted up from beneath the desk.

"Who?" Karuna lifted the steel weight higher.

"I don't know!" The weight came down crushing the bones of his left. "Voivode Cneajna," he squeaked, curling his hands in agony. "A boat will be waiting for you when you get to the docks."

Karuna reached around the desk and withdrew the handgun Boris had in his drawer, stuffing it in her purse.

"Thank you, Boris. Store the Mercedes for me, if you would be so kind." Karuna refilled the glasses and downed hers before walking out. The question of why Vlad Cneajna would want to keep her under control would have to wait.

✱✱✱

Dino arrived as promised. The morning sun had yet to fully breach the horizon when his rig pulled into the parking area. Sechra was there with a cup of coffee in each hand. The garage door was up with the motorcycle inside, seat removed and panniers being loaded. The old battery sat on a workbench. The blinking red light on the charger indicated it was still futilely attempting to bring the battery to life.

"Good morning Dino," she said, handing him a cup of coffee. "The old one won't even take a charge."

"Haven't been riding much, huh?" he replied in between sips.

"Too busy getting ready for the show."

"Yeah, sorry to hear about that. I finally saw some pictures of your work, though. Geez! Where do you come up with that stuff? Guess it freaked a few folks out. More," he asked reaching out his empty cup.

"Sure, come on in." When he was seated and Sechra pouring, she said, "There is more to it than what you read in the papers."

"No doubt there. Where is Karuna?"

"How did you know she was gone?" Sechra was suddenly paranoid.

Dino picked up on it. "She's usually here. I always enjoyed talking with her after the boat. Hey, lighten up kid. I'm not one of the bad guys."

"I know. It's just that things have gotten a little strange lately." Sechra wasn't sure how much to reveal, so she kept it to the minimum.

"No shit," Dino replied sarcastically. Then a bit more wryly, "I just see it from my end. People are stocking up on oil and getting their cars ready for something. I'm working my ass off to keep up with it. What bugs me is where is it going?"

"Straight to hell if something isn't done," Sechra said darkly.

"Well that's reassuring, coming from the stepdaughter of the Prime Minister. Anything else I should know about?"

"Igor stole my machine gun."

"He won't be using it for a while. You want me to get it back?"

"I don't care about the gun. It's just that..." Sechra's face had concern written all over it.

"When I get a chance, I'll swing by his place and snoop around. If it's there I'll find it. Where ya going?" Dino stood.

"Into the mountains. It's been years since I've been back."

"Getting a little late in the season. The heated handle bars working?"

"Yes thanks, just the battery."

"Got a fresh one in the truck, fully charged. Where did you go with the Dracul?" Dino was fishing while he went to his rig and retrieved the battery.

"Didn't feel like walking home. What does Riana want you to do with it?"

He was fishing, but nothing was biting. "Pull the ignition switch so she can't be taken again."

"You going to do it?"

"She pays my bills, honey. But I'll show you a way to bypass it, fair enough? Besides with your toy stolen, you'll need something with more punch than the peashooter you carry. Come on..." Dino tightened the battery connections, pocketed the wrench, picked up his toolbox and headed to the boat. "Must have been a hell of a scene in Bucharest," he said making small talk.

"Worse than that I'm afraid. Funny thing was it was the Boyars who did all the shooting. They were all armed coming into it." Sechra was unsure of the disclosure, so she watched for Dino's reaction.

"Now that wasn't in the papers. Usually it's the other way around." He stopped at an electrical panel on the shore side of the pier. "You want to take her out again, disable the alarm first." He thumbed a few screws, swinging the weather door open. "I never remember the code so I leave it hidden here." Dino pulled a slip of paper from in between two breakers. He unfolded it, tapped a keypad, "Now it's yours."

His body language remained neutral.

"Simple as that," she said absent-mindedly.

"Yup."

The Dracul rocked easily at the mooring while Dino went about his usual maintenance routine. When he was ready, he took the captain's chair and deftly removed the ignition switch. "All you have to do is join these two wires to give her juice then tap these two together to start her up."

"That's it?" Sechra was shocked at the ease in which magic turned to mechanics.

"Yeah, but if it gets out I showed you all this stuff..."

"It won't, Dino, thanks. Listen I'm going to go finish packing the bike. Come on up if you need more coffee."

"Wait just a second, let me get it." Dino went on all fours reaching for something under the dashboard. "Uhhn, here we go!" In his hands was a weapon wrapped in a filthy oilcloth. He slid the pistol grip shotgun from a body harness and handed it to Sechra. "Twelve gauge semi-auto. You can get ammo for it anywhere." He unrolled the cloth revealing a holster and body harness.

Sechra checked the action. "Where did you get this?"

"Found it when they brought her back from Istanbul, stashed in the same place. I don't think anybody knows about it. So I keep it in good condition along with the boat. Figure the owner may be back some day."

"That's pretty doubtful, but I don't think Jake would mind. This gun has quite a history you know."

"No I don't, but it's obvious it's seen plenty of action."

"It has. Hmmm. Thanks again, Dino."

"Just be careful out there. If you need 'anything' call and I'll come."

After Dino departed, Sechra dressed in her cold-weather riding gear to wear under her Aerostitch one–piece. The suit was designed to be worn year-round and was virtually waterproof. The bike was loaded and so there was no reason to stay. To stay would be to live in the safety of a prison. To leave would be risking her life in a quest to find out what began when she finished her last piece. She had to know. The darkness that entered her when she was a young girl had been gestating till the final blow of the hammer and chisel opened a way for it to once again be amongst men. Surely her extended family in the mountains would know of a way, a way out of the nightmare she aided in creating.

Out of Stone

PART TWO

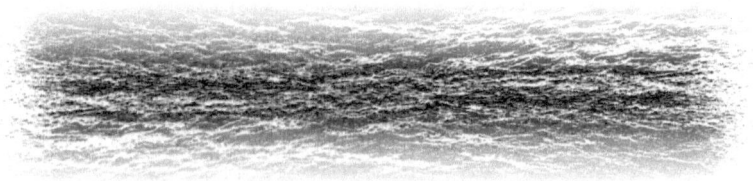

***

The darkened alleys in the old town of Istanbul were caked with centuries of dust along with the wind blown detritus of a modern world. An old woman, bent at the waist from scoliosis, leaned heavily on a staff as she hobbled the cobbles. She stopped: haggling with a produce vendor before procuring some wilted cabbage and stewed lamb. The vendor offered to carry her groceries. Dracine declined, gripped her walking staff firmly and painfully made her way down the alley, stopping at other roving merchants purchasing herbs and an occasional trinket that usually found an eager street urchin. The bauble, if for a moment, would reignite the life in the young eyes. The poor in Istanbul had little to look forward to.

Dracine came to a cul-de-sac. The dun colored walls of the back alleys seemed all the same to the untrained eye; the scars of time being the only difference. Clothes hung from lines stretched from building to building. They dried not by sunlight, but by the oppressive heat of the city. A rat's nest of crazed wiring zigzagged through the open spaces overhead. If there was a plan, it had long been forgotten. When an old wire couldn't be retraced, a new one was installed adding to the nest. It was nothing short of a disaster waiting to happen. But within the madness there was a plan. The end of each wire terminated in a household, tying and locking an ever-bourgeoning population into the virtual world. As mentioned before, the streets held little to look forward to. The escape was high-speed broadband. There was no wire above a short wooden door to the left at the end of the alley that led into her tiny pension. She ducked to enter. Once the door was closed, the cane was set aside and Karuna arched her back to straighten her body from being bent over for so long. The room was two meters by four. The previous occupants had been a family of seven.

Karuna had wanted a place to hide away, disappear from not only those that may have followed, but from herself. Istanbul had always been a city of the world much like Paris, New York or Hong Kong. And though the dominant religion was Islam, Istanbul, at that time, had yet become prey to fundamentalism. In other words, Karuna could roam freely with only a veil to cover her head. This was one of the reasons she chose to stay here. To live in a fundamentalist country is less than living, for any woman. It was also an easy place to disappear in, especially if you're poor.

Karuna could have stayed at any of the high-end hotels, even bought a house if that was what she wanted. But what she wanted now was different. She wanted invisibility, which would give her time to read the diaries of Vlad Tepes III. Her previous forays into these macabre writings had been specific to her circumstance. The goal now was no less different, with the exception that it was more personal. Karuna had an intellectual knowledge of what she had become. Her experience in the reality of it, however, was just beginning. The nightmare began with her first 'call of the wild'. Since then, it has been an ongoing battle to control her urges and still survive.

A sleeping cot, rickety writing table and chair and a two burner hot plate were the only real furniture and they looked about as old as the building, which had been in use as a pension since it was built more than a thousand years ago. The walls were covered in etched graffiti hundreds of years old. The one item that looked out of place was the laptop, its keys blackened from continual use.

Karuna made a pot of coffee before settling into the chair that rebelled at the weight, lashings squeaking loudly as they strained to near breaking. The computer crowed before coming to life and lighting the screen with the dark writings of Tepes. His cursive was nearly illegible, requiring all of her concentration just to read the words, let alone pull meaning from the mind of a madman.

Karuna began reading the journals chronologically, regardless of whether she had read it before. Why this was so even she was not sure. Since crossing the line and taking a life, Karuna felt driven to understand the man who created a living, breathing hell on earth.

His earliest writings were the cries and demands of a spoiled child that wanted the trappings of his father without having to work for it. By the age of ten, he wanted the throne. Vlad would conspire with his brothers against his father only to be made a fool of by his siblings. They would play along with the bourgeoning psychopath only to bail on the ploys at the last minute, leaving Vlad holding the bag, so to speak. Vlad was slow to learn in the beginning and there are rumors that his being a royal pain in the ass was one of the reasons he was bartered to Mehmed the II of Turkey, ruler of the Ottoman Empire. The deal was an attempt by Tepes' father to forestall an invasion. A weak attempt at best that bought Vlad the II a few years of peace. Of course this was at the expense of his son's asshole and mind. Vlad's younger brother Radu was also part of the deal. But rather than suffer the brutal affections of Mehmed's court, he converted to Islam and became one.

For what Karuna had planned, she needed to be fluent in the old language. Current Romani bears little resemblance to the language spoken a thousand years ago and she would need it down rote along with Persian and Arabic.

In her studies Karuna had yet to come across the name Dracine. It was only after returning from his forced internship with Mehmed and the change that came along with it was she ever mentioned. Dracine was a few months younger than Vlad as well as being his half-sister. When Vlad's mother became pregnant with him, his father's urges were directed elsewhere. In this case, it was the royal mid-wife. Dracine lived on long after the mid-wife had been put to death. Being of the blood of the Draculs, Vlad the II would not allow her to be put to death. Rather she would serve the family for the remainder of her life.

***

Sechra headed north to Constanta. She wanted her grandfather's blessing before journeying into the old country. Of course Dray Kcirb had long been in the ground. No doubt the worms had finished with him by now. It was a respect thing. Dray was all the family she could really remember. The details of her loved ones deaths would be etched in her memory forever, but the love and caresses of both parents were lost in the fuzziness that time creates. Only the calloused hands of her grandfather, as he held her little ones, were remembered. The gnarled old man had once been all the world to her, protecting

Sechra from the evil that unfolded around them. But that was long ago. The wretchedness of the past had been put to rest.

The Zapar estate overlooking Constanta harbor had been torn down. In its place was the Harbor Master's residence and office. Behind the structure was a well kept trail that led to a sitting area with expansive views of the coast. A brass plaque explained the locations' points of interest and asked that visitors not disturb the graves. Set back in a few meters from the bluff were two granite headstones. One stone held just a name, no dates or epitaph – 'ZAPAR'. The other – 'DRAY KCIRB – Father of the Romanian Constitution'. Again no dates. Sechra sat on the moldy sandstone bench and wept for herself.

"Help me grandpapa." Sechra wanted to say more but the words did not come. Tears fell onto her hands, soaking into the beaten and hardened skin. In her hands, she saw grandpapa's leathered digits from a life of working with stone. In the silence, only the wind blowing in off the sea was her answer. Sechra zipped her suit and pulled on her gloves.

By nightfall, the coast was far behind. Since noon she had been on back roads and wagon trails, switchbacking through the foothills to the base of the Alps. The going was slow, but it was not speed she had in mind, more a regaining of the mindset necessary to survive in the mountains without modern comforts. The length of the semi-automatic shotgun was cold comfort enough. Sechra practiced with the weapon after setting up camp for the night. Were it not for the upper body strength, from years of sculpting, the shotgun would have been too much to handle. Bracing herself each time she squeezed the trigger kept Sechra from having to step backwards from the recoil. As the days and nights wore on, she became adept at pulling it from the body holster and accurately unleashing a barrage of death. At the time, the practice was something to idle away the few hours before sleep.

The rumble of the twin cylinder motorcycle was the only disturbance that marked her passage. Sechra was not fool enough to think she was traveling unseen through the foothills. 'The hills have eyes,' she thought and knew she was being tracked. To ditch the tail, she would have to ditch the bike. 'Only if I have to.' Besides, it was not as if she was being followed, per se, as she kept an eye on as she passed through hamlets and mini-caravans. Word was sent along ahead of her. The mountain wireless worked as well or better than modern forms of communication.

Pulling into a roadside café one rainy afternoon in the forest, Sechra felt as if she was expected. Though the seating was full to capacity and other hungry people were waiting to eat, there was one empty table and chair next to a hot wood stove. As Sechra got off the bike, she thumbed the safety off on the shotgun and unsnapped the tab holding it secure. She knew these people, just not personally, and was playing it safe. Cold and wet, she hung her leather 'Stitch' near the stove, taking the seat that was meant for her. Icy neutral eyes watched her every move. A waiter handed her a towel and set a cup of coffee on the table. She nodded to a bowl of goulash a patron was intent on devouring. Message understood, she went to drying her face and hair. When she took the towel away, a man with horrendous facial scarring and one eye replaced the waiter. For a flash of a moment, she thought it was Jake. The man was not the diver. Jake lost his other eye. He looked her over carefully before pulling a chair and sitting, never taking his eye off of her.

"Good afternoon," Sechra said raising a carafe of coffee left by the waiter. "Café?"

"Please. I have been waiting for you. Urloff is my name." He extended his hand. When Sechra took it he felt the texture of her skin. A yellow smile punctuated by missing teeth spread across his face. "You have hands like your grandfather, Madame Kcirb."

"I work with stone as did he. Why have you been waiting?"

"Because you travel so slowly." Urloff burst out laughing, "If you had a mule...?"

Sechra looked hard at the man and the laughter dwindled. In fact the whole café had become silent, intent on hearing what came next.

"We knew you would come. The question is why?"

Sechra scanned the diners, all of whom pretended to be eating at the moment. "Are you sure, Urloff, that this is the best place to be asking?"

"Do you think these people are here by chance?" he replied sternly.

"I guess not. I have noticed you following me for some time now."

"We are not so much watching you as making sure you have not been followed. There is change coming. You can almost smell it," Urloff sniffed the air.

"Which is why I have come. What can I do?"

"You must kill it."

***

Four months passed before Karuna felt the eyes of Ahmed in the back streets of Istanbul. During this time, she had become fluent in the old languages. Persian and the old Arabic were still used in the ancient city. High-speed internet had yet to infect all of the slums where the forgotten ways still existed. Here she practiced in full burqa attire, for otherwise she would have been shunned as an outsider. The disguise was never complete, requiring her to give a mental push to get people to talk.

At other times she would dress as an old man, poor, but not a beggar, to enter the Hagia Sophia in order to study the vaults of knowledge that it held.

Time had wasted most of the magnificent structure. The restoration of the ancient church, now a mosque, never really happened. Feeble, under-funded attempts in the late 1900s and early 2000s were failures. Scaffolding still stood where efforts were started then abandoned. Humidity and salt air, however, was ever at work crumbling the mosaics, fracturing and collapsing the domes and toppling minarets.

For more than a thousand years, she had stood as the greatest hall of knowledge the world had ever seen. At that time, around A.D. 330, Istanbul, or Constantinople if you will, was already a major hub of the known world and capitol of the Eastern Roman Empire. A small version of the Hagia Sophia was already existent. Skip ahead two hundred years. Emperor Justinian expands the Roman Empire into the whole of the Mediterranean and Black Sea regions, Byzantium. During his reign, he reconstructed the Hagia Sophia into the largest structure ever built in the world. Scholars would travel for years to get to its doors. So would the armies of those who wished to control it. The Crusaders had their chance, the Ottoman Empire crushed Istanbul time and time again, but the Hagia Sophia was left alone, relatively. It wasn't until the mid–1400s that Mehmed II wrested control of Constantinople from Christian powers and in effect destroyed Byzantium. A moderate form of Islam would rule Turkey and Istanbul from then on.

Karuna read from crumbling parchment scrolls, pieced together fallen tile work and cleaned works that still remained intact, all in an effort to bring herself up to date on current affairs during the fifteenth century. Every day until the evening call to prayer, Karuna devoted herself to the task. This day she was reading a graphic description of Mehmed's conquering of Constantinople. For Christians everywhere, his victory was the death knell of Byzantium. When he stormed the city for the final time, the faithful hid behind the Hagia's massive wood and bronze doors, believing they would be protected by the sacred structure. Though Mehmed would save the Hagia Sophia, the frightened citizens would not be so lucky. Those who survived were sold into slavery. Most were savagely butchered or put to the pike and cross.

Feeling the call to prayer at hand, Karuna began to wrap up the scroll and gather her things to leave, when a familiar voice came from a darkened corner of the vestibule. She had not heard anyone enter or felt someone's presence.

"Please do not run or push yourself from my mind. I can help you, Voivode Danesti," came Ahmed's voice, speaking the ancient Romanian dialect.

Karuna reached into her purse and jacked a round into the gun, stood and faced the shadow. "Good evening, Ahmed. We should leave." The call to prayer sounded from minarets all around the city. Together they left the one hall into a larger one with prayer rugs in rows across the floor. For the next twenty minutes they prayed. To have left the mosque without praying would have drawn attention to themselves, something neither wanted to do, ever.

Karuna did not push him away mentally. She sensed something in what Ahmed said about 'helping her'. Instead she made them invisible to those around as they wove their way back to the hovel she called home. Not so much invisible, as they could not be seen, but forgotten in a blending with the market crowds and becoming the nameless faces of the masses. Only after they ducked through the doorway into the cool darkness did she break the silence.

"How did you find me?" she asked, making tea for both of them.

"I waited and watched. For the last 22 days you have been going to the Hagia, though what you wish to gain from studying there is beyond me. The place no longer holds the mysteries you seek to divine." Ahmed coughed and rolled a couple cigarettes.

Karuna had given up the habit when she arrived in Istanbul. Now she savored the dark tobacco before responding. Her words tumbled through the haze of smoke that hung in layers of air. "Fascinating as it was, I fear your words are true. I have been biding my time."

"You have been wasting your time!" Ahmed's statement came like a deserved slap in the face.

"Of that I am aware. You said you could help. What did you mean?"

"You know what you have to do. Why do you wait?" he asked.

"Because I am not sure it can be done."

"You of all people, Voivode Danesti, know that anything is possible. When you return to the estate, I will be there waiting for you. Together I will show you how."

"When?"

"In three days." With that Ahmed got up, bowed curtly to Karuna and left.

Karuna wasted no more time. By nightfall she had her things packed. She sat at a beachside café, sipping strong coffee until the darkness was complete and the shoreline empty of traffic. She had never traveled by sheer will alone, but knew it could be done. Centering herself, she looked up and down the beach. Seeing no one, Karuna kicked up the sand sprinting across the shore to the waters edge, leaping into the night sky on her way back to Eforie Sud...

✳✳✳

And what dear reader, you might ask, happened to Frederick, who got his dick cut off and Igor, his hands? Not to mention the plight of poor Thora Wozniak.

When Frederick Cezar was released from the hospital there was no time to worry about his loss. Cezar got caught up in the world of sensational art. Since the riot, the Kcirb exhibit received international recognition. Everyone now wanted to see it. With Sechra MIA, he stepped up to the plate and took over. Zurich, Moscow, Munich, Paris, and New York were cities at the top of the list. Since he could no longer think with his dick, his brain took over and Frederick Cezar was making more money than he ever dreamed of.

The exhibit itself, eleven massive sculptures, to say the least, was a monumental effort to relocate. Cezar was a delagator, not a doer. His skills at juggling people and events allowed him time to spend a few weeks in Copenhagen getting a new dick and arranging for an exhibit there as well. Thora, he thought, would be pleased at the new arrangement, that is, if he only knew where she was. The windfall that the riots in Bucharest created, however, kept him from dwelling on her plight as the exhibits kept him busy during the day and his new, oversized member the nights. Success like this he had always hoped to achieve. He was only aware of the upside, never once considering what fate may have in store. As yet no one had noticed the changes in the exhibit that happened that first night, nor the macabre additions in Zurich or Moscow.

Igor returned to the beach cottage he shared with Sechra with the stipulation he was not allowed on the estate grounds or into the building itself. With Karuna gone, Riana had the place shut down. Steel roll downs covered all the windows and doors sealed the estate from all possible entry. The Dracul had been rendered useless by Dino.

Igor spent his time rehabilitating. Reinstalling his hands required excessive physical therapy. After the first few weeks, he could feed himself and wipe his ass, poorly. Ironically, it was the ones footing the bill of his rehab that he plotted against. It would be months before he could use the gun, if ever. This however gave him time to study his history and devise a way to destroy the Draculs. In the meantime, he searched for an entrance into the estate. The old ones always had escape routes in case of a siege. Underground tunnels that ran for kilometers before ending in a hidden exit. The searching didn't require the use of his hands, yet.

Thora Wozniak had discovered hell, while still alive. Trapped beneath the outhouse sculpture, she wallowed in the filth along with the child. Every moment was filled with terror. There was no respite. The price of murder is different for everyone. The price of greed is what got her there.

***

Karuna tumbled into the sand on the beachfront in Eforie Sud. Not realizing the effort it took to travel by will, the journey left her spent and wasted. She made no effort to get up, that is until the sun came over the horizon and turned the shadeless stretch of sand into a scorching torch. Her burning skin brought Karuna back into the moment. Even though Jake and Johnny had taught her about such things, it takes experience to truly glom the reality.

The closest shade was the gazebo. From there, she saw the estate closed down and locked up tight. 'Shit,' she thought, 'I have no keys.'

That didn't mean she couldn't get in. It would just take a little more effort. Karuna dug into her shoulder bag and produced a thermos. We'll call it red coffee. The thermos kept it cool. A half hour later, she was able to twist the lock off of one of the roll ups. The red coffee had keyed her senses as well as rejuvenating her will. Karuna disabled the alarm before rolling up the steel door. Once inside, the door was put back in place. She didn't want anyone to know she had returned.

Even with the jolt of red coffee, Karuna remained wasted. 'How did Jake and Johnny keep going all the time when they did this sort of thing? A man's will surely had something to do with it.' Then she laughed wryly to herself, remembering the amount of drugs they consumed on a regular basis. It wasn't her way, yet. She crashed on the couch in the main room as the physical realization of the effort took hold and put her down.

The scent of a demitasse of strong Turkish coffee roused her from the slumber of the dead. So sound was the sleep, Karuna never heard Ahmed as he made himself at home. He sat across from her in a large overstuffed chair with feet upon an ottoman, as at ease as a man can be when in comfortable surroundings.

"Good evening, Karuna," Ahmed said, toasting her with his little cup as she opened her eyes.

Her senses became immediately keyed into the fight or flight reflex. She saw her demitasse before Ahmed and in that moment was able to reel in a violent reaction. Too often she had seen Jake go off half-cocked; she was, after all, an academic and professor, but more importantly, a student. Karuna fought the urge to fly from the couch and tear the throat out of whoever it was, as she had been taught to do, just as Jake struggled with subduing the sudden urges with a shot of heroin.

Instead she thought of nothing and settled her mind into a state of clarity.

"Good evening, Ahmed. I take it three days have passed."

"Actually four. I have been waiting for you to come around naturally. I understand the toll such travel takes on your body and mind."

"I am just becoming aware of it. Thank you for the consideration. How do you know of such things?"

"Like you, I am a student. Unlike yourself, I am not of the blood. Voivode, yes, the darkness no. Many times, back in the day, my father would come to me as you have and I would wait, like now, until he was himself again."

"Your father? I do not understand." Karuna tipped her demitasse, shooting the coffee and reaching for the carafe for more.

"You know him. And though we have not been formally introduced, I have seen you before coming into the service of the Prime Minister. I fear you did not see me, as I did not wish to be." Ahmed glanced in the direction of the mosaics, "It was in there."

Karuna's moment of clarity expanded. Putting two and two together had never been one of her shortcomings.

"But your eyes, they had been put to the red hot iron," Karuna realized who he was. Facial features were similar but the skin color would suggest Arabic origin rather than Romanian, a requirement for being Voivode.

Ahmed read this in her eyes. "My mother was Turkish. Vlad after all was a trader. To be successful, which he was, required blood connections for things to work properly. Back then it was easy to have several families."

"That still doesn't explain why you are sitting here." Karuna sat up and poured more coffee.

"No, no it doesn't. In fact I cannot truly explain it myself. When I created the mosaics, I depicted myself with eyes. Throughout the centuries, I lived within the broken pieces of ceramic, studying all within the borders. It was my world. Then some twenty years ago, I stepped out of the walls into reality, this one anyway."

"But why are you a guard, carry guns, help old women and..."

"And work for my father? Because he does not know."

"How could he not?"

"Vlad is no longer as you are. He is aware that I am from the mosaics, but is not as good at math as you. Besides the country and its stability consume him."

"May I ask why he asked that you watch over me?"

"To protect you from yourself and to keep you from damaging his political image," Ahmed explained.

"The accident on the highway?" Karuna was referring to saving the family, but mostly 'the call of the wild.'

"Exactly that sort of thing."

"How did you travel from Istanbul?"

"I drove. It's the only thing I like about the modern world. I love cars."

"Do you wish you could go back?"

"I do. All the time. It is one of the reasons I contacted you. You entered months ago when Igor's hands were removed and focused on Dracine.

Of course it was not actually Igor at the time, but one of his ancestors."
Answering her unspoken question, "I was the axeman."

"I had to know more."

"Understandably, but Dracine? She makes Tepes look like a boy scout."

"What more can you tell me about her?"

"She is cruel, heartless, basically a Dracul by definition. But I can tell you nothing that will help you. For that you must continue what you started. I will be with you."

They both looked towards the mosaic tiling. "When would you like to start?" asked Karuna.

***

I t was late one evening along the coast. Igor was wrapping up a long day hiking the woods, hills and valleys in the vicinity of the estate. He had been searching for weeks already. During his years living on the coast, teaching Sechra, Igor had often taken long walks, usually along the beach, but not always. He knew the countryside well and didn't require the use of a GPS to track his movements.

Now he was searching for the exit or entrance, depending on how you look at it. Long forgotten, he was certain years of overgrowth had further hidden the access. The last light of day was a few blinks away when he caught a movement out of the corner of his eye. When all around you is still, any movement will capture your attention. The figure had crested a rise and dropped quickly into a darkened ravine. Having never seen anyone on his walks before, Igor quickly and silently stole through the woods to where the person had disappeared. He waited, listening. If someone were down there, he would hear them.

Nothing but the chirping of crickets. Igor squatted for hours, perfectly still for fear his own noise would give him away. The night was moonless, the darkness impenetrable. When his haunches could no longer withstand the position, Igor rose painfully, into an upright position. Hard as he could, he tried to remember the location. Doubting his accuracy he tied a handkerchief to the branch of a tree, looked to the stars to get his bearings and headed back to the studio. He would return tomorrow. Most likely it was the hovel of a shepherd or homeless waif. Either way he intended to find out, armed.

***

'Kill what?' Sechra wondered as she dipped into the goulash with a piece of bread while buying herself some time with the chewing.

"I thought that business had been taken care of years ago," replied Sechra after swallowing.

"As did we all, but I think you know better, yes?" Seeing her bowl half-finished, Urloff called for more. When it came Sechra did not object; off-road riding is harder than it looks and she hadn't had a decent meal since heading to the mountains.

She hung her head, wet hair stringing over her face helped to hide the shame. "Yes, something did happen. I was a child, I didn't know."

"There is no fault or blame, Sechra," she had not mentioned her first name. "You were set up from the beginning. The horrors you witnessed as a child opened the doors of hate and revenge. It was only natural and has happened to us all." For the first time there was a murmur of agreement amongst the others in the diner. It did little to relieve Sechra's feelings. "As they say, you were at the wrong place at the wrong time. The essence of evil that lingered needed one with the deepest of hatred and fear. It found you." Urloff paused to let the thought sink in. "You see, we are all human. Even the Kcirbs who have been of the greatest service to the peoples of Romania had their axe to grind."

"I don't understand. What has my heritage to do with it?" Sechra finished her bowl and pushed it away. A cup of strong coffee was put in its place.

"Everything. You are Kcirb. How much do you know of your lineage?"

"Of our history as a people, I know a good deal. My grandfather never spoke that much of our family other than what we could do to help."

"That sounds like Dray. If it were not for the Kcirbs, our country would be illiterate. But I get ahead of myself. In the back there is a sitting room, we can be more comfortable."

They both got up. Urloff took the coffee while Sechra gathered her leathers, following him to the back.

After removing the shotgun harness, Sechra settled into an easy chair and rolled a cigarette while waiting for Urloff to finish whatever it was he was doing. She had anticipated some research while getting back to her roots, but what he said about killing 'it' had her more than a little concerned about what was actually going on. Her art was just that, her art. It acted as a catharsis to relieve her of the many images that still assaulted her mind. She had been a child, and like many children saw things during this time that no one should ever see, least of all a kid. No, she was not unique with the version of PTSD that haunted her daily. Many, too many, over the years had had similar experiences and no way to work them out. Sechra considered herself lucky in this respect. That is until now.

Her heritage, along with an unforgiving kismet, had her revise the situation. Somehow, somewhere the Kcirbs had always had to deal with these kinds of issues. With Dray long dead and buried, Sechra was the last of a family whose history stretched back so far. And unbeknownst to her, went further back than even the Draculs.

Urloff entered the room with the two coffee cups and a full carafe of more. Reading her mind to a certain degree, the big man said, "Did you not know that the Kcirbs were the original Voivodes of Romania? It was your family that traveled far to educate themselves, but never left the homeland behind. The idea was not to rule the country, but educate the population, so they may rule themselves without a traditional royal family to dictate the rules and suck the people dry of their work and self-respect." Urloff refilled his cup and topped off Sechra's. "In the beginning, that is to say before we civilized the country, we were just a band of nomads, like everyone else. The earliest Kcirbs settled in the mountains of Tirgoviste. Once a farm and stability was established, a few traveled to Istanbul in the south, Germany to the north and Paris and London to the west. During these expeditions, they not only observed other cultures that were farther along the civilization curve, but stayed on for years at a time to study their language, art and ways of life. Each would return and share the knowledge they gained within the clan. This was all well and good for them, but there was one, we will call him Grandpapa who had a vision." Urloff drank his coffee in one gulp, refilling the cup while he gathered his words. There was no way to tell the whole of the history, for it had never been written down, but passed on from generation to generation.

We've all played the game of whispering a thought to the person next to you. They in turn told the person next to them, and so on until the thought came full circle to the one who started it. Then the laughter would begin as the thought had changed so much around the circle that it hardly resembled the original, if at all. Thus Urloff found himself repeating what he had been told over and over again until he had it down rote. Now he shuffled through the history, trying to separate fact from fiction and reach his audience, Sechra.

"The vision, which I had mentioned before, was to teach the burgeoning population and consolidate them into a people, a nation. Grandpapa's vision was good, but lacked the caveat that not all who learned would be fair and just with the knowledge."

"So let me see if I'm getting this correctly. Landowners and peasants were treated the same," Sechra began.

"Correct," replied Urloff.

"But some used the knowledge to make others subservient. I assume we will call them Boyars."

"Correct again."

"Nothing new there. Not a damn thing has changed in thousands of years." Sechra drank deeply from her cup.

"No doubt. But it worked. It wasn't your perfect socialism, yet there was harmony and fairness. We lacked a monetary system and relied on barter and need. Those who did well shared with those who didn't. Amazing is what it was. Greed and hoarding were nonexistent."

"What happened to our utopia?" Sechra asked mildly sarcastic.

"The world became smaller. Trade and shipping brought it down, along with the rest of the shit that has ruined our world ever since. What we called our country was smack dab in the middle of the trade routes. At first, it was the riches traders brought with them that sparked a flame of greed into our hearts. But we had no money, or thought we had none. As the language barrier was broken, we learned that gold was what was needed to acquire the shiny silks and trinkets that enamored everyone."

"They still do. America stole their country from the Indians for little more than a handful of glass beads. But since the natives were 'paid' that made everything okay. That they got screwed wasn't an issue. Megacorp works the same way." Sechra was wondering where this talk was going. The creatively challenged wealthy do it to artists all the time. They wave a wad of cash, far below the value of an artist's sweat and blood, until they cave, never understanding that artists have bills to pay and need to eat once in a while. Sechra understood this well. She didn't mind the history lesson and Dray had taught her to be patient. Besides she was still cold, the riding gear wet, and the chair comfortable. There didn't seem to be any reason to push Urloff into rushing his tale. She topped her coffee, sat back and put her feet up. "Go on."

"There wasn't much, gold that is, but the rush was on. For the first time ever, those that scored kept it to themselves. There was no sharing. That in itself was enough to topple the rows of dominoes that had been our life. Greed is not just for the rich alone. The poor have it in equal measure, just not the means to satisfy it. Then again, is greed ever sated?"

"Almost overnight we wanted more. More of what the ships and caravans had to offer. Ironically none of it was needed. We had everything. What more could one want? A full belly, bountiful harvests, good hunting; the earth had provided us with all that was necessary. But now we wanted more and the more of it, the better."

"It was at this time that the Boyar class invented itself. They used their knowledge to become clever in acquiring 'more.' For trinkets, they bought up the land from those who lived farther from the action, thus the ignorant never understood how they were taken and suddenly the land they had worked for generations now belonged to another. The farmers who stayed after the sale worked for the Boyar to live on the property. It's a simple form of indentured slavery. Where else was the farmer to go?"

"The land barons however were ever at each other, too, with no cohesive bond besides acquisition. At the same time that the Boyars were at each other's throats, the poor and less clever were rising up against the ones who had taken advantage of them."

"Some things will never change," drolled Sechra.

"True enough. Be that as it may, there was one who stood apart from either side to view the situation from a neutral perspective."

"Grandpapa?"

"Yes Sechra, your ancestor. He had what we now call 'savoir faire.' Grandpapa was able to discuss the issues with the poor as well as the Boyars. Both groups saw the need to stabilize the volatile situation, but neither could grasp a way to do it. The old Kcirb was able to see a way. The trick was to get both sides to agree to it."

"Grandpapa knew there was no going back to the way things were. The lines had been drawn. The 'haves' had no intention of having less, of redistributing 'their' wealth. The 'have nots' just wanted to survive, and of course have a way to rise above their status. And so, like Dray, your grandfather, the old Kcirb studied the ways of other countries. What he discovered did little to raise his confidence that there was a way. Every country he delved into was a monarchy that did little or nothing to find a balance between the 'haves' and 'have nots.' Instead they used the power to nurture and grow their own greed. A cabal formed around the monarchs for protection from the common people and invaders bent on taking their stuff from them. The cabal, in turn, supported the monarch's decrees and made sure the demands were met with the sweat and toil of the 'have nots.'"

"Grandpapa knew this wouldn't fly for his people. Of course they could be forced into it, a.k.a. feudalism, which was already happening, or by forming an army, like the other countries, to enforce the laws. At the time, the Boyars were ruling the country and when not busy attacking each other, they united and went after their own people. The internal strife was bad and getting worse, causing problems in the shipping industry, which in turn affected their newfound wealth. There were other ports, but they were not connected to the Danube, a major route into Western Europe. Something had to be done before Romania destroyed itself or worse, was taken over by a greedier nation. Then it wouldn't matter who you were. There is little or no distinction amongst slaves."

"So instead he began writing his own constitution. Democracy had yet to be invented, nor did he invent it then. But it was a loose form of the political idea. A leader put in place by a consensus. In this case, it would be a vote by the Boyars, the landowners. Even the poorest, who still held title to their property, had an equal say."

"Since more than a generation had lived since the 'need' for more stuff began, so dwindled the opportunity of using the educational efforts initiated by the Kcirbs. His thinking was that by having the Boyars do the voting, at least you would have the educated making the choices. It was a sad state of affairs, but he could see no other way."

"Grandpapa Kcirb was a Boyar. His plan was to do good and he did very well. On the surface, it would appear as if he was no better than the others in buying up the land for a pittance and requiring the previous owners to work it for the privilege of staying on. But, there was a difference, and not all that subtle either. What he was doing was saving the farmers from being gobbled up by the bastards and forced into indentured slavery. Sure he owned the land on paper, but set no quota on his share of the crops, required no rent or taxes. In other words, he let them live on as usual. The only stipulation he placed upon his tenants was that they never speak of the arrangement, for surely if word got out there would be revolution."

"The old Kcirb bided his time, waiting for the right moment to unveil his plan. He didn't have to wait long. The Persian Empire was failing. And had been for some time. In the throes of its death, the armies and navies were dispatched to secure whatever foothold they could in a world that was changing faster than they could keep up. With no plan other than to divide and conquer, the divided forces failed in every attempt. Jerusalem, Cairo, Athens, Istanbul, all swatted the once mighty Persians as one would a fly. A naval contingent was sent to the mouth of the Danube to hold it for no good reason."

"Romania was, nevertheless, unprepared for such an assault. When the Persians hit the beaches, there was little if any resistance. Only the landowners held their ground, however briefly, against the onslaught of a few trained men. Word traveled fast throughout the lands, fortunately coming to the ears of Grandpapa sooner than later. His grasp of the reality was swift, for though I call him Grandpapa he was still a young man, then. Realizing that it was only the Boyars that had anything to lose, then surely they would band together to save what they had. With the added incentive that they may acquire more land and power by aiding than running, well, let us say greed has an upside. Within weeks, the Boyars gathered upstream from the mouth of the Danube. Steel and the skill to use it came with them. A plan was made."

"Twelve small skiffs each holding ten men, paddled silently in the darkness of the night towards the sea. Six boats along one shore and six along the other. On foot, two hundred men on each side of the river paced the boats downstream. The sounds of the battle that took the port had long since quieted. The echo of drunkenness now drifted on the breeze signaling the men that the time was close and also good, raising their confidence now that they needed it most."

"Kcirb had always been a man of the land. He led the shore party that would initiate the attack. Fishermen manned the boats. It only seemed logical. A man named Zapar was in charge of the water. On the other side of the river a Dracul led his six boats and a Cneajna, the forces on land."

"The little boats slipped silently across the black water of the wharves.

Each went to a moored Persian warship. Eight men would then get out, waiting for their moment. The two men remaining in the boats began painting the warship hulls with a flammable accelerant."

Urloff paused to drink from his cup. Sechra took advantage of the break in the monologue. "So Urloff, your jaw must be tired. Math has never been one of my weak points. Let me see if I can fill in the rest. Grandpapa had done his homework. They surrounded the Persians on three sides. The sea taking care of the fourth." Urloff nodded, Sechra continued, "So they attacked, raising all the hell they could muster. In the dark, a few can seem like many. Like rats, in a reverse analogy, the Persians ran for the protection of their ships. At which point they were lit afire."

"You left out all the good parts, but yes, that is what happened. This was the event that the old Kcirb had been waiting for. Shortly thereafter, he submitted his proposal, his constitution."

When he did, there was little if any resistance. Everyone had had enough. Volunteers were asked to step up for the election process. There were few willing to take on the responsibility, but also a few who saw the opportunity, which presented itself in the position. The Cneajna's and Dracul's were among the first to avail themselves of a life in the service of the people of Romania. Oddly enough, Grandpapa did not want the position for himself, withdrawing from the competition. Ironically, however, when the vote was cast, it was Kcirb who was elected Voivode."

"But we are no longer, nor have we ever been considered one."

"Ah yes, the foibles of men fuck things up once again. Needless to say, there are always some who considered themselves more fit for the position and conspire to get it. Who it was, is as forgotten as your family's position and no longer matters. After some years of relative peace, it was decided there be another vote. The incumbent did not win. The treachery of politics is ever in vogue. It matters not who, whether Dracul or Cneajna, or Danesti, but they wiped the record of the Kcirbs from every document of the times. Why this was so is unknown."

"Yeah well, life's a bitch," Sechra murmured, remember something Jake once said.

"It will get worse."

"Always does. Now don't get me wrong, I appreciate the history lesson, but just what the hell does that have to do with me and killing 'it'?

I could stick the barrel of this shotgun in my mouth and splatter my brains across the décor, but I don't think that is what you have in mind."

"You are correct. But what a visual, whoo!"

"And just what is this evil, this shit that entered me as a child and comes out in my sculpting? Is it something that can be killed or is that a metaphor?"

"No, and yes. It has spread so thin it appears to be a metaphor. You see it did not only enter you, but the hearts of all Romanians. That's why your sculptures have taken on a life of their own."

"Then you know of the changes. I thought only I knew."

"An old one told me. She sees things. Did you know only Roma's are added to or affect the works?"

"No I did not. There have been more?" Sechra replied with surprise. "The original additions were of a crude nature. Surely someone has seen the changes."

"If they have, they have been absorbed or the changes more subtle, who knows," replied Urloff.

"Then I must see them!"

"No, that is unless you want to, but there is nothing you can do."

"I can destroy them," demanded Sechra. "They are mine!"

"I don't think you can anymore. Before you finished the final piece, perhaps. But now you must find another way."

"But how?" For the first time in a long time, Sechra felt helpless.

"It is within you. You must find the way of peace. Your work has always been of pain, hatred and ruthlessness. No more! Find it, Sechra, and deal with it before the tide of madness destroys us all."

"Then I must return."

"Yes, at some point. Sorry for the long drive, guess I could have called," Urloff added to lighten the moment.

"Thanks Urloff, I needed that. Is there a place I can spend the night? The sun is setting and well I'd rather not ride in freezing rain wearing wet leathers."

"Arrangements have been made," he pointed to a door behind Sechra. "It is small..."

"Thank you Urloff, I have slept in far worse places."

"I know."

***

Karuna sat alone at the kitchen counter nursing her first cup of the day when Ahmed entered the dining area. Like a shadow, he poured himself a cup from the French press and slid out the oak doors to sit alone at the gazebo. He himself was a true drinker of the black life offered by the little bean, too. Twenty minutes later he returned for a second.

"Good morning, Karuna. Rest well?"

"Slept like the dead," she responded with a Jakeism in an effort to keep it positive.

It took Ahmed a moment or two to catch the joke, "Oh I get it, slept like the dead, very funny."

"That's the first time I think I've seen you laugh, Ahmed."

"There is not much to laugh about any more."

"No, there isn't, but I used to know a few guys who could make a joke out of anything. Sick but funny, you know."

"Americans and their wry sense of humor." Karuna looked at him questioningly. "I've read your dossier," he added.

"I see. You don't seem to have one, but then how could you? That you are here is what matters. I would like to hear your story one day, but alas, there is no time for it."

"Not yet, but one day perhaps. It's worth hearing."

"I'm sure it is. What's your plan?" Karuna cut to the chase.

"We enter the mosaics and learn what we can. I recommend that we go with Dracine again. I will be her personal assistant. Your personal assistant, that is. I can keep you from making breaches of protocol that you would inevitably make, being yourself."

"By the way, how did you get in here? I would have heard the roll ups," Karuna asked.

"Ahh – the secret entrance. That is why no one knows where it is. Because it's a secret. It is possible that Vlad does not even remember having it constructed. Come on, I will show you."

Karuna followed Ahmed to what would be considered the kitchen's pantry. The original use for the room had been obliterated by remodeling.

"This was the sleeping quarters for the kitchen staff." He saw the look in Karuna's eyes, disbelief. The room was only three meters square.

"Not the entire staff," Ahmed laughed again, "Just for the ones off duty. The kitchen ran 24/7."

Karuna expected a hidden latch or torch holder that turned to open a wall. Instead Ahmed rolled back an ancient oriental rug to reveal a hatch. He bent over, raising the recessed handle and put his back into lifting the wooden portal. "Now you know the secret."

"Where is the exit?"

"In the forest, deep in a ravine. Should you ever need to use it, when you emerge head south, it will lead you to the highway."

"Let's hope it doesn't come to that."

"With any luck, but it can't hurt to be prepared. When we have time I will take you down there. The artifacts of our heritage have been kept safe for centuries. You would be amazed, even with your experience."

Ahmed closed the hatch and replaced the rug. They then went to the mosaic panels.

"It is here where our work truly begins. When we enter, we must have no intention of ever returning. Having an escape route keeps you from truly being in the moment."

"Okay Ahmed, I understand the meaning of commitment better than most and will, without hesitation, do what has to be done regardless of the personal consequences."

"That is good, for that is what it takes. Were you not Danesti, you would not understand."

"But how? Our bodies are left on the floor before the images. They would die of dehydration in a few days."

"How very insightful and true, according to your understanding, but not complete," Ahmed knew he was losing her. "It took me many years to learn what I am about to tell you. You see Karuna, when you entered the mosaics before it was with your mind. You focused on a subject and soon found your conscious mind living in the experience."

"Both Jake and I were nearly killed with just our minds hypnotized into the images."

"The wounds that happened there of course were reflected in this reality. Why? Because it is real – not a dream, not mesmerization. When you are there, you are there. You have gone back in time."

"Tell me something I don't know, Ahmed!"

"I was getting to that." He poured some more coffee, cleaned the press and started another pot while Karuna rolled a cigarette. "Entering with the mind is just one way. There is another." Ahmed finished the coffee ritual, topping off both cups. "Come I will show you."

Karuna fell into step behind Ahmed. From behind, he looked just like his father. Gait, set of the shoulders, and swinging of the arms was a dead ringer for Vlad Cneajna. He stopped before a particularly placid scene. There was no death or vile circumstances in the panel. It was a wedding party in full swing. In contrast to many of the panels, there was joy and light, peace and happiness amongst the revelers. It was as pleasant as one could possibly imagine. Karuna had never paid any attention to it in the past.

"This is as good a place to start as any. Now watch, it's as easy as it looks. See that man pouring wine?" Karuna nodded. "Try not to lose yourself in the image just yet. The theory is the same. It's just way more intense. Watch me. Once I'm in, I will wave for you to enter. Just do as I do. You focus on the woman I am pouring for. Got it?"

"I still don't," Karuna began.

"You will." Ahmed's attention went into the mosaic panel. Karuna watched him go calm as he became one with the object of his aspiration. His steps were slow and sure. He walked directly at the image. When his body met the tile he kept going, leaving the estate and entering the past. Karuna looked around. He was gone. She went back to viewing the mosaic. The barkeep set down his pitcher before finishing filling the woman's goblet. He looked directly at Karuna and waved to her. Not like a hello wave, more of a come on wave.

The woman became Karuna's focal point, immediately feeling her intoxication and mild impatience at her cup not being full. The hot air filled her nostrils as the wind blew at the veil she wore. Karuna walked towards the image as she had seen Ahmed do. At the moment of contact she thought 'I did it,' and promptly clocked her forehead on the hard surface, bringing her to her knees and stars to her head. A weak stream of blood ran out her nose as a knot raised on her forehead. She used a hanky to wipe the blood, rubbing the bump with her other hand as she got back into position to try again. She saw the error. The little thought pulled her out just enough to cancel total commitment. When she looked back the woman was just getting up off the ground, more embarrassed than drunk. Ahmed waved again.

Karuna's stare was intense. Few were the times in this life when she had been this 'in the moment'. She stepped forward, her eyes intent on the woman and didn't give in to another thought until she felt the sand beneath her feet and goblet outstretched to a waiting Ahmed.

"Welcome to my world," he said lightheartedly.

Karuna had heard the phrase before, but never with such kindness. When her cup was full, Ahmed quit being the barkeep, extended his hand and took her for a walk away from the people. Not too far as to draw suspicion, hanging at the periphery. When Ahmed spoke, it was in the old tongue. Karuna's time in Istanbul, on the lam, was not a complete waste. The words of a dead language did not come naturally, but they did come correctly. They spoke of the weather, the changes in landscape, food, and in general ran the gamut of a normal conversation. They could not speak of things important, as this was practice, for Karuna. Ahmed would correct her when pronunciation or grammar conflicted with current usage, all the while laughing and in general being an ideal guest.

It was only later, as the torches were lit that he was able to spirit her away from the crowd. His demeanor had become serious.

"It is time to leave. This was just an excursion to show you that it was possible. Soon the husband will come to find his wife, you. No doubt word has been passed that you have been flirting with me all night. You do not want to be in her shoes, nor I these." He glanced down at the leather sandals.

"What do we do?" Karuna asked hastily.

"PASHA YOU WHORE! You have shamed me for the last time," came the voice of the husband, yelling as he strode in their direction.

"Right now I'd say run!" Ahmed grabbed her arm, bolting for the dark stretch of sand, then into the maze of buildings that was the port town. Already a posse was being formed to run down the lovers. The chase was on and Karuna and Ahmed were losing. Forced by darkness and men who knew the streets, they found themselves with their backs to the sea.

"Can you swim?" asked Ahmed. Karuna nodded. "Then I'd dump the burka and make like the Olympics." Answering her other question, "We can do it out there. We just need some peace."

Few were the times that Karuna was thankful for her decision and Jake's compliance with her request. It's a complicated issue, but right now it meant she could swim like the devil. As Ahmed became tired, Karuna towed him.

Torches held from the bows of fishing vessels zigzagged the harbor in search of the two. More than once they had to dive down while the slow moving boats passed overhead. Time was passing. Dawn was etched on the horizon when the search was called off. By then, Ahmed was going the way of hypothermia.

"How do we do it?" Karuna begged. Ahmed was getting light-headed, one of the final stages of freezing to death.

"You will it, baby! You will it!" With that Ahmed went comatose.

The effort began to take its toll on Karuna, too. Her legs were tiring and she had stopped shivering. 'This is no good,' she thought. Her will was weakening as well. Holding on to Ahmed she began to imagine the hallway of the mosaics. Every detail she could remember was put into the dream. The hard edges of broken ceramic, granite floor, skylights through which stars shone, colors, the colors of the party in full swing.

Water splashed into Karuna's mouth. Her nose went under, inhaling the sea. She was drowning but did not care or give it a second thought, for if she had...

Ahmed was dead. As soon as Karuna finished coughing up what seemed to be half of the Black Sea she began CPR. Within minutes that were like hours, Ahmed was soon coughing his guts out and before he was through, the laughter began and didn't stop.

***

Igor was up before the sun. With coffee on, he did his physical therapy, working and stretching his hands. Since having them replaced, he practiced diligently to regain the use of them. He could not swing a hammer or grip a chisel to any useful degree. He could however make coffee and wipe his ass, not bad considering...

This morning he would try and load the magazines for the machine gun. His fingers could hold a bullet but the manual dexterity and strength required to insert it into the mag, against the tension of the spring required all his concentration. After getting three rounds in and picking up the thirty or forty that hit the floor, due to poor coordination, Igor found the pill bottle. Not only was it damn near impossible to load the mags, it hurt like hell. He did a triple dose and went back to work. As the pain dissolved, motivation returned and though the floor was littered with bullets, he had three 50 round mags filled and was rather proud of himself.

Igor loaded the gun and mags into his pack. Water, dried fruit, some bread and a big knife. He didn't plan on doing any more than looking. His hands wouldn't let him. As the sun broke free of the horizon, Igor was already moving. Halfway to his goal, the painkillers started to wear off. He did not eat any more. Pain was his reminder, not that he could ever forget, but it maintained his anger, so he used it –only taking the pills when he had to, like this morning. God forbid he should have to fire the damn thing. The recoil of 800 rounds a minute would probably tear his hands off.

He was wrong in the assessment of his hands. He was a strong man and healed well. It was the pain that made him think otherwise. In another month or two, he would be able to begin carving again. Igor was insane, but still an artist.

Coming to the top of a low hill he spied his handkerchief blowing in the breeze. He had never been in the military, but had seen enough vids to help him pretend he had. Staying low within the treeline, Igor circled the ravine. On the second time around, he spotted the fresh prints made by the person he saw last night. The reason it took two circuits was that he was not a tracker either and the trail was virtually nonexistent, for it had only been used several times. Of course he didn't know this. Unshouldering his pack, he withdrew the little machine gun and inserted a mag. Jacking a round into the chamber was merely agonizing.

With his pack on and gun slung around his neck, Igor began the steep descent into the ravine. The weather had been wet; the ground in the hollow was soggy from the lack of sunlight due to the overhanging trees. Cautiously stepping down didn't help when the wet moss acted like grease, sliding his feet from under him. Igor reacted naturally, grabbing for the nearest limb or tree to stop his fall. His right hand hit a sapling as his fingers curled around it. Like a steel clamp they held tight. He screamed mightily as his other hand fought for a hold. Suspended three meters above the ground, Igor found a moment to be amazed. His hands held. It hurt beyond imagination, but that no longer mattered. He had his hands back. The first thing he did with them was let go only to land in the cushioning comfort of a blackberry bush. The canes broke the fall while the spines poked a hundred holes into his skin. He could care less. Madness is that way. After extricating himself from the natural barbed wire, his eyes had adjusted to the gloom of the deep ravine. There, farthest back and set into the rock was a doorway.

Tree roots and saplings had once obscured the opening. Now, they had been pulled away from the ancient door, not cut away, as if whoever was using it intended to keep it hidden. For whatever reason, the person who used it the night before did not return the shrubs and roots back in place. Igor didn't care, happy as he was in an insane sort of way. The Cneajna crest, long worn by time and the elements, was still visible in the shallow relief carving on the door. His smile changed in the craziest way. Neither upturned nor down, the lips pulled tight as he watched his plan play out in his mind.

Igor reached out and took the door handle in both hands and pulled. It was not locked, but took more effort than he would have liked. His hands ached painfully from the fall and opening the door didn't help any. He had to sit, resting his hands in his lap. Each beat of his heart was like a hammer blow on both wrists. A metronome of pain conjured a cruel image of his hands taking the life from his enemies. The idea was so much more satisfying, than say, using a gun. To take the Voivode by the throat and squeeze, with powerful hands, until the soft tissue and bone were crushed between them. He didn't realize that while dreaming he had unzipped his pants and jerked the Voivode to death. You don't call them crazy for nothing.

The darkness was impenetrable beyond the faint illumination cast in the doorway. He could see nothing until he pulled a headlamp from his pack. After the initial blindness of the light and his eyes adjusted, Igor staggered back, lost his balance and hit the ground hard. Three rounds escaped from the machine gun on impact, echoing deafeningly in the cavernous tunnel. What made him stagger? The relics of the past stacked from floor to ceiling on both sides, leaving just a path meandering through the artifacts had surprised him.

'Where did all this stuff come from?' he thought to himself. Igor got to his feet and began to examine the menagerie, all of which had been placed and stored with obvious care. But the pieces of furniture themselves were from different time periods, like an estate that had been in use for centuries then it was all put down here. Thoughts whirled around in his demented mind, losing for a moment the reason behind his being here and replacing it with thoughts of greed. The little he had seen so far was worth a fortune and there was far more beyond the limits of his light. Before he realized it, he was stuffing golden statuettes and anything else that glinted yellow and could be jammed into his pack. 'I'm going to need a bigger pack.' Seeing only what he wanted to see, Igor missed the shattered glass that now littered the floor. Pieces of mirror and ceramic destroyed by the three bullets were everywhere. But since he had never been here before, he did not think the damage was of his doing.

Someone would though. That thought sank into his mind causing him to return several of the pieces to their original location. 'No reason to be greedy,' he mused. 'There is time, all the time in the world. Just a few of these trinkets will buy it for me.' He covered his tracks and left.

Upon returning to the art studio, Igor drove to Eforie Sud in time to catch an antiques merchant before he closed for lunch.

"They have been in the family for as long as I can remember. Times are hard. What do you think they are worth?"

"These candlesticks are Goth. A guess would be around $100,000. Certainly you don't wish to sell them," replied Mr. Heuweler.

"I do. When can I collect?"

"I wish it were that easy, Igor. They must be cleaned, inspected by a specialist, and then ran through the Interpol list of stolen art."

"I didn't steal these," Igor demanded.

"Calm down, Igor. I didn't say you did. These are just the requirements of this sort of thing. We do it all the time."

Igor calmed himself. 'I almost lost it there. I must control myself.' "And there is no way around this protocol," he replied slyly.

Heuweler had heard the rap a million times. When people want fast cash they mean it and would be willing to take considerably less than the value if the 'fast' part was met with.

"I can give you $10,000 right now for them." Heuweler was no fool either, having been in the family business all his life. The relics were worth at least a million. He would take advantage of Igor, but not for greed.

"I'll take it!" Igor knew he could get more. The seed of greed fell upon fertile soil.

When Igor left the gold merchant with a pocketful of money, he headed to a camping supply store to purchase more lights and a bigger pack.

***

Karuna could only wait until Ahmed finished with his fit of laughter. She went to the bathroom gathering a couple of towels to dry themselves with. By the time she got back, Ahmed was still chuckling, but busy making a pot of coffee.

"I fail to see what's so funny about this. We both nearly..." Karuna paused, "never mind. What happened to the two people we accessed?"

"Let's go see." Ahmed rose from his chair at the counter and went to the particular panel of the mosaics. "They look fine to me."

The scene had altered. No longer was the woman alone getting her cup filled. Now her husband was with her and by the looks on their faces there was no fallout from the intervention. The bartender however had a black eye.

"The simple justice of the old days for making a pass at another man's wife," said Karuna.

"Some things will never change. A flirt, a punch, and back to normal. Notice how the husband's hand rests lightly on the shoulder of the bartender. It's a guy thing."

"Male bonding," Karuna replied sarcastically.

"Well yes. The flirt was an affront to the husband's ego, which was satisfied with a blackened eye. The friendly touch on the shoulder is a way of saying, 'thanks for noticing my hot wife. For it made everyone else behold her as well.' Sometimes it doesn't work out so well."

"Yes, I know." She still had a question and Ahmed picked up on it.

"The laughter bothers you from the intensity of the moment," he inquired.

"There are not too many who enjoy a ride on the razor's edge. I've known a few."

"For me, I must humbly admit, that after a thousand years of solitude, that I do relish the rush perhaps a bit too much," Ahmed added somberly, "Unlike you, I can die. Having seen more than my fair share of it...what was it that someone said, 'It's better to burn out, than to fade away,' – just my take on it, that's all."

"I understand and take no offense, but now that the escapade is over, what is it we intend to do?"

"The 'escapade', as you call it, had at least one lesson to be learned..."

"Beyond finding out that you can die?" Karuna began to lose her patience.

"Yes, true enough. But did you not notice that the scene had changed. Reality had changed. Not much and probably would have happened anyway, but enough to show you it can be done."

"But what is the point? It is clever, but if that is all you have to show, then you have wasted both yours and my time."

"I'm sorry you see it that way." Ahmed pointed at the mosaics. "In there is a chance to save what is becoming of our country. It is dying. Unless something is done, there will be no future. Everything you fought for will have been wasted."

"The battle with Vlad Tepes is ov..." Karuna was cut off.

"This is not about Vlad Tepes the third." There was no more humor in Ahmed's voice. "It is about you, Sechra and Dracine. Why do you think the Prime Minister had me look over you?"

"Vlad Cneajna is aware of what is happening?" demanded Karuna.

"Since the beginning, but there is nothing he can do about it anymore, beyond being a good head of state. Twenty years ago, you took on the world and won, but nothing changed."

"My young man, you were not there..." Karuna stopped in mid-sentence.

"But I was." Ahmed pointed to the mosaics, "In there. It's the evil and greed in men's hearts that keep it alive. You and your friends merely shifted the balance of power."

"How can you say that?" Karuna was exasperated.

"Easy, because it is true. Look around you! It is all turning decrepit. Even the land runs foul with the effluence of evil. Are you a fool not to see it?" he demanded rhetorically. "Since Sechra struck the last hammer on her art, it has begun to grow. The riot at the exhibition in Bucharest was its birth. Now it travels the world in the form of Sechra's sculptures. They become more grotesque all the time. Feeding off the filth of hatred, jealousy and greed, it has become an entity unto itself with its own motives and goals."

"Then we must stop the show and bring it home where we can deal with it." Karuna was nonplussed. This was all news to her.

"That is no more possible than passing a camel through the eye of a needle. It feeds off the world now. It will not come home."

"Then what is it we can do, Ahmed?"

"We must find someone willing to bear the burden."

"Then it is done. I will," Karuna spoke without hesitation.

"Were it that easy I would have already stepped up," Ahmed replied. He looked Karuna over. The events over the last twenty-four hours or so had wasted her energy. She needed rest and a little pick me up of a dark nature. Rather than point out the obvious, he said, "Listen Karuna, I'm beat and need to sleep. I suggest you take the time to refresh yourself, too. Where we have to go there will be little time for rest. Take the opportunity now while you still can." Ahmed bowed curtly, "Good night, Voivode Danesti."

"Thank you Ahmed, I think?"

Karuna went to her room and bolted the door. She had no intention of going to sleep. Underneath the stacks of boxes in her closet was a shoulder bag of Mexican design. She had purchased it years ago while staying with Jake and Johnny in Baja. Before leaving them to their endless summer, they had filled the bag with a plethora of nasty drugs. Karuna set the bag on her bed, wiped away her tears and opened it.

***

Heuweler, the gold merchant, turned the gilt candlestick over in his hands, studying the design. Stamped into the bottom, next to the manufacturer's symbol, was the crest of the Cneajna family. 'These do not belong to Igor.' Heuweler's phone call was not to Interpol or any 'specialists' concerning the objet d'art. It was to the museum/estate on the coast. This was where Igor lodged and most certainly where the 'sticks' came from. He knew about Igor's recent misfortune, as had most of the coastal town, but did not think that he would stoop so low as to steal from his employers. Heuweler himself had just fired one of his own long-term employees for doing just the same thing. He had been shocked at the time but now, 'even the Cneajna's have their problems.' Heuweler was not gloating. In fact, quite the opposite. He hung up the phone before it was answered.

Heuweler had been watching the downward spiral of the country for the last few years. 'Everything had been going so well,' he thought. But now the big money was pouring out of the country. If you want to know what is going on in a country, follow the money. It is a very accurate barometer of a nation's health and in this case, it was dropping like a rock. 'Ever since that big art exposition,' Heuweler said to himself.

He talked to himself a lot. Gold and money make for poor conversation. 'I will put these in the safe and return them to the museum before I leave.' He looked at the mobile safe. 'Well my friend, it is time for us to leave again. When the weather changes we shall return. But now I fear, the time has come to run.'

Heuweler, like many of Romania's wealthy, returned to the country after the revolution. They did this not only out of love for their country, but also for the profiteering that inevitably follows these things. All the gold that Deep Salvage Inc. brought up from the bottom of the Black Sea went through Heuweler for documentation before being delivered to the coffers of the government. He got one percent. The Heuweler family in general went from filthy rich to fabulously wealthy almost overnight. He wasn't going to lose it all with some misbegotten loyalty to a failing regime. "It's tonight, my dear," he said to the safe. 'A delivery van is en route to take you to the family jet. I have already waited too long. That business with Igor was the last straw. After the safe is picked up, I will drive out to the coast and return them,' he said to no one, referring to the candlesticks.

While waiting for the delivery van, Heuweler packed his stuff. One suitcase was filled with cash, another, his clothing. Another, smaller, the gold; another, smaller yet, his laptop. It was by far, the most valuable item of all. Into a small canvas sack went the 'sticks,' two relatively worthless pieces of gold that would cost him his life.

With the delivery van finally on its way to the airport, Heuweler finished packing his little sports car with his personal items. He said goodbye to all his stuff that was being left behind. There was a lot of it. His farewell took a while. The sun had long since set by the time he hit the road and headed up the coast to the estate.

'Shit!' he said to his car, or his briefcase. 'This gate has never been closed before. What was I thinking?' This last phrase he said to himself, while pacing back and forth before the entrance. Only by chance did he stop to lean his weight against the door in a pause to his pacing. Heuweler stumbled as the big gate swung inwards on well-greased hinges. 'Well, I'll be damned,' he said, turning around as he pushed the gate fully open.

His spirit was lifted again with discovering the gate unlocked. He drove the few hundred meters through the estate to the mansion, only to find it darkened and locked up tight.

'Well, son of a bitch. Okay, Heuweler, you tried. Leave the 'sticks' and get the hell out of here. Now!'

He snatched the bag containing the candlesticks from the passenger seat and unfolded himself out of the cockpit. Close to the house, sensor lights picked up his movement and came on. Heuweler jumped at the sudden illumination. 'Jesus, this place is freaky at night.'

The lights lit the entry, revealing the roll down protection doors in place. 'Jesus! This is not my night.' He spotted the twisted, broken hasp at the lower right hand corner of the roll down. "So that is how Igor got in," he mused aloud.

"No, that's not how I got in, but since it is open...." Igor let the thought trail off as he raised the little machine gun. Heuweler turned on his heels before backing up and flattening against the roll up.

"Jesus, Igor, you half scared me to death." He saw the gun now in the sculptor's hands. "Jesus – what are you doing?"

"Protecting my investment. And you?" Igor inquired. Igor chinned at the obvious bag. One of the candlesticks was sticking out.

"Jesus, I, I..." For once Heuweler was at a loss for words.

"Just open the door. You wanted to return them, yes?" Igor motioned with the gun that Heuweler should get to it.

"Well yes I was, but I wasn't going to say anything, Igor," Heuweler stammered.

"Yeah, yeah, yeah, get the door."

Heuweler started to squirm away. The muzzle of the gun, however, kept him from going far. "Listen Igor, what do you want? Money? It's in the car. Just take me to the airport. Keep it all."

"Get the door. You'll be taking your trip, once we take care of a few things. Now get the fucking door before I splatter your brains all over it!" He held the gun tight and fired three rounds into the empty night sky. Igor stepped forward, lowering the gun and inspiring the gold merchant to act. Heuweler looked at the sack on the ground then at the broken hasp. He reached down to grab the handle and not being used to such effort, it caused him to strain himself before the door began to move. Heuweler broke an instant sweat, as well he should have considering, but it wasn't the wet in his armpits that worried him. The smell of strong urine filled the air. Then, like magic, the door began to roll itself up. It wasn't magic, but a simple mechanical application. The door was self-winding; you just had to assist it in the beginning. The barrel of the gun pushed Heuweler into the foyer. Another shove of the hard steel had Heuweler opening the door into the mansion. Another got him to cross the threshold into the darkness.

Igor stopped to pick up the bag of 'sticks' before following him in. Doom had filled Heuweler's pants. The gloom of the interior of the house was deep and penetrating, filling his very soul as the shit did his tight underwear.

"Geez, I haven't done anything yet," snided Igor at the odor. "Now walk forward." He stabbed the barrel into the man's back again to get him moving.

"But I can't see," whined Heuweler as he shuffled a few feet away from the gun and the madman right into a coffee table, shinning himself painfully. Something crashed to the floor in the dark.

" Ow! Jesus, Igor, let's get out of here." He bent to rub his shin and was rewarded with an awful jab to his ass.

"Keep moving forward. There is something I would like you to see first. Then you can go."

Another warm rush slaked his pants. The words did not inspire him with confidence that this issue would be resolved. He moved ahead, slowly. He stumbled into the dining chairs that surrounded a big table and was just barely able to catch himself on the railback of a chair before another poke of motivation forced him onward.

Igor knew the layout and could walk it with his eyes closed if he had to. At his urging, Heuweler kept making progress. He neglected to inform the man that two granite steps were just ahead. He heard the sound of a pair of Gucci loafers hit the risers, tangle together in a rush of soft leather before dull multiple thumps of a body taking a fall. 'It had to hurt,' Igor said to himself and smiled. 'But nothing like it's gonna.'

Now the warm puddle Heuweler was lying in was not his piss, but his blood as it flooded from a broken nose. He had done a classic faceplant. His arms had reached out, not down, in order to protect himself. His face took the full force of the impact. He moaned as stars danced in his vision.

"Oh yeah, the stairs. Watch out for the stairs," he laughed. This time he let his foot urge Heuweler on. "Let's go we don't have all night. If you still wish to take your trip I suggest you motivate yourself."

"Oh Jesus, Igor, let me go," Heuweler was pleading for his life. The words fell on deaf ears.

"You should have just left, but you let your conscience get in the way. I lost mine when I lost my hands. Funny though, I got my hands back, but the conscience has not returned. Now down the hallway. We will have light in a moment." A few tentative steps later, activated sensors lit the hall lights. They came on slowly; refinement only money can buy.

The relief brought on in chasing away the dark was flushed away in a vision of horror. On the wall before him was a mosaic panel depicting the impaling of a man accused of hoarding in a time of war. Heavy gold rings covered the fingers of the hands that were tied to ground. The rest of his body was curved over a barrel, face down with his feet also tied to stakes. Golden ankle bracelets stuck out from beneath his trousers that were down around his feet. Everywhere was gold, coming out the pockets, around the neck, pierced in the ears and scattered on the ground where it had fallen from him when they had secured him in position.

Six men, three on either side of a long pole, were busy shoving it into a well-greased ass. The hoarder's face was raised, neck arched, and face grimaced in agony. Heuweler pulled away. The sight sickened him. He bent over as bile surged up his throat before splattering his shoes, adding to the stench of human fear.

Igor let the gun drop on its sling as he reached out and grabbed a handful of Heuweler's hair and yanking him back into an upright position. While holding the terrified man's head, he pulled his handful back and slammed Heuweler's face into the image.

"Now look!" Blood streamed across his face, glazing the mosaics in shades of red as it washed over his eyes. He clenched them shut. Igor was no fool. He withdrew a pocketknife with his free hand and thumbed the blade open. Igor was also a very strong man. The handful of hair twisted and the body turned with it. Heuweler was now facing him, his eyes a blur of terror.

With the deftness that comes from a life of using your hands for careful work, Igor slit Heuweler's eyelids so he could not close them. The strong arm twisted again. Now the vision would not go away, or ever for that matter. Igor stared at the back of Heuweler's head as he held it inches from the damnable hoarder. Heuweler could see nothing else.

It didn't take long. Within a few short minutes Heuweler's body went limp as his mind went into the mosaics. Igor let go of him and stepped backwards a few paces but not before stuffing the 'sticks' in

Heuweler's hands. He lurched forward putting all he had into a kick that would have slammed the gold merchant into the wall, that is, if it had been a normal wall. Heuweler's body instead went into the image and for a moment you could hear him screaming as he took the place of the hoarder.

Igor stayed just long enough to observe his work, like an artist who had just finished a piece. There on the ground next to the barrel were the two candlesticks that had fallen from Heuweler's hands. The face had morphed to a caricature of Heuweler that sent chills running down Igor's spine. Reflected in his eyes was Igor standing there with a gun. Of course you had to look close, but it was there.

Igor wasted no more time. He retraced his footsteps, rolled the door down, and folded himself into Heuweler's sports car. The roar of the twelve-cylinder Ferrari engine nearly scared the crap right out him. It was the sound of the car along with the blinding night driving lights that brought him here in the first place. He had been just closing up the studio, getting ready to head to the secret entrance when he heard the car and flash of lights in the night sky as it pulled off the highway, changing his mind and direction.

Igor sped north along the coastal highway. He had gotten more caught up in the rush of dealing with Heuweler than he realized. Now, behind the wheel of one of the most powerful cars ever made, he tried to calm himself. He didn't catch on that trying to mellow out while driving a car like this was impossible. Even with the night lights on, the curves and hairpins in the road kept catching him by surprise. He was overdriving his lights and abilities, but of course didn't know this. Sooner or later...

There was a sudden screeching of rubber as the car spun out of control and smashed through a guardrail that was the only defense against a 300 meter drop into the sea. It never occurred to him to take his foot off the gas. C'est la vie.

Years later the car would see the light of day again as salvage operations along the coast worked their way north. On that day, there will be a few very lucky divers.

***

Sechra was alone at the inn when she woke in the small backroom, which had remained warm, surprisingly, throughout the night. Only the innkeeper was there, busy as he was with the day's food preparations. She followed the smells of morning to the kitchen, which, after a circuitous route, was just on the other side of the wall that separated the sleeping stall from the big oven. It explained the warm night. Coffee was waiting.

"Good morning, Ms. Kcirb," the innkeeper said, not looking up from the cutting board.

"Good morning, and thank you," she replied pouring a cup. She went into the dining area before getting caught in a conversation. After all it was the first cup of the day.

The clouds had lifted and the first rays of the sun shone brightly on the wet outside.

'Could be worse,' she mumbled. And she was right with the exception of making an incredible understatement.

Sechra stared out the windows as the dawn waxed into morning. Pots and pans clanged in the kitchen as the first round of hungry came in for breakfast. She had expected Urloff to be among them. He was not. The inn was filling fast. Soon all the tables were full with the exception of Sechra's. They gave her her space, or kept her from invading theirs. Either way, she sat alone. It was only after a line began to form that Sechra got up to make room for them. She navigated the aisles of tables, nodding to people she had seen yesterday, but otherwise was invisible. A few heads bobbed to her in passing. There was neither a negative or positive attitude, just acknowledgement.

Sechra slipped out the front door with her cup to find a group of gypsies ogling her motorcycle. The group parted for her, revealing another bike parked next to hers. A tall thin man in leather was inspecting something on his bike. He stood upright when she arrived.

"Ms. Kcirb, a beautiful day for riding, yes?" He extended his hand. "My name is Skender. I am Urloff's son."

She reached out and took his hand firmly. "A pleasure, Skender." She gave the hand a solid shake and disengaged contact. "It's Sechra and where is Urloff? I half-expected him to be here this morning."

"He is busy and besides, he doesn't ride. Nice bike, ever take it off road?"

Sechra looked back and forth from his bike to hers. Though hers was dirty, his was caked in mud. "Little bit."

"Better than none. The roads gradually get worse from here on out. You'll have plenty of time to get through the learning curve, or not. There is always walking."

"I think I'm missing a piece of the equation, Skender. What do you mean?"

"When it is time to go, I will be your guide."

"When is that?"

"Anytime you're ready. Breakfast first? I've already had mine, but I will share some coffee with you while you eat."

They both took a last glance at the bikes before heading inside. All the tables were full now and didn't appear as if anyone was about to give up their seats when the innkeeper waved to them from the kitchen. Within the kitchen was a table set for the staff to eat at. It was now set for two. The innkeeper poured for both of them, while Skender peeled out of his leather riding gear.

"Damn, these things are great for riding but that's about it." Skender wiped the sheen of sweat from his brow. Sechra knew he was right about that. Add the heat of a kitchen and riding suits turn into an all too confining sweatbox. He hung the suit on a hook and bent himself into the chair.

"Urloff didn't mention anything about this," Sechra said, as she reached for the coffee pot.

"He is a man of few words." Skender saw the perplexed Sechra who had received a filibuster of a monologue from Urloff the day before. He burst out laughing, understanding his understatement. "We're kind of making this up as we go along. Everything is changing so fast, it's the only way we can keep ahead of it. Wing it, shoot from the hip, take it as it comes, doesn't matter how you put it, but it keeps us dancing. For now we will head west and north deeper into the mountains. Are your riding boots good for hiking?"

Sechra shook her head. The boots were like the suits and really had only one purpose.

"Then that is our start. We will pick you up a pair on the way out of town."

"There's a shoe store here?" she asked cynically.

"No, but there is a place that has them. It is where 'we' get our needs and where you used to." Skender scarfed his plateful of food as if it would be taken from him. 'There are a few things I need to attend to. Meet you at the bikes in a half hour. Good enough?"

Sechra grunted with a mouthful of food. Unconvinced he got her reply, she gave him a thumbs up. Skender smiled and returned the gesture before grabbing his suit and leaving Sechra to her meal and thoughts. Finishing both, Sechra paid for the meal, not that any was asked for. The food came from somewhere and cost either someone's time or money. She added a little more for the warm bed, which she was certain had been vacated for her. 'It cost them more,' she thought, strapping on Zapar's shotgun, which was then buried beneath the top of her riding suit. A vent under the arm allowed her to draw the gun with the suit fully on. It would be cold comfort in the days ahead, but better than none at all.

Skender was filling his gas tank from a can when she arrived.

"That's got to be a pretty expensive commodity this far out," Sechra said as she started to load her bike. She laughed to herself as she took the moment to really examine the two bikes. Hers was new, a top of the line BMW adventure model. It had integrated panniers and all the fancy shit that money can buy. His was an old thumper whose age was indeterminate beyond old, really old. A mismatched assortment of luggage was tied onto it like a pack mule. It looked like shit.

"It is. Pop your tank and let me top yours off. Could you carry a few things?"

"Yeah sure, what ya got?" Sechra replied. She got a chin to the space behind her bike. There was a twenty-five liter full gas can and two crates. She got another laugh when she lifted the crates and can to check for weight in helping to decide where to put them. The crates were full of chickens that clucked wildly when their space was hoisted up.

"They have gas deeper in the mountains, but they need some layers. We'll still have to pay for the gas, but at least there will be some for us," Skender explained closing the cap to her tank. He handed the can into the crowd. Hands appeared, the can disappeared.

"Mountain economics?" inquired Sechra wryly.

"A little. Must be getting hot in that suit. Peel the top down and we'll go to the store. We'll need some bread and sweets. The chickens will give us eggs."

Sechra was just a little nervous revealing her gun in this crowd. Then she remembered they had all seen it yesterday and for those who maybe missed the show there was the gypsy grapevine. Still when she pulled the top down the crowd went quiet. The pistol grip semi-automatic was an impressive thing. That is if you're into things like that. Mountain peoples generally are.

"Come on," Skender spouted as he led the way.

To say there was an inn implied there was a village, hamlet or town. Once, this area had been the estate of a long dead and forgotten Voivode. The master may have been gone, but the people remained. The 'inn' had been the crumbling remains of a stable or other utilitarian structure. Being boarded up with scraps of plywood nailed to pallets with its roof tin, cankerous with rust, kept the establishment from dissolving into the forest floor. It looked like its people; worn shabby and thin against an abrasive environment. Like Skender's motorcycle, however, they endured. How, was another question. The chickens' wire cages that were scratching the shit out her bike's paint job explained this to some degree. They helped each other. For certain this band of gypsies will have fewer eggs this coming winter, but rather than hoard, they shared so that another band could survive. They depended upon each other.

Sechra and Skender meandered through the defunct mobile homes, military tents, and other hardscrabble dwellings on the way to the store. Dirty children at play scattered when they passed by, leaving their toys where they fell. They weren't toys so much as pieces of toys that took an incredible amount of imagination to fill in the blanks. The little pieces of broken, colorful plastic could have been anything. That it could be played with made it a toy. When you have very little and most of that is used to survive, there is little to play with. Sechra saw herself in the young faces that scrupled her from behind rain barrels and through the shattered, whitened windows of junker cars. At least the child she used to be before all of it was ruined. Before the vacation at the outhouse Marriot and all the death, when she was clean, with only the dirt of the forest to contend with. Before the filth that would never wash away entered her very soul.

The yurt would have been passed by unnoticed if not for the telltale smoke that issued from its chimney. The flap door of the yurt, made from the hides of mountain goats, parted and a small head full of black hair, bright eyes and big teeth poked out.

"Daddy," the little boy squealed as he bolted from the door and charged Skender, who was already squatting to catch him. Sechra held back, not wanting to encroach on the father and son moment. Skender waved her to come closer.

He turned to face her with his son in his arms. "Sechra, I would like you to meet my son, Skender Jr. – Skender Jr., Sechra."

"Good morning, Skender Jr., I need a pair of hiking boots. You have some?"

The little boy looked down at her feet and scrunched up his face in deep thought, "Maybe."

Within the yurt was a combination of army surplus, farm supply, pharmacy, liquor and food store all in one. Once Skender Jr. was set down, he promptly took Sechra's hand and said, "Follow me." His two little hands pulled her through the mountains of clothing and material to where the shoes could be found, sort of. There was nothing new, with the exception of food and some of that was questionable. Most of the footwear was military issue. 'Combat boots are practical,' Sechra thought sifting through the mismatches and sniffing the insides.

"Practical, yes," responded Skender as he peered over a pile of green jackets, "but you will need something with more support. Skender Jr., get the good boots. She has money."

Skender Jr.'s face lit up at the sound of 'money,' the corners of his mouth turned down.

"We don't have any that will fit her." Skender Jr. knew his stock. "Except..." The little boy's eyes filled with tears, but did not cry. "I will get them." He hurried away before letting the woman see his tears fall. The boots were his mother's and sat beneath a small shrine devoted to her.

Skender Jr. brought them back and began re-lacing them, occasionally wiping his eyes with his forearm. Sechra looked to Skender with a 'what am I missing here,' expression her face. He returned it with one that said, 'just go with it. I will tell you later.' She did.

"I don't know, Skender Jr., those are some awfully nice boots. You sure they are the right size?"

"Once I saw your feet I was certain." There was no small amount of pride in the boy's voice.

'Another time, another place and this boy could have gone to college,' Sechra thought.

"But it is not, Sechra. And we are poor," Skender said picking up on her thoughts.

Slipping her feet into the boots had that good feeling you get when the fit is right. Skender Jr. went to work lacing them up for her. While he was busy, she thought back to when she had first met Voivode Karuna, Aunty Karuna who without hesitation had offered her an education. It was something Sechra had always been thankful for. She had that same feeling right now.

"Go ahead, stand up and give them a walk," Skender Jr. said, backing up and giving Sechra some room. The boots were the heavy-duty mountain climbing kind that came up over your ankle giving a good deal of support, stiffness and protection. Walking around in them was more like clumping on the wooden floor, but like the riding boots they served but one real function, climbing.

"Thanks, Skender Jr., these will do just fine. How much do I owe you?"

"There is no charge for these, ma'am. Return them when you are done is all I ask."

"That seems hardly fair, young man," Sechra protested.

"Hmm," Skender Jr. paused, "You are right." He paused again, thinking. "Then perhaps that schooling you were thinking about a few minutes ago should do," he finished like an adult.

Sechra shot a glance to Skender, 'WHAT?'

"It runs in the family," he replied, shrugging his shoulders as if he had said it for the millionth time.

"Sounds like a bargain," Sechra said in return.

"It is," Skender Jr. said, "But not just for me. All the kids in the village must go, too!"

Sechra pretended to think about it for a few tense moments that lacked any real tension.

"It's a deal." She extended her hand.

"You know, education for thirty or more kids can be pretty expensive."

"It's all relative, Skender," she said after shaking hands with Skender Jr. on the deal.

"Yeah, I suppose so," he heaved as he dropped all his weight onto his right foot, kick starting the old bike. It chugged once with a puff of white smoke and no noise for the effort. Whatever the bike might have been when it began its life, it was now a combination of a half a dozen other bikes that had been 'parted' to keep this one going. The single cylinder fired on the second try. Sechra on the other hand tapped a switch next to her right thumb. She smiled as the big motorcycle came to life, effortlessly. Skender gave her the chin and dropped his bike into first gear and headed west along the trail. She followed a few seconds behind to avoid the mud that flung from his knobby rear tire.

Long distance and short become relative when you've been in the saddle all day long. There were no highways here to kick back and let it out with a long visible stretch of clean road ahead. Pot holes, puddles of indeterminate depth, slushes of mud and debris, broken pavement, no pavement, packed gravel and loose rivers that were roads and roads that were rivers; all required an intense mind and a loose body. It's hard to put the two together.

After two hours of non-stop bobbing and weaving the bikes along a pathway meant for foot traffic, Skender pulled over as the road opened up for as far as the eyes could see, which is to say not all that far, maybe two hundred meters. It looked sweet to Sechra. Her arches were already killing her from riding in a stand up position for the last hour as the footpath turned into a mudded rut.

"Some of the chickens laid. Should I take the eggs?" Sechra yelled to Skender.

"Leave'em. They are safer where they are. Want some coffee?"

Sechra left the chickens and limped over to where Skender was pouring into two cups that sat on the seat of his bike.

"Been meaning to talk to you about that."

"About what?"

"Your riding style. Don't get me wrong; you're doing really well. It's just that... You need to loosen up. That's why I stopped here."

"I don't know. It was taking all I had just to keep the bike tracking."

"That's what I'm saying. You can't keep it up all day, let alone the week it will take us to get there."

"So what do we do?"

"The stretch ahead is fifty kilometers of hard pack with a surface of pea gravel. You got to stay loose or you'll lose it." Skender made like chicken wings with his arms, sort of flapping without tension. "We can make up some time here."

"Okay, stay loose, huh?"

"Yup. Lock up and I can guarantee you'll go down. Or, we ride slow."

Sechra had her boots off and was rubbing her feet in the shade at the side of the road. Skender bent over and picked up one of her boots and bent the sole.

"Carbon fiber shank. High tech and don't weigh jack, but they flex too much for this kind of riding. You want to keep standing, put the mountain boots on. The steel shank won't bend around the footpegs."

"Speaking of the boots, just what was that all about?" Sechra jerked a thumb in the direction they had come from.

"His mother died a few years ago while guiding a group up on a mountain trek."

"His mother? Not your wife? What happened?"

"You're quick. I didn't think you would catch it. No, she was not my wife. Nor am I Skender Jr.'s father. Marion was a single mom. She ran the store. When the wasted mountaineers returned half-starved and frozen to death, there was no one to take care of young Skender. I stepped up. You see, Urloff is not my real father either, so I was just balancing the scales. As far as the details of what happened on the mountain, no one really knows. The survivors claimed she saved their lives, but could not save herself. All they returned with were the boots."

"That is a very honorable thing you did for Skender."

"It is tradition, nothing more. But I have grown to love the boy, and he makes more money at the store than his mother ever did."

"That's why I offered an education. He's a sharp kid."

"No internet."

"No doubt. But there has got to be more to the ruined expedition than that," Sechra replied incredulously.

"There is. It is where we are headed." Skender began reloading his bike while Sechra put her mountain climbing boots on.

The road was six meters across and relatively level with only a slight incline. Sechra followed Skender's instructions to the letter. He took off. She waited for Skender to get a few hundred meters ahead before letting out the clutch, spinning the rear tire as it fought for a grip on the pea gravel surface. The idea behind waiting was to let the ejecta from his rear tire settle instead of taking it in the face. It also helped to hide her embarrassment as she struggled to control her machine. The tires simply would not grab hold of the road. You were in a constant slide. As she picked up speed, Sechra relaxed her arms and grip on the handlebars. It helped with control by controlling less and letting the bike run. Her breath was next. Let it flow in and out and quit with the huffing and puffing, relax. She wiggled her elbows every time she felt them tightening up.

She laughed at herself. Sechra was a good road rider; this off-road riding, however, was a whole different animal.

Ten minutes into the ride, she was just getting used to it when she rounded a right hand sweeping curve. The windblast coming down off the mountains hit when she reached the apex of the turn. She was already hugging the inside edge of the road when it happened. All the while she had been thinking about what Skender had said, 'Steep cliff on the left, stay far to the right.' As it was, her riding profile acted as a sail when the wind plowed into her. The 'sail' effect pushed her from the right side in a gradual but unrelenting slide to the left while still moving forward. She leaned hard to the right, into the wind, to counter the gust. It's a pretty effective maneuver on pavement. The stronger the wind, the more you lean. At forty-five degrees over, she was just barely holding against the wind. Still she was inching over to the shoulder and there wasn't a damn thing she could do about it. Then it happened. Sechra could feel the tires going out from underneath her. In a desperate move she turned into the wind knowing she would go down. Had she not, the drop-off would have surely taken them both – the bike and Sechra, that is. It was working. The motorcycle veered from the edge as the tires lost their grip. She screamed. The next thing she knew she was sliding down the middle of the road, the opposing boxer cylinders and oversized saddlebags kept her right leg from being crushed and ground cruelly underneath the weight of the bike. Sechra held on, hoping the bike wouldn't flip. It didn't. By the time she came to a stop and was extricating herself from the downed machine, Skender was pulling up next to her. He pointed his machine into the wind before dropping the kickstand and attending to Sechra. By now she was standing, but a little wobbly from shock. Gloves off, Skender removed her helmet and looked deep into her eyes.

"Are you all right?" The question was variable in that he wanted more than the stock answer.

"I think so," Sechra replied, not all that certain herself.

"Go through a range of motions, one limb at a time."

It was her right elbow.

"Peel down the top of your suit so I can get a look at it. If it was broken you wouldn't be able to move it." Skender took his helmet off and put a pair of reading glasses on.

"What did I do wrong?"

"Nothing. If you were at the bottom of the cliff, the answer would have been, everything." He never took his eyes off Sechra. After the movements and elbow inspection, "Let's have a seat and a smoke," he said, relieved she hadn't busted anything beyond her rider's pride. "We've all done it, but you never get used to dropping your bike. Nor should you."

Spiked with a cup of cold coffee and dose of nicotine, Skender got up to look over Sechra's bike. There was no apparent damage from his point of view. The 'adventure' models are overpowered dirt bikes and designed to take a hit like this one. You just never know, though. With the road slightly banked in the wrong direction, that is, toward the drop, Skender grabbed the handlebars and spun the bike around so that the tires were parallel to the downside of the bank. This assists in righting a motorcycle by using gravity instead of fighting it. The wind would also help.

"This is why it was so tough." He pointed to the reverse banking of the curve. Sechra nodded understanding. "Your bike has a super-low center of gravity, so we shouldn't have to unload her. Ready? On three. One, two, three, heave!"

With their feet planted and a secure grip, they both put their backs into the effort. Getting an upward motion started was the hard part. After that it just took all you had to give. Bike up, kickstand down, they began inspecting. Skender concentrated on the engine, while Sechra went through the luggage.

"I was told when I bought the bike that the hard cases would take a hit."

"That's Kevlar for you. Lousy in boots but great for cases. It didn't do the paintjob any good though."

"That's just tough shit. Now what do I do if that happens again? Slow down a little, maybe even stop and move along at a crawl?" Sechra was searching for a pearl of wisdom.

"Tough to say. Like you said a while back, it's a relativity thing. If it happens again, I think you will know what to do. There's nothing like a little experience for learning stuff like this. You ready? We could take some more time if you want."

"Another smoke and then we'll hit it while I still have the adrenalin."

Skender smiled and began rolling.

Skender let Sechra take the lead so he could watch her and keep her from developing too many bad habits. They still had a long way to go. Sechra lowered her speed in an effort to battle the wind more effectively. It worked, but it was hard. How long she could keep it up was another question. Once she had a handle on maintaining course and hugging the hill side of the road, Sechra began increasing speed a few kilometers an hour every minute or so. Soon she was back at the original speed they had been traveling with skill and finesse, easing the strain of the effort.

Rounding a hairpin turn, the wind stopped. Sechra got the bike upright in time to avoid a repeat but reverse performance. She was able to relax as the road stretched on straight for a few kilometers. Not. As soon as the turn ended, Skender accelerated, passing Sechra in a cloud of dust and pebbles that pelted her like hail. Sechra let him go before pouring it on. The loose surface had its desirable aspects, too. It's a little too close to the edge for most, but two-wheel drifting is a decent rush, as long as nothing goes wrong.

This time it was rounding a lefthand hairpin when Skender suddenly appeared standing on the road waving his arms to slow her down. She had already downshifted in preparation for making the turn and continued more aggressively seeing Skender. Less than one hundred meters past her riding partner was a herd of sheep filling the road from edge to edge. Her bike came to a halt not a meter from the closet sheep. Whooo!

Sechra dropped her kickstand, removing her helmet and took a deep breath. 'Man, that was close,' she said to herself.

"This is why I moved ahead of you. It's one of the few passes a shepherd can get his herd through to the other side of the road. And it never fails to happen when vehicles are approaching. You'd almost think they waited for traffic to make their move."

He was right, somehow. Even though his bike made enough noise to raise the dead, the herdsman did not hear it.

"A little early to be moving the sheep down for the winter, eh, Glerk?" Skender knew the man and was making conversation. Glerk was a poor shepherd with only a smallish shoulder bag and bedroll.

"The high pastures are dead. Rain yes, but nothing grows. And even the rain is as undrinkable as the mountain streams."

"Is this the only place affected?" interjected Sechra.

"No, we are all having to move and not only for the dearth of food and water."

Sechra could sense there was more that he wasn't telling. If you don't ask you will never know. "What? What else is it, Glerk?"

"Something is killing our sheep, too. A something that does not eat, but only kills, like men do to each other. My herd is big because many of the sheep belong to another and I am returning them for him." Glerk looked at the two motorcycles and the direction they were headed. "Do not go into the mountains. Our presence is no longer tolerated." He returned his attention to the herd, which had stalled when Sechra and Skender arrived.

"When was the last time you ate?" Skender had lived his whole life in the mountains and knew what hunger was and what it looked like.

"Three days. We have been running. There is no time to forage and nothing to forage for," Glerk said as he applied a switch to the hind of a stalled sheep.

Skender walked over to Sechra's bike and opened up one of the little chicken coops. His arm slipped through the gap while his hand fished around under the birds. Despite their squawking, he produced three large eggs and brought them over to Glerk. Sechra, not to be outdone, opened up a bag on Skender's bike and tore a loaf of bread in half.

Glerk was a man on the move. He cracked the end of one of the eggs and slurped the yolk and albumen in one shot. Then another, before ripping the loaf in half and stuffing his mouth full. Sechra set a water bottle next to him. Chewing, swallowing, and chewing some more. When he finished the bottle he handed it back to Sechra.

"Thank you, Ms. Kcirb."

"How do you...?" She had not spoken her family name.

"Everyone knows who you are. Even shepherds." He was humbled by her presence.

Having a history and roots deep in these mountains, Sechra understood, intimately, what was going on in the man's head. She was not impatient at the delay, nor aloof in her demeanor. After all, she was one of them and an education and money could never change that.

"I still can't believe the eggs made it through the crash."

"Hens are very protective of their eggs, as sheep are with their young. They would give their lives to keep them intact. Would you be willing to give your life, so that others may survive, Ms. Kcirb?"

'What an odd question, odder still the one who uttered it, a shepherd with no education or real connection to the outside world, yet he understands what is happening to a deeper level than even me,' Sechra thought.

"If it comes to that I suppose I would," she replied.

"But you are not sure."

"How can one be until the moment arrives?"

"It is in the heart, Voivode Kcirb. Let us hope you have it in you."

"You are mistaken. The Kcirbs are not Voivode."

"Not now perhaps, but a long time ago. The Kcirbs were the first. Unfortunately treachery and intrigue expunged the knowledge from all written record. Time took care of the rest."

"Then how do you know?"

"We in the mountains have never forgotten. We lived and worked under the guidance and protection of your forefathers. We still do. Enough of the trivialities. Would you like a young lamb to butcher and fill yourselves for the long journey ahead?"

Sechra glanced in Skender's direction with a 'what, huh?' He nodded to accept. She carefully looked the herd over, admiring the shepherd's obvious care of the animals. "Why have you not taken one for yourself instead of starving?" she asked in a voice befitting her position.

"They are not mine and what few are will be needed to survive the winter and breed more sheep."

"Then how can you offer me one without suffering yourself?" Sechra was cool but assertive.

"Everything from the land is yours. It belongs to you, not us. Whichever you choose, mine or another's, we will be proud to have been of service. It has been so very long since you have come home. Do you understand?" The shepherd may have never seen the modern world, but that didn't mean he was a dullard or slow. His education was obvious.

"It is a tradition passed down through the centuries that never died out. Your great, great, great, great, great whatever started it. You Kcirbs are educators."

Sechra eyed Skender to step away for a word in confidence. He shook his head no. There was nothing to hide. She sucked it up.

"Well Glerk, I have never chosen a sheep before and so I could use your help in deciding which to choose." Sechra tried mild diplomacy.

"That depends on what you want to do with it. The young are the most delicious, but an older female will give you milk and more sheep."

"Hmm. We just ate a while ago, hmmm. What would be a good choice for going into the unknown? We may need it for ourselves or give it to someone who needs it more."

"You think quickly, clearly, and wisely. Perhaps a yearling female would be best. One that has had its first birthing and yet is not full grown. In this country there is always a wild billy goat to do the honors. Of course if the winter is hard, it will also provide plenty of meat."

"I accept your offer, on the condition that you choose the animal. I defer to your experience and knowledge in the matter."

Glerk began wandering through the herd after gauging the motorcycle's ability to carry a sheep. He chose a smallish female with a pleasant demeanor. Skender nodded, smiling as he produced a rope and began to weave a harness for the animal. To tow the animal behind would hamper progress and eventually kill the sheep. Sheep were loiterers and vagrants that only ran when they had to. Sechra and Skender had many kilometers to go and a walking pace would not do.

Sechra had rolled a cigarette and was trying to decide where to put the sheep. Skender's bike was already loaded beyond capacity. That left her BMW. Skender walked up to her.

"We can put the chickens on top of the gas can and the sheep behind you. Talk about a sweet backrest. You'll be a little top heavy, but on that bike you will hardly notice."

"Yeah right," Sechra replied as she bent over to adjust the rear shocks to accommodate the extra weight of the sheep. By the time she was through with both the adjustment and her cigarette, Glerk had gotten his herd to the other side of the road and was preparing to leave.

"Madame Kcirb, it is an honor," Glerk said snapping the heels of his worn out boots together with less snap than they should have produced. Of course being covered in sheep dung will do that. Regardless, the message was received. It was that of respect and the support of the mountain gypsies in her quest. "Thank you for the lunch. It will get me home." With that he turned, shook hands with Skender and headed down the hill after the sheep. Sechra watched on in awe at the simple man's departure. She had never before seen anything like it. Well, not in a long time anyway.

"He will spread the word." Skender cut in on her reverie, bringing her back into the moment. In his hands was the net he had been weaving. "We'll tie this around her and secure the net to the frame of your bike."

"Very clever, Skender."

"Not really. I've done this before."

In those few words Sechra saw the hard life that had been Skender's lot. There was little in his life beyond survival, his people came first – himself, a sorry second. In looking him over as he tied the sheep down, she saw he had nothing beyond his freedom and pride. From her point of view, it was more than most would ever have; regardless of how much stuff they accumulated. His personal wealth outweighed her portfolio any day. Which, by the way, was growing more and more. The exhibit was the biggest thing to hit Paris since the Germans during WWII. Part was due to one of her 'artist' stipulations in the contract, no pictures. Even in the modern times of button-sized cameras that could capture an image without pointing and shooting, the devices were rendered useless by the quality of the low lighting used for the displays. The eyes could see the sculptures, but digital and film could not. For this reason also, no one noticed the changes that were occurring to the art. That is except for a few that traveled with the exhibit, and even they could not be 100% sure. The images were so disturbing, you did not want to look too close and yet were compelled to. After viewing, all you wanted to do was forget, and that wouldn't happen either.

The next twenty kilometers sped by uneventfully and ended all too soon as far as Sechra was concerned, as she had gained confidence in her abilities as a rider and the ease that comes with it. Through the mud that coated Skender's taillight, a dim red flashing glow penetrated the muck and let Sechra know that something was about to change. She had been lagging behind, enjoying the late afternoon view. She spotted the lights just before he rounded a corner and, being more cautious than bold, Sechra slowed to an idle. When she heard the gunshot, she stopped altogether and withdrew the shotgun. Without thinking, Sechra grabbed a bungee cord and cinched the barrel to the handlebars. The bungee would help control the recoil while allowing her one hand on the handlebars.

Her bike was quiet compared to Skender's and twice as powerful. There was no need to rev the engine for a ripping entry. Instead she turned around and headed back the way they came for a few hundred meters. Turning around again, she paused to check there was a round in the chamber. There was. Sechra rocked back on the throttle while engaging the clutch. The bike was quick. In fourth gear, she banked around the corner doing a good sixty kilometers an hour, well over the safety limit on this road surface. Insanely over the limit, I might add. It was the element of surprise that she hoped to attain. Of course, if there were a bus on the other side of the curve, death would be highly attainable, too.

It all happened so fast. One moment she was leaning hard into a righthand hairpin. The next she saw Skender with his hands raised and half a dozen mean looking bastards bearing down on him. Only one of the men had a gun. As the BMW came around the corner, Sechra pulled it upright, aimed in the direction of the other gun and squeezed off three rounds of buckshot before she zoomed passed them. Unlike birdshot, which is comprised of hundreds of small BB's the diameter of a pencil lead, buckshot contains no more than a dozen or so nine-millimeter ball bearings, any one of which will tear your arm off. At the distance she fired from, the pattern of shot would have expanded to several feet in diameter. It helps when you can't shoot straight. Sechra hoped Skender was not within the kill zone. She kept going until making another turn. Out of sight she replenished the spent shells, turned around for a repeat performance after making a few adjustments to the placement of the bungee cord. If she hadn't scared them off, they would be waiting. This time she really put the guns to it. Sechra came around the corner doing over a hundred K.P.H. The bike was fishtailing wildly until the road straightened. When it did, she started shooting, fanning the shots from right to left, across the roadway and into the shrubs that bordered the high side. On the left side, there was nothing that would provide cover. That is unless the bottom of the cliff was cover enough. Sechra tried to make sure not to hit Skender's bike. The man himself was nowhere to be seen. There were three men on the ground. This pass left a fourth clutching his abdomen to keep his guts inside where they belonged. She could not see the other two. Around the corner again Sechra reloaded. This time the bungee was taken off. Putting down the kickstand she locked the forks so the bike couldn't be taken and started walking towards Skender, hugging the wall that was the high side of the road. The protection it afforded was an illusion, but better than none at all.

Sechra peeked around the last outcropping that separated her from the scene. All was quiet. 'A little too quiet,' she thought as the hard steel of a gun barrel was jammed into her back.

"Hand me your gun," demanded the voice behind her.

"No," Sechra responded.

"Then unload here and now. I have no desire to kill a Kcirb but then I am not above it either. Now empty it!" He added a little incentive with another poke of the barrel of his gun. Eleven unfired rounds hit the ground as she ejected them.

"I can count, Ms. Kcirb. It is a gift from your family, which is why you are not dead right now. Eject the last bullet." It was not a request and Sechra complied without hesitating any further. "Now put it away in your holster. I don't want to have to keep this thing pointed at you. Let's go and keep moving until we get to Skender's bike."

"You know him?" Sechra asked.

"No, but when he was pleading for his life he was kind enough to make introductions."

"Does he still have it?"

"Keep walking."

***

'So this is how it begins,' Karuna said to herself as she withdrew the needle from her arm. She lay back in to the bed to receive the rush from what Jake would call a speedball. It was too much. She made a dash for the bathroom holding her vomit until she was suspended over the toilet. Sitting on the tile floor, wiping the puke from her face, Karuna had to laugh. Junkies never tell you about the downsides. These you have to find out for yourself. After a few minutes Karuna was able to function again and began packing a shoulder bag that she would take with her into the mosaics with Ahmed. A few handfuls of the goodies from the Mexican satchel went in there, too.

At dawn she was already in the kitchen working on her second cup of coffee when Ahmed showed up. He also had a satchel along with an armload of clothes dated from another era.

"Good morning, Karuna, you look refreshed," Ahmed said kindly.

"I am, and you?"

"I fear I did not take my own advice. I spent the night in the cellar digging up a few things for us." He raised the clothes then set them on a chair. "I also discovered something very disturbing."

"What, Ahmed?" Karuna could sense the unease in his voice.

"Someone has accessed the cellar through the secret escape passage cut in to the hills."

"Was anything taken?" Karuna asked, somewhat perplexed.

"Perhaps. It is the violation of space that rankles me. Only I have used the passage in recent times. Someone has either discovered it by chance or saw me gain access to its location. My guess is the latter, as the entrance is well hidden and we own the land it sits upon."

"Then you should lock the door securely from the inside and then block it, in case the door is torn off."

Ahmed laughed wryly to himself, "What do you think I have been doing all night, Karuna?" He raised his blistered hands, cut and dirty.

"Then you have done all you can. Now as a friend of mine used to say, you need a chill pill." Karuna reached into her bag and withdrew a medicine bottle. She dumped a few in her hand, fingering through the assortment to get the ones she wanted. The rest went back in the bottle. "Here, take these and have your first cup in peace. Everything will be all right."

She left the kitchen and stepped out into the morning light, making a beeline to the gazebo. Karuna had never fixed the wall Jake had been knocked through by Johnny when he learned the awful truth. Their works would be spread across the table along with an overflowing ashtray and coffee cups, both of them nodding in relinquishing the constraints of who they were. It was a good memory. She drank deeply from her coffee and lit a cigarette. So much has changed since then. For the last twenty years, she had survived comfortably on the kindness of others. Now that had all changed with the taking of a life on the highway. The alteration was subtle, lurking just behind her eyes, waiting, waiting for the moment to become crystal clear. Then without warning it would emerge and take. Karuna, in that moment was just a vehicle for the madness. Or was it the other way around?

She wanted to call Jake or Johnny. Either or both would drop what they were doing to come to her aid. This was a battle within herself and help would not help. Both of them had earned their independence after considerable personal sacrifice. Though they fought battles for others, it was not in their nature to ask for assistance in theirs.

Karuna decided she could do no less and returned her cell phone to her bag. 'Besides, if I need help it will be there. If the future is beyond my control, they will know. She walked the grounds of the estate as if it were the last time she would ever see it, remembering the history as it unfolded in her passing. Stepping out onto the dock, she was able to view the top floor of the building; Jake's room, from where hell unleashed its fury against the forces of the damned. Then there was the Dracul. The mighty speedboat was a far cry from its predecessor as was its history. The original had been a vessel of death. The newer was death incarnate, but for better reasons.

Over the stretch of sea was a Deep Salvage Inc. barge sitting on the horizon. Their help over the years was one of the reasons Romania was able to maintain its economy and independence. It was not just the gold and artifacts Deep Salvage delivered to the country that kept it afloat. Tons of money in the wrong hands just gets wasted. With the bounty came the financial specialists employed by Deep Salvage to train and ensure the country's stability. After all, Constanta was their home port and they didn't want to lose it. In recent years, however, internal problems within the borders, that had nothing to do with politics or finances, were sending ripples of uncertainty throughout Eastern Europe and Deep Salvage, in particular.

The synchronicity of the universe is, at times, uncanny. Karuna's cell phone rang while she was staring out to sea.

"Good morning," she answered.

"Karuna Danesti?"

"Yes."

"This is Chief Tobias Kuchta of Deep Salvage."

"There is no need to be so formal, Tobi."

"Perhaps, but it has been some time and the times are changing. I was being careful." Chief Tobi was choosing his words very carefully.

"Thank you and I understand your concern. I assume this call is a peremptory strike to avoid a call to the Prime Minister." Karuna had always been good at reading between the lines.

"You still wield a keen edge, Karuna. The corporation is concerned with the troubling news developing in Romania."

"As well they should, but there is nothing you can do." Karuna's assurance was not assuring.

"That's what bothers them. I volunteered to discuss the matter with you before the official channels get activated." Tobi was relieved so far with the reception, but they had not reached the heart of the matter either.

"I imagine once they do, the process is difficult to stop," Karuna replied with her take on it.

"More like impossible. They need some reassurance. Those that remember the revolution with Tepes still reel with PTSD. I mean some strange shit happened, the likes of which were never meant to be seen, ever."

"There was a time when Deep Salvage stepped up to the challenge. You are right, times change and so do people and their values. I wish you were here to speak with you face to face. This will have to do. I leave today on a journey into I do not know what. The purpose is to discover the source of the current unrest, which, if left unresolved will result in the death of thousands and the inevitable return of Megacorp rule."

"Where are you going? Is there anything you need?" Tobi was sincere in his offer. His memories of her strength and bravery were indelibly etched in his memory. How could he ever forget? The question was rhetorical.

"I cannot tell you, nor do I require anything." Karuna paused, mentalating. "Hold your people off for as long as you can. The wheels have been put in motion. I leave today. Sechra left a week ago, heading into the mountains to find out what she can and do something about it, if she can. A great deal of what is going on is her doing." Karuna heard the uneasy pause at the other end of the line. "No, Tobi, she has not gone anarchist or plotting to subvert all that has been accomplished. It is her art. When she finished the final piece, something happened, an evil found a way into our world."

"My God! What do I tell the board?"

"Tell them anything you want, but stall them."

Tobi was having déjà vu. When he recovered, "I'll do what I can. Good luck, Karuna."

"Thank you, Tobi, for everything." Karuna pushed the 'end' button, rose from her seat and memories, grabbed her coffee cup and downed the dregs and headed back to the house. 'Enough of the past,' she said to herself, seeing the irony at the same moment, for it was the past that she was destined to go in the hope of salvaging the future.

Ahmed was working on another pot of coffee by the time Karuna reached to door.

"Thank you for the moment with my first cup. We will miss it where we are going."

"What! No coffee!" Karuna was serious, yet added levity to her voice. "What will we do?"

"Oh they have coffee. It's just nothing like what you are used to."

"Then we shall have to bring some."

Ahmed smiled and shrugged his shoulders, 'At least she does not want to bring a gun.'

"But I am, Ahmed," Karuna said pulling a nine-millimeter semi auto from her bag.

"I do not advise it. We are messing with the past you know."

"Of that I am fully aware, but these things come in awfully handy at times." Karuna saw the look in his eyes. "I have no intention of using it, Ahmed, just as I have no intention of dying while we are in there. While we're on the subject—just how do we take over Dracine and whomever you choose?"

"They are long dead. Nothing inhabits the images anymore, but your question is not without validity. You see although the person no longer remains, the spirit or essence of them does. Dracine was an egotistical and cruel administrator. The half-sister of Vlad II, she copied his ruthlessness to maintain her position in the royal court. That she could not rise above governor of a small coastal township, for she was a woman, was at the root of her reign of terror. Having fallen into the trap of opium, hashish, alcohol and coffee, she lived in a vain dreamworld. That which didn't blend with her vision was crushed. And like a man in drag, Dracine overplayed her role to keep the illusion that she was a man in power. Meaning no offense, Karuna, you should get a sports bra or wrap to confine your breasts. If it is ever discovered, you will be put to death."

"None taken. Thank you though, Ahmed. I have already arranged for such. What more can you tell me?"

"To be careful to not let her will affect yours. It will happen, but if you remain aware, it will not control you. It's like having a split personality. You must be vigilant."

"What about you?" Karuna asked, concerning the split personality business.

"I am experienced and though not totally free from the effects, I have a better handle on dealing with it. Plus my role is that of a servant with little or no ego to cope with. I will be your P.A."

Karuna leaned on the French press, delivering the last good coffee she would have in a long time. "No coffee, huh," Karuna said absentmindedly. Ahmed shook his head. "Bummer," the Jakeism seemed appropriate. "So what is the plan, Ahmed? When I entered the mosaics previously, it was to learn."

"This time it is to act and observe. You must play the role of Dracine, not simply walk around in her form. You understand what cruelty is. Now you will have a chance to dish it out. To do otherwise, or according to your nature, would expose you."

"So I finally get to be the evil bitch."

"Yes, but what is more important is that you get into Dracine's head. Unlike her half-brother, who discovered the darkness and made it his, Dracine willed the darkest part of her soul, that which is normally suppressed by our human nature, into the dominance of her personality. What she created and nurtured before being buried alive has been gestating in the vapid souls of our people. Although Sechra did not know it at the time, she was creating an outlet for the evil to once again wreak havoc upon the face of the earth."

"Then I must stop this 'thing' that Dracine had conjured."

"Or die trying," Ahmed finished the sentence for her. "In there," Ahmed pointed at the mosaics, "YOU can die." The only sound was coffee being thoughtfully sipped.

"Anytime you are ready," Ahmed said picking up on Karuna's thoughts.

"Let's do this thing."

Together they rose from the chairs at the kitchen counter. After rinsing the coffee cups and carafe they walked into the hallway. Karuna eyed the panels she knew so well and realized how little actual knowledge she had of them. 'That will change,' she thought as Ahmed came to a stop.

"Here is the scene I have chosen to enter. Dracine is shopping amongst the vendors in the marketplace."

Karuna inspected it closely. The merchants near Dracine groveled for her attention amidst a plethora of wares. Fine silks and cottons dominated this end of the market. Dracine was examining a bolt of black silk interwoven with gold threads. One eye marveled at the material while the other ripped the merchant into fearing for his life along with the rest of the shoppers in the vicinity. Their eyes were like that of a frightened animal, trapped and nowhere to run. Although the market was packed, a bubble of space surrounded Dracine that no one ventured to enter.

Dracine herself was dressed to the tens, as the fashions of the times were. When not in the role of magistrate, she dressed more feminine. But butch, you know. Black leather slippers with pointed toes that curled up, the tips were gold. Puffy pantaloons cinched at the ankle, again black. A flowing black and red sari wrapped her torso and was secured with a wide belt. A heavy-handed application of kohl around the eyes was dramatic and disturbing at the same time. You were compelled to look closely yet were repulsed by what you saw – it was totally unnerving. Rock stars use it for the same reason. Her fingernails were black as well, sharpened to points like claws. They matched her fuscous thin lips, which the ink turned into a drastic maw that you did not wish to see open, for fear it would devour you.

In this particular image, Dracine was pleased with the silk and so was smiling. There was nothing endearing about it, for it was a smile that smiled inward, not an outward expression of pleasure. It also revealed her teeth. The incisors both upper and lower had been filed to a point. Beyond the shock value, Karuna wondered what the point was.

Once again Ahmed stepped in to put words to her thoughts. "Unwritten history says she was a cannibal."

"And the written history?" Karuna inquired further.

"There is none. You see the man standing between you and the silk merchant?"

"Yes."

"That is who I will enter. Please understand I will be a eunuch and with you at all times."

"At 'all' times?"

"Yes."

Karuna took a last, longing look at the coffee carafe, sighed and looked up to Ahmed.

"Let's go." As they both began to gaze into their characters Karuna took Ahmed's hand and squeezed it firmly. After he squeezed back she let go and together they step forward into the past.

***

Urged at the point of his gun, Sechra walked into the middle of the road in the direction of Skender's bike. Skender himself was still nowhere to be seen. Three dead men lay in puddles of their own blood. Whether they took the full blast of her weapon or just part of it didn't matter. A fourth moaned his last in a gurgle of his final breath. Was it her imagination or did he recognize her, for in that last gasp he voiced, 'my God, it is Sechra Kcirb.' His eyes registered recognition just as they glazed over and became still.

Sechra turned to face the man who took her. He was gnarled from a hard life in the mountains, but the scars and hair could not hide the tattoos. Arcane symbols of ancient design covered his face. He was a witch or a child of one. The 'tats' were used to protect the wearer from harm. 'So far they did,' thought Sechra. None of the dead men had the markings.

"Where is the other bandit? There were six of you."

The man with the tattoos pointed his gun towards the edge of the cliff. "Your first shot blew him clear off the road. I imagine he is at the bottom, dead as these men. Look if you don't believe me."

She had been scanning the hillside for the other when he said this. Sechra walked slowly to the edge of the road. It was a foolish thing to do for he could push her over with little effort as Sechra had to get to the very edge to peer down. Three hundred meters below was the fourth. His body had been destroyed in the fall as it bounced off outcroppings and boulders on the way down. She shook her head in sorrow. 'This shouldn't have happened,' she said to herself. The movement of her head however gave her a glimpse of hope. Three meters below the edge was Skender clinging to a shrub that was clinging to the rock face. The effort to maintain his grip was taking its toll. His face said that much. She turned away not wanting to expose his position.

"So what is it you want?"

"I'll take that bike of yours. Empty your pockets as I'll take your money too."

"Is that what this is about? You are thieves, stealing from your own."

"No. But yes. As the mountains are becoming polluted, so are we. The Roma have always been at one with the land; when it is damaged, we are damaged. It is out of our control. I see you've noticed the tats. They are new and not for protection. They are a warning. You are to go no further. I was sent to stop you."

"Can you fight it?"

"To a degree. I have not killed you, yet."

"Then can you help me instead?"

"To do what?"

"Stop this madness."

"No, for I am part of it."

"Then can you help me save Skender? He will fall to his death if we don't. I cannot do it by myself. Look if you don't believe me!"

All Sechra needed was three seconds. She looked to the ground and exuded an air of harmlessness. The man was wary, but nevertheless inched his way to the cliff to get a look. He was more concerned with being pushed over than any thing else and so was tuned in to listen for

Sechra's feet to begin moving. Not hearing that, he craned his neck out over the drop off for the better look, and got one. There was Skender. Blood ran down his sleeves and dripped from his elbows to the valley below. In those few seconds Sechra pulled her shotgun, rammed a speed loader, and had one in the pipe before the man was able to turn and aim his gun. Instead he dropped it. Practice makes perfect and Sechra had it done in two seconds.

"Get the rope from Skender's bike. Tie it to the frame and toss it over to him. Now!"

Sechra got the drop on him and wasn't about to lose the moment. A coil of rope was stuffed under some bungees. He hesitated, but only for a fraction of a second as the barrel of Sechra's shotgun held a bead on his chest. He did as he was told. She watched as he tied the knot to make sure it was secure, then followed him to the edge to make sure the rope fell next to Skender.

He was hanging in there, but could not change his grip from the shrub to the rope. Skender's eyes told his story. He was losing it and fast. Sechra dashed to his bike and hopped on it, turned the key, shifted it into neutral and pounced hard on the kickstarter. 'Thank God the engine was still warm.' It fired on the first try. Off the bike, she stuffed the shotgun back in its holster and slung the bandit's gun over her shoulder.

In a commanding voice she said, "I'm going to climb down and get him. When I yell to you put the bike in gear and move it!"

"Why should I?" he questioned fearlessly, now that there was not a gun pointed at him.

"Because I am Kcirb, and I will hunt you down and kill you and your entire family if you don't." She left no doubt that she meant what she said.

Sechra grabbed hold of the rope and disappeared over the edge of the cliff. The face of the escarpment was shear, with nothing to hold on to. Her arms were strong from a life of sculpting; her grip, solid. Skender was barely aware when she reached him. All of his effort was put into holding tight.

With the rope twirled around her left arm and holding, Sechra wrapped the bitter end around Skender's waist two times before tying it off with a bowline on the bight. By now she was pushing her own limits of strength and endurance. There was a sudden jerk and the rope dropped them a few meters before going tight.

"Son of a bitch! Go man go!" Sechra screamed from her dangling. Skender was tied on. She was not and nothing happened. She hurled a few more expletives at the cliff top knowing only the birds would hear her. She had to climb back up. Each reach upward was an effort Sechra had never experienced before. She understood survival, but fighting for your life was something altogether different. The physical part where every move matters and each one meaning life or death. "Fuck you," she yelled at no one this time as her hands finally got hold of the lip of the cliff. The surge of adrenalin as she hit the top gave her the energy she needed to finish climbing over. Just then a foot stepped on her left hand, crushing it cruelly into the rock.

"I admire your tenacity, Madame Kcirb, but you have reached the end of your journey." He pulled a knife and thumbed the blade open. The shiny steel flickered in the sunlight for a moment as he began to bend over to cut the rope. There was no time to pull her gun, just enough to kiss your ass goodbye. Instead, she reached down and put her finger on the trigger of the man's own gun, secured her lefthand grip, tilted the barrel and fired. The explosion blew out her eardrum while the bullet hit the man in the face and consequently blew his head to pieces. Sechra pulled herself over the edge only to find Skender's bike lying on its side. Were it not for the adrenalin and overall rush from the experience, she would not have been able to do it.

The road surface was level, a plus – as she could not have spun the bike around with the rope tied to it. Squeezing the front brake, she tied a hanky around the lever to keep the wheel locked. That was the easy part. She grabbed the frame, bent her knees, and put her back into lifting the machine upright. It started to come up. Every muscle in her wanted to stop, for the exertion would surely be too much. Her will was stronger. The higher the bike came, the harder it was to keep it going. 'Oh God," she screamed as her back began to collapse under the strain. Something popped. Sechra almost froze and let go as the pain was so sudden and severe. She couldn't. A life depended on her. Regardless of the agony, she kept pushing until the motorcycle was vertical, put the kickstand down and dropped to her knees.

Tears ran down her face as she pulled herself back up to a standing position and spastically got on it. There was no electric starter. Kicking over the six hundred c.c. engine would merely be unbearable. Each kick was an exercise in masochism. She got into it. There was no other way.

Pain can stop you or be the incentive to get the job done. On the fourth attempt, the motor sputtered and came to life. Sechra leaned on the rear brake as she untied the front, squeezed the clutch and dropped it into first gear. She put the gas to it and released the clutch.

With all she had left to give, Sechra revved the engine as the rear tire spun, shooting gravel out like water from a hose, but the bike moved forward. Her momentum increased until coming to a jerking dead stop. Sechra lost control and the bike went over again. In a panic move, as the bike fell to the left, she leapt to the right to avoid being pinned under the machine. This time though she could not get back on her feet.

The will of the human spirit, however, is an unusual thing. The pain had consumed her. Her thought processes no longer functioned beyond the pain barrier. Something though, something stronger, willed her to crawl back to the edge of the cliff. There was Skender, pulled halfway over the top and not doing so well himself. Sechra reached out, took his hand and pulled. It was the last thing she remembered.

It was dark when she woke, but it had nothing to do with the sun. She was lying on a sleeping roll and through the pain felt a cold compress underneath her lower spine. Regardless, she had to go to the bathroom. Sechra rolled to the right and used her hands to push up into a sitting position that didn't last very long as she collapsed back onto the bag of packed and melting snow. Her moan was replied to.

"You are awake. How are you feeling?" Skender had been tending to her, but with Sechra unconscious it was difficult to know what to do. She had ripped up her back pretty good saving his life, but she was still not through with that yet. Skender had been hit by several of the ball bearings that shot from Sechra's gun. He could not remove them himself. His question was responded to with, 'like I have been stabbed in the back.' The words were unintelligible, but he got the meaning.

"There is a bowl next to you. I must go and tend to the animals. Make use of it. I will clean it when I get back. Then I will need your help." Skender got up within the dark cave and limped to the exit. A flashlight was left next to the bowl along with some toilet paper. Sechra struggled to use the makeshift bedpan. At least her shit hit the bowl. Wiping her ass, however, was next to impossible. The pain caused by the simple movement, that all of us do every day, was unbearable. After several attempts she gave up, considering it was good enough and pulled her pants up just as Skender, with chickens and a sheep in tow hobbled back into the cave. She was not about to ask him to finish the job. The sheep curled up next to Sechra while Skender dealt with the bowl of waste. The coarse curly hair of the animal was comforting in a strange sort of way. She petted its head, absorbing the animal's peace. It did little for the ache in her back, but did wonders for her head.

When Skender returned the bowl was full of snow.

"If you could roll to the side I can renew the cold pack for you. You must have slipped a disc lifting the bike."

Sechra didn't question, but rolled away while Skender poured out the water and replaced it with the snow. "Now comes the hard part. I need you to sit up so I can tie the ice pack in place around you."

Sucking it up Sechra said, "Okay, oh God!" She bit into her lips to help sustain the position. With the ice came comfort, some anyway, and some is better than none.

"I need your help, Sechra. I was hit by some of the shot when you came at them. You have to get the bearings out. Close your eyes. I am going to light a lantern." She heard a match strike and burst into flame, followed by the hiss of gas before it ignited. He adjusted the flame saying, "Go ahead and open them, slowly." Sechra gasped.

Skender noticed her notice and said, "Had you not come around the corner shooting they would have beaten me to death."

Skender was black and blue wherever his skin showed and Sechra was sure that which was covered looked the same. "Why would they have done this, Skender? Weren't they just a gang of roving thieves?"

"No. They are what remain of the family that we were to deliver chickens to. I recognized one of the boys before you blew his face off. The leader I have never seen before. Thank you for giving him what he deserved. Now, I have two of those big bb's in my ass and one in my thigh. I cannot reach them. If you do not get them out I will die. Gangrene, ya know."

"Do you have any booze?" Sechra inquired. "We are both going to need some to get this done."

Skender reached beyond the circle of light and pulled a pack back into it. Within it was a liter of grain alcohol, a limited first aid kit, and a roll of tools for road repairs. He unscrewed the cap and handed the bottle to Sechra. "You're going to need it as much as me." They tipped the bottle back and forth a few times before getting down to business.

Skender unrolled his sleeping mat, pulled down his pants and underwear, and lay prone, preparing himself mentally. Surgery without an anesthetic sucks.

The tool kit did indeed have what she needed, a pair of needle-nose pliers and a pocketknife. Sechra took another hit from the bottle and ran her thumb across the edge of the knife. It was sharp enough. She only hoped she was.

Just before making the first incision she gave Skender one of her riding gloves. "Here, bite on this." She didn't wait any longer for fear she would lose her nerve. After fanning the flame of a cigarette lighter to sterilize the knife, Sechra sunk the tip of the blade into the hole on his right butt cheek a few centimeters, then cut the skin twice the width of the puncture – big enough to get the pliers in and find the ball. The pliers were filthy. Scrubbing them with water and her t-shirt didn't appear to help, then the flame. Blood flowed feely from the incision. Sechra knew she had to work quickly. Spreading the gash open with the thumb and forefinger of her left hand she inserted the pliers, ends closed, into the pulpy mass that used to be muscle tissue. Skender groaned, but did not call out or flinch when she felt the ball. Opening the pliers and trying to grab it was another thing all together. The bearing had not flattened, like many bullets do, making the grab that much harder. Working blind gave Sechra a greater appreciation for the skills of those who could not see what they were doing, using their minds to visualize the manipulations necessary to complete the work.

The little teeth at the end of the pliers finally caught, allowing Sechra to slide the pliers out without losing control. Using duct tape, she created a butterfly bandage to close the wound temporarily. She had to keep the blood loss to a minimum as there wasn't any extra around and no means to transfer it if there was. She scooted over a little to get to the other cheek and regretted it immediately. So focused was Sechra on the little surgery that she forgot about her back, almost. The movement brought that reality back into focus. She took another swig from the bottle and handed it to Skender. He would be needing it, too.

Working on his ass first gave her a little experience at the process. It was the thigh that worried her. Too many horror stories of cutting the main artery and the subsequent rapid bleed out had her imagination in overdrive. That the hole in his leg was not pulsing blood was a good sign, but then again what did she know? Nothing, that's what.

Before making the incision, she filed down the sharp edges of the pliers at the tip. The tool was old and she didn't want any burrs nicking something she couldn't see while searching around.

Resterilized, Sechra made the cut, but not as big or deep as the ones in his butt. Just enough to open up the puncture. The plan was to follow the path of the ball, wiggling the tip of the pliers until she found it. Which she did, eventually. In finding the spent round, she also discovered Skender's limit to what he could endure, which in Sechra's mind at least, was anything, anything at all. After applying the final butterfly, he rolled onto his side, smiled, and said, "Got a cigarette? You should have been a surgeon, honey. How's the back?"

"I should get some more ice."

"Not right away. Let the blood flow back into the area for a while and warm up some. In the meantime, let's make camp. We'll be here for a few days. The bikes will be safe enough, we just need a few items."

Sechra started to get up, dropping to her knees as the stenosis in her spine let her know in no uncertain terms that she had indeed done some serious damage.

"We don't need it now. Lie back on your bag and put your feet up. I'm saying this for both of us. And I also suggest we get hammered on that alcohol."

"I won't argue with that, but shouldn't we ration it?" Sechra asked knowing she would need it tomorrow too. Igor threw his back out, from time to time while teaching and muscling rocks, so she knew the score.

"There's more," responded Skender with a wry smile. They both did a big shot. After recovering from the burn, they did it again, and again and again. Were it not for the last few days events, they would have been laughing and getting to know each other in the way drunks do. Instead, they passed out in the way that drunks do, too.

Sechra woke to the warmth and light of a fire, the smell of coffee and frying eggs. Handing a steaming cup to Sechra he asked, "How would you like them, sunny or over easy?"

"What? Huh? You mean the eggs didn't break?"

"Nope. Parents could learn much by watching chickens. People in general, too." He set a perfect pair of easy over eggs and a hunk of bread next to the coffee. "I'll be back in a few minutes," giving Sechra some time with her first cup and a little space.

Skender followed the narrow trail back to the road. The bikes were stashed in a cleft in the rock hillside, hidden from view. That is, if nobody looked too close. He was now about to make sure no one had a reason to. Three bodies lay in the road. Two were faceless. The third, on the other hand, could conceivably be recognized. Skender solved that with the forceful application of a good sized rock before dumping the bodies over the cliff at a spot that would go unseen, if you didn't look too close. He scuffed the bloodstains into the dirt and mud and dragged a branch over the tire tracks to further camouflage their presence. Nature would take care of the rest.

After tossing the last body over the cliff, Skender felt a warm wetness crawling down his left leg. It wasn't his urine but it reminded him he had to go. Standing at the edge he let his stream fall upon the bodies. It's a guy thing. He stopped at the bikes on the way back and retrieved another bottle and made a big snowball.

Once in the warmth and feeble light, "Sechra?"

"Yes," she replied wiping up the last of the yolk on her plate with remaining bread.

"I think you're going to have to stitch me up. The tape pulled." He drank the rest of his coffee and refilled it with what was left of the first bottle. Taking a big gulp, 'There's some thread and a needle in the tool kit."

The needle was rusted and thread worthless. Sechra dug in her pack for the toiletry kit and withdrew a roll of dental floss. Using a smooth stone she ground the needle to clean steel and re-point it. "Better finish that cup. This is gonna hurt." Sechra poured some for herself and drank deeply before dropping the needle and floss into the liquid. "Thanks for the ice." Sechra drained the water, refilled the bag with snow, belted it on and went to work. As a child she had done this many times during the course of her clan's survival. 'It's like riding a bike,' she said to herself. A horrible and evil bike, that is. The stitching brought back the memories of men and women whose bodies had been ruined by the tyrannical Voivode and left them both passed out, again, when the wet work was through.

Three days went by before Skender felt well enough to ride. The only physical activity either of them had was to answer the call of nature, gathering more snow for the ice pack, eating and drinking water. That was it. Skender knew Sechra needed the time off her feet to heal as quickly as possible. The problem was that time was of the essence. Winter was quickly approaching as evidenced by the pockets of snow they had been surviving on.

"We leave tomorrow."

Sechra had no desire to agree, but agree she did. Sechra thought she knew what sucking it up meant. She had no idea.

The following morning Sechra was able to stand, walking was merely unbearable. As the early morning progressed, her back loosened up a little. Skender did all the carrying of supplies. It was Sechra's job to secure them to the bikes.

Finishing the last of their coffee Skender said, "I would ask if you are really ready to ride, but we have no choice. A couple shots of alcohol might help some."

"I'd rather not. The road is shit and I need to be 'all here' if you know what I mean."

"I do. Soften your rear suspension as much as you can so the bumps won't hammer your back. It's still going to hurt like hell. We'll keep you on ice all day. Sorry I don't have painkillers. They are hard to come by, but some of the villages may have something. We have the chickens and the sheep to trade with."

"I have money," Sechra replied concerning the conundrum.

"No good. Money is useless up here. Speaking of, I used a few hundred to get the fire started. I didn't mean to go through your stuff but we needed some dry paper."

"Not an issue, Skender. There is plenty more where that came from."

"Good, because we're not done yet. You ready?" Skender asked zipping up his suit.

"No." Sechra made sure the shotgun was loaded before putting it away and putting on her helmet. "Can you get it off the center stand for me?"

With a grunt, Skender shoved her bike forward until the stand sprung back into place and put the kickstand down. Sechra eased herself into the saddle, a maneuver that was as natural as tying your boots, which Skender had to do for her also, as she couldn't bend over to tie them. She watched Skender as he pounced on the kickstarter of his bike, thankful she didn't have to do the same. Sechra gave Skender the chin, the go ahead.

With the sun to their backs, the two headed deeper into the mountains. The riding itself was better than Sechra thought it would be, as long as she stood up a little when the bumps and dips were unavoidable. Three hours into the ride, they came across the remains of a gypsy encampment. Skender pulled over on some hard packed ground and stopped. By the looks of it, the camp had been abandoned hastily and recently, if the smoldering cook fire was any clue. The scene was a flashback from her youth that buckled her knees as bile rose to her mouth. She recovered by grabbing onto the bike.

"What happened?" Sechra asked after swallowing hard, taking her helmet off, visibly shaken and happy she had not thrown up in the helmet.

Skender shrugged his shoulders with a look of, 'how the fuck am I supposed to know?'

Sechra pulled her gun from the sleeve vent in her suit and for the first time saw Skender pull a nine-millimeter pistol from his thigh pocket. Since he had kept it out of sight until now...best to stay alert and keep her distance. Two people together are easier to kill than separated.

Sechra found the trail first, whistling to Skender using two fingers. It could have led anywhere, to the latrine, a still, water, or just a nice spot to be. It was none of the above. The trail ended in a clearing circled by tall black walnut trees, whose branches kept the open space in near darkness. Within the gloom was the band of gypsies. All were dead. Their bodies formed a pentagram, five to a line. Four more formed a square within the star. And three, a circle within the square. The sight was beyond appalling. All the dead were naked and mutilated. Sliced and diced on the open skin were arcane symbols, ancient in origin and beyond the comprehension of Sechra and Skender, other than they meant something horrible and evil.

"Witch symbols," Skender muttered as he crossed himself, then made another sign with his right hand and fingers forming a sort of mudra to ward off evil.

"And by the looks of them, not the kind of clairvoyant you'd go to, to read your palm," replied Sechra sarcastically. Though Romania was a country of witches, she believed none of it, but apparently Skender did.

"Usually they use chickens or at worst, a beast. People haven't been used since the dark ages, before the inquisitions, and during them, in an attempt to stop the Christian madness."

"It didn't work then so what would force them to try it again?"

"I don't know, but I think we'll be finding out..." Skender raised his weapon and pointed it in the direction of Sechra. She began to scream when an explosion ripped through the clearing. Sechra felt the brush of the bullet across her cheek as Skender ran forward, following the bullet, charging Sechra. He took a flying leap; she ducked as Skender went over her tackling a man to the ground. The man was crazed and Skender could barley contain him, even though he had shot him in the shoulder.

"GET THE KNIFE OUT OF HIS HAND," Skender yelled to Sechra.

She did one better and brought the butt of her gun down hard on the nut's head. The man went limp. Skender rolled off of him and using the man's belt to tie the still hands together, he then tied the shoelaces of the still boots together before stepping back and taking a breath.

"Thank you," he breathed heavily. "I couldn't hold him any longer."

Sechra rubbed her cheek. A light smear of blood covered her fingers. "Nice shot."

"A little close, but there was no time. He came out from behind that big walnut and was just about to take your head off."

"Why didn't you kill him?"

"Because I know him and dead men can tell you nothing but how they died."

"Who is he to you, and why is he alive?" Sechra asked.

"A cousin. In the mountains pretty much everyone is a cousin. But why? Maybe he can tell us. Besides whoever did this," Skender waved at the meticulous massacre, "didn't need any more people." Sechra gave him a perplexed look so he went on. "Twenty-five to form the pentagram, four to the square, and three to the circle. Thirty-two."

"I can add, Skender," Sechra replied sarcastically, "but what does it add up to?" The question was more metaphorical.

"Thirty-two. Twenty-two for the letters of the Hebrew alphabet, and ten for the – tree of life. It has nothing to do with the Jews as a people, but the Kabala. It must be read and used in the original language for it to make any sense. Only a few are willing to give their lives to its understanding. It is what it takes."

"I take it you haven't."

"No. It was my father..."

"I thought Urloff..."

"It's all relative. He is not my real father, but father to many who lost theirs during the revolution."

"I understand," Sechra replied with complete commiseration for she had lost her entire family around that time. "So what do you know?"

"Not much I fear. At least not as much as you would like me to. He died before I came of age when the real teaching begins. It was the rule of those who studied properly that one must live, truly live for a short while before giving up the self in pursuit of, well, whatever it is they pursue. But I have picked up a few things and can read the signs. It may help." Skender turned to face the carnage. "At face value," he chuckled at the pun, for very few of the dead had their face left intact. Sechra smiled darkly, indicating she 'got it.' "It appears to be an extreme ritual to ward off an impending evil but," he looked closely at several of the symbols carved into the flesh of some of the dead, "they are backwards, a mirrored image. I shouldn't have to tell you that this is bad, like really fucking bad."

"And just how bad would that be? Have we lost already?"

"Good question. Depends on whether it worked or not. You see, instead of trying to stave off evil, they were attempting to call it into being. There aren't too many reasons to do this for the good of mankind. When I read the history of the revolution, twenty odd years ago was one of the few times it was done for the right reason. Your guardians, in a bold effort to put an end to Tepes and his rule, had to do just this. It was the Prime Minister's wife, Riana. To end it..."

Sechra finished the thought for him. "She had to call the fetid malevolence into being before being able to destroy it. I know. I was there. I can also tell you she did not destroy it, merely disabling it. The thing, now a wisp of evil, searched for a soul with all the right requirements, to enter and grow."

"And what would the basics of those requirements be, Sechra?"

"A deep seated hatred within the undeveloped mind of a child."

"You were that child?"

"Yes."

Skender began to make the sign to dispel the evil again and thought better of it, brushing his hair back instead.

"I would if I were you, Skender." The slight of hand did not go unnoticed.

"Sorry, habit."

"I would like to think of you as a friend and friendship can overcome most anything. You are a brave man, Skender. Thank you. Now what else can we learn from these bodies? And then what do we do with them?"

"Frankly, it's getting a little rank, ya think? You have a camera?" Skender asked.

"In my phone."

"Good. Get a full line of shots. Each individual and a few of the whole scene. Think you can do it? I mean, is your back holding out?"

"As long as we don't have to bury them I should do all right."

"Wasn't planning on it."

The man who had attacked them was still unconscious. While Sechra did the photo shoot, Skender examined each body closely for the details that were missed on the cursory survey. Every body was disfigured beyond recognition. He searched for tattoos and scars that would aid in identification. Nothing. The dead had even been robbed, not only of their lives, but also of gold teeth, fillings and piercings that had been torn from their implantation. Whether this was done before or after the ritual didn't matter much, except that witches would not have taken the items for the karma that came along with such things.

There was a rustling and thrashing of clothes. Both Sechra and Skender turned as one to see the man coming to. Unable to free his hands he went to stand and without hesitating tried to run away from the two people who were now heading his way. Adolf went down, succumbing naturally to the simple booby trap of tangled laces.

"Kill her, Skender," he began to scream, "Before she kills us all!"

Skender was at Adolf's side, restraining him, while he was still screaming.

"Kill her! Kill her! Kill her," he ranted.

Skender slapped him hard across the face. "Calm down, Adolf, the killing is over."

"No, it isn't," Adolf bellowed. "It has just begun. She has come back and taken the form of a succubus!" Adolf pointed wildly at Sechra.

Two things happened at this moment. Skender looked toward Sechra, questions forming in his mind and Adolf's shoestrings snapped. Before Skender could secure his grip, Adolf scrambled from beneath him and bolted for the woods beyond the circle. The forest was nearly impenetrable and Skender did not give chase. He would get no more information from Adolf. He had lost his mind, but part of what he said in those few moments bore remembering. That this business had 'just begun' bothered him more than the possibility of Sechra being a succubus.

A succubus normally uses her femininity to sway things in her direction. Sechra did not. In fact, she acted more like a man than most men do, without being a dyke, too. Times change however and evil evolves like everything else. Skender would have to remain vigilant, to watch for the signs. By this time, Sechra had hobbled up to him.

"What did he say?"

Skender raised his hands to show they were empty. "He said I should kill you before you kill us all."

"There was more than that Skender. Give it up. I need to know." Sechra meant every word.

"That this nightmare, for what else could you call it, has just begun."

"And...?"

"That you are the source of this evil. Something or someone has taken over you."

"I believe I just told you that not so long ago."

"Perhaps, but the confirmation of it, well..."

"I understand, Skender. You see I have lived with this all my life. And yet you have awakened thoughts that I had long ago buried, to survive. I did not create the sculptures. She/it did, through me. At the time, and my shrinks agreed, that it was good therapy to create and face my reality. Oh my God ... they were so wrong and so was I."

"Have you been following the news of your exhibition?" Skender asked.

"No. My manager is taking care of it and I have little interest in it now."

"Well you should. I have. Everywhere the show goes, insanity in the form of bigotry, hatred and anything else you can think of, affects the region."

"The exhibit's on a world tour..." Sechra let her thoughts trail off.

Skender on the other hand was good at picking up the threads and weaving them into understanding. "You will not be able to stop the tour. You must travel into the heart of the matter. And that, my dear Sechra, is not just a metaphor. I suggest we get the hell out here and right now! This ritual was for you. The sigil of the Kcirbs is drawn in blood in the center of the circle. Untie the gas can and top us off. The rest we'll spread over the bodies. One good ritual deserves another, ya think?"

Sechra wasted no time in following the orders. Chickens squawked and feathers flew as she yanked the gas can from under the woven bungee tie-down. Filling both bikes left about half the can with fuel. She paused looking at Skender for an answer.

"You must do it. Every body must go up in flames. Save the last..." Sechra interrupted Skender.

"For me," she demanded.

"We should be so lucky, but killing yourself will not stop what has begun." Skender was busy reaching into the chicken pen, eventually withdrawing one by the legs. "This one is old and will not lay much longer." Sechra stood there, stunned. "Get moving, Sechra, we have no time."

She snapped out of it and began drizzling gasoline on the corpses while Skender tied the chicken to the center of the circle. The gas did not gush from the can as it had to be rationed. Tears however poured in torrents from her eyes as she did what she was told.

"What do I do with the last of it?"

"Pour it on the chicken."

"What!"

"Sechra, we have just entered the world of the bizarre, it will get worse. Now please."

Again she did as she was told. Sechra dropped the empty can, as empty as her soul and walked toward the bikes and began to suit up. Skender came up to her, his face passive and stern.

"You did well, now you got a cigarette?

"But I thought we had to split?"

"There is always time for a smoke."

Sechra pulled a case from her breast pocket, pressed a tab that flipped the cover open to reveal a dozen hand rolled cigarettes. She offered one to Skender. He picked one out and put it to his nose inhaling deeply.

"This is good tobacco," he smiled. "As we smoke, think kind thoughts. Push hatred and anger from your mind." He produced a lighter, the old kind that smelled funny. The case was engraved in a writing that Sechra could not read.

"It is a special lighter." Skender flipped the top and struck the wheel in a practiced clever move while mumbling what could have been a prayer. He lit Sechra's first. They smoked in silence. While Sechra tried to stop the internal chatter and think nice thoughts in the face of horror, Skender just stood there with a smile on his face. Sechra took the hint. A few minutes passed while smoke filled the still air. Then, without communicating verbally they both reached out with the smoldering stubs and flicked them at the chicken.

They did not wait to enjoy the conflagration but rode hard and fast into the mountains, never looking back.

***

T he wind blowing down the beach captured the smells of the
marketplace and entered Karuna's nostrils. Spice mixed with
rotting fish and meat, the scent of roses, the sweat of unwashed
bodies, incense, flatulence, filth and halitosis. But it was the heat that
nearly melted her into the sand. It was summer. They were as blistering as
the winters were cold. A hand reached out carefully grasping her elbow
to steady her until she regained her composure. The hand was Ahmed's.
Or the hand of the man that Ahmed now occupied.

"Drache," Ahmed began, Drache being the male nomenclature for
Dracine. "Would you like some water? The heat is most oppressive today."
To the cadre of attendants that were ever at Dracine's side to comfort
her every need, he yelled, "Water, more shade, fans!" The cadre went
into double time at the command. A gold trimmed goblet was passed
forward. Dracine did not have to reach for it as the water was poured
into her mouth for her. The water bearer, Aquin, was a nervous, little,
overweight man. His hand shook, spilling some water down the front
of Dracine's outfit.

Karuna looked down as the water droplets beaded and absorbed into the
silk before evaporating as if the dribble had never happened and thought
nothing of it. Ahmed on the other hand had been playing this game for
more than a thousand years. He stepped forward, giving Aquin a backhand
that tumbled the man head over heels backwards. Ahmed's hand had hit
the glass first before slamming it into Aquin's face, which now bled freely
through shards of glass. The display of Ahmed's strength was formidable
and apparently used quite often when you looked upon the faces of the
service people.

Nevertheless he dropped to one knee next to Aquin. While deftly
removing the broken glass from the man's face, he bent close and whispered
into Aquin's ear.

"You must calm yourself, Aquin, when in Drache's presence. Or would
you like to be invited to dinner? Why do you think we feed you so well?"
The laugh that followed from Ahmed's lips was dark and sent ripples of
fear into all that heard it. Aquin, on the other hand, had the eyes of a lamb
about to be slaughtered. In a heartbeat, Ahmed was back at Dracine's side.

To the linen merchant, Ahmed asked in a voice that was not to be
contested, "Is this the best you have to offer?"

"Ye, yo, yes sir," he replied shitting his pants, "does it please the magistrate?"

Ahmed looked to Dracine. Receiving the slightest nod of approval, Ahmed withdrew a pouch that hung from his side and withdrew several gold coins, dropping them on a bolt of cotton muslin.

"Th th th thank you," he bowed eyeing the money and knowing better, from experience, as his scars attested to. "P p please forgive m m m me, k k kind s sir. You h h have p paid too m m m much."

"Think nothing of it. Provide us with your best and it is the reward. You have pleased Drache and so you can sleep well knowing your family will still be with you in the morning."

Karuna made a movement with her hand. It was something she had never done before and made her wonder if it was Dracine's personality was slipping through. She didn't have to wonder long. Ahmed was at her side as if he always had one eye on her.

"Yes master, what is it you desire?" he leaned in close, his ear nearly touching her lips.

"Ahmed, I need to go to the bathroom. All that coffee this morning."

His fingers snapped when he raised his hand above his head. Within moments a dark age version of a port-a-potty was being erected and moments after that, the two entered. Ahmed removed the lid of a porcelain commode. Karuna studied the design for a moment before deciding how to use it. When she undid the belt around her trousers, the pants fell to the ground, which of course was not sand but an oriental carpet. A small embarrassment before the urge to pee overrode it.

When she was through, Ahmed handed her a damp towel. "I am supposed to do it, but under the circumstances..."

"Thank you, Ahmed." He turned around to face the wall of the enclosure.

Securing her wide belt in place she asked, "And what is your name? So I don't blow our cover."

"I have no name and am no one but your personal servant. You, however, almost 'blew our cover,' as you so aptly put it. Had I not stepped in and disgraced Aquin..."

"I was supposed to do that? It was just a few drops of water."

"Precisely. To have his family killed for such lack of care would not have been out of line. You are a cruel woman. It is now your nature and you must step it up. The only time you can let your guard down is when we are alone, and even then the walls have eyes and ears." Then in a loud voice, for their conversation had been barely a whisper, as Ahmed knew someone would be listening, "And if anyone is even close to this tent when we exit, they will be made an example of." No one was. Before Ahmed opened the flap of the loo, "Be arrogant, abusive and have no patience. Even I bear the scars of your intolerance. We are done shopping for the day. Look at them hungrily and watch the peasants try and look skinny. If it brings a wicked laugh to your lips, let it be heard."

From the doorway of the loo to an umbrellaed litter ran an oriental runner so that Dracine's feet would not have to feel the heat of the sand. A wrinkle in the fabric caused her to stumble. Ahmed was there, naturally to catch her and keep her from making an unroyal-like tumble.

As soon a she was upright Karuna said in a voice that was loud but not yelling, deep but not a bellow, "Who is in charge here?" she demanded.

A nearly naked slave was pushed before Karuna. She pretended not to notice him. Rather she admired the pointed, razor edges of her fingernails. She straightened her hand until they formed the ridges of a serrated blade and without hesitation drove her stiffened fingers into the man's throat. The skin and esophagus parted under pressure of the four scalpels. Hot blood sprayed her face before he fell to the sand and died. Karuna licked her lips and stepped into the carriage. Ahmed was right behind in the litter, as befitted his position.

"Well done," he mouthed the words, but uttered no sound.

Six burly slaves lifted the carriage without the passengers feeling the slightest movement. They moved in unison as their muscles strained with the overadorned mode of transportation. Another slave bearing the bolt of silk followed behind.

Half an hour later, the assembly arrived at Castle Drache, a Gothic structure two hundred and fifty meters above the beach on a bluff with an uninterrupted view overlooking the Black Sea. The carriage was set down, on granite blocks carved into the shape of devilish gargoyles, with as much care as it was lifted. Two of the carriers got down on all fours to create steps for Dracine and Ahmed. Once, it was suggested that steps be built for this purpose. And only once. The man with the clever idea, a stonemason who went by the name of Kcirb, was the bottom tread until the day he died. He learned the hard way that human flesh is easier on the feet than, let us say, stone.

For the duration of the ride, Ahmed and Karuna said nothing to each other. Instead Ahmed scribbled rapidly on papyrus paper with a piece of coal. The note involved how Karuna should conduct herself at home, the names and descriptions of people and slaves she needed to know and the schedule of the magistrate's business for the next few days. That Karuna had picked up on his advice while in the bathroom, delivering the lethal blow with unfailing accuracy and the cold-hearted look on her face, the licking of the lips being the coup de grace, gave Ahmed confidence she could pull off the charade. He watched as she got out of the carriage. Already he could see Dracine's influence developing in Karuna. The set of the shoulders, a slow yet powerful gait with an air of affluence that comes with the position of magistrate. The real Dracine would have ground the heels of her shoes into the backs of the human stairs for no good reason other than to relish in their pain.

Karuna on the other hand was struggling desperately to maintain control of her mind. Dracine's impact was more powerful than she had expected. That she liked what happened on the carpet runway bothered her most. Without the support of Ahmed...She had only enough time to read through the first part of Ahmed's notes when the carriage stopped. Luckily the first order of the day was to retire to her den. This was to be done without giving anyone or anything her slightest countenance. Dracine was an opium addict and everyone in the castle, and I mean everyone, knew the routine. That being to make sure everything was perfect for her arrival and stay out of sight until she had begun to smoke. Even then hours would pass before she would be considered approachable.

Ahmed opened the door into the den for Karuna and closed it behind them. As he had mentioned before, the walls have ears and eyes. Ahmed set about the ritual of filling the pipe as well as making some tea, into which a small ball of opium was allowed to steep. Karuna lay down on a Kashmir woolen bed, resting her head lightly on a carved ivory headrest. When Ahmed was finished with his ritual he held the pipe to her mouth and applied the flame of a candle to the bowl. When heated sufficiently he murmured, 'smoke.'

Ritualistic smoking of opium was one of those traditions that had survived throughout the ages. In modern times, it had been reduced to 'chasing the dragon' as so many addicts called it. Yet there were havens where the old ways were still adhered to – but you had to search them out and avoid the lure of the quick fix. Once you'd found one and experienced what Karuna was now learning, you understood what it was all about. Drug addicts didn't have a clue.

She inhaled deeply. The urge to cough was cancelled. Karuna held her breath until Ahmed quietly uttered 'breathe.' Ahmed, knowing Karuna was not experienced, repeated the smoking less often than the real Dracine would have wanted. That would come in time. The trick now was finding the fine line between a heavy dose and overdosing. With nausea being an indicator of overdosing, Ahmed observed her closely. When a sheen of sweat glistened on her forehead, he stopped.

The sun sat far in the west by the time Karuna came out of her nod and said, "Ahmed, thank..." His hand quickly clasped over her mouth. He bent close to her ear.

"The old language, only. And never call me by name. I know both of you very well and am somewhat of a clairvoyant. When I cannot anticipate your needs or desire, strike me and don't hold back."

There was a knock at the door. Ahmed unfolded himself into an upright position, slowly, for he had been partaking of the satisfying smoke as well. A female slave stood on the other side, waiting patiently. In her hands was a tray with an assortment of dates, fruits, honeyed breads and a bowl of small black beans with a beckoning pungent odor. Her face stared at nothing for she was blind, as were most of the castle's servants.

With the exception of the cooks, guards, and carriage carriers, the internal staff were all blind. If they were born that way they were lucky. If not, one day was allowed for them to memorize the layout of their work areas and duties before a red-hot iron was put to their eyes, bursting their liquid-filled orbs in an explosion of pain and darkness. The reason for this is obvious. Dracine was a woman in drag. Her paranoia of being found out dictated her actions.

Ahmed nodded to the servant before taking the tray. He cursed himself silently for the breach of protocol. Why would he gesture to a person who couldn't see? He glanced around to see if anyone had seen what he did. There was no one. He was relieved and reminded himself that his tutelage of Karuna applied to himself also. So he listened up. The servant was gone. Ahmed backed into the room, closing the door behind him. He set the tray on a low stool.

"Lunch has been served, master. Would you like me to feed you?"

Karuna was a little stoned. She looked up at him and broke out laughing, not only at the request, but at their situation in general. Nevertheless, the tittering was not Karuna's, at least not completely. There was a curl, a barb, an edge to the sound that frightened Ahmed more than he was prepared for. But for the wickedness, the woman still showed through.

"What is that smell?" The roasted coffee beans glistened black and oily in their dish. "Is it, is it..." Karuna asked excitedly. Well not all that excitedly, considering, but the smell of fresh roasted coffee has been known to lure a junkie back into the here and now.

Ahmed held the still warm bowl of beans out to her. Karuna picked a few, rolling them in her hand beneath her nose before popping a couple in her mouth and began to chew.

"Mmmmm, now if there were only some chocolate." No sooner had she finished the request when another bowl of roasted seed came before her.

"It is not the milk chocolate of your youth, but I think you will enjoy the combination." Ahmed was being the perfect servant. The bitter cacao had been dipped in evaporated sugar cane juice. Karuna smiled as she savored the unusual but familiar flavors.

"Fabulous. The taste. The future has nothing on this. So much has been lost in mass processing."

Ahmed gave her the eye, indicating she was straying from the moment. "Perhaps," he paused, "but the flavor of starvation is ever the same."

"Speaking of, I will be meeting with a delegation of farmers tomorrow concerning the new tax I burdened them with." Remembering the walls have ears, she raised her hands upward in a supplicating gesture.

"You want more, my lord Drache?" replied Ahmed while he peeled a banana, perfectly, and handed it to Karuna.

"More of what?" she asked with a mouthful.

"Of everything." Ahmed stirred the tea and placed the cup before Karuna.

"But I already have everything. Paying the merchant for that silk was an act of kindness on your part. I had nothing to do with it, for it already belonged to me."

"That is not the point, my lord Drache."

"We will do away with the tax. Men with full bellies have more to lose, work harder and suffer more."

"The law is in place, they come to pay tribute."

"Are you questioning me?" her hand was quick, arm strong. The half empty cup of tea was smashed into Ahmed's face. A gash below his left eye began to flow crimson.

"Fill another glass with the drippings from your face and prepare another pipe. We are done for the day." The two personalities were clashing like plaid and stripes, with the schizo switch being flipped by a madwoman. Ahmed was having a difficult time keeping up with it. The rules of the game were changing, but he was still a servant and did as he was told. Late in the evening, Dracine succumbed to drug and sleep, giving Ahmed a chance to address his wound and collect his thoughts. He did not leave the room, but retired to an alcove from where he could still hear her breathing and be of immediate assistance. He himself would not get much sleep tonight. Ahmed was worried for Karuna, as Dracine's will dominated the evening. But then Ahmed did not know Karuna Danesti/Talian as well as he thought he did.

The morning was bright behind heavy black and red curtains that shut the brilliance out of the sleeping chamber. Dracine was not a late riser, but had a habit of waking and baking. When she finally opened her eyes, Ahmed was at the bedside, waiting patiently in meditation. He heard her eyelids raise. With the sound, his hands, which had been folded on his lap, picked up a smoking pipe. This one was different in style and function than the afternoon pipe, a hookah. Within the bowl had been prepared a mélange of hashish, tobacco and opium.

An hour passed before Karuna got out of bed to dress and the heavy curtains could be opened to light the room. Ahmed leaned into the windows to get a breeze blowing to dissipate the reek. The wraithlike layers of smoke swirled together as the tail of the dragon wisped out the widow. With that came a slight knock that was breakfast being served, similar to lunch, but this morning was something new, something the dark ages had yet to see, taste, indulge in and/or profit on.

In the wee hours before dawn, Ahmed silently left Dracine's chambers to go to the kitchen and teach the staff how to make coffee. It was an effort to please the demand before it was spoken. It also allowed Ahmed to view the staff in the relative safety of their kitchen, where they could let their hair down, so to speak. They did not suppress their feelings when he was in their midst. After all, he was one of them and bore the scars of equality. The man with no name, Ahmed, was also not a snitch and had developed an unspoken reputation for covering the staff's collective ass, when he could. Of course there were times like yesterday in the market when he disciplined Aquin. The fact was he did the man a favor, saved his life and his family's. At least for one more day. The act of cruel kindness did not go unobserved. He was greeted with smiles and the freshest of the morning's sweetbreads. Ahmed showed his thanks by eating well. That the staff was in a reasonably good mood was something of a miracle in itself. Perhaps it was that Dracine had not ripped a few of them a new asshole last night by staying in her chambers, or maybe they felt the change of goodness. How long it would last is the real question. Since he had their confidence, Ahmed swore them to secrecy. The conspiracy was making coffee, which he explained, was why Drache was in such a good mood yesterday after sampling some at the market. It was a lie, but who cares? Ahmed went through the entire process. Roasting they knew, having been taught by the Turkish importer of the bean. Coffee, as we know it, was something altogether different. He needed a fresh mortar and pestle. These tools were for grinding the coffee 'only', he explained to the eager staff who would do anything that made the master happy. 'Only the roasted coffee. Use it for any other spice and you will ruin the flavor.' Ahmed didn't have to repeat himself. The staff fully understood the consequences.

Karuna exited her dressing room with a flourish of black and gold silk. The seamstress had been up all night creating the outfit and was sweating bullets as she pulled the final stitch through, for she heard Ahmed putting the hookah away. The garment was hung with care to display the finished product at its best. And not a moment too soon. The curtain, behind which led to servant's quarters, had just finished swaying when Karuna came in to dress. This, of course, came after a sponge bath by Ahmed. Karuna's self-consciousness was not so much slipping away as being overlaid by Dracine's.

'I'll be wiping her ass next,' smiled Ahmed as he brought the breakfast tray into the room. "Your outfit is stunning," he said placing the tray next to a table by the windows. "And your ability to spy such fine material amongst the many bolts..." Ahmed was interrupted, but by whom he was not sure.

"You didn't," Karuna smiled.

"I did, though you will hear it was your idea. It will take Europe by storm." Ahmed poured a cup of rich, double roasted black coffee and set it in place before holding the chair for Karuna to sit.

"Must we be so formal," Karuna asked politely sipping from the cup. "Mmmmm. An old friend of mine likes his coffee this way."

"The man knows his coffee. And yes, we must. You see I am having trouble knowing who I am talking to. This morning I gave you a sponge bath. I believe 'you' would have preferred to do it yourself. And last night you kept shifting back and forth so often... As you can see," he brushed his fingers across his cheek, "it was not easy to keep up."

"I am sor..."

"Never say you are sorry, never. It is part of the game and I have accepted my part. The staff, on the other hand, worked very hard to make that coffee you are drinking, and they will keep your secret until you are ready to share it."

"The secret of coffee," she laughed, but there was an edge to it. "They had better."

Ahmed set the breakfast before Dracine. Breads, eggs, seasonal fruit, and strange looking bacon.

"This brew is absolutely delicious. Why didn't I think of it before?"

"Would you like me to feed you, master?"

"Am I a child now?" she spat. "No, this coffee makes me feel up for the task. Go prepare some more and ready the court room." Dracine picked up a piece of the unctuous bacon and sank her pointed teeth into it. "God I love the bacon of a fat man." A little hot fat dribbled down her chin. Before Ahmed could wipe it away, Dracine caught the drip with her thumb and licked it off. "Be gone!" Ahmed was already halfway to the door.

It was noon by the time Dracine entered the court of the magistrate. The high ceilings made the room appear larger than it actually was. Vents in the gables allowed heat to escape and created a draft that brought cool air up from the catacombs beneath the floor. It made for a simple yet effective air conditioning. Churches with their tall steeples are built that way for the same reason.

Ahmed held Dracine's hand as she eased herself into the overstuffed chair. A portly slave followed behind, who was dressed in the attire of a wealthy landowner of the day. When Dracine was seated, Ahmed signaled to the slave who went down on all fours to be an ottoman. She sighed putting her feet up. Ahmed handed her a cup of coffee, Dracine taking it as if he didn't exist. She sipped slowly and smiled.

"You can open the doors. But only the farmers, the rest must remain outside."

The court of the magistrate was no church, but like one, everyone who entered usually suffered. Those with appointments had been waiting for hours. No cell phones, no hotels, café's, you just waited. Most had been there all night, waiting and watching their taxes lest they be stolen. Some had been waiting all week for their chance. All were cold and tired at the morning's first light. Now they sweat, smelled and bickered with each other, waiting, in the unrelenting hot sunshine.

Ahmed leaned into the massive door until it yielded under his weight. He then stood in the sunshine for the first time that day. It hit like a frying pan. The patrons were literally withering in the heat.

He held up his hands. "Only the farmers. The rest of you will wait." There was no grumbling as one might expect when reservations are disrupted. Even those who had waited the longest just hung their heads, accepting their fate. The group of farmers divided like an amoeba. Half remained to watch the beasts and grain that were their lay of the taxes.

Thirty men stood, hats in hand, before the divan and Drache, sitting at royal ease, eyed them hungrily. "There are thirty of you. I cannot speak to you all. Is there one among you that can?" That the formality of these things was cast to the wind was nothing compared to the question. It was totally out of character. Karuna smiled at Ahmed and gave him a curt nod that meant, 'go with it.' He bowed respectfully in return and started praying.

One man stepped forward from the cluster of sodbusters. He held a scroll in one hand, his hat in the other. He waited for permission to speak.

"What is your name?"

"Kcirb, magistrate," replied the farmer firmly, but not disrespectfully.

"It seems I know that name from somewhere?"

"You knew my father. He was a stonemason and worked for you until the day he died."

"I see," Karuna knew the story. "What is it you have in your hands?"

"The records of our crops and taxes due."

Karuna reached out for them and Kcirb stepped forward and handed them over. Ahmed guffawed at the breach of protocol. Everything went through him. No one approaches the magistrate. Drache did not flip out, so Ahmed held his cool. The catch was everyone knew Drache was illiterate.

Karuna took the document and unrolled it. You could hear a pin drop, instead it was the sound of the scroll being scrolled.

"Your record keeping is extraordinary," said Karuna.

"We try," replied Kcirb. He could tell she was reading it.

"And honest. It appears you have come up short on your quotas in several areas of field production. I suppose you have an explanation."

"We have been under drought conditions for the last five years, sir."

"Five years you say, yet the rivers have not run dry, nor our wells to be deepened. What more is it that a farmer needs?"

"Rain. Wells do not supply enough and the river is too far to carry." Kcirb knew he had gone too far, but there was something in the air, in the very presence of their nemesis that spurred him on. "We have a plan, of course it would require your approval. It was your idea that brought it to our attention in the first place." Kcirb may have been pushing it, but he was no fool.

"Let us hear it, while you still have my interest," Karuna yawned and sipped from her coffee. She 'was' interested but couldn't show it.

"You wanted the cold fresh mountain waters brought to the castle via an aqueduct based on the old Roman design."

"Yes...the expense. I remember now."

"We have one design, it is simple and functional but lacks the flair and expense of the ancient stonework."

"And you can bring this to my door?"

"And water our crops to increase our yield."

"What stops you?"

"Your permission, and... "

"Do not try my patience, Kcirb. You would need relief from the taxes until it is built. Why is it so difficult to say something so simple?"

The entire congregation considered the question rhetorical.

"Your request is granted. Build your aqueduct." She chinned to Ahmed. "He will supply any funding that is deemed necessary."

"Thank you," Kcirb said bowing and stepping back into the group at the same time.

Karuna looked to her wrist out of habit. Laughing to herself, she looked at Ahmed.

"We have time for one more round of groveling. Take these men out and make sure they have sufficient funding to start the project."

As Ahmed and the farmers left, Drache snapped his fingers. Instantly there was the tube of a hookah within her reach. Another pair of hands held a glass of cool water. Drache partook of both. A cloud of smoke enveloped her like an aura or body halo. However there was no goodness in it as Dracine had taken over. The oral fixes disappeared as the door once again opened and Ahmed led a family of Boyars into the court. He could tell immediately that the moment of grace beheld by the farmers was gone. Once the Boyars were in position, he was back at his master's side.

"Magistrate, Boyar Lenes."

"Well, Lenes, what is your grievance, for you never show your face when you have good news, that is unless the meal is free." Dracine wasted no time in cutting him down to size. But Lenes was a fool and didn't pick up on it.

"Why was I forced to wait outside while farmers, of all people, were allowed to..."

"To what Lenes? Precede someone of noble birth like yourself?"

"Yes, exactly," replied the idiot who began to shuffle some paper into a semblance of order.

"Before you say anymore, let me explain something to you." The Boyar was impatient and showed it. Drache savored the disrespect in a sick sort of way and allowed it. "It was your grandfather that originally bought and worked the land so that you could have the chance to stand before me. He worked hard and earned the respect of the court. Likewise, your father was also diligent, and smart, too, for he was able to employ many of the local people to help work on the estate. And, I might add, he treated them fairly." Now the Boyar was shuffling nervously. Drache liked this even more. "Then, 'you' came along. Since your father died, you have run the estate, farmlands and pastures into the ground."

"The workers are lazy," interrupted Lenes.

Dracine looked at Ahmed with surprise. "Did you hear that? 'The workers are lazy' he says. Bring him to me!"

Two guards led the now distraught landowner to within a foot of the dais upon which Drache sat.

"Hold out his hands!" Each guard grabbed an arm, forcing the arms before Dracine, palms up. Drache inspected each hand visually then ran her fingertips across the palms and puffy parts of the fingers.

"My, you take good care of your hands. It must require a great deal of effort to never use them. Your father's hands were hard as rock, calloused over from helping in the fields and doing what had to be done to succeed. Your grandfather's, legendary." She raked her nails across the soft flesh, cutting deeply and painfully.

The Boyar screamed, "I tell you it is the workers, not me!"

"It's definitely not you. You do nothing but bleed the people dry."

He thrust his paperwork at Drache. "Here – this explains everything."

The magistrate thumbed through the paper pretending to read it. Although Dracine couldn't read she had no trouble putting two and two together.

"It does explain a great many things. You, Lenes, are a liar and a lazy one at that." To Ahmed, "Have his tongue bifurcated and schedule him to have his hands removed since they do him no good. Seize his lands and let those farmers that just left work it for me."

"But what will I do?" asked Lenes using up his last words foolishly.

"Die, I suppose."

"We are done for the time being. Get him out of my sight!"

Lenes began to grovel like the beggar he had just become. The diktat of the magistrate was given. There was no recourse but to beg. The pleadings of the damned fell on deaf ears but her eyes inspected the overweight Boyar. It was his corpulence that brought a smile to Dracine's face. Lenes' loins and steaks would be marbled with succulent fat, like a cow that finished its life eating corn; the meat would be tender, moist and unctuous.

The guards and Ahmed were dragging the screaming man away so he would not spoil the magistrate's new clothing with the pawing of sweaty hands. When Dracine spoke, it was clear whom she was talking to for she used no name. Ahmed looked up.

"Invite him to dinner this evening. Perhaps he can teach us how a good meal is supposed to taste."

Relief washed over the liar, as he did not understand the statement.

"Oh thank you, thank you, magistrate. I knew you would understand. We eat well on our estate and I can show the cooks a thing or two to make your meal the most desirable that you could think of."

"Of that there is no doubt. I'm sure they will surprise you, too." Dracine smiled revealing all her teeth as her eyes fed on the fat man. Dracine rose from her seat and left the Boyar wondering many wonderful and terrible thoughts. "Take care of this business and return to my quarters," she said to Ahmed.

Lenes was allowed to stand and walk freely. The guards were at his side as Ahmed led the way to the kitchen.

"There are appointments that I need to keep before tonight's dinner. If I can keep them, I will return at sunset," Lenes begged, wanting to get away. That smile scared him half to death, which was exactly what it does to everyone. Of course he missed the innuendo.

"I was listening during your discussion with the magistrate. You are a liar and I would be a fool to believe you. Had you not been invited, I would slice your tongue in half at this very moment for your insolence. But since you are to eat, I believe your 'appointments' can wait until tomorrow. I wouldn't want you to not be able to enjoy the feast that you will be a part of. Now, to the kitchen." Ahmed was reading Lenes' body language. "You would be a fool to try and run. At your weight I doubt you could."

They walked around to the rear of the castle where the service entrance was located. Within the thick rock walls it was cool, like a butcher shop.

"In here," Ahmed pointed. The room was empty except for the hooks that hung from the ceiling and a thick slab of polished granite that served as a cutting board. The top of the granite table was about waist high with a wide groove ground into the surface just inside the perimeter. The groove was a gutter of sorts to capture the fluids. Every estate has one, though none were better than this place where the animals are butchered. Lenes turned to run. The guards blocked his way as two of the cooks came in bearing the tools of their trade.

"Tie him to the table," Ahmed said to the guards. To the cooks/ butchers, "Not only is he dinner, but also a guest." He needed to say no more as this was de rigueur, usually. The cooks knew how to remove the flesh without killing. Once Lenes was secure, a guard strangled him, cutting off the flow of blood to the brain until he passed out. Strong cords were used as a tourniquet around the tops of the thighs, at the crotch, to stem the bleeding. With a flash of steel, the wet work began with a bone deep incision below the cord circumnavigating the thigh. The meat was spread apart by one cook, the other hefted a two handed cleaver, bringing it down hard with a bone crunching blow that separated the leg from the body. They worked quickly and kept the blood loss to what was in the legs. He would survive to eat dinner. The stumps were cauterized with a hot iron, after which the severed legs were skinned and hung on the hooks. Ahmed did not wait and watch, but returned to his master's room where she was waiting for him to fill the pipe.

Dracine inhaled deeply, capturing the blessed smoke and held it a long time before exhaling. It was Karuna that needed instructions on how to smoke, Dracine had it wired. After a few hits she asked Ahmed, "That business with Lenes was disturbing. Who came before him, I can't seem to recall."

"Farmers, with legitimate grievances. You let them live so they could continue with their work."

"We learned long ago not to kill too many farmers. That is unless you eat them."

Ahmed shook off the weirds at the thought, then remembered what was for dinner, and started planning how he could get out of it. Refilling the container that stored several days' worth of smoke, he saw they were running low and had his excuse. Once Dracine was high enough, Ahmed broached the subject. "I need to acquire more and must go out this evening to get it. Do I have your permission?"

"Always. You will miss out on a feast," she gloated.

"Duty first, pleasure second."

"I couldn't agree more. Fill the pipe again." The afternoon's schedule was busy, but Ahmed knew better than to bring it up. It could wait. In fact, everything waited until Dracine was high enough to deal with it or too high and couldn't. Either way it waited, whatever it was, until she was ready.

Eventually they went back to work. The remainder of the day was similar to the beginning with the exception that the poor bastards had to deal with Dracine. Ahmed had never seen anyone enjoy what they did as much as she. Her logic was as insane as the vicious justice she meted out.

The last was a woman burdened with nine or ten kids. She was a prostitute and even after that many children, she still produced wood wherever she went. Dracine even felt lust surge through her. Atoli, the mother, exuded sex; it was her nature. She wanted a handout.

Aroused, Dracine felt generous, among other things.

"The court does not gift moneys. You would spend it feeding those hungry mouths and find yourself back here when it was gone. There is recourse for you, however. I shall appoint you court whore. You will teach the ones we have and should your daughters come beautifully to age, you would teach them, too. Your children, in the meantime, will become wards of the court and put to work according to their abilities."

The woman bowed her head and cried bittersweet tears of joy for her children and hatred of what she was. Sucking it up she said, "I will do my best."

"I am sure you will. Tonight you and the children are invited to dine with us. Since you cannot say no, I will accept your family into ours. There is one thing."

"Anything, Lord Drache."

"Anything? I suppose that comes with your occupation. All members of the court have their primary senses rendered useless, blind, deaf and mute. In your case, we will leave everything intact. Your eyes are quite beautiful and it would take away from you, your allure. Your voice is also enchanting. We will leave your tongue intact, as I'm sure you use it quite well. The ears, I suppose you will need those, too. Your children will be left as they are. They must learn first. Do you agree?"

"Yes," the court whore replied instantly. "May I have the evening to talk to my children?"

"Naturally, besides it would interfere with dinner." To Ahmed, "Take them to the harem. The children may stay with her tonight. After that the children will sleep in the servants' quarters." Dracine took a long look at the beautiful woman. "What is your name?"

"Atoli, magistrate."

Dracine's eyes glazed over as she fantasized about being with Atoli the whore. When she came out of the nod, the court was empty. Only Ahmed stood patiently waiting for her to come back from wherever she dreamt off to. When the eyes opened, it was Karuna that stared out of them.

"Where are they?" she asked referring to the faces in the court that were no longer present.

"Gone, to prepare for dinner as should we." Ahmed reached out his hand, guiding the stoned Karuna off the dais, out of court and to her quarters, in silence. Laying Karuna on the soft wool, he set about the ritual of filling the pipe. Karuna did not stop his ministrations nor the pipe when it was offered.

"What are we doing here?" she asked. "I watched through the eyes of madness and there was nothing I could do. Am I going insane?"

"No, but the person you inhabit is. You did some good things before Dracine overwhelmed you. I was not sure if you would ever return."

"How do you maintain?" Karuna took another hit.

"The personality I have taken over is a servant. There is no ego to contend with. You on the other hand do have to struggle to maintain control, a position I do not envy. If you cannot handle it, then we must leave or your personality will be subdued. If that happens you will be stuck here forever. Speaking of, Dracine did some pretty horrible things today. Most of which you will have to deal with at dinner. I will not be there."

"Why?"

"There is something I need to do for the real Dracine," replied Ahmed.

"You can't, I forbid it! What will I do?"

"Endure. If you can make it through tonight, then we have a chance. If not, I will get us out of here at the first opportunity."

Karuna entered the dining hall long after the appointed hour. She had spent too much time trying to decide what to wear. The clothes that Ahmed had chosen for her, looked like a clown outfit. Considering the dinner arrangements, she thought black would be more appropriate, but the folds in the clown suit would allow her to hide the nine-millimeter within easy reach. Ahmed recommended she not take the gun because of the potential of a personality shift. Karuna thought otherwise. The cold steel would help to remind her of who she was, and flying solo, as Jake used to say, she wanted to be packing.

The guests had assembled hours before and had been waiting. Dracine was a notorious latecomer due to her habit and the desire to have all the diners disarmed by the delay. Doctor's offices usually made patients wait for the same reason. An hour of absolute boredom dissolved the will and made the doc's job that much easier as patients no longer had the ability to bitch and moan. Karuna entered with a splash of color, in fact the only color beyond the dun colored fabrics of the whore's children and the coarse wool serape that hung over the foreshortened form of Lenes. He was doped to the gills, marginally coherent of his situation and was praying quietly for death. Atoli was dressed in a blue silk sari that went with her eyes. Eyes that showed thanks, acceptance, worry for her children. 'She is beautiful,' Karuna thought as a blind servant held her chair.

Before her were the opposite ends of Dracine's justice. Compassion and cruelty are part of the same thing. Had the whore been ugly with a gaggle of rotten little bastards, the outcome of the court would have been significantly different. Karuna was a bit slow, the side effects of Dracine's habit. It took her a moment to see Lenes' feet set on the table as part of the arrangements. She put two and two together pretty quickly though. Aside from her suit of clothes, the only color was the deep red meat piled high in puddles of crimson on silver trays. Her thoughts now were of the children. What sort of sick mind would have the starving

kids eat the man who sat at the end of the table? Not only that, but
they had been waiting for hours, staring at the relief the food would
bring. Fear kept their hands on their laps. Instinct took over for Karuna.
A mother's instinct. And another inherent urge took the form of mental
clarity and an expansion of time. She looked at all the faces before rising
from her chair and heading into the kitchen. The head cook had her
senses intact.

"Bring the children and mother into this kitchen and feed them real
food." A wave of relief washed over Karuna and the cook. An understanding
of sorts took place, but words were not necessary to explain it. "No one
enters the dining room, no one. I am to be left alone with Lenes." There
was no need to further elucidate the cook.

Following Karuna back into the dining room, the chef spoke with
Atoli. The hungry children didn't whine, but followed their mother into
the kitchen. They did not want to eat the man, but would have.

Alone now, Karuna walked up to Lenes. "My poor Boyar. Not only
are you lazy, but your timing, sucks." Karuna plunged a carving knife into
Lenes' neck. Karuna knew Lenes' knowledge would come along with
consuming his life. She had prepared herself mentally for this. Besides,
Lenes was stupid and all she would have to deal with would be the terror
of his inevitable fate. Withdrawing the blade brought on a fountain of
blood that Karuna used to slake her thirst. If she wanted to maintain the
upper hand of a battle of personalities, then she needed to be proactive
about it. To be herself was the only way.

She drank the life away until the last beat of his heart. Lenes' head
lolled to one side, exposing the gash that tore through his jugular. A cut
on the neck, like this one, was a dead give away. Whether the dark ages or
the modern, the signature is always the same. People would talk, rumors
arise. Dracine was wicked beyond your wildest imagination, and insane,
but that is all it was. Her cannibalism was part of her mental deformity
and it was not in her nature to drink fresh blood. If word got out, it
could get ugly, so Karuna decided to destroy the evidence.

After making sure both doors to the dining room were locked from
her side, Karuna withdrew the nine-millimeter and lined up the sight
dots on Lenes' head before squeezing the trigger and emptying the
clip. Eighteen hollow-point rounds blew the head to smithereens. She
reloaded before tucking the hot barrel into the folds of her clothes. No
one would know just what had happened other than now they had one

more reason to fear Dracine. Confidence surged through Karuna as she imposed her will into the mind of Dracine. There would be no more personality shifts. Karuna had found her way to maintain control. The shit that has been going on in Castle Drache was about to go through a radical change.

***

Sechra put the kickstand down, leaned forward and put her chest on the tank bag. She was too tired to get off the bike. Skender pulled up alongside, flipping the face shield so he could talk.

"Why'd you stop?"

"I can't go any farther. We've been riding for sixteen hours." Sechra sounded exhausted.

"We can rest when we get there."

"Get where, Skender? And maybe the witches have been there, too. What's the point?"

Skender shuffled around in his tank bag, withdrawing a thermos. The coffee was old and cold, but like beer, as long as it's wet... He reached over tapping her shoulder with it.

"Here it's from the last time we made. I know you're tired, but it's not much farther."

"Time, Skender, give me a time reference," Sechra asked while unscrewing the cap/cup and pouring the dregs.

"Two hours, give or take."

Sechra shot the whole cup in one gulp, "I'll give you three. If we haven't made it by then, well then, I suppose it will be four. Just get us there tonight."

"Your wish is my command. We made a good one hundred and fifty kilometers so far."

"Well that's got to be some kind of record," jested Sechra. "Time for a smoke?"

"Always."

Sechra got off her biked and began walking in large circles, the width of the road, while she pulled a couple smokes from her case. She lit both, handing one to Skender on the second circuit. She worked her hands, making fists then relaxing them and stretching them backwards, over and over while flexing her fingers. Skender was doing similar stuff but different, as different as men and women. Both were preparing mentally and physically for the next leg. Endurance riding is as hard as it gets. Sixteen to twenty hours in the saddle is a long ass day. She smoked hers down till the stub burnt the tips of her fingers, stretching the moment. For once it was finished, there was only one thing to do.

Sechra took the lead once the sun went down. Her BMW was what they call an adventure model. Huge gas tank, big knobby rubber, and lots of ground clearance. But it was the headlight array that had her take point. The world lit up around the front of her bike like day. Skender traveled close behind. His headlight was old and wouldn't stay pointed in the right direction. He would have to fix that, but not tonight. Skender's far sight was good as he watched the road ahead of Sechra more than her taillight. When the red light bobbed up and down, he knew a pothole or bump was coming and would stand up when he got there, for his ass was sore as hell, too. He dreamed of skinning the sheep tied behind Sechra, just for that layer of curly wool to ease the unending ache. It made for a pleasant diversion in an otherwise undesirable situation. He also dreamed of Sechra, there would be no skinning involved, but there would be lots of skin.

Two hours passed and they were still rolling, or rather bumping along slowly. At two and a half, Sechra started to grind her jaw. It was taking all she had to remain focused on the road ahead, when suddenly Skender started beeping his horn. Sechra eased over to the side of the road and slowed down preparing to stop, wondering what the problem was, as Skender accelerated around her leaning on the horn button. But it wasn't a continuous blaring. Intermittent beeps, they were, like Morse code, but not the code, but definitely a signal of some kind. The brilliance of her headlights kept her from seeing the small lights in the forest, that were actually lanterns being lit. Skender stopped in a clearing where the road widened considerably. Pulling up near Skender and turning off the bank of lights, she was stunned by what seemed to be fireflies all around them. The lights, with voices and people came out of the trees.

"Is that you, Skender?" asked the first voice.

"Yeah we made it, father." Skender turned to Sechra, "Untie the sheep, quick!"

With lights everywhere now, Sechra could easily see the knots that reinforced the bungee net that covered the animal. By the time 'father' had made it to the bikes, Sechra was handing the sheep over to Skender. He spoke in a language that Sechra did not understand. It was more of a strong dialect than another language, but it was hard to tell. What she could tell was that it was a formal greeting of some kind, where an offering was part of it. She laughed quietly to herself thinking a chicken would have been an insult.

By now, the village people had surrounded them. Sechra coolly unzipped the vent in her riding suit that would allow her access to her gun, if needed. Scratching her armpit, she undid the clasp that held the gun secure and lifted it an inch or two to make sure it was free sliding. One more thing before the good itching was over. She pressed the safety to the off position. Now she eyed the crowd while waiting for Skender to finish. She smiled politely, but was looking for weapons and aggressive body language in the villagers. Something suggested that this was more than a spontaneous social gathering.

The villagers were pressed shoulder to shoulder, but gave Sechra some space. Skender was not so lucky. With the passing of the 'gift,' the air of oppression lifted from the peoples and snippets of conversations began to filter about the crowd. 'Who is that Skender brought with him?' 'Is it her?' 'Has our village been protected with a spell?' 'They rode all this way? They must be tired and hungry.' Sechra perked at this last statement and made eye contact with the woman who said it. She stepped forward extending her hand to the gypsy woman.

"I am Sechra Kcirb." There was collective gasp amongst the people who heard it and word travels fast. Skender was quickly being abandoned, as all wanted to see the Kcirb. "We are both very hungry and could use a meal if there is any to spare."

The old gypsy took Sechra's hand and led her away from the people and bright lights to the dull illumination of the cook fire. A huge pot of goulash was suspended above the fire while flatbreads cooked on the inside of a dome-shaped stone oven, where the breads were slapped on the ceiling. The old woman poured a bowl and peeled one of the bread rounds from the oven. The dish was handed over.

"Thank you. What is your name?"

"Greta Kcirb. We are cousins of sorts, distant relations, extended family, whatever you want to call it. Welcome home."

Sechra was standing up and pacing. She just couldn't imagine sitting down yet. Her ass had never been this sore before. At least her back wasn't bothering her as much. 'The adrenalin perhaps,' she thought.

Skender extracted himself from the thousands of questions. He was hungry, too. "I see you have met the most important member of the village. It has been too long, Greta," he said hugging the woman, like you would your mother.

"I knew your grandfather, Dray. We lived together for a long time before, before it all went to hell. Then he had to leave 'to save his country,' I never saw him again." Greta's eyes filled with tears, they did not fall.

"You knew my grandpapa?" Sechra asked.

A sly smile crossed Greta's face. "Yes, he was quite a man in more ways than one."

"He was. He passed away delivering the final draft of our constitution."

"Dray was smart, too, and had a love for his people that is beyond description."

"No doubt," Sechra replied with a mouthful of goulash that was washed down with a beer. After eating a second bowl and before feeling like sitting, she polished off a third bowl, washed her dishes then wrapped her hands around another home brew, as she finally painfully sat.

Greta finished whatever she was doing and approached Sechra. "Come, we must talk, away from the others." Greta reached out her arm to lend Sechra a hand getting to her feet. "Lean on me, I can tell you're hurting, though you do a good job of faking it."

Sechra took hold of her forearm and pulled herself up into an almost upright position, hunched just a little to favor her back. On the way out of the camp, Greta palmed Sechra some pills. "Eat these, they will help temporarily."

Sechra didn't ask what it was, but swallowed them all, chasing the tablets with her beer.

"It's just a little morphine to help you get some rest tonight. You will be leaving in the morning and the road gets worse."

Sechra rolled her eyes sarcastically, 'great'.

"Are you armed?" Greta asked.

Sechra slid the shotgun from her holster and let it drop back in. "12 gauge semi auto."

"It was Zapar's, yes?"

"How did you know?"

"That gun has a reputation. What kind of ammo?"

"#Two buck shot."

"Here, put these in your pocket." Greta handed her a handful of magnum rounds. "Slugs. You're going to need something with more punch. That popgun of Skender's is pretty worthless. We shot an aggressive bear with those rounds and the bullet blew it back a good five meters before it hit the ground."

"What about the shooter?"

"Broke his wrist and gave him a concussion from the recoil."

"What are we heading into to justify all the firepower?" Sechra asked.

"We don't know, but guns won't stop it. They are just for confidence."

"Cold comfort," replied Sechra.

"Better than none at all."

"I suppose. What is it you want to tell me?"

Greta shifted her feet nervously. "There is a great deal of hatred within you, Sechra. It's only natural, I guess, considering what you had to deal with as a kid, but you must, and I mean must, put it behind you. Hatred only breeds more of the same. Why did you think Skender had you clear your mind and smile when you lit the chicken and witches circle afire?"

"I don't know really, I just followed orders."

"Then follow mine as well or our country will die and so will you."

"What do you mean 'our country will die'?"

"The peoples of Romanian descent will cease to exist, period."

"What is it I need to do?"

"The moment will speak for itself and you must listen with your heart of hearts and then decide."

"Kind of vague, Greta," Sechra replied.

"Nothing is clear anymore. I am a seer and the fog has rolled in. Come, let us get back to camp, sleeping arrangements have been made and I am sure you are beat." Greta picked up a stick and handed it to Sechra. "Use this to lean on."

The old and young hobbled back to the now dispersing group of gypsies. Life goes on. Skender and 'father' were the only two left at the bikes, with the exception of curious youngsters who had never seen anything like them before. Sechra's bike was by far the most interesting, as far as they were concerned.

"Sechra, I would like you to meet my father, Gnurl."

"It is an honor," Sechra replied reaching out her hand.

"The honor is all mine," Gnurl said in response.

"Listen Gnurl, I'm tired. Could we continue this in the morning? I don't mean to be rude, but my back is killing me." Greta took her hand and together went to a one-person tent that was already made up, complete with a sack of packed snow to help reduce the swelling of the discs in her back.

"Good night, Sechra, dream good things."

"I will try, Greta, thank you." They nodded to each other. Sechra pulled a flashlight from her pocket, stripped and climbed into bed, adjusted the ice pack and was asleep by the time her head hit the pillow.

Skender, Greta and Gnurl did not go to bed. Instead they sat around the small cook fire passing news back and forth. There was no internet up here and the information they were passing wouldn't be on the media anyway.

"We've become blind, Skender," stated Greta. "This 'was' a band of seers. That is why we lived so far from everything. Being too close, you see too much and thus cannot see what you are supposed to. With distance one is able to focus on the things that were important. Even the present is unclear. That you have brought Sechra is auspicious and I believe there was some peril involved."

"Just riding these roads is dangerous enough, but it's faster than walking. But to answer your question, yes. We were attacked by a band of thieves, but there was more to it than stealing. They were twisted, somehow."

"How did they get away?" Gnurl had just been listening until now.

"They didn't, Sechra killed them. It was an us or them situation. Action not hatred," explained Skender.

"How did she handle it, on a personal level?"

"Sechra knows death and how to deal."

"What else?" prompted Greta.

"We ran across a ritual that had been used to ward us off. Everything was backwards, the writing, layout. Instead of animals they used people."

"It has gone that far," said Gnurl thoughtfully. "I didn't think it would be so soon."

"What did you do?" Greta was holding the line while Gnurl's mind wandered.

"Undid the hex, I think, but it sure as hell will scare the shit out of anyone who sees it now."

"You used a chicken, didn't ya?"

"Yeah. The sheep was for you. And we have a couple more chickens, too, good layers. They were for another village, but it had been wiped out. We were supposed to get fuel there. You have any?"

"Some," Gnurl said. He was a man of few words.

"Can we get some tomorrow? All we have is the sheep and chickens, unless you want money. That we have more than enough of."

"We'll take some of that, too. You never know anymore."

"Hopefully, we'll fix that," Skender replied positively, trying to lighten the gloom. When seers can't see they are blind; like losing one of your physical senses, it's depressing.

"I wish we could be of more help," Greta said disappointedly.

"You already have been. You are here. We'll figure things out somehow. How bad does the road get? We have farther to go."

"The same. Wait, wait a minute..." Gnurl closed his eyes, the others remained silent. He was 'seeing' something.

Skender poured some more coffee and waited patiently while Greta poured some brandy into his cup then did the same to hers.

"You've got about a hundred kilometers before a landslide blocks the road. You may be able to get around it..." Gnurl was unsure of himself.

"Or over it if we can. There is always walking. Thank you, Gnurl."

"It was the first thing I've 'seen' in weeks, thank you," Gnurl replied.

"What can we do for you and Sechra, Skender?" asked Greta.

"The fuel, some bread. Whatever you can spare. We will be unloading a bunch of stuff to make the bikes lighter. You can have whatever we leave behind."

This was the gypsy way. Sharing. A certain quid pro quo. To give the riders bread would leave less for the camp. To not give them bread would be to break a tradition that had lasted centuries. No thought was put into, 'how much does it cost?' Everyone knew the cost and money wouldn't cover it, you can't eat money. The sheep and chickens would more than make up for the loaves of bread. The loose barter is a strange concept to the western mind. It's always value, value, value. Even without the animals for trade, Greta and Gnurl would have helped anyway. It was a small something of beauty and love in the midst of madness.

Around midnight, Skender hit the sack. Greta stayed up a little longer to finish the baking and renew Sechra's snow pack for her back. After leashing the sheep to a nearby tree, she put the chickens with the others of their flock. She then peeled the flatbread from the oven and wrapped them before sitting alone by the fire. There was something in Sechra's arrival that lifted the blindness from her mind. The images weren't clear, nor any answers given, but what she saw made her cry. Not for herself but for Skender and Sechra. They would not be coming back.

Morning broke with a staggering brightness, not a cloud in the sky. Skender had been working on the bikes since dawn, allowing Sechra to sleep in. When she woke, a cup of coffee was put in her cold hands without a word, giving her some peace while she packed up her personal belongings and strapped on the shotgun harness. Without the riding suit to cover it, she looked like one mean ass bitch that you didn't want to fuck with.

Gnurl did a double take when Sechra entered the 'kitchen' with her riding suit over one shoulder, the gun over the other and an empty cup of coffee. It was a hardcore look that Sechra had earned over the years shaping rock. Her hands, forearms, shoulders, and upper body were all oversized, for a woman, that is. It was her fingers though that impressed Gnurl, each a little sausage of muscle and callous. He wanted to shake her hands hard and put the squeeze on, but didn't, and not only out of respect. Gnurl figured he would lose.

"You have beautiful hands," he said taking her cup and refilling it.

"Thank you, Gnurl," she said taking the full cup. "Not many people would call them that."

"I can use a hand here," yelled Skender from the bikes.

Gnurl broke out laughing and Sechra joined in to enjoy the moment of synchronicity. Skender had removed his rear wheel and was in the process of changing the tire. Sechra's bike had dual-purpose rubber already.

"Ever use a tire iron before?"

"The riding course I took years ago explained how to use them."

"You remember?"

"Yeah."

"Well, have at it. Set the wheel on that 55 gallon drum so you don't have to work in the dirt."

Tire irons were pry bars and used to peel the tire from the rim. The bigger the iron, the easier it was to do. Skender had a small set. Sechra rolled the wheel to the drum and went to work. She remembered the basics, but her instructor didn't tell the class that it was really hard to do, which was the reason most people took their bikes to a shop. Fieldwork was always a challenge. Rarely did you have everything you needed and creativity was key to a successful repair.

Struggling with the small irons, Gnurl came over with a couple large screwdrivers to give her a hand.

"Ahh, leverage. Once again, thank you, Gnurl."

During the course of Gnurl's life he had done this particular operation many times. The motorcycle was easy as far as he was concerned. That is, compared to a car or a truck tire. Plus he wanted to get a feel for the girl. It helped to 'see' someone more clearly when you knew them. And there was nothing like working together to get to know someone. Verbal communication was one way to achieve this, but a poor one, for words were just so much bullshit. It wasn't necessary in this particular instance. He watched her hands, face, and, to a certain extent, her mind. Sechra's sense of purpose and determination stood out like neon signs. There was no dearth of strength and bravery. From what he could 'see' from her guarded expression and equally fortified mind, there was no fear either. He could feel the hatred and anger of the young girl who watched as she lost everything, paving the way for a darker thing to steal what remained. He saw a bitterness so strong it could carve itself into stone, immortalizing itself and wreaking havoc and madness on its world tour. He saw the words come out of his mouth before he could stop them.

"Are you prepared to die?"

"No," Sechra replied with a grunt as she shoved the new tire bead over the rim. "I don't plan on it. But neither am I afraid of losing it." She finished, answering his next question. A rushing hiss of air followed as Sechra filled the new tire with air from Gnurl's portable compressor. With a loud pop, the tire seated itself on the rim. Hearing it, Skender came over to inspect the work. It's a guy thing.

"Mmmm, not bad," he said.

"There is no way to balance it, but if the road ahead is anything like what we've already been on, it won't really matter..."

"But it does," Gnurl interrupted. "Skender, get the axle shaft. We'll get the balance close. Balance always matters, Sechra. You must never forget this. Darkness is balanced by light. You have been the darkness, Sechra. Now you must be the light."

"I'm missing something here."

"No, you are not, just hearing it for the first time." Gnurl was setting up a jury-rigged wheel balancer while Sechra learned about balancing a tire and her life. "The young know very little about balance and care even less. Strength and agility is all that is required to keep up the juggling act. It is only when you get older and can no longer keep up the pace that you try and find some balance. By then it is usually too late. The habits are set and there is less flexibility. You are at the mid-point between young and old and have a wicked karma to deal with. If you wish to grow old, then you need to understand balance, now!"

Skender brought the axle over and handed it to Gnurl, who slid the shaft into the wheel and lifted it into a cradle, giving the wheel a spin.

"Like you, Sechra," Gnurl began as he watched the spinning rubber. "Some men work hard all their lives never really taking the time for rest and when it comes, they cannot deal with it."

The tire came to a slow stop, rocking back and forth a few times. Gnurl took a small piece of lead and wrapped a spoke before giving it another spin.

"They are out of balance, having never spent enough time, doing nothing to appreciate it. There is a difference to doing nothing and doing nothing well." The wheel slowed, eventually coming completely still without any rocking motion. "That should do you, Skender."

"You sure made that look easy," responded Sechra.

"Years of practice, Sechra," Gnurl replied as he looked at his gnarly digits. "When my life was torn from me during the revolution twenty odd years ago, I was a man out of balance. Since then, I work on it every day. You, dear, won't have the opportunity. You have to get it right the first time. No learning curve for you."

"What are you talking about, Gnurl? Your metaphors work, but you are losing me."

"Not surprising. Words are no good for this kind of stuff. You are a woman of action. There will come a time when your mind will scream like a banshee to do something, when what you will need to do is nothing..."

"And do it well," Sechra finished for him.

"Yes."

"But it ain't now, Sechra. Come on – it's time to go." Skender was bolting the wheel back in place. "Gnurl topped the tanks this morning. Should be enough to get there and back. Will you and Greta be around here for a while?"

"The harvest is still a few weeks away. If you have not succeeded by that time it won't really matter."

"Just a little bright spot in everyone's day today, eh, Gnurl?" said Greta coming around from the cooking area with a bag in her hands. "It's not much, but it should be enough for a few days." From the weight it felt like more than a few days thought Sechra. Gnurl noticed the size of the bag, too.

"What are we going to eat?" he asked helplessly.

"Love, dear. It's all we've ever needed." She kicked Gnurl out of his melancholia. "You kids be careful."

Greta hugged them both and planted kisses on their foreheads. Tears formed in her eyes, dripping soundlessly into the dirt. She held Gnurl's hand as the two bikes weaved down the path and onto the road. The old couple held on to each other long after the sound of their engines had disappeared.

"What was that taradiddle I heard you telling Sechra about balance?" Greta asked Gnurl.

"I didn't know what else to say. It beat, 'you know you're going to die in those there mountains' and 'that it will be more horrible than anything you have ever lived through,' just didn't seem to cut it."

"It would have been the truth."

"I didn't hear you stepping up for it," Gnurl bickered lightly.

"It's because you are right. I have seen something," Greta said hesitantly.

"What is it?"

"I don't know," Greta replied solemnly.

Skender and Sechra rode on into the mountains. There were times when twin tracks would stretch out ahead and they would be able to open the throttles and make up for lost time. When the sun was overhead, they stopped for the first break, but it wasn't by intention. The tracks were mudded out and Sechra found herself on the wrong rut. In trying to cross over her bike bottomed out and slid sideways, and she went down in the muck. Once again, the horizontally opposed pistons saved her leg from getting crushed beneath the bike, but she was pinned to the ground. Skender had taken the lead an hour before and she hadn't seen him in the last forty-five minutes. At least she was on her back. Face down; she would have been in a really unfortunate position.

Adrenalin rushed through her like liquid fire when she felt the bike going out from under her. She had to use it and use it now, before the fight or flight instinct left her spent and wasted. Sechra tried the bench press to push the bike more vertical and slide her leg out. Her upper body strength didn't fail her but God, in his infinite wisdom, made her arms too short. Sechra felt very alone after the third try and alone could kill you. Already the muddy water was soaking through the open vents in her suit. If she was not free soon, hypothermia would start and that would be the end.

A flash, a moment of clarity as alcoholics called it, lit her mind with a possibility. It was a stretch, but that is what she needed. She reached around with her right arm and fully unzipped the vent under her left pit. As the zipper parted cold mud washed into the opening, inspiring Sechra with the freezing jolt. Pulling the shotgun, Sechra ejected the round in the pipe. She didn't want the thing to go off and kill the bike. She pressed the barrel of the gun into the side of the seat and started pushing, using the gun as a short pole to give her the extra centimeters the bike would need to be lifted to extract her leg. Her hands were slipping. With a final surge, the bike went upright before falling the other way. Sechra was scrambling just the same to get herself out of the mud and onto some dry ground to assess the situation and get her breath. A wise choice and one that is always forgotten in the moment. In the rush of dropping a bike, the first thing the rider wants to do is get it upright and right away, too. Pride, a little shame and embarrassment keep you from looking the situation over. Once it's down, it's not going anywhere, so what's the rush?

Skender's long strides carried him to the bottom of the gulch Sechra was stuck in. She was sitting on a rock smoking a cigarette when he loped up to her out of breath. Like Sechra he was covered in mud.

"What happened to you?" she asked flipping the stub of her smoke.

"Same as you. Just over the hill and around the bend. You okay?"

"Yeah."

"I'm surprised we haven't been doing this all day. It's just the shits," Skender exclaimed.

"Where are we going, Skender?"

"To the end of the road."

"And how far would that be?"

"Around the next corner, over the next hill. Basically that way." He pointed towards the cloud-shrouded mountaintops. We'll know when we get there."

"How come I get the feeling we're going nowhere, Skender?"

"Sometimes that is the best place to go." He paused, "Now let's see if we can get the bike up."

Curses turned to laughter after slipping in the mud and struggling to get it back on its wheels.

"You know you really had me there, Sechra. I thought you were going to pull that thing of yours and blow me to pieces."

"Plenty of time for that later, ya think?"

Skender didn't know what to think of the sardonic reply, so he shrugged his shoulders and said, "Get on. I'll give you a push to get you going."

"Nah, you ride it up, Skender. You can plant your feet better than me." It was a matter of trust. She had to trust him. There was no one else. He could leave her to freeze to death or be at the top of the hill when she finished slogging her way up.

Sechra leaned into the rear of the bike pushing as Skender slipped it into first gear. She learned how useless those little fenders were when it came to mud. She struggled to maintain control and push. And was losing. Later than sooner, the tires grabbed while Skender bobbed and weaved the bike up the mountain. She grabbed her gear and followed.

Indeed Skender did leave her bike at the top of the rise, idling in neutral, but he was nowhere to be seen. A trail of muddy footprints led down the road. Sechra tied on her gear and hopped on the bike and followed in slow pursuit. Road conditions were so bad you simply couldn't go any faster than a quick walking pace. Ahead she spied Skender starting his thumper. He waved that she should just keep going, so she did.

After another ten kilometers of the worst riding of her life, Sechra – cold, tired and hungry – had little more to give when the sight of four lanes of asphalt, lit shiny black by the sun, stretched out ahead of her. 'What the fuck?' Sechra uttered in the confines of her helmet as Skender's machine roared up beside her. He gave her a thumb's up followed by an 'okay' sign. She responded in kind. The 'okay' sign is one of those things that require a response. No response means things are not okay. Divers use it. Bikers use it. Any time you can't talk, the 'okay' sign puts it all in a nutshell. When Skender got it in reply, he signaled she should open it up and enjoy the road. Her big bike ate up the white lines at an ever quickening pace, leaving Skender just a speck in the rearview mirror.

Nine kilometers after the asphalt started large, aged, cracked, orange signs stood akilter, warning drivers that the road was ending. At ten kilometers exactly, a barrier of giant concrete blocks crossed the road. Sechra came to a stop. 'What the fuck?'

She had a cigarette lit and was pacing the block line when Skender came up. He shut his machine off and sat in the silence while he took off his helmet and gloves. Pulling a leather pouch from his pocket, he rolled a cigarette, lighting it. Sechra walked up to him.

"The mentality behind it was, if they started in the middle then it's halfway done already."

"Pretty fucking stupid."

"Well, it wasn't the greatest idea..." Skender began.

"I mean of me, to follow you all the way out here without more information," Sechra laughed, more to herself than with Skender.

"She said if we gave you the least amount of information, innocently enough, you would follow along like a trained dog. You'll have to understand that the phrase about the dog was in the old language, meaning that if you didn't know, you wouldn't sniff it out."

"I know the expression, Skender. I grew up in these mountains, remember? Who was it that told you to bring me here?"

"Out of respect, I gave my word that I would bring you here. There were no other stipulations."

"Who was it, Skender?" Sechra did not have to reach for her gun, though she did consider it.

"Your mother."

"My mother is dead. Killed by the minion of the bastard that ruled Romania for a while."

"The old castle is not far from here you know. Maybe thirty kilometers as the crow flies."

"Who is it, Skender?"

"Your other mother, Riana Cneajna."

"That bitch," Sechra said vehemently.

"She has been called worse and worse yet before this thing is over. This much I know, she wanted to get you here as quickly as possible."

"To keep me out of the way..." demanded Sechra.

"To keep you from being distracted. We are stuck here now until winter is spring. There is something you need to locate. It is hidden in a cave or catacomb." Skender pointed into the mountains.

"More disinformation?" asked Sechra sarcastically, as her mind labored to accept the reality. There was no going back. She flipped her cell phone and checked the weather. The first serious weather front of the season had been chasing them into the mountains. She closed the phone and her eyes. 'Goddamnit!'

"No, more like the end of it. I know how to find the cave, but you must help me."

"What is it that I am supposed to find?"

"You'll know when you see it," Skender squeaked, cringing away just a little, like a kid that had just been too clever with an adult and understood that sometimes the reaction was more like tough love without the love part.

"You got anything to drink, Skender?"

"Yeah, but let's unload first. There are some construction trailers on the other side of these." He waved his hand at the concrete barrier. The gaps between the blocks were wide enough to walk through but too narrow for the motorcycles.

The trailers were typical mobile construction offices, two of which had been converted to dorms. The 'office' was the only livable space, as it hadn't been lived in. Inside were crates and cartons of canned and boxed food filling one end and desks at the other end. It was obvious that someone had brought the goods up relatively recently and cleaned the place. There was no reason to ask Skender about this. She had been set up.

Sechra had known Riana most of her life. That Karuna and Riana had saved her, so many years ago, from a fate worse than death, was beyond a doubt. For this reason alone Sechra would do what was asked. She lit a fire in the small wood stove that would serve as heater and stove for the next few months. She warmed her hands over the crackling tinder as Skender brought in more wood, handing her a liter bottle with the second load.

"Pure grain alcohol. Should cure whatever ails you." He left for more wood with a couple of plastic tarps to throw over the bikes, but mostly to give Sechra some time to come to terms with the news. Besides he was stuck here, too, and had to find a way to cope as well. Aside from his front as a cocky biker dude, he was scared. His father would know what to do. Would he? He had not told Sechra that his family name was inscribed within the witches' circles along with the Kcirb's. Was any of his family still alive? 'Probably not,' he thought morosely. The darkness was moving too fast. They had barely gotten away in time...

The setting sun silhouetted pieces of heavy equipment left behind when the road building stopped. Skender felt like shit and heavy as the cold steel sitting on the frosted ground. Keeping his word had cost more than he realized at the time. He had grown to like Sechra and the deception had been killing him. At least it was over and out in the open now. Well, most of it anyway. His hand unconsciously went to an outer pocket where he kept the nine-millimeter pistol.

***

A hmed sat back on his heels next to the woolen bed as he set the pipe into its resting place. As Karuna drifted off in a nod, he shook his head trying to decide what to do. When he returned in the morning after spending the night procuring more opium of the highest quality, it didn't take him long to realize there had been some serious changes taking place while he was away.

At the crack of dawn, he entered the sleeping chamber to find Karuna pacing the floor. She was flush from a feeding, that much was obvious, but he had expected to come back to Dracine, not Karuna. There was a knock at the door. Small footsteps brought a large carafe of coffee. Ahmed took it from the child, closed the door, then set the tray on a low table and poured for both of them.

"Good morning," he said handing Karuna a cup. "I take it there is no need for formalities this morning."

"Nor will there be in the future. I have taken control. I have found a way."

"I see. I didn't think you would take my advice so literally."

"I have no desire to be stuck here. And this shit at this time and place has gone on long enough."

"Are you sure it's such a good idea?"

"What else did we come here for if not to change things? You just said it best. Things have to change, literally."

"It can't be done."

"It can, I am already doing it. But I can't do it alone for long."

Ahmed sat back, unsure of himself for the first time in, let's say, a long time. For lifetimes, centuries, millennia or two, he had lived within the realm of the mosaics, never really doing anything. Simply experiencing without living. Without the risks and dangers, responsibilities and duties that come with life, living is barely tolerable. Forever it seemed, he had contented himself with every pleasure known to man and a few we only dream of. But in the end, it was masturbation, physical or mental and therefore, of no consequence. When the pleasures no longer satisfied, he tasted the suffering. Of this he knew but a little. His torture had been short and death not long after. But the flavor of endurance sufferers was not as sweet as he could bear. When your next breath could be your last goes on for years, it becomes a sour, rancid spoilage of the human soul. They endured not because they could but because they had to. 'Why' is too deep a question to fathom here.

Here, now, before Ahmed was a chance, his chance to live. It did not come as he expected or dreamed it would be or even thought that it could really possibly happen. Opportunity yawned before him and he recoiled in fear. It was the one thing he really wanted. All he had to do was reach out and take it. Make a decision to make a difference. Take the chance. He saw himself failing and it scared the shit right out of him.

"Just tell me what it is you need and I will try and be of service." Ahmed was lying to Karuna and himself. When he was out procuring the opium, the dealer had offered him the finest available. Ahmed sampled the product only to wake hours later, highly satisfied; this would come in handy for his plans to work. He was preparing to have to dope the daylights out of Dracine. The twist of fate, that now left Karuna in place, changed dramatically what Ahmed had in mind, but either way he would have had to deal with a strong-willed woman. Luckily what worked for the one would also work for the other. All Ahmed wanted right now was to keep his world intact. He had tasted living and did not like it.

"There will be no court today. I want to review the contracts and laws before making any more judgments."

"I can get the scrolls together, say, after lunch?"

Karuna looked at her wrist, but the watch that would normally be there, of course, wasn't. "Sure, I suppose that would do."

"Good," Ahmed smiled, "more smoke?" He smiled bigger with all the charm he could muster.

"Sure, again? More coffee too?"

"Sure," he laughed conspiratorially. Ahmed took the pipe to a table to prepare the mélange. The sticky black opium created an ass-kicking concoction that Karuna would never suspect. He would be able to effectively thwart her newfound enthusiasm with regular dosing. If she became a problem, the dealer also taught him about overdosing.

Ahmed left after filling the pipe for Karuna. He did not notice that Karuna, after her infusion the night before, had become hyper-aware. When he lied to her she had felt it, bringing her into a focus on Ahmed. She couldn't tell what was on his mind, but deception stood out like flashing red light. He was also intent upon the pipe, like a person that's told not to use their cell phone. They just can't stop thinking about it. When he filled the pipe she watched him, even though his back was turned. She watched his reflection in a mirror and saw him dump in the new product. Jake and Johnny had taught her much about such things. Their bad habits just might save her life.

Three slaves, burdened with scrolls returned with Ahmed just after lunch. They had been waiting the last hour for Karuna/Dracine to finish the meal. Karuna may have cast protocol to the wind, but Ahmed wasn't about to. 'If Karuna goes down pursuing her own agenda she will go down alone,' he thought. All morning long he had been thinking of ways to cover his ass. He still had a few aces up his sleeve. Karuna's own dark nature could be used as a tool for her demise. He knocked.

"Come," said Karuna as she paced the floor. Pacing was not Karuna. It was a Dracine thing and Dracine's body. Body memory kept the habits alive. Karuna knew she would have to be vigilant in watching herself for more signs of intrusion. How often she would have to take the life of another to keep the charade intact was another question. The knock. 'And then there is Ahmed,' who had gone from confidant to a burden in the course of a few hours. She questioned herself for being the problem, but found no answers. It had to be Ahmed.

The door opened with Ahmed stepping in to the sort of living room. The slaves waited to be called. The pipe sat on the table where he had left it. It was still full, unburned.

"I see you have had a busy morning," he said trying not to look at the pipe.

"Highly educational to say the least. I had the cook make me some coffee."

"Perhaps we should get some more then." Ahmed waved to the slaves, who, with heads down came into the living room and placed the parcels where Ahmed indicated. After they departed he said, "You haven't smoked?

May I? God knows the marketplace was a nightmare this morning," he added to cover his anxiety.

"Go ahead. You know Ahmed, that smoking business is more of a Dracine thing than me. I think I'll pass for a while."

"That is not such a good idea, Karuna. You may inhabit her body and mind, but it is her body. If you do not smoke soon you will go into withdrawal."

"Hmmm. Nope don't want to go there," she replied affecting a Jakeism. She had seen this moment coming. Some time before Ahmed returned, she had done a little speed from Jake's medical kit so that when they did sit to smoke she would still be able to function. Ahmed offered her the pipe and she took several big hits before handing it back. Sweat beaded on her forehead as a nauseating feeling accompanied the rush. She lurched for the commode.

Usually Ahmed would have been there with a cool cloth and gilt bowl for her to relieve the unpleasant side effects of a heavy dose. He was not. In this single act of insolence, she saw the dark side of the man she thought she knew. 'Would this have happened had I not taken Lenes' life?' Her answer was 'probably.' There are times when the universe acts in synchronicity with our lives. And times when it does not. Either way, the timing couldn't be worse. She needed him on her side, not someone who will feed her rope until she hangs herself. He was now a saboteur of her plans and had to be treated with kid gloves, for she still needed him. Karuna was knowledgeable about twelfth century Romania, but not fluent. 'I can always kill him,' she thought puking into the clean commode. The irony of her idea brought a sardonic laughter to her lips along with the bile and coffee. Her plan involved no more killing. Even Jake did not kill indiscriminately, normally. Only when it was necessary and even then it took its toll on his soul.

'The problem with killing people is you remember each and every one down to the finest detail,' Jake once admitted, 'and you can't stop thinking about it.' Karuna did not want her mind filled with the dead. It was already getting cluttered. Lenes' cracked, split and chewed toenails were the screensaver of her imagination. She had looked at them when she drained the life from the Boyar's body as they sat on the dining table next to his plate. Now she couldn't get rid of the imagery.

"Ay carumba," she said getting to her feet. She laughed to herself again, a little lighter this time. Why was it that when she was stoned, she said things Jake would say? Little stupidisms, that seemed to lighten the load. Dumb private jokes to keep yourself from screaming into the depths of madness. Idiotic reminders to stave the desire to take everything too personally. She would use them a lot in the coming months.

"Very nice, Ahmed. I should have taken your advice earlier," Karuna amended in an attempt to mollify Ahmed's attitude.

"I always have your best interests in mind," he replied with a touch of condescension that was so common in a P.A.'s demeanor. When you have seen your boss at their worst and let them get away with it without calling them out, you have to rise above it somehow. Combined with his change of heart, the phrase was downright insulting. The dope helped Karuna blow it off and smile instead as she wiped the sweat away. The rush was settling. She had plateaued and eyed the stacks of scrolls.

Ahmed was ever in touch with the nuance of royalty. "The pile on your left are the laws. The center is the current state of affairs of the court. The one on the right are your past judgments."

"You don't have it on a computer, do you?"

The query put Ahmed in neutral. He looked at her incredulously. "What?"

"Geez Ahmed, I was just joking. Lighten up." Karuna moved the laws to her day bed and spread them out. She did not however take her own advice and spent the next six hours reading the laws of the state and how they were to be applied.

That each and every law favored the Boyar class came as no shock. 'Some things will never change,' she thought. The laws were for the peasants, not the upper class. In fact, there were no laws for Boyars. They could do anything they wanted, within reason, and sometimes, even reason didn't matter. As an example, Lenes was an overweight, out of shape and lazy Boyar. He could not have chewed his own toenails if he wanted to. Someone had to do it.

The only time the Boyars got into trouble was when there were personal conflicts with the magistrate, or worse the Voivode, as in the case of Lenes. The reasons though were always the same. Jealousy, avarice, power, were always the prime culprits. What is it that makes us always want more than we need? There it was, the word 'more'. There was never enough of it. The more you had the more you wanted to have. In the early 2000s, two percent of the world's population consumed twenty-five percent of the resources. Go figure. Did that two percent have enough? Never!

This was where the magistrate, and ultimately the Voivode, acted as a meat grinder to keep the balance correct. To check the greed and stupidity before the two toppled the empire and the country fell into anarchy, again. Dracine's half brother, Vlad the III, had already set the precedence of a cruel yet insanely just system. Dracine merely applied the new tools extremely effectively, retooled the definition of cruelty and rewrote the protocol to administer it, in order to maintain control over her district.

Karuna was going to change things, but she had to know the rules of the game first. The trick was making the change without anyone realizing it was happening. Use the rules to change the way the game was played, then change the rules. That was the plan in a nutshell. She knew her history. Vlad III would only be in power another year or two; he would be assassinated by his brother, Radu. Though Vlad would hang around for a few more centuries, he would never again return to power. Karuna had no desire to mess with the bigger history any more than she had to. Just this one little piece of it.

She needed time to find out what it was that Dracine did to tap the depths of evil that lie within us all. How did she do it? What did she do? Had it already happened? Was there still time to keep it from manifesting? Karuna did not know how long it would take to discover the answers. 'If I can keep it from happening in the first place, the web of darkness spreading across the globe in the form of Sechra's sculptures would not be.'

It hit Karuna with a flash. "Ahmed, I need to go back."

He had been sitting in the other room, waiting to be called. "But your work here, I thought..."

"This work will take more than a weekend to attend to. I must go back to my time and stop someone who will get herself killed uselessly if I don't," Karuna said assertively.

"The girl, Sechra?"

"Yes. She will take it upon herself to resolve what she considers her doing."

"Yes. She was a tool."

"And I am a fool," Karuna laughed to herself remembering the last time she heard someone say that. "How do you do it?"

"In my experience, the return takes you back to where you started. From the moment you left, time has stopped, but just for you. In your reality several days have passed. But when you go back you still have to live out that time. Making any sense?" he asked.

"Sort of. What about coming back here?"

"It is the same. You pick up where you left off. Before you leave here you must memorize every aspect of this moment in time so that you may recall it again, clearly, when you stand before the mosaics."

"So it is the tiles that create the phenomenon?"

"No," Ahmed continued his lesson, "It is the location. I do not know how it works. It just does."

"But the doorway never worked prior to the revolution?"

"No. Not the way it does now. Since creating it, I have always had the ability to travel between the frames of the mosaics but never into the present. When you removed, or shall I say your daughter removed the one evil called Tepes, that simply made space for another to takes its place. Like the corporate ladder, when the rung above you is suddenly clear, you climb to take it. Thus, Tepes' hoarded the upper rungs. When he was deposed...it's the unnatural response."

"That's a strange way to put it."

"Yes, but it works. Business is as far from nature as man can get. Notice how he gives up everything in the pursuit of the filthy lucre. Man cannot control nature, so he unnaturally gravitates to that which he thinks he can control. The ironic part is that, at the end of the day, man is no longer in control. Never was."

"An illusion?"

"Everything is illusion, Karuna. You above all should know that."

"Thank you for opening my eyes," Karuna replied wryly. In Ahmed's attempt to be helpful and charming he let it slip, intimating that even he was an illusion and therefore not to be trusted. He noticed her notice and cursed himself for the faux pas. The walls came down again; like a lion tamer whose lions have escaped, he locks the door of the empty cage.

"Do you wish to come with me? I could use some help." Karuna did not rub it in, but tried to use it to keep him from retreating entirely within his paranoid mind. It almost worked.

Ahmed hesitated before replying. Karuna could 'see' he was trying to spin the current affairs to his advantage. 'He's overthinking it,' she thought.

"No. No, this is your affair. I only travel when my presence is truly needed," Ahmed mocked, respectfully. "Since you will return to this moment, I have but to wait."

"I respect your choice, Ahmed," replied Karuna, who made every effort to remove the barbs and points from her words after being dissed. Ahmed would read enough between the lines without her help.

Karuna poured the last of the coffee while she paced the room. The pacing, once again, was pure Dracine, but Karuna was using it to create a picture of the room. The window treatments were pulled wide to let in the warm sea breeze that ruffled them lightly. Spots of illumination were candles lit atop furniture. All was gloomy. They weren't called the 'dark ages' for nothing. The dim lighting at night was a thing you had to get used to after a lifetime of intense illumination. Furniture, what little there was, tended to be clusters of pillows around low tables. The southeastern Mediterranean influence was obvious, made for comfort and practicality. In the sunlight, the colors were deep and bright. But at night the hues went fuscous with only the darkest reds adding color, forest greens and burnt umber shining through. The whole effect was easy on the eyes. Considering Dracine's habit...Stars twinkled weakly beyond the open window as if they too passed through a layer of shadow and smut before being allowed to enter. When she felt she had it, Karuna drained her cup and set it on the table next to Ahmed and the pipe. She didn't want to leave him, but she had to.

"Be back in a few moments." She tried to make light as she concentrated on the hallway of the estate at Eforie Sud. Karuna, using her imagination, brought up the image around her. When it was as complete as she could get it, Karuna stepped into the illusion.

The warm summer night was whisked away to be replaced with the chill of the late fall along the coast. The estate had never been heated. She rubbed at the goose bumps on her arms and headed to the kitchen. The first order of the day was coffee. Good coffee.

In the fridge was the second order. Bags of crimson fluid were stacked to one side within easy reach. She checked the dates and made a cocktail of one, with another going into a slim cooler and then into her bag. She was going to be traveling fast and light. Karuna chased away the iron taste with the last of the coffee she had made earlier. Dawn was still a few hours away as she left the estate through a side entrance. Karuna did not want to go through the ritual of rolling up the big steel doors and dealing with the alarm system. In fact she didn't want anyone to know she was here to begin with. With the door locked behind her, Karuna went to the courtyard. Her memory played back the despicable events that had occurred out here over the years. 'They're not over yet,' laughed Karuna at something that wasn't all that funny. Horrible things had happened. That's an infusion for you. Like getting high, you were able to find humor in just about any situation. A sick sort of black humor, that was. Couple that with the feeling that you could do anything, made you do just that. Karuna cleared her head and sprinted for the far wall. Just before reaching it, she leapt into the cold morning air. A shadow headed north along the coast, away from the estate. Karuna used the lights along the waterfront towns to guide her. When she reached the port at Constanta she turned west, into the mountains. From here, there would be no more 'sign posts'. She would be 'flying by the seat of her pants,' as Jake would say. This time the laugh was wild, echoing into the void of night.

Ahmed jumped from his seat moments after Karuna set her coffee cup down, to catch the falling Dracine. Karuna's inhabitation left the magistrate spent and unconscious. He carried her to the sleeping quarters, undressed her and put Dracine to bed. Two heavyish pouches were concealed in the folds of her clothing. One held the gun, the other, a bag of drugs. Ahmed inspected the contents to find it full of 'up' drugs. The kind that inhibit sleep. 'So that's how she did it,' he exclaimed to no one. He began to laugh, loud, hard and ugly. The sound of it warbled through the castle halls, chilling even the most hardened of slaves for it was the laugh of death. With Karuna gone, his plan could now be put into effect. Ahmed figured he had several days to a week before she would return. Time enough to corrupt Dracine with the powerful mixture of opiates and make her useless for Karuna to manipulate. Shortly after her return, the drugs would take their toll on Karuna, too, ruining the woman and making her a puppet for Ahmed to use.

***

Sechra woke to shivering cold and a brutal hangover. She was pissed. If anger could light a fire, the trailer would have been burning. Instead, she crawled to the woodstove and lit new wood off the smoldering embers. Looking around in the eerie light of dawn, she saw the place had been well stocked. Riana must have anticipated her arrival. Skender was snoring as the fire took hold. Sechra wasted little time bundling up in cold weather gear and putting on the hiking boots. She waited impatiently for a cup of yesterday's coffee to warm. Stepping outside, Sechra was blasted by a frigid wind blowing down the mountain's side, stopping her in her tracks. Autumn was over. Since the trailer was well supplied, she decided to take stock of what else was available in the old road-building yard. Heavy equipment dominated the scene. Dozers, forklifts, graders, dump trucks and front-end loaders were all parked in neat rows. Dusted with a layer of debris from sitting for a dozen years, they looked liked they were still ready to roll. The place had the feeling that it was deserted. The previous occupants had packed up in a hurry, taking only their personal gear and leaving the company equipment to rot, this much was obvious.

'Men,' she thought, angry, her head pounding. 'Women would not have left the place like this.' The tools had been stored carefully. The rest was a shambles. Sechra wandered between the rows of machinery and housing in the still of the morning. The more she looked, the more it seemed that the evacuation was more immediate than she had originally surmised. The personal belongings of the work crew were still where they had been dropped, not taken but buried beneath the debris of seasons. The morning's breeze carried more than the smell of smoke issuing from the trailer's woodstove. The smell of rotten meat wafted into her nostrils. Sechra followed her nose.

Set back from the construction yard, in the woods, was another structure. It was old, much older than the trailers and storage sheds. The closer Sechra came to it, the stronger the smell. She circled the building. Generators were stored behind the granite-blocked bunker. It had no windows and only one door. Heavy iron hinges and lock secured the entry. The odor which brought her here was now overwhelming. The smell coupling with her hangover brought Sechra to her knees, puking for all she was worth. Remnants of last night's dinner, booze and coffee flushed from her onto the ground until she was left spent, still vomiting, but there was no more to come out. One more heave and she was sure her guts would be left at the door as well. They weren't. Puking seemed to revive her to a certain degree. Enough to see the crevices, between the granite stones, where the grout had been worn away by time. One gap was deep enough. Her fingers swept the opening, searching for something, the key. The skin peeled back across her knuckles as it chafed the rough rock. There! She couldn't see it, but her fingers felt the smooth surface of a man-made object. The key. Sechra placed her fingers on top of it and slid the metal skeleton key out. Her frosted digits were not quick enough to grab it before the key fell into her gelid vomit. Fishing through the slush she retrieved it and inserted it into the lock. Sechra took a deep breath and turned the key.

The rusted mechanism resisted, but time and the elements had not ruined the action. With a snap the bolt opened and the door began to screech on its hinges as it swung inward. A gust of fetid air assaulted her again, as her eyes watered to the gasses emitted during decomposition and adjusted to the gloom within. Sechra gagged at the smell, but held it down. At least most of it. The acrid taste of bile swirled in the back of her throat before she forced it back where it belonged. Her head spun as the light from the open door penetrated the single room. Expecting no less than bodies piled high, she was shocked and relieved to find it empty with the exception of a peculiarly large stone set in the center of the room, a table with a half full bottle of vodka on it, and a broken chair, that was all. Stepping toward the table, Sechra tripped on a hasp that held closed a hatch in the floor, near the wall. The table and chair were forgotten.

On her hands and knees Sechra fumbled with the hasp. There was no lock, just a pin slid through a hole kept it secure. She pulled the pin. There was no doubt in her mind that the source of the stench was underneath. There were no handles or way to gain a purchase on the lid to raise it. She needed tools. A pry bar would do. Suddenly the light was gone. Sechra spun around to see if the door had closed, as she grabbed for her shotgun. In her haze she had forgotten it. 'Shit!' Sechra stood and backed up a few paces to give her more room only to see that Skender had found her. His stature filled the doorway.

"I suppose you'll be needing one of these," he said, leaning on a flat bladed shovel.

"Jesus Christ, Skender! You nearly scared the shit of me!"

"Smells like it." His sarcasm was lost in the darkness of the moment. Skender stepped into the room and away from the door. The light returned. "I found this place on one of the supply runs. Never had as much curiosity as you though."

"What happened here, Skender?"

"I don't know but I think we're going to find out," he replied as he dug the blade into the space at the perimeter of the hatchway. He leaned into the lever, gradually putting all of his weight onto it. The wooden door in the floor did not budge. "Unnnh, son of a bitch!" He tried several other points with no success. "There's got to be a way," he said more to himself than Sechra, while he pulled out a flashlight.

Skender panned the light over the floor and across the walls. Nothing. It wasn't until he shone the light into the rafters that his question was answered. Directly above the hatch was a block and tackle rig that must have been used to raise and lower it.

"Sechra, here, hold this." Skender handed the light to her while he lifted the shovel to dislodge the coil of rope that ran through the blocks. It fell to the floor, bringing a cascade of dust along with it. They both coughed and spit the smut from their mouths as the cloud settled. "Keep the light on my hands while I rig this."

Sechra held the light steady while her mind wandered to the darkness that entered her as a child. At eight, she had been too young to make such a decision. She thought she had hidden from the wisp of darkness as it pursued her below the deck of Barge#22. In the moment, Sechra had forgotten the extended family that Karuna offered her. She only remembered the loss of her own and the morbid feelings that came along with it. Alone and afraid, she gasped when the curl of blackness discovered her hiding place. It paused at the door and did not dash at her as she had remembered. It called out to Sechra. I call it 'it', for there is no name for the malevolence that swirled in the darkness before the girl. It, too, was alone and fearful that it would cease to exist, and so naturally gravitated to one of a like nature. Sechra, with her family destroyed before her eyes, had nurtured the deepest of hatred for what had been done, along with a vengeful wrath that was so like 'it'. The two, in their twisted despair, reached out for one another for the satisfaction of a kindred spirit. As mentioned, Sechra was too young to make such a choice.

Skender broke her ruminations. "There's no lifting 'eye', Skender said half to himself.

"What, huh? I was thinking about something else. What did you say?" replied Sechra.

"The lid has no way to attach a rope. I mean there was one, but it's gone now."

Sechra got down on her knees next to Skender, shining her light closer to where he was examining.

"See these bolt holes?"

Sechra nodded, "Mmmhmmm..."

"Well they must have secured a lifting hook or eye to the lid. Whoever closed it didn't want it to be opened again."

"Considering what must be under there..."

"Come on, let's go have breakfast. Then we can look around the tool shop for something to bolt to the hatch."

"You go along, I'll be right behind you."

"Don't take too long. Fresh coffee and eggs. After the drinking we did last night we could sure use it."

"Just give me a few minutes." Sechra began to look closely at the stone in the middle of the floor. It was a perfect piece of granite. In all her years of carving, Sechra had never seen one as ready for the chisel as this.

"All right, fifteen minutes and eggs are on." With little reluctance Skender left the stinking confines of what he considered a brick shithouse.

With Skender's departure, a deep silence settled into the room, giving Sechra's mind a chance to wander further into the gash that revealed memories she had long since hidden. The manic way at which she delved into her carvings allowed her to bury the recollections of her youth beneath a pile of rock chips. Each blow of the hammer put them farther out of touch. That is until this moment. Then, like the undead, the horror reached up through the burial mound, exposing the hideous nature that had been the basis for her sculpting.

Sechra chilled at the sudden emergence of her past and insidious relationship with the darkness that lives in some small way within us all. Except with Sechra, it was a full measure, to overflowing. She had been running her hands across the face of the stone, feeling its mana, which was great, and was drawn to it. 'What did it want to be?' she mused darkly and turned to leave.

Suddenly the screeching of rusted iron hinges was deafening in the confines of the building. Just as quickly, the light was gone with the resounding slam of the big entry door. Sechra closed the space between the door and herself a little too expeditiously, misjudging the distance and faceplanting into the solid oak planks. Stars shone briefly, spinning around inside her head, before succumbing to unconsciousness.

The darkness was so complete she couldn't see her hand in front of her face and wasn't entirely sure she was even awake. A solid pinch to her thigh solved that issue. Not only was she awake, but the knots on her forehead ached painfully where the door connected with her face.

Perhaps it was best that Sechra woke to the pain, giving her something to focus on before the reality of her situation took hold. When it did, she cringed in despair. The memory of the present threw her back 20 years into the nightmare beneath the outhouse seating with her grandfather. The memory brought up the remainder of the previous night's debauchery, leaving her spent, in the cold sweat of fear. Her eyes searched the darkness for light, any light. There was none. The weather may have worn the chinking on the outside but the inside was tight, the roof solid. It was morning when she entered. How long had she been out? It could very well be night.

Sechra's mind was a black scream that would not stop. Using the wall as a guide she followed it around the room to the table, where the vodka was. Sechra had to silence herself and tilted the bottle. Two healthy slugs later, the alcohol began doing what it does so well. As her mind went still, the sound of distant pounding came from the other side of the door. Walking carefully to the door, Sechra laid her palms on the planks, feeling the banging of what she assumed was Skender, futilely trying to open the door. She could almost hear him yelling her name, almost. Her hands felt about the perimeter of the door for a locking mechanism. There was none, only a ring meant for pulling the door open. Sechra grabbed the handle and put her weight into the pull. She strained for all she was worth. At one point both her feet were on the doorjamb while both hands put their all into the unforgiving moment. The ring wiggled before popping free, sending Sechra crashing to the floor. She cried quietly.

After a time of self-pity and desperation her brain came back online; the thinking, logical, problem solving part, that is. Of course the only thing that did was have her realize the hopelessness of her situation. As the vodka soothed her fried nerves, Sechra was beginning to get a handle on her emotions when the sound of metal against rock grated loudly into the room. For a moment a pulse of hope surged through her, but when the floor began to tilt all hope was dashed. She had been standing on the hatch in the floor. It opened with a belch of foul air. Sechra coughed, stumbling off the hatch and scrambling behind the granite boulder. Even though she could not see, a presence, darker than the blackness that surrounded her, rose from the opening in the floor.

Its voice sounded like entrails being crushed between two stones. Sechra had heard it before.

"Welcome to my world, dear Sechra," it rasped.

With a sudden intake of breath, Sechra realized what it was. It was the darkness that comforted her so long ago.

"You remember. I was wondering if you would."

"How could I not? I have done your work for more than twenty years and I regret it."

"You have done our work, dear one. I still remember how you embraced me."

"I was a child," spat Sechra.

"As was I, long before you were a glimmer in your father's eye."

Sechra slapped the air before her at the crude remark.

It laughed, dark, slow and foul. "Your emotions still fail you. Aeons before you, as a child, I accepted the darkness, not unlike yourself, and have become it. Now it is your turn. That you were a child when you made the choice is somewhat of a moot point."

"I refuse to accept this. I did not know what I was doing, or understand the consequences." Sechra was coming to the realization that she was suckered.

"Why do think I chose you, a child? Look at what your hatred, with my guidance, has created. Works of art unlike anything the world has ever witnessed. And now it spreads like an oil slick across the sea of humanity."

"My God, what have I done?" Sechra asked of herself.

"Your God didn't have anything to do with it. You have laid the ground work for your final sculpture." A banging and clanging ensued, sounding like metal being dropped on the floor.

Sechra knew the clunks to be sculpting tools as she had heard the sounds before when she would drop or fling a hammer and chisel away in frustration.

"I won't carve for you anymore!"

"Perhaps not, but you will carve if you have any desire to leave this place."

"Never," Sechra screamed at the darkness.

"Never means you will. That is unless you wish to starve to death in this oubliette, this place where prisoners are left to die. It scares you, does it not, to be in a shithole again after all these years? Where you first nurtured your dreams of hatred and revenge, knee deep in your enemies' excrement."

"I wish I had died..." Sechra was cut off abruptly.

"You did not. You survived and together we will rule the world!"

"Never!"

"Ever the child, dear Sechra," it said quietly. "Accept your fate!" The bellow of incipient evil bowled her across the floor, into the pile of tools and against the rotting mire that was 'it'.

Sechra recoiled at her proximity to the stench and mass of death that kept her from falling into the opening in the floor. She crawled away to the comfort of the stone and embraced the granite.

"That is good. Hold the rock. Get to know it. Feel my form within it so that you may remove the parts that do not belong and thus release me. Tomorrow I will come to guide you in your work. There is food and water on the table. Do not waste it. You will need your energy."

"I will need coffee, lots of it."

With that said, there was a wet sucking sound followed by the grating of rock against steel. It was gone.

Sechra sat back against the granite boulder in disbelief. Well, not disbelief in that she didn't believe it; more stunned that it was actually happening would be more appropriate. A part of her had always known this day would come, when she would have to face what was behind her eyes. That it did not come as she imagined would be an understatement. Her carvings bore the nature of the worst man had to offer. Cruelty and agony executed with extreme detail were her trademarks.

What she was realizing now was that the last twenty years were spent mastering the skills necessary to carve that which man was never meant to gaze upon; the essence of evil, personified.

***

High above the mountains Karuna fought against the cold as she followed the path/road that Sechra had ridden deep into the unknown. Far below she spied the settlement where Sechra had met with Urloff. She spiraled down, following a flock of ravens to a clearing in the woods about a kilometer from the village of gypsies. Karuna hit the ground, dropping to her knees in exhaustion. For the life of her, she couldn't figure how Jake and Johnny did this sort of thing and continued to function. Then she remembered their drug intake. Standing, Karuna realized it wasn't the drugs so much as will power, overcoming your personal limitations in pursuit of that which had to be done.

Will power separates the men from the boys, the doers from the wannabees. She took a few moments to stretch out the kinks of traveling, while giving her mind a chance to get on the same page as her desire. With her wits gathered, Karuna made the first steps along the trail that would take her to the heart of the village.

Her will kept her moving forward and also transformed her into the garb and look of a traveling gypsy. All she had to do was concentrate to keep the illusion from disappearing. One hundred meters from the encampment, the trees began to move, or rather, men who been at watch emerged from the foliage until she was surrounded. One man stepped forward into the clearing to face Karuna.

"This is gypsy land. What business do have you being here?"

"I am looking for my daughter," said the hag in rags.

"You will not find her here," came the stern voice of Urloff.

"I know, but she did come this way." Karuna pointed at the ground where the tire tracks of Sechra's motorcycle were frozen in the gelid mud.

"There are those who have passed through, but it is doubtful that they made it to wherever they were going," admitted Urloff.

"Why?"

"Because there is nothing alive past this point. What is your name?" asked Urloff.

"My name is of no importance. I only ask which direction they were headed."

"Your name, or you will go no further."

Karuna hesitated for a moment while she read into Urloff's statement. Her disguise of a peasant should not have brought the trees to life with guns. These people were afraid. Karuna felt the nervous sweat of the men hidden in the shadows and heard their weapons as the safeties were switched off.

"I am but an old woman searching for..."

"Yes, your daughter, your name please. I will not ask again."

Karuna stepped towards Urloff. "My name is Dracine..."

BANG! The shot blasted through the trees hitting Karuna in the chest, just above the heart. The large caliber round knocked her backwards, head over heels into the darkness at the side of the road.

"Who fired?" Urloff yelled at his companions. But it was too late, the screaming had begun. Like a bat eating bugs out of the night sky,

Karuna whirled through the surrounding forest disabling all the men hidden in the woods. Not killing, mind you, just leaving them unable to cope for a little while. She smashed their guns and put an elbow to the backs of their heads in the moments that followed. Urloff was the last. He had turned to run, pistol still in its holster, when Karuna was suddenly standing before him. She reached out, grabbing Urloff by the collar and raising him off the ground until his feet were dangling. Blood poured from her wound, thick and black. The smell of Urloff's fear dripped from his pantlegs.

"Why, Urloff, when I meant no harm?" Karuna flung him to the ground violently. Urloff's head bounced off a rock, leaving him dazed and bleeding.

"We are dying," he said weakly as the blood leaked from a split in his scalp. "One of my men panicked when he heard your name."

"Is this the same treatment my daughter received?"

"No, no, no! We fed her and gave her a guide into the mountains. It is where she wanted to go."

'At least he is telling the truth,' Karuna said to herself, 'but there is no reason to let him know that.'

"Which way did they go?" Karuna coughed up a copious amount of blood onto Urloff's face, as the bullet had gone through her lung. It was not her desire to puke on the old fool, but it would keep up his truth quotient.

Urloff pointed in a westerly direction. "Winter has taken hold on the mountains. There is no way to get there, or them back. We must wait until spring."

"The road conditions matter not to such as I."

"It's not the weather that I speak of. A barrier has been put in place. It is not a physical blockade, but it stops all who would try to pass it. I sent some men to follow Sechra Kcirb and keep her safe. After three days of trying to circumnavigate the blockade they returned. No one knows where she is or even if she is alive." Urloff was sticking to the truth, this much Karuna could tell, but was still not about to let her guard down.

"I will find out whether you are lying or not. Pray for your family that you speak the truth."

Through the glaze of blood that ran down his face, Urloff saw the shadow rise above him and disappear into the dusk.

Karuna continued heading west, clutching her breast to keep the hole from pumping too much blood out. The pain of the bullet lodged between two of her back ribs was nothing compared to the torment in her heart. For some reason she could not 'feel' Sechra as she always had been able to do. Searching as hard with her mind as she could, Karuna was drawing blanks. Some thing was blocking it.

She settled into an abandoned camp. The only structure, a dilapidated house that had collapsed into a lean-to of sorts, would serve her needs well enough. Karuna had to stop the bleeding and get the bullet out before she could travel further. Like Jake and Johnny, Karuna carried a kit. A medical kit with all sorts of must haves, that is with the exception of another hand. She pulled a scalpel, her longest pair of forceps, some gauze, a suture needle and dental floss. From a hip flask, Karuna took a long pull on the little container of bourbon, flushing her with warmth and calm. The hole in her chest was round and somewhat larger than the diameter of her thumb. Blushing at her vanity, she was, however glad the bullet had missed her breasts. Four stitches later Karuna took another shot and considered the bullet between her back ribs. With her left had she was able to reach around and feel with her fingertips. After a little searching Karuna felt the flattened nose of the bullet sticking out. Not through the skin mind you, more like a boil that the skin stretched painfully over.

Working blind is always tricky, but working with your left hand, in a contorted position was next to impossible. Karuna imagined her back and hand. When she had them fully in her mental grasp. She closed her eyes and went to work. The scalpel blade brushed over the bump back and forth several times until Karuna was sure of her mark. At that point she turned the blade perpendicular to the skin, slicing across the protrusion, through the skin until she felt the blade dragging on the lead.

Groaning loudly, Karuna set the scalpel down. Picking up the forceps, she checked the action and grip before pretzeling her arm into position. Hunt and peck. Hunt and peck. After pinching herself good a few times, she was finally able to grab the full metal jacket. She pulled on it. The pain almost forced her to stop, but the forceps slipped, stopping the procedure instead. Karuna poured sweat and grunted between clenched teeth. 'Goddamnit!' she yelled, more for the release than for anyone to hear. The bullet was stuck. She had to spread her ribs a little for the next try. Another shot, another try. Karuna bent forward, putting her chest on her lap. This made the pretzeling of her arm next to impossible. To do it right, she needed to dislocate her shoulder.

There was nothing in the lean-to that would bear her weight. After searching the campgrounds, she found a tree of an appropriate height, with a stout branch that formed a 'y'. Karuna put her arm in the crotch and dropped her weight in a freefall to the ground.

"AAAAHHHHHHH, SHIT THAT HURT!" the surrounding forest echoed her cries as her left arm hung limp and useless at her side.

The rest of the operation was merely unbearable.

After getting her shoulder back where it belonged, Karuna unrolled a blanket to settle in for the day and give herself a chance to heal. Before sleep, she downed the last of the blood she had brought with her. Now that she was no longer leaking it at an unhealthy rate, it could be consumed without waste.

Karuna dreamed the dream of death. It was not her death, but that of Sechra. Something was consuming her, keeping her, forcing her...Karuna woke to a cold profuse sweat. She wiped her face and shoulders, checked the bandages, wrapped her knees with her arms and wept. The dream brought glimpses, flash freeze frames of the nightmare enveloping Sechra. Black on black, it was hideous and foul, strange, yet oddly familiar. The images told her less than the vibes that emanated from them. It had been gestating, metamorphosing within Sechra and was now waiting to be born. Sechra in her horror would be its lover, mother and midwife. Karuna had seen it before in the eyes of a madman. She wept, not only for Sechra, but for herself. There was nothing she could do to help or save Sechra. The dream had made that much clear. It was up to Sechra to birth or abort the madness and for Karuna to continue on with the work in another time.

Karuna slept through the next three days within the comforts of the lean-to. When she woke, she was parched in more ways than one. She was dehydrated and the last of her blood had been spent on the healing, leaving her wasted. It was near noon, the sky leaden and filled with water. It would rain soon. Karuna knew she had to leave. Getting up off her knees sent her head spinning, as she tumbled out from under the fallen roof into the mud. Karuna controlled the urge to regurgitate, while the world slowed and came to a stop. She had been hurt before, just never this severely. Now on her hands and knees, Karuna raised her mud-stained face to scan the surroundings.

Tears rolled down her cheeks again creating clean rivulets in the mud. She was not crying. She was savoring traditions that have stood the test of time. Not three meters away were a jug of clean water and a lamb, tied loosely to a piece of junk so it wouldn't wander. The smell of Urloff and his clan came strongly from the animal and water bottle. She was sure he had each member pet the yearling and handle the container, so that Karuna would know where the kindness came from and where their hearts lay. They would always take care of their own.

After sating several urgent thirsts, Karuna digested on a number of levels while eyeing the mountains. The overcast was unbroken in all directions while the chill indicated the rains were turning to snow. She covered the carcass with rocks as she couldn't dig worth a damn, what with the big hole in her chest and damaged ribs. Karuna gathered what little she had into a pack, buttoned her jacket, and willed herself to the treetops. She sent her love west, deep into the mountains, while her body headed east, back to the coast. Not, however, before a stop at the nation's capitol for an unannounced visit with her daughter.

During the journey to Bucharest, Karuna saw what Urloff spoke about in the eyes, bedraggled faces and bent shoulders of the people. He was right. They were dying, a cancer of the soul that was metastasizing around the world in the form of Sechra's infamous exhibit.

Karuna had been sitting on the veranda of the prime ministers' house for an hour before being noticed by security. She had swirled in with the leaves of late autumn that now lay at her feet. The door to the balcony squeaked on its hinges.

"How long have you been here, mother?" asked Riana, both confused and surprised by her mother's presence.

"Long enough to know that your security is sadly lacking," Karuna replied. She turned on the seat to face Riana. The motion activated the light sensors flooding the space with illumination. The contrast between the women couldn't have been more drastic. Riana was groomed to the tens while Karuna looked a mess of a bag lady. Riana was immediately at her side.

"Mom! Are you all right! What happened?"

"I was in the wrong place at the wrong time, then I fell in some mud," replied Karuna sardonically.

Riana picked up on it. "Anytime you sound like Jake...You haven't killed anyone, have you?"

"No, but you may have!"

Riana's righteousness rose. "Just what do you mean by that, Karuna?"

"Why have you and Vlad conspired to keep Sechra and I out of the picture?"

"We haven't..."

"You have! And now Sechra's life is in danger!"

"She is not. They have more than enough food and comforts to wait out the winter. She was born there remember?"

"You have no idea what you have done." Karuna shook her matted hair morosely.

"We wanted her out of the picture until the crisis is over. She has caused enough trouble."

"So you sent her back to 'her people', is that it?"

"Yes," Riana said, losing her conviction.

"How quickly you have forgotten. 'They' are your people, too," retorted Karuna.

"You know what I mean..."

"No, I don't. Nor did I ever expect to hear it from my daughter."

"That is just about enough, Mother."

"I haven't even begun, but you no longer hear, so I will not waste my breath. Once you stood against the darkness. Now you send Sechra into hell because she is inconvenient."

"I have no idea what you are talking about," Riana wavered.

"What do you think happened to that thing you destroyed? It entered the only innocent it could find!"

"Sechra," awed Riana, then, "Wait, wait..." But Karuna was gone, only a swirl of desiccated leaves settling where she had been sitting.

The bolt to the private entrance of the beach estate snapped open. Karuna had that to hell and back look about her. Feeling like it, too, she made for the fridge, checked the dates and made the tallest and bloodiest of Mary's. She laughed, lightly remembering the first time she drank one. Karuna settled into a hot bath and fond memories. It would be the last of either for a long time.

***

S echra woke to a halting, heavy breathing, the kind you hear in the dark corners of a strip joint. Her head was resting on the sack that the tools had been dumped from. She did not move, but listened for it to finish. With a slobbering gasp, the filth that was 'it' sighed.

"Good morning, my child, I was just thinking of you. Or rather, of you creating me."

Sechra rolled into a defensive, non-aggressive crouch as her right hand silently grasped one of the mauls. She tried not to think about what it had said. The scent of fresh coffee caused her to stand, sidestepping around the thing to the table. There was bread, boiled eggs, the meat she would not eat. Without acknowledging it, she ate ravenously. When she was full, the leftovers went into her pocket. Sechra poured the last of the coffee and returned to the comfort of the large granite boulder. She set the hammer down and began to run her hands across the stone's surface.

"Do you not need to feel me, all of me, so that my features will be perfect?" it asked lecherously, slapping its wet lips in satisfaction.

"I already know what you look like," spat Sechra. "Get me more coffee!"

"You have had your food. It is time to begin."

"I don't work without an unlimited supply of good coffee. You should know this if you have been watching over me all this time!" Sechra spit her mouthful at the darkness, the cup was right behind it. Since the cup did not smash against the wall Sechra figured her aim good.

"You will begin or you will die here..."

Sechra did not let it finish. "I died in a shithole long ago. Now do what I say or you will die here as well."

"I cannot die. As long as there are men, I will be among them."

"If you don't want to watch from the cheap seats, I suggest more coffee. Turkish and burnt."

"The Turks," it mumbled as it sloughed beneath the floor, leaving Sechra alone.

A trail of sweat ran down her back. She pushed and it did not push back. Normally she would have laughed at the situation. It was comedy, but a black comedy devoid of mirth. With both hands she felt the boulder again, feeling the grains and texture. As mentioned before, it was a perfect stone, a thing of great beauty. To carve a thing of baseness and cruelty would turn perfection to shit. Sechra sat next to the stone, leaning her back against it and closed her eyes.

For certain this piece of rock came from deep within the mountain, the foundation on which Romania was built. It was of the land and like the people; hard, enduring and perfect. Her mind slid back to her childhood, to the times of happiness during the hardship of those days. Filthy clothes, but clean smiles. Grimy faces held the clear, cool eyes of free men. They fought and died for that right. Tears of happiness rolled down her cheeks. She had forgotten, and now in the darkest depths, Sechra saw the light.

Never once had she carved of her people's triumphs, only their failure and debasement, their pain and agony. It would help. Sechra walked round and round the boulder, memorizing it by touch. In her mind she could see it clearly. Within the clarity of darkness, her inner light beheld two distinctly different, yet similar images that the stone would yield itself to.

The first was familiar, akin to all of her work, wretched and horrible, executed with such skill that the viewers could hardly pull themselves away from viewing. Instead of the plight of the damned, however, the image in Sechra's mind bore no small likeness to the slave master, the sinister side of man himself that inflicts pain and anguish upon his fellow man. Was it human? In form perhaps, but exaggerated to bring the essence to the surface. The essence of what? No less than the darkness that resides within us all. Which is the main reason why it is so familiar and captivating – our morbid nature yearns for it. 'The image of the coffee boy,' Sechra laughed darkly, for there was nothing really funny about it. The kicker for Sechra was that there was no fear either, she had seen and experienced far worse, or so she thought. This piece could be carved in a full sculpture, not shallow relief, or deep, or even pierced, but the most damnable 'David' Michelangelo never dreamed of.

The second, naturally, was the polar opposite of the first. As close as she could figure, the boulder was about three meters in diameter and nearly perfectly round. Through her calloused hands, Sechra could feel the shallow and deep relief cuts the stone would give her. Because the stone was round she could tell the tale of the gypsy peoples in elliptical panels. Each panel would be bordered, yet merging with the next; the final panel would blend with the first in the never-ending cycle of life. The tale would include the trials, tribulations, and triumphs of the Romanian peoples, of its close ties to the earth and the simple truths of men and woman who did not want 'more'. Life was enough and a chance to live it cleanly with the sweat of your brow and toil in the soil. From the earth, they took what was needed and left the rest. In the end, a worn out bag of bones and sinewy muscle was all that was left. It, too, was buried beneath the dirt to rot and become the soil for future generations, completing the cycle, or starting a new one, depending upon your point of view.

In the dark, Sechra's life stretched out before her in a panoramic view, not unlike the potential second carving. As far back as she could remember to the present, freeze frame images depicted the high and low points. When she would focus on them, the frames would start to unreel.

Sechra watched her life unfold in what we call an 'out of body' experience. There was little emotion to obscure the details as she watched herself watch. Each frame coalesced with the one next to it creating a continuity, a continuum. For the first time, she saw that every step, every moment, every tear, every pain, every happiness, every failure and triumph of will had led her to this moment.

Twenty years of sculpting had given her an intimate knowledge of the tools and their function. More importantly, she knew how to use them. After two decades of calloused hands and carpal tunnel issues, Sechra concluded, 'I could do this in the dark.' She would have to.

With the span of her hands, Sechra accurately measured the rock, dividing it like a globe into eleven identical ellipses. Using a coarse chisel, she scratched, ever so lightly, the shapes onto the stone surface. Sechra had decided which of the two sculptures she would do. She tried to hold on to the out of body thing. It helped with seeing clearly. 'It' was a client. Her work a commissioned piece, which she had already paid dearly for, in direct opposition of the way it usually works. She was the artist. It would not, could not tell her what to create or how to do it. If it could, it surely wouldn't need her.

Sechra lined up her tools. The chisels that need to be sharp were sharp, the dull, dull. Half a dozen hammers for a dozen uses were well worn, but not damaged. One hammer had a chip in the feel, which had been overlaid with duct taped. These were her tools! Who, how, what?! Somehow...it didn't matter. The unctuous mass came up the stairs from below, smell preceding the liquid footsteps.

"I see you have done something, but there are no chips upon the floor. Pray that you are neither a lazy or slow sculptor."

"Pray that you brought some decent coffee or the work goes no further," Sechra deadpanned.

Out of the darkness came a whistling sound that ended when the cold wet fleshy hand struck Sechra a sound blow that sent her over backwards into the far wall. Her head cracked loudly on the granite blocks, cutting her scalp. Blood poured from her brow and merged with the crimson river the came from a split lip. Sechra was not one to give in. She pulled herself upright and walked to the table. Since becoming trapped, Sechra had learned the room and had it down rote, like a blind person. She knew exactly where the hole in the floor was, the table, the chair, where 'it' usually stood, the boulder, her tools and the exit door. So it was with a strange sort of confidence that Sechra brushed passed it and poured some of her dark master. She savored the flavor, aroma, and the silence.

It moved with a slithering, dragging of the feet. Sechra could hear the flesh of its unchallenged hands moving carefully over the abrasive surface of the sculpture.

"I feel nothing. I see nothing that is akin to my likeness," it growled.

"That is because there is nothing in this world that comes near to what it is you are." Sechra was emotionless.

"Yet. I have brought you what you requested. More than enough and a way to make it. Now create me!"

The movement of air caused Sechra to step back, flattening against the wall, but not quick enough. A powerful fist smashed into her face, turning the nose to one side. Blood gushed from both nostrils as Sechra struggled to remain on her feet. She waited for the next blow. It did not come. It was gone. Sechra was just beginning to understand its methods of communication. It would get no satisfaction from her. Her anger rose, but Sechra realized it would not serve her. Instead she would use it. Anger gives strength. Strength gets things done. Not only physical power but that of the mind firming her resolve. She would do what it wanted.

Sechra refilled her cup and lit one of the few remaining cigarettes from the coal box meant for heating water. The glow was the first light she had seen since entering the old structure. The dull orange, the smoke, coffee, brought a sense of calm to the situation as mundane tasks usually do. She stretched the moment until the stub of smoke burnt her fingertips. When the light winked out, she flexed her hands.

With a chisel, suitable for the work at hand, and hammer of the right heft, Sechra went to work. Hours passed, days even, she did not know. After the tenth pot of coffee, she quit counting. First she set to cutting the boulder into a perfect globe. How long this took is anybody's guess.

She slept twice before considering it complete. Remeasuring the ball, Sechra chiseled in the ellipses again as completing the roundness had removed some of her original etchings. Part of her wanted to leave it irregular. But no one had ever carved a perfect sphere, freehand, in the dark. She would. For what she wished to create required an extraordinary amount of exactitude. To fail in the beginning would be to fail in the end. There were no shortcuts.

Time became meaningless as Sechra chipped way at the borders of each panel. Her hammer became a metronome. Each time she struck the chisel, she knew she was alive. It struck often. The borders would describe the images contained therein. The symbols of their lives. In what one would consider the first in the series of eleven, the allegory was arcane and not readily understandable. The panels in the middle were obviously religious with a heavy dose of Christianity, it being the primary belief from the dark ages until the end of the twentieth century. The end panels' motif was primarily money oriented, with the final panel, next to the first, left blank. Sechra dug deep into her ancestral memory to access the signs, trademarks and icons of long forgotten history. She did not so much conjure them up, more, the images coursed through her. Sechra had become the carver; her personality only came through at the edges. She did not think, she cut rock. It was what surfers call being in the zone, when one was at one with what they were doing.

✳✳✳

Skender had worked his hands until they were raw and bleeding before stopping his assault on the door. The power equipment had been sitting for too long to be serviceable in the moment. Carbs gummed up, injectors frozen, batteries dead and fuel turned to varnish or sludge. The door itself had been made of the strongest of oak and seemed to have petrified over the years making it hard as steel. Saws and axes blunted when used against it. He cradled his hands and made his way back to the trailer. It was dusk, the sky was clear as the sun burnt low over the mountains, the color of a lit cigarette in the dark.

Skender stirred the fire in the woodstove. He sat and rested. Skender knew what hard labor was. He had done his share during the first thirty years of his life, sharing in the satisfaction after a long day at the end of a long tool. Today he poured all he had into an unforgiving effort and little to show for it. He worried about Sechra, no food, no light in a place of rancid death.

He had done as he was instructed. Over the course of the summer Skender had shuttled all the food and supplies Sechra and he would need to ride the winter out. 'Get her far into the mountains, and keep her there.' So he did, and now he regretted it. 'Why did I bring her here?' Skender thought silently. The crackling embers did not have an answer. "Because it was as far away as you could get. The road ends," he mumbled to himself.

We all have fantasies. His personal one of being trapped in the mountains with a famous babe had been innocent enough. Enough to get her here. But now what? The dream had turned into a nightmare of which he knew he had the lighter end. His clairvoyant nature had failed him. How could he have not seen it, felt it or had an inkling that things would turn sour.

Skender reached out with his mind, searching the cloud of mass thought for Sechra. Nothing. And not only nothing, but he couldn't pick up anything. The ether was usually jabbering its head off, making it difficult to pull out an individual from the masses. What was once full was now an empty void. He had never had to deal with the lack of perception and it scared the shit out him. Leaving was not an option, not yet anyway. Skender's long dead father had given a bit of advice on this matter. He had blown it off at the time as young men often do with advice. 'Go with it, Skender. You will always have what you need if you but look. And never, never give up, son.' It was the last thing his father said to Skender before the old man was swallowed by the revolution twenty years ago.

Skender wrapped his hands in gauze, made some rice and opened a can of beans. He ate, but there was no pleasure as Skender imagined Sechra trapped in the dark. Even lighting lanterns came with a certain amount of guilt. This was his place. He brought her here, therefore it was his fault. Skender knew better, but still...

Dad's words of wisdom shed some small amount of illumination over the pall that was settling over him, just as one of the lanterns cast its beam upon Sechra's gear. 'You will always have what you need if you but look.' Skender had never been a snoopy person as far as people's stuff was concerned. It was easier for him to pick their minds than their pocketbooks and far more lucrative. Most of it was typical motorcycle touring equipment, top end, fancy shit. The tank bag was kind of like a big purse, a little of everything went into it. Basic toiletries, water, snacks, cell phone, sunglasses, maps and a first aid kit. The med kit had already come in handy, so he left it out. Saddlebags and stuff sacks held clothes, sleeping bag, tent, a high tech little burner, flashlights, and rain gear. Pretty normal stuff for backcountry riding and nothing he needed.

Skender was a mountain gypsy. They lived with the necessities and little more. There was no virtual world up here. No computers, no cell phones, no wireless hot spots or a thousand other gizmos and gadgetry that served no real purpose other than to pacify one's need for instant gratification. If you wanted that, you jacked off. There was little enough of indulgence and none of it was instant. Skender was also nobody's fool, which he would be, if he thought the little pieces of plastic and lithium batteries were useless. They just seemed out of place. He went back to the tank bag and pulled out the cell phone. Flipping it open made all the little lights come to life.

A neophyte in the world of buttons, it took Skender some time to figure out the basics. Trial and error. Push a button. See what happens. Mostly nothing happened. Skender half-expected the world to explode if he pushed the wrong one. So…he was extra careful. The batteries were charged but there weren't too many bars. Throwing on his jacket he went outside, another bar popped up, still not enough. Walking to an open area brought another bar. It wasn't until he climbed to the top of the trailer that all the bars popped up.

But who was he going to call? He didn't know anyone, anyone who carried one of these things. The mysteries of the phone book eluded him. Skender couldn't figure out the sequence of buttons to open it up. He was however, literate and pressed the redial.

"Dino. Sechra where are you?" answered the mechanic.

"Hello?"

"Sechra are you all right?"

"Hello?"

"Hey who is this? And what are doing with Sechra Kcirb's phone!"

Skender had the phone upside down. "My name is Skender. I am Sechra's guide into the mountains."

"So what are you calling me for? How come Sechra didn't call? Where is she?" Dino was suddenly on edge. "What the fuck have you done with her?"

"Nothing, Mr. Dino. She is trapped. We have equipment but I lack the skills necessary to make them run."

"How did you get my number?"

"I press redial."

"Oh... Where are you and what kind of trouble is she in?"

"At the end of highway one. I believe it would be the kind of trouble you die from."

"What the fuck," screamed Dino over the phone. "That's deep in the mountains, the road was never really built. Just what kind of scam are you trying to pull?"

"No scam, we are snowed in and she is inside a fortress of sorts, locked in, no food, no water. If you cannot help, direct me to someone who can."

"All right, all right. Give me directions."

Skender did as he was asked. When the road signs ended, he gave Dino landmarks. There wasn't much and he knew it and ended with, 'keep heading west.'

"Okay, this is what I want you to do," instructed Dino. "Call me every night at this time. Leave her cell phone on. There is a charger outlet built into her bike, I think it's on the left side. Her phone has a GPS and I can track it. Keep trying to get her out. I've known Sechra since she was a girl."

"Yes sir," responded Skender.

"One more thing. If you're fucking with me I will kill you dead."

Skender didn't have to be a mind reader to know that Dino meant every word. He hung up and climbed off the trailer and into the compunction of a warm bed.

***

Dino ran his hands through his hair, his mind a blur with the multitude of things he had to get together in short order. After making a pot of coffee, he left his little house and went around back to a warehouse of a garage. The five meter tall roll-up door raised at the touch of a button as the light came on. He walked through the maze of toolboxes, cars and works in progress to the rear of the building and began to pull the plastic sheeting off a huge military transport vehicle that had tracks instead of rear wheels. Dino was the Eforie Sud plowman when winter extended its grip this far south. He didn't use it very often and it was more of a town joke than an asset. That is until now. All through the night he loaded everything he could think of to be ready for a dawn departure.

***

Karuna slept the sleep of the dead for three days, healing the hole in her chest. A distant pounding pulled her awake. It took a few moments to remember where she was and what the noise was. Someone was banging on the steel doors. In the kitchen Karuna disabled the alarm, flipped three deadbolts on a side door, turned the knob and stuck her head out in the chill dawn.

"What are you doing here, Dino? It's six o'clock in the morning," Karuna yawned.

"Sechra is in trouble. Why didn't you call me?"

"I know. There is nothing that can be done," replied Karuna forlornly.

"Bullshit," Dino began, stressing the bond of their relationship. "I got a call from a guy named Skender last night. He apparently feels differently about this than you do, and so do I. What the hell is the matter with you?"

At that moment Karuna's housecoat opened at the top. His eyes would normally have fallen to the cleavage but the bruise and crude stitch work above her heart broke his.

"Jesus, Karuna, I'm sorry, what happened?"

"I went up there. I was shot."

"Is that what this guy Skender and Sechra are up against? He didn't say anything about fighting."

"There isn't any."

"But the wound? Should I drive you into town?"

"No, no, I made a mistake is all. I will be fine. Maybe you can help Sechra, I don't know. I just know that I cannot. You can trust Skender. Would you like some coffee?"

The door went wide as Dino stomped the crud off his boots before entering. Something bad had happened, real bad. Even at the break of day, Karuna was a stunner, but not today. She looked old, pale, and beaten down. Her eyes were dull as she went through the motions of making the new day's elixir.

"What route did you take up? Skender's direction would be good enough if I knew the country," Dino said accepting the first cup. "Thank you, but I don't. I know the first half of the way. Any helpers?"

"Huh, what?" Karuna asked, somewhat obliviously.

"When you went to find Sechra, can you help me with directions? Geez..." Dino had never seen her so unfocused.

"No, I didn't take the roads."

"You took a chopper?"

"Well, something like that I guess. When my mode of transportation could go no further, I had to turn around."

"I'll call Riana. She could get me one and it would be a hell of a lot faster."

"She can, but she won't," glummed Karuna.

"What the hell?" Dino was floored.

"Please Dino. I wish I could tell you, but I can't. It's a family issue. Hand me the map, let's see what we can do."

"Okay... " Dino replied slowly and warily, pulling the map out. He unfolded it. "I can get to here." A grease-packed fingernail pointed to the middle of nowhere.

A pale hand, fingernails a peculiar yet unhealthy color, pointed further into the mountains. "I was able to get this far. I remember the rivers here," she pointed. "There is a gypsy encampment where the rivers meet. Your road primarily follows the river and it's not much of one."

"The river or the road?" Dino asked, removing his cap and scratching his head.

"The road. It's just a meander through the mountains that follows the contour of the terrain."

"As long as there is some kind of road I can make. If not I'll make my own. The trans-country highway was a stupid idea to begin with. Connect the people from the mountains with those in the cities. It can't be done. Like oil and water, you know?"

Karuna had been lost in the flow of his blood, pulsing warm just beneath his skin. Almost feeling it. Karuna wanted to feel it. She pulled herself back into the moment as he finished talking.

"Yes, yes. A metaphor for the plight of our people, you could say."

"I suppose," Dino replied as he finished the cup of coffee. He was getting that real nervous spike of adrenalin, like a rat must feel when cornered by a cat. All he wanted to do was run. 'Why?' he thought.

'Who the fuck cares why, just get the fuck out of here Dino,' the other side of his brain said. He was on his feet.

Karuna reached out feebly. "No stay," she rasped.

"I really should go, thanks for the help with the map." He couldn't say it fast enough as he backed out the door. The sharp, brisk wind blew in off the Black Sea. 'It's warmer than what awaited you if you had stayed a moment longer.' He was sweating bullets as he hopped into his rig, heading out of the damnable place, into he knew not what.

✳✳✳

Skender woke early after a worrisome sleep that was more staring at the ceiling than anything else. The sun had barely risen as he kindled the coals of the night's previous burn, bringing the woodstove to life. Skender imagined Sechra asleep in the oversized mausoleum, curled up on the stone floor. His imagination wasn't that far from reality. With water on the boil, he headed out to install the phone in Sechra's bike. The early winter sun was bright enough for him to find the charging socket on the left side, just as Dino said it would be. He started the bike, making a mental note turn it off after an hour, and went back to make some coffee.

First cup in hand, Skender went through Sechra's stuff again. It was all just as he remembered it to be, with the exception of the shotgun still in its sheath and harness. Stuffed into loops on the outside were the rounds she received from the gypsy woman. Skender noticed the palm off a few days ago and 'heard' what was said with his third ear, so to say. He pulled one of the shells out. The writing on the side was worn with only a faded EX... on the slug. 'Heavy,' was his first thought. High brass, over pressure, with a solid stainless steel slug. 'Goddamn.' What he didn't know was that it was an exploding anti-personnel round meant to do more damage than punching a huge hole in something.

He finished his first cup looking at the shotgun shell. With the second, he withdrew the shotgun and unloaded it. Skender stuffed the menacing round in the pipe, closed the chamber, and put the safety on.

"Maybe this is what I was supposed to find," he said to no one, pulling on his coat.

Skender had already found it – the phone. The discovery of the gun however, sent him on a course of events that had nothing to do with what needed to be done. He had already done what was necessary with the call. What he needed to do now was nothing.

Shotgun in one hand, coffee in the other, Skender headed back to where Sechra was. There was no reason to wait. He downed the last of the cup and set it on the ground. The pistol grip felt good in his hands but he unfolded the stock to give him better control. 'Those 'plus p plus' shells kick a hell of a lot more than bird shot.' He held tight and brought the gun to bear on the door. His feet were braced when he pulled the trigger.

The oversized bullet exploded into the morning, kicking Skender back a few meters while the stainless steel slug left the barrel at supersonic speed. He had been unprepared for the recoil as the barrel slammed into the center of his forehead, splitting the skin from the eyebrow clear to his hairline. Blood gushed from the open wound. The slug went wide and high slamming into the rock jamb and exploding on impact. Fleshettes embedded into the slug sprayed out from the blast zone in all direction shredding Skender's heavy winter clothes like a thousand little razors. As bad luck would have it, Skender was still standing. All that energy needed somewhere to go. Chunks of rock flew backwards, hammering Skender with shards that tore through his clothing and smashed into his bones. The largest hit him in the chest, fracturing the sternum, crushing it inwards against his heart. Another in the forearm created a new joint, while a fleshette split his right eye like an egg yolk. He hit the ground, bits of rock and razors protruding from crimson gashes like an insane mosaic. The clouds of fog released with each breath in the cold morning became less and less as the chill went deep into his near lifeless body. He closed his eyes with the words 'fuck me' on his breath. He had heard Sechra say it a few times, and surely she had heard it from someone else. It seemed appropriate.

No one heard. Only the silence of a winter's mourning returned to comfort the dead.

***

Sechra jumped from the table she was standing on when the explosion rocked the building. She crouched at the base of the sculpture, waiting for the structure to come down. A cascade of dust drifted down from the rafters sprinkling everything with yet another layer of accumulated smut to the floor, table and Sechra. She spit the grit and rubbed it from her eyes. All was still.

A coating of fines floated atop her coffee. Sechra rinsed the cup and poured the last of the pot and downed it in one fluid motion. The movement was crude and graceful at the same time. She wiped her mouth on her sleeve and climbed back on top of the table, her makeshift scaffold. A chisel wedged under one leg kept the thing from wobbling. Sechra closed her eyes and began feeling the surface so she could pick up where she left off. The dividing panels had been relieved of the unwanted surface, except for the patterns. These, the under drawings, still needed to be refined and polished. The first of the panels was well underway. The figures were sinewy, as hunter/gatherers were wont to be. Simple gardens of root food were tended while a high mountain elk was being skinned. Open fires, buildings of sticks and hides. A group of hungry, cooking sticks in hand, waited for the butchering to finish. This was a tight-knit clan consisting of half a dozen families. Their faces were dirty from a life spent close to the earth, but the smiles and eyes were clear and unblemished, as yet unstained by their humanity. One couple stretched their arms across from the first panel to the second, handing over a newborn child.

A celebration was in progress to receive the child. A feast of sorts had been set on crude tables with benches for seating. Meat and seasonal vegetables were strewn across the surface while a piglet roasted on a stick. After being gutted, it was impaled upon the spit and turned. Eager eyes watched the sizzling fat. On the other side of the panel was another gathering. They seemed to be part of the first party, but cleverness on the part of the artist made them distant at the same time. While the first party was in a pastoral valley, the second was in the mountains. Instead of a birth, it was burial of a child. The food was scarce and the faces of the people were harder, as life in the mountains tends to be. Looking closely, one noticed the faces in both parties were similar, if not the same. The differences were environmental. One people, divided only by the terrain of their lives.

At the end of the second panel the baby is being interred. Arms are lowering the child into the bowels of the earth, only to be received in the third panel, a stillbirth. The faces mourned a lost future. Religious symbols begin to appear at the periphery, twisting the lives within into something self-serving, feeding off the guilt and hatred. These places were heavily populated micro-metropolises along the trade routes.

Deep in the mountains were a people out of touch with the outside world. Their miscarriage was born alive, but its life was not to be spent among the living. Tunnels, man-excavated and natural, led to the depths of the mountainside. Here the abortion was allowed to live, tended by the mountain people. It existed within the dark confines of the earth, unable to free itself into the domain of men. Only by invitation could it leave the lair to do the dark bidding of men, the work they themselves could not or would not do. They called it the Drac. Men like to give things names, especially when they fear them.

The Drac was a dark elemental, the death side of the life equation. It was born at a time when man himself was still becoming what he is today. It wanted the life that was its polar opposite. A perfectly natural desire. Our genes were still confused. It slipped in. The crude caesarian abortion, led to the brutal death of the mother. In her screams of agony and motherhood, it was born.

Nine months earlier, a mother was raped by another mistake of genes, a grotesque abomination of nature with male genitals. This was before the age of the Drac. The misfortune had been allowed to live among men, surviving off the scraps and throwaways of its limited society. No one had put any thought to what would happen when it came of age. It nurtured a bitter hatred and loathing as it watched the other children grow, full and healthy. Worse than a dog it was treated. And so like a dog it sniffed out the woman when she was in her moon, repeatedly raping her until he was sure his seed took. It was an animal act, with a little brutality thrown in for spite. When she began to show, the inhuman spawn was hunted down and killed. For all their limited knowledge, the clan knew where the baby came from, for the fetus was unnaturally active and caused the mother great pain until the time of birth. When it came, there was no mucous plug or losing the water. The child would not wait to be born. It began to rip away at the mother's belly, tearing itself out with sharp little claws. Blood was everywhere.

Small mine shafts dotted the mountainside where the men dug for meager deposits of coal and whatever precious metals they might find along the way. After birthing itself, the baby chewed through the umbilical cord as it gazed at the horror-struck men and women who had gathered. It began to suck on the mother's end of the umbilical, draining what remained of the life that carried it around for so long. In that moment of mother and child bonding, or what should have been, it nuzzled around the still-bleeding umbilical like a tit. And at that moment, the presence of mind returned to one of the men. Hefting a hard-sided barrel he captured the thing, securing the lid while all around him were faces agape and gasping. It was borne by a pall of men and women to one of the deepest mines and hidden from the light and eyes of man. The access to the shaft was blocked by a huge roundish boulder, with only enough room at one spot to lower food and water, using only the thinnest of threads so it could not climb out. But there was something more than just the depiction of a very sad affair. In the faces and hands, the body language of the people, was a righteousness born in the acceptance of one's fate. It was not bad, it was not good, it was acceded.

Sechra squatted above a small hole in the floor to drop her little demons from sight and mind. When the steaming stream finished, she carefully wiped herself, folding the rag for reuse. She had never regretted finding a place she could relieve herself without shitting on the floor, or worse, to hang her ass over the big hole in the floor and expose herself to that which lurked below. No sooner had she begun carving than the grating of the hatchway was heard, it was returning. Sechra knew it would. The explosion surely roused it from its despicable meditations. An unhappy laughter heralded it presence. The sound was that of one enjoying the pain of others. She had heard it before, in real life, and horrid dreams forever after. The explosion had to have been Skender trying to get her out. Apparently the effort failed.

"Good morning," it rasped in ancient Romanian. "We are alone, finally."

Sechra picked up on it. "What did you do to him?" she asked, all kindness gone from her voice.

"Why nothing, dear one. Leave you to your own devices and sooner or later you will kill yourselves. Why do you think humanity is still alive after all these years? Their fear of me, and things like me, keeps the stupidity at bay. But enough of me! I hear you tinkering away at all hours. Your drive is admirable. It arouses me."

"Go satisfy yourself. Your being here distracts me. I work alone!" Sechra shuddered and put the table between them.

"After I see what you have done."

Sechra moved again, keeping the space between them at the extreme limit.

"Ah... ahhh, ... Ahhh." The ahh's became a heavy panting while a rhythmic slapping closed the air around Sechra. The beat increased with a final, AHHHHHHHH, as it climaxed, splurching on the stone its slobber and cum. A rancid musk filled the air. "Where am I?"

Sechra knew the inquiry was not rhetorical nor an utter of confusion. Its vanity wanted to see what he looked like. She slumped her shoulders and sat on the floor. She had done this many times, explaining her vision to the client.

"You have more than one face, more than one existence..." she drolled.

To the untrained hand, lips curled in happiness feel similar to agony. Eyes of genuine sorrow and joy are akin to pain and degradation. "Where you feel pain, the cruel hardships of life, there you are. Touch it! See with your fingers and smile. I create you!"

It did. It felt and saw what it wanted to see. "Very clever, a me for every season, every reason."

Sechra smirked, rolled her eyes and shook her head. She had heard it all before.

"Something like that," she snided.

"When will I be done?" Greed was already creeping into its voice.

"As soon as I finish it and not a moment before." She was ready for the response to her wisecrack, simple as it was. The close air pushed towards her. Sechra dropped to her knees as its arm whipped the spot where she stood, fluffing her hair. The follow up backhand was a killing blow that struck nothing.

Its laugh was sick, foul, the sounds you hear in an insane asylum and during a cholera epidemic.

"You move quick. But the room is only so big and I can be everywhere."

Its hand shot through the blackest air and grabbed Sechra by the throat, dragging her towards him. Its acrid breath made Sechra gag in wheezing gasps. They touched foreheads. The thoughts of it entered her mind. She saw Skender lying on the ground, a crater in his chest. His skin was blue and freezing, hands still clenching the shotgun in rigor mortis.

Horrible as the image was Sechra tried to look beyond, into its mind. Suddenly she felt as if she was walking on broken glass with bare feet. Its fried nerve endings recoiled at her presence. Its nerves had never felt the calm before death, as Sechra felt now; the blood supply to her brain was being cut off for too long. She reached out to soothe the nerves. The nerves went moue for a moment before stabbing out with barbed tendrils. The shock pulled Sechra back into the present as her head knocked the floor soundly, sending stars flying in all directions. She rolled into a sitting position cradling her head. Warm blood seeped under her fingers.

'Why was I not afraid? Why was the child so familiar? Am I, are we – some sort of twisted twins? An anomaly of two?' Soon the chill of inactivity forced Sechra to her feet. She cupped her hands around the coal burner while boiling water for coffee. Five minutes later a coffee cup steamed atop the granite boulder. Chip and feel, chip and feel. Her mind's eye was bright with the image. She would feel it with inner hands and the outers would carve until the feelings were the same. It was a godawful, slow process but Sechra kept at it. At this point it was coming out the way she wanted. Exacting detail was one of her trademarks and satisfied her right brain. The left side however controlled what the reliefs revealed. Instead of the horrors that the Roma lived through, it was how they lived that was the revelation. Hard work, pride, life with all its beauty's and sorrows, acceptance and the courage to bear it righteously. Thus was the life of the people of this rugged land. The simplicity of a life well lived was what she wanted to capture and never before had Sechra done it so well. This is what it was. Now all she wanted to do was finish it. Steel met steel as it gouged and scraped the rock into a thing of infinite beauty.

✱✱✱

Karuna collapsed into herself after Dino left. Deep inside she felt the endless void of failure. It consumed her. First with Riana, for bringing her into this sordid world and now, losing her to it. Then, of course, was the child Sechra. She, too, was lost to the darkness and would have to endure the hardships she so diligently recreated in stone. 'I should have seen it coming,' she chastised herself. Lastly for herself, for accepting the foul gift in a moment of death and despair, and, as she realized now under the influence of overblown guilt, vanity. The inability to rectify the situation was overwhelming. Jake had once tried to explain that there was a time to act and a time to not. Not acting was by far a most difficult and shameful thing to endure. Especially when your life was one of action.

Tears of blood dripped soundlessly onto the kitchen counter. Karuna was frozen in grief. It wasn't until a warm, malodorous stream crept into her underwear that she came out of it. She curled the bathrobe around her thighs and made a shameful dash for the bathroom. Her sweat had been thick when she fell into the stream of Dino's pulsing blood; loosening the adhesive on the butterfly bandage she used to seal the incision in her back. She had tried but couldn't pull a stitch.

Her relief was small but enough so it would seem to pull her out of the 'funk', as Giovanni used to call it. Stepping into the shower, Karuna realized it wasn't the time in the funk so much as the depth of it that brought on unendurable despair. 'Is that why Jake and Johnny did so many drugs, to block the wretchedness?' They had a hundred years on her in the world of darkness. She was but a neophyte. Karuna couldn't imagine it being any worse.

After re-taping her back, Karuna made a cocktail, a pot of coffee, and began gathering her stuff to leave, again. There was nothing she could do here and no reason to stay. There was, however, something she could do for others in another time. Certain that Ahmed would have gone through her belongings she repacked, using a carpetbag made from old oriental rugs. It wouldn't exactly match the times but it wouldn't stand out either. Into the bag went the rest of Jake's drugs and the .44 single shot pistol he had given her so long ago and some clothes. There really wasn't much she would need. The fridge had three bags of blood, which were good for another few days. These went into a sleeve cooler and into the carpetbag along with a transfusion kit and spare points.

Karuna stood at the kitchen counter looking out over the living room and through the windows to the yard and gazebo. She was filled with sublime emotion. So much good had happened here. She smiled and wiped a crimson tear before turning away and heading into the halls of mosaics.

Karuna knew not to look too hard into the mosaics to find a suitable point of entry. 'Let it find me,' she mused silently, slowly strolling the lengths of the maze of hallways. Suddenly she stopped. Blood and the detritus of a fight lay on the floor before one particular scene. She looked closely, not too close mind you, and kept her analytical mind to the forefront of her thinking in order not to be drawn in. The clothes were wrong on a man who had just had his hands removed with an axe. The expression on his face was more than perplexed. He was dazed with being in the wrong time at the wrong time. A nightmare was just beginning for him. Imagine being caught in that terror of the moment, forever.

The face was familiar but she couldn't place it. Horrible as it was, her attention was drawn further up the coast where the sun had set. There was something, another out of time issue in mosaics over a thousand years old. It was difficult to make out with the coming of night, but surely it was a car plunging from a high cliff into the sea. The driver's face and bandaged hands bore the likeness of Igor, Sechra's sculpting teacher. 'What had happened here?' In a moment of clarity she realized someone else knew how to use the images. But who, how? Perhaps she could learn this from Ahmed. After all he created them.

Karuna moved on. She was looking for a panel depicting Dracine at some point after Karuna's previous visit. Five minutes later she was pulled to a stop. It depicted Eforie Sud just prior to the battle that took place on its shores a thousand or so years ago. The port was active as it prepared for hell's arrival. On the horizon were the Turkish warships, as yet holding off, instilling the land's populace with fear as sails stretched across the water as far as the eye could see.

While all prepared for a fury, the likes of which mankind has rarely had a chance to witness, a party was being thrown away from the port. On the beach below the Castle Drache tents with no walls had been erected under which the revelers were showing weariness after having been at for too long. On a raised dais, within a darkened enclosure sat Dracine, nodding amidst the goings on. Ahmed was nowhere to be seen. Karuna concentrated on the sleeping figure, the look of bliss on her face, the black silk robes and loose pantaloons, shear but not too shear. Just enough to let the breeze blow through, yet cut full to hide her smallish breasts within the folds.

Karuna closed her eyes and stepped forward. It wasn't until she felt the silk against her skin and exotic spices enter her nose did she open her eyes. Her first reaction was unfortunate but unavoidable. Karuna lurched to one side and began to throw up. A slave was ready with adorned puking bucket and damp towel. Her reaction couldn't have been more 'normal' if she tried. After being wiped clean and refreshed with cool water Karuna felt just how wasted Dracine had become. Before letting her thoughts get carried away, she double-checked that the carpetbag was still in her possession. Relieved, she signaled she needed to use the loo. Karuna leaned on the shoulder of a blind slavewoman as she was led to another tent. She took the time while seated to go through the bag.

The .44 went into her waistband. Rummaging through the drugs, she found some speed and popped a couple of the amphetamines to pull her out of the doped haze. Her years of watching Jake and Johnny do just this same thing helped her now, as she never thought it would.

The speed kicked in quick, bringing on another round of nausea. All perfectly normal, as far as her attendants were concerned. Now she had to control herself and remain in character. Right now that meant being cool when she felt like jumping out of her skin. She lifted a limp wrist, raising a weak finger as she did. Immediately there was a servant at hand.

"Where is my man?" she snapped, grinding her jaw, hopefully unnoticeable.

"He is gone for the next few days on an errand for you."

"Yes, yes," she forced herself to say slowly, almost slurring. "I tire of this affair. It is time to leave."

"The guests..."

"Let them enjoy the evening. Bring food and wine until they tire. Have the scrap food given to the poor." Now this was out of character for Dracine, yet the servant couldn't help but let a glint of hope shine through her dead eyes. Dracine snapped her fingers.

Dracine settled onto the mohair divan, the evening's cool breeze blowing through the den's windows, carrying the sound of people enjoying themselves on the beach below. 'They are probably having more fun now that I am gone.' Dracine smiled to herself. Though the sharpened teeth took away from the look of pleasure, it was the first time Dracine ever felt happy. She called to the servants to bring her the records of last week's court decisions and the coming week's schedule. She would spend the rest of the night studying them by lamplight.

The affairs of state and local issues had stagnated since her departure. Dracine assumed it was because of Ahmed's control of the pipe. She was far more addicted than her earlier experience, and that does take some work. Dracine would have to wean herself down. Knowing how difficult it can be she was thankful for 'quick clean; it won't be any fun, but it works.' It was a concoction Johnny had devised years ago in his lab. Dracine would not use it now, but when the time came. She smiled at their forethought. It felt so strange on a face that was not used to feeling it, reminding Dracine to be careful and not use the smile in public.

That is unless you want to see people tremble, when the pointed teeth tore into their souls, loosening their bowels with fear and nowhere to run.

Dracine, both of them needed sleep. Dracine had not had a decent sleep since heading into the mountains. Resting while healing doesn't count, nor is Dracine's nodding on opium equivalent to a decent REM. With the sun coming up after a night deep in an ancient language studying her new life, and with no urgent duties planned for the day, she decided to retire. She went through the ritual, smoking some opium, inhaling just enough to keep withdrawal at bay but not get blasted, and to keep up appearances. The walls have ears and eyes, Ahmed had once said. 'But who's?' questioned Dracine. She rifled through the drug bag for some sleeping pills. One bottle was labeled 'sleeping clowns; two mgs, out like a light for six hours.' She popped one 2mg pill. Half an hour later the jagged edge of the speed was worn out as Dracine dropped into the deepest sleep either of them had ever had.

Dracine woke with her hand resting lightly on the .44. She palmed it, rising to a sitting position feeling refreshed, unburdened, ready for the day. It was when she took her first few steps that she felt the clown's residual in her system. It was not undesirable, just making her a little slow. 'Perfect,' she thought. But coffee was first before any more 'thinking' could be accomplished.

The noon meal had been laid out earlier in the den, along with a filled pipe, with multiple reloads lined up on a golden tray. Moving at a leisurely pace, she crossed the room and took a small hit off the pipe to satisfy the walls and a bourgeoning jones. Then came coffee. Fifteen minutes passed in silence as Dracine savored the brew like never before.

You see, the two personalities were living together in one body. So far, it was symbiotic, acceptable to both parties. Dracine disdained matters of court and Karuna liked them. Karuna's own nasty habits satisfied most of Dracine's, and then some. 'Will it last?' Dracine mused. 'Probably not, but let's enjoy it while it's there.'

An inner dialogue was already initiating a rapport between the two. 'That we have merged so well... should come as no surprise. Ahmed as you call him has been in many of the people in these scenes...so you know where you are...in my reality...yes, yes and now I have become part of your reality...I had always wondered if I would be infiltrated. Thank you for your intelligence; it will be needed in the days ahead. How long do you plan on sticking around for this time...As long as I am needed...You know what happens to people I have no need for...in detail.'

Dracine enjoyed the afternoon without the meddlesome ministrations of Ahmed. He was ever underfoot and always with the pipe in the face. For the first time, she realized what a pain in the ass he had become. Yet he had also become a necessary evil. He knew the secret of her identity and covered for her. Dracine could trust no one else and should she cast him away surely he would spill the beans before his tongue could be cut out.

These realizations were part of the merging of the two personalities. To the extreme nature of her temper would be added intelligence to use it, well, well. Their dark natures were harmonious. Dracine was thrilled and frightened at the new aspect of her persona. Her cannibalism had been more for show than an actual desire to eat human flesh. But now – to drink from the living to survive – whet her appetite considerably. Unfortunately for Dracine, the reality of these dark impulses were far less desirable than the dream. This, hopefully, will be constrained with discipline and discretion. Hopefully. One untimely call of the wild could ruin everything.

Here was the spoiled child and the observant adult. Impulsiveness would be tempered with thoughtful consideration. Cruelty would be dealt to those who deserved it; otherwise it would be saved for demonstration and education. The two personalities only seemed to be in polar opposition, when in fact they were not so dissimilar at all.

We all have blank spots in who we are. Areas of our persona became less developed while others were paid more attention to. With these two temperaments, the blanks of one fit with the excess of the other. Although it did create a semblance of balance, the fit was not always perfect. Like a normal person, almost.

For some time now, Ahmed had been using Dracine as a puppet dictator. Her lack of a decent education, even for the times, was atrocious. Then again during the 1400s, a woman of any status was lucky to have any tutoring at all, let alone being able to read or write. It just wasn't done. Dracine may have been illiterate but she was not stupid. She was clever. As a child, Dracine was ever in the shadows of her father's court, fascinated as she was by the goings on and especially the reverence with which her father was held. Men groveled before the old Dracul, begging for their lives, their farms and families. Dracine saw a smallness in these beggars of forgiveness and their pleas for mercy. In her young imagination, she showed them none. Each was whipped, torn or mutilated for their weakness and failure.

Where this vicious nature came from is a good question. Certainly not Vlad II's court. He was a fair, if heavy handed, Voivode. With his eyes on the crown of Walachia he thought not to destroy the people but rally them to him, a trait that would sadly be lost in the future generations of the Draculs. His three sons, Vlad III, Radu, and Mircea received the bulk of his attention, spoiling them with the desire for power and rule. The firm hand he held to the people was withheld from the boys' rearing. As they grew older, they would vie for their father's attention with cruelty and treachery.

Ultimately, Dracine's nature developed from neglect. As the bastard child of the Monarch, she was the oddball. Dracine neither fit with the family, naturally, or with the staff, or with the common man. An outcast that could not be disposed of. A hemorrhoid, a piece of luggage, a wart, a boil, Dracine was ignored, like trash in the yard that has been there so long, it does not register when you do see it.

Although she could not read or write, Dracine picked up on the spoken word and through the context was able to, in time, understand all that she heard. Her chosen schoolroom was the court.

It was a scorching summer. The hot wind blew down the beachfront and into the open doors of the court. Her father wore a light silk tunic and pants while a slave waved a fan back and forth creating a comfort zone for the judge and his cronies. Those with a grievance or offenders of the law waited patiently as the sweltering heat stole their will to argue.

A peasant, Grippens, stood before the judiciary bench. Stood is perhaps a poor word. Grippens had been chained to a pillar outside, waiting his day in court. Four days had passed since he was caught stealing stalks of rye from a farmer's field. His body was burnt from the unrelenting sun. Grippens stank of sweat and filth, his shoulders hunched over in submission as he rocked from foot to foot, unable to stand still on his crippled feet. When Grippens was caught, there was no way to secure him so the farmer smashed the thief's feet with a rock to keep him from running. It was a pitiful sight of what can happen to a man driven to starvation and madness.

Dracine watched and listened from her place within the comfort zone. She was in the process of changing her sitting position, as her foot had fallen asleep, when she spotted Vlad III waving to her from deeper in the shadows. She acknowledged him, but did not move. Her presence was just barely tolerated in the court as it was. If she should move about during the proceedings, it would be her last day. She wouldn't risk it, so she signaled for him to wait, not knowing she would pay dearly for doing so.

Vlad III had begun to pay more attention to Dracine ever since she began to bleed on a monthly basis and her breasts began to swell. Since no one had ever explained to Dracine about being a woman, she had no idea what was with the sudden interest.

Grippens wobbled before the court. His eyes rolled back in his head and he keeled over. Dehydration had gotten the best of him. The prisoner lay on the floor in the cold sweat of heat stroke. Moments later he died, his brain cooked by the sun. The death however was timely, coming as it did at the midday break. First her father and the other Voivode in attendance departed, followed by the next in rank until the chambers were empty with the exception of Dracine and Vlad. She rose from the squatted position and walked over to where her half-brother stood, her footsteps echoing loudly in the vacant hall.

"Why did you not come to me when I hailed you?" Vlad was condescending and bitter at her lack of obedience.

"I am not allowed to make any disturbance while the cour..." Dracine began before being cutoff by a wicked backhand from Vlad that sent her sprawling across the floor.

"When I call, you will come! Do you understand?"

"Yes Vlad," Dracine lisped around her swollen, split lips and freshly chipped front teeth. "What is it you want?"

"I want you. Have you not heard, Dracine? My father is sending Radu and I to Turkey in hopes of finding a way around a war between our two countries. I will be an emissary of Romania," Vlad said with complete vanity and false bravado.

"What do you wish of me?" Dracine wiped the blood from her mouth, spitting the chipped tooth on the floor.

"The one thing I have yet to obtain."

For a skinny little runt, Vlad III was quick. He grabbed hold of Dracine's hair, using the leverage to drop her to the floor. Her body slid across the polished granite into a darkened corner.

"STOP IT," Dracine screamed. Once again, her plea was cut short with Vlad's fist. He hit her again and again before getting down to business. That he cared little for Dracine was obvious, even less for her clothing.

It wasn't sex, or Dracine, for that matter that he wanted. It was the taste of power; dominance over another individual is what he craved. This he learned from the adults.

"Please let me get the clo..." Again came Vlad's fist. The next time she spoke, he took her head by the hair again and smashed it on the floor over and over until her eyes glazed over. She was still conscious but knew better than to scream anymore. Her arms and legs went limp as he tore the clothes from her.

His erection was weak. Even the sight of the nubile Dracine failed to bring on the wood. He spread her legs as he had seen the men do and plunged his dick into the apex. Something was wrong. It wasn't disappearing inside her. His ignorance turned to frustration as he jabbed his hips forward thrusting into nothing. A moment later, he went hard and splurched across her stomach, instantly losing the erection. The stupidity of youth was full on in Vlad. Seeing no reason why he should have failed, he blamed it on Dracine and beat her until he heard the court awakening. Vlad disappeared into the shadows of the court. No one saw him, or Dracine.

By the time Dracine was conscious, court was already in session. She pulled herself deeper into the corner, drawing up her clothes around her body in an attempt to hide. From the men she was able to, and if not, none of them were moved to mention the magistrate's bastard child. But it was from herself that she could not hide. Her body bore witness to Vlad's failure. From head to toe she was black and blue. This was the price of not knowing what to do. Her shame redoubled its effort when she realized she had wet herself in the process. Yet the stench of urine did not envelop her. The wetness was hers. The ignominy went deeper as she realized she liked it, part of it anyway. The attention. The undivided attention of another had her mesmerized. It was something she had never known. Like a good drug, she knew that she wanted more of it. 'I will take it again,' Dracine thought as she rubbed her sore groin. What was he looking for? She found it but still did not understand.

Her body ached long into the afternoon until the orange sun brought an end to the day's proceedings. As the last of the court departed, Dracine struggled into a standing position. Leaning against the wall for support, she staggered from the court to the kitchen; surely the cook would help.

Dracine fell into the chicken pen, outside the kitchen. She could go no further. Moira, the head cook's daughter was bringing in water when she found the young girl, beaten half to death. Moira was about the same age as Dracine, and though technically a slave, the young cook's apprentice had had a far more thorough upbringing than Dracine. She was also experienced in the things that Dracine was just becoming aware of.

Moira dropped to her knees while dipping a clean rag into the water. She squeezed out the excess water and began to clean the young royal's face. The smell of a man was heavy on the limp body. She looked at the torn clothing, garments too good for her to ever wear, now in shreds. It was the beating though that captured her attention. Purple, blues, black with scatters of deep shaded crimson, the colors of a morbid rainbow were spread across the young body. As Moira was putting two and two together, Dracine's eyes opened. One of them anyway, the other was swollen shut.

"Help me," rasped a damaged voice. It would be the first and last time Dracine ever used those two words together. Her eye closed and she was out again. Moira checked for wounds and bleeders before running to the kitchen to get her mother.

Mother had a piece of cloth tied around her head to catch the sweat as she leaned over the big pot suspended above a fire. Her body was plump, stretching the seams in her dress, as strong hands pushed the ladle, stirring the stew. Behind her was the cutting board with a dozen different knives hanging around it. Earthenware bowls held hardy root vegetables, herbs, and wild crafted edibles. Smoked pig belly hung from the ceiling along with a dozen rabbits that had been gutted, waiting to be skinned. The walls and overheads were covered with soot and grime.

The kitchen door slammed open into the dinge. "Mother come! Someone has hurt Dracine!" Moira was back out the way she came, while her mother, also Moira, set the ladle aside and wiped her hands on a dirty apron. 'What could it be now?' she muttered to herself, fully aware of her daughter's youthful overexaggeration.

"Oh my God," the mother said as she crossed herself in the Christian tradition. Her daughter's understatement had caught her by surprise. "Come Moira, we must get her inside, quickly." The two women picked up the still supine form of Dracine and carried her to the servant's rooms next to the kitchen.

"Put her in my bed," Mother said. They turned the body around and laid her down. "Now let's get her clothes off and see how badly she is hurt.

There were sudden intakes of breath and gasps while they did this. Neither Moira had ever seen a beating this severe. Even though there was very little skin surface that was not an unhealthy color, there were no broken bones either.

'It must have been one of the boys,' mother said under her breath. A larger man would have broken her, but all the bones seemed intact, indicating a weak individual. She checked between Dracine's legs for other damage. There was none, just bruising to the inside of the thighs. Her hymen was not broken. This brought a strange little laugh from mother.

"What is it, Mother?"

"For all the suffering this poor child went through, her abductor didn't even find the hole."

"Radu doesn't have that problem," Moira blurted, before realizing her faux pas.

"I know, Moira, I have been watching you. You know he will be leaving with Vlad soon."

"He told me last night," Moira replied quietly.

"Watch yourself with him, Moira. The Draculs have treated us kindly, but there are limitations."

"I know."

"Now clean her up so she doesn't have to wake like this." Mother waved her hands at the girl's disarray. "When she does, and if she can still think, you will explain to her the functions of her body so she doesn't, hopefully, have to go through this again."

"But mother," contested Moira.

"She will listen to you. If things were different, you would have been friends."

Moira retrieved more water and followed her mother's orders while she thought about what her mother had said and what she was going to say. She was bound and determined to make Dracine a friend in this life.

***

Dino's rig ground its way forward along the road into the mountains. He got coffee and fuel every chance he could, which is to say not often. He had enough of both for the round trip, so the stops gave him a reason, a chance, to grill the locals for information. They remembered Sechra passing through, but it made the mountain people uncomfortable to talk about it and they were forever with making the sign of the cross whenever her name was mentioned. Dino got the distinct impression they were very fearful of her or for her, but not sure which.

Dino drove on into the pall that oppressed the deep mountain region. At the last stop, he was told there would be no more supplies available from there on out. The mountain folk had abandoned the high pastures early this year. The reasons revolved around the weather and seemed more metaphoric than say a forecast. Dino was navigating by the seat of his pants. He checked on the signal from Sechra's cell phone every few hours. He was making progress in the right direction; unfortunately the road followed the contour of the mountains rather than boring straight through them as they do in modern times. The road that rose before him had been in use from time immemorial and was the only passage that went this deep into the mountains.

He stopped for lunch at the opening of a tunnel that went beneath an impassible peak. He got out of the rig to stretch his legs and breathe some fresh air when he noticed a brass plaque bolted to one side of the opening. It read, 'Built sometime in the mid-1400s by Vlad Tepes III, using the indigenous peoples as slave labor to construct the tunnel. No dynamite was used.' Dino's jaw dropped just a bit as he read the last sentence. He stood back to get a good look at the opening, which he guessed at thirty meters wide by ten high. Even by today's standards it was huge. The face of the tunnel had a block facade in Goth fashion complete with gargoyles to divert the snowmelt away from the opening. Looking inside the dark shaft, he felt the suction of the wind. It seemed to be trying to pull him into the depths. But it was the foul odor of death that made him grab the walls, dragging and clawing his way out. He retched in the light.

"Jesus Christ," he said to no one in particular.

Back in the truck, Dino pulled out his computer to track the road he was on. At the final fuel stop, the locals had directed him this way. He scratched his head. 'The road split here. I went right, the shorter route. Yet both roads go to the same place.' His hand went back to scratch beneath his wool cap again, he then rubbed his face. Dino took a slug of coffee, 'How could I have been so stupid? They were on motorcycles. This way, although shorter, was too steep for them to climb, what with the shitty weather and all.' He flipped the night driving light toggles and pressed the clutch, racking the shifter into first gear. The rig lurched forward, its tracks digging deep into the snow pack before entering the tunnel with an annoyingly loud, nerve-racking, clickity clack on the smooth basalt floor.

As the light of the entry faded, two banks of high intensity discharge lamps lit the scene before him as the stench of the deep passage seeped into the truck. Dino lit a cigarette as he concentrated on the road before him. It was a perfect surface. The debris of the seasons dissipated the deeper he went. The smell increased in direct proportion. He filled his handkerchief with a handful of tobacco and tied it around his nose and mouth. It helped, a little.

A whining sound that began as a distant shriek was growing louder. Dino stopped and listened. 'Is it the truck? A fanbelt? A bearing?' He got out of the rig holding the hanky to his face with one hand and a flashlight in the other. He cocked his good ear towards the rig and walked around it, panning the flashlight under the lifted vehicle to check for leaks. The dry surface of the road would certainly have a telltale puddle if there were. Dino backed up to get a good look. He was closer to the wall than he expected and bumped into it. Something jabbed into his back and rattled at his shoulders, clinging to folds of his jacket and grasping his limbs. He flailed, jumped, freaked and spun around to face the wall while pulling a handgun.

"Son of a bitch," he gasped, stumbling backwards over his heels, to wind up on the ground looking at the wall. Human bodies had been smashed into the gaps between the cut blocks that surfaced the walls and ceiling. Arms, legs and heads stuck out randomly all over the place. A more gruesome scene he could not imagine. Only bone remained, creating a loathsome form of grout. His coffee surged up his throat and he was just able to get himself out of the way of the splatter.

While driving, Dino had been so focused on the road that he didn't spare a glance to the walls. Had he, most certainly he would have turned around. As it was, he looked upon the panorama the H.I.D. truck lights lit all to well. Hundreds if not thousands of bodies reached out from the walls. Suddenly it all seemed to be closing in on him and he hopped back into the relative safety of the truck. All was normal again, just difficult to look at. But now that Dino had seen it, he could hardly watch the road in front of him as the phantasmagoria assaulted him. The scream got louder as the truck crawled along the passage. He wanted to go faster but couldn't stay focused enough, with the walls grabbing his attention. An hour passed in a brilliantly lit dark fascination. Several times he bounced the truck off the walls when he could not pull his eyes from some grotesque figure. When this would happen, the scream increased, bringing Dino back into the bleak. It was then he realized the walls and ceiling were screaming. It was still alive and suffering after all the years, howling into the black void.

Lost in the madness, the rig began to tilt downwards at a precipitous angle. The hardpacked surface was now a loose black gravel with no traction or support. Dino jammed it into reverse in an attempt to back out. The tracks began to slip on the shards of lava. He stepped on the accelerator as a cold sweat ran down the center of his back. There was no other way to go. Instead of escaping he concentrated on controlling his descent. The slope steepened. With the truck sliding down past the point of no return, Dino stole a look out the window. A whitish pile loomed ahead, or downwards as the case may be. The rate of descent was increasing with no way to slow it. The rig careened down the tunnel bouncing off the walls, which were no longer adorned with the dead. Relatively speaking, this portion of the roadway was crude and unfinished. Driving lights lit up the pale mound he was going to smash into. The brilliant beams raked a wicked glare over the immediate future. A pile of bones filling most of the mineshaft lay directly ahead.

With nothing he could do and no time to do it in, Dino lowered the plow smashing into the heap. His momentum slowed gradually as the plow and tracks crushed into the skeletons. Dino shifted into low gear, pushing on until he broke through the mound's other side into the open tunnel. He stopped, pulled his cap and raked his hands through his hair.

"Jesus fucking Christ," Dino breathed in relief. Despite the carnage, the smell was gone and the screaming could only be heard in the distance. He took a few deep breaths before lighting a cigarette to rid himself of the last of the odor and calm down. Dino started to laugh at himself and the situation he was in. It was no laughing matter, but there simply wasn't any other way of dealing with it. Maybe that's why some lunatics are always laughing. It was their way of coping. Dino wasn't crazy but the chortle was the relief he was looking for.

He walked to the limit of the rig's lights. The roadway was clear and less demented. 'Okay, Dino, let's keep this train moving.'

The day ground on into the night. Not that you could tell without looking at a watch. He tried not to look at it too much. 'The tunnel will end when it ends,' he told himself with some reluctance. 'It has to.' He wouldn't let himself think about the alternative. Another day passed in silence and darkness. The sound of the engine and tracks across the rock's surface had blended into a background of black growling. The lights but a weak defense against the darkness. It's all relative. The tunnel turned a sweeping right-hander when Dino clasped his hands over his eyes. The glare of a cloudy bright day beckoned before him. Dino stepped on it bursting into daylight a few moments later. He drove another hundred meters into the light and away from the cave before stopping. Before he could jump from the truck screaming like a kid, his inner voice insinuated itself. 'Now what?'

He scratched at the week's growth on his chin. "I made it, but to where?" he questioned the cold dawn, opening the door of the rig and stepping onto the crunchy snow. With map in hand, Dino walked back towards the exit of the tunnel. He scanned the surroundings. 'Where is it?' It was only by watching the tracks of his truck that suddenly the exit loomed before him. 'What the fuck?' He took a few steps backwards and the mouth disappeared. He stepped forwards and back a few times, confused with the illusion. 'I better log this place into my GPS, otherwise I'll never find it again.' Dino hopped back into the truck and played with the little computer for a few minutes. Before heading onward, he did a damage survey of the truck and checked all the fluid levels. The county of Eforie Sud would be none too pleased with condition of their rig. "Nothing I can't fix," he said to no one, shrugging his shoulders as he jumped back inside the warmth of the cab.

The road cut around several low peaks before merging with another road. A snow pack covered the asphalt as Dino put the hammer down. A kilometer later he shut the rig down. An avalanche covered the road. Dino got out of the rig again and looked at the mess of snow, ice, trees and boulders. 'Shit.' He grabbed a pair of binoculars and went to climbing the tumult of snow to get an idea of how big it was and what it would take to get past it. More than once the snow at his feet caved and he would have to spread his arms to keep from being swallowed whole.

Dino finally made his way to the top. The whole avalanche had that unstable feeling about it. And it was fresh. A week or two tops. The freshly broken snow pack and ice had yet to begin sublimating. Using the glasses he spied the road ahead. After the snow was clean road, but there was another barrier at the far end of it. The blockade appeared manmade. Was it? No it couldn't be. It had to be Dino's imagination, seeing what he wanted to see. Were there two motorcycles parked in front of the roadblock?

With his goal in sight, Dino had to curb his enthusiasm. To crank it up now would be a fool's response. It was a tender balance between pushing it and pushing it too far. First he had to get over the mountain of snow and rubbish before him. It took an hour of creative plowing to build a ramp up the side of the frozen plateau. That was the easy part. From here it was a simple matter of finding a solid lane from point A to point B. At sunset, Dino found himself surrounded by snow about midway across the avalanche. He was beat. The combination of a series of adrenalin rushes along with having the shit frightened out of him more times in one day than he had in a lifetime, left him dazed and confused. This was a condition he was not comfortable with at all. And the worst frame of mind to cross a treacherous terrain, in the dark. He forced himself to stay away from the coffee and did a few shots of brandy to help bend his will to his desire. Right now that meant sleep. Dino couldn't remember the last time he had a good night's rest. He wrestled with the bones of the dead, before falling into a fitful black state.

Dino woke a few hours before dawn. Stuffed inside a sleeping bag and curled up on the front seat, he didn't want to move, knowing that when he did it would be the beginning of another marathon. Dino stared at the dashboard mindlessly for as long as he could.

With sunrise still an hour away, he sat up and started the little burner to make a pot of coffee. Dino hopped from the cab to fill his pot with snow for the water, when he saw the footprints of something big that had circled the truck in the middle of the night. He dropped the morning's coffee water and pulled his gun. Looking at the size of the tracks and puniness of the gun started the day off with a laugh, albeit an uneasy one. Refilling the pot, he got back in the truck and finished making a hasty brew. He tried to blow it off by thinking of the abominable snowman and yeti stories. But for some reason, the thing that made the prints outside was darker than the sludge at bottom of his cup, than the images of a snowman. Dino swirled the dregs, downed them and poured another, and then rolled a cigarette. With no gun larger than his pistol, he double checked the magazine and put a round in the pipe. As ready as he could be, Dino left the rig to scout the route he would take. Naturally, oddly, morbidly, he began to follow the trail left in the wake of the beast. It had taken the same way to and away from the truck. Still thinking it was maybe an animal of considerable size, and that animals somehow can find the safest path, Dino followed along. It was indeed solid beneath his feet and wide enough for his rig to scrape through the narrows. His spirits lifted cresting the final rise and seeing the open road.

'If I am being led into a trap, then so be it,' he said to himself. Dino stopped himself from firing his weapon into the air to announce his presence. Something about 'not being a complete fool' controlled his actions.

But time was of the essence. He did not come all this way for a little adventure; someone's life was at stake. A friend's life. That's what he was here for. Not a client, nor a contract, but a friend in need.

The rig started with a clatter of valves and puff of black diesel smoke. Dino poured another cup, rolled the window down, lit a cigarette and headed on. The going was slow, he was used to that by now. The trail across the moraine held tight. An hour later, Dino drove off the slide onto the roadway. Ten minutes later he pulled up next to Sechra's bike. The motor was out of gas but the dash lights were still on. Dino smiled. That new battery he installed held its charge, delivering the signal from Sechra's cell phone. He turned the key to the 'off' position. 'Deal with that later."

Now he was excited and on firm enough ground to show it. He started his rig up, set the plow and pushed his way through the concrete roadblock. Dino followed the road to the center of the camp, honking his air horn in loud bursts. 'Enough to wake the dead,' he thought. It woke nothing. Birds scattered in the trees as deer bolted for the cover of the forest. All around was quiet. Dead quiet as Dino climbed down from the truck.

"SECHRA," he yelled. It was too still. There was no one here and no reason for him to waste his breath. He looked over the ground before his own footprints destroyed other prints. There weren't many. A few led to a trailer. Dino knocked before entering, expecting the worst.

"They were here." A pot of cold coffee sat atop the woodstove. He relit the fire and started a fresh pot while examining the contents of the mobile home. There were no real signs that a living situation had been established. Like a hotel room, the luggage and gear had been dumped on the floor, but nothing was arranged. Sechra's toiletries were still rolled up, not used at all. Her empty holster lay on the floor surrounded by eleven unused shells. 'Well, if she had her gun, she had a chance.'

Once coffee was ready, he poured a mug, rolled a smoke and went outside. Inclement weather conditions had all but obliterated the tracks left by Sechra and Skender. Dino wandered through the heavy equipment that was left at the site. Most of it looked operational, just neglected. But he was not here to play with some old toys, not yet at least. Faded footprints led away from the bone yard before disappearing completely. Dino kept walking in the direction the steps had been going.

By the smell of it, they probably led to a poorly engineered outhouse. With each step the smell grew stronger. It was worse by far than the stench within the tunnel. He had hoped to never smell such a thing again and was about to leave when something caught his eye.

There were a dozen ravens fifty meters ahead busy doing what carrion do. Dino sucked it up and kept moving forward. At twenty meters the birds took off as one, screeching and cawing at the intrusion on their meal. They circled once before settling in the branches of leafless black oaks and towering pines, watching.

With the scavengers gone, Dino was able to see the form of someone on the ground. He raced forward. Ravens usually fed off the dead, but not always. He dropped to his knees next to Skender's body. Cruel wounds covered the body and blood had soaked the surrounding soil before freezing. The birds fed on the open wounds, and were having the ruined eye for dessert. Peck marks gouged and tore bits of flesh away from every place skin was exposed. It was the face, however, a face only the damned could love. Dino looked away, it was just too much.

The stink wafted into his nostrils again. He realized it did not come from the body. With the cold, it may very well have been in a morgue. The rot seemed to come from the building not six meters away.

The massive door was solid and locked tight. Holding a lit cigarette next to the edge of the door and the jamb, a slight breeze blew the smoke away from the door. Dino put his nose to the gap.

"Whoo! Jesus," he exclaimed. He pulled his head away. Dino had found the source. He went back to the body. Sechra's shotgun lay next to the dead man's right hand, which was no longer clutching the gun but pointing at the door. The extended forefinger had been chewed to the bone by the ravens.

'Who was this guy? Is it Skender? What the hell happened here? A spent shell casing was lying on the ground next to Skender. Who or what

was he shooting at?' These and a thousand other questions roiled around
in Dino's head. He began searching Skender for identification. Removing
the rock embedded in Skender's chest revealed a ghastly wound but no
I.D. Only after rolling him over and digging into the back pocket did he
pull a wallet. There wasn't much. A couple worn family pictures, a few
bucks, an old pass for the med school in Bucharest, and a driver's license.
It was Skender. Dino's heart dropped a few feet. "Shit," he said to the
corpse. "Couldn't you have waited a couple of days?"

Getting no reply, Dino squatted and took Skender by the shoulders.
The dead finger waved as if saying, 'notice me, notice me,' as it pointed
at the door to the oubliette. Dino did and got the message. What he was
looking for was behind that door. He dragged Skender's lightened body away
from the smell to a pile of rocks he spotted earlier. Laying Skender on the
earth, Dino forced the arms to bend, folding the dead man's hands across
the chest and rolling him up with an old blanket. When the rocks were
piled over the body to protect it from scavengers, Dino folded his hands,
saying a made up prayer. "Dear God, I don't know what this poor bastard
did to deserve such a fate. Forgive him, he was just a man. I don't know
what you've got in store for me and I don't much care. If you want to help,
I could sure use a hand. If not, just stay out of the fucking way. Amen."

Dino wasn't one for long goodbyes or the drama that goes along with
them. "Thanks for calling, Skender." Dino returned to the trailer for
more coffee and to make a plan.

***

Sechra hammered on. She no longer slept. Driven by coffee, desire,
and a son of hell, Sechra's assault on the granite began to come
into being. The central panels were complete. Each portrayed an
era specific to the evolution of Romania.

They began in the time before the crusades and the infiltration of
Christianity, the reign of Vlad Tepes III, and with the Inquisitions that
followed them. It was important for Sechra to show in detail the horrors
of these time periods, with a skill that exceeded her hideous exhibition
that was scourging the world on its tour. More still, to capture the glimmer
of hope in the people's endurance and survival.

There was another reason why she no longer slept. Early on in her
confinement, she had paused in her sculpting to give her hands a rest.

They were cramping and it affected her control of the tools. In her mind, there was no room for error. Sechra set her tools down, drank from her cup, sat in the broken chair and promptly fell asleep. She had let her guard down. She did not hear the rasping shriek that was the floor door opening, nor smell the gust of fetid air that came with it. She did however feel the wetness of its drool as it splashed on her face while grotesque hips tried to ram a flaccid penis into her. It seemed more a pantomime of rape than a real one with the exception of the total fear and loathing that came with it. Sechra screamed into the darkness that now wished to become part of her. Her hands reached out for her hammer, a chisel, anything GODDAMNIT! She flailed at the embodiment of evil. The more she fought the more it laughed. She felt it becoming hard. 'Oh God nooooooo!'

"Your God can't help you now!" Spittle and phlegm fell from its mouth as he pounded on her, forcing penetration.

The more she fought, the more it became enraged and violent in its repulsive intent. As part of her recoiled at the horror of what was happening, another part said, 'Stop! It feeds off of you, your fear, your disgust. Stop!' The one thing she did not want to do was 'give in'. Yet the reality was, it was the only thing Sechra 'could' do. A moment passed in confusion and fear before she went all Ghandi.

It screamed deafeningly within the confines of the oubliette, shaking the building, sending a rain of dust and grit down from the rafters. Like a jilted lover, it cursed its failure at Sechra. The rabid pounding stopped as its wet sticky mass lifted from her supine and motionless form. It kicked her hard in the stomach. "WORK!" Tears of thankfulness rolled down her cheeks as she gathered her torn clothing.

Since then it was all Sechra did. She fought through the cramps, broken fingers and gouged flesh, from missed hits. 'Better to hit my hand than the rock in the wrong place.' To look at them, if you could, her hands were a wreck. If you were to look at her, you would see a similar reflection. She had grown hard and sinewy. Her face and body caked in rock dust made her appear to be made of the stone itself. In a way, she was.

With no pauses of any considerable length, beyond eating, drinking and shitting, the work progressed quickly. It was pleased with what it saw but no longer bothered Sechra physically. Since its failure at dominating her, he kept the conversation to understanding the sculpture. The conversations were one-sided as well. Sechra maintained a vigilant intermittent silence. When it would ask about a certain detail or why a child seemed to be smiling, she would take its hand and pressed it to the spot in question.

"Feel the pain, it is there." She would say no more. The pain it would feel was Sechra's, surging through her hand into its.

"Yes, yes, there is much in the way of suffering here," it would slobber, understanding nothing.

She would then pull her hand away and return to work. Sechra was closing in on the final panels, the rough out etchings were in place. The second to last was a fantastic collage of images, detailing the revolution twenty years ago. A few panels before this one showed the original battle of Eforie Sud back in the 1400's. Though the two images shared a certain familiarity, the outcome of the latter was considerably different then the former. There was Jake and Bela gunning down the parade of the damned. Riana aboard Barge#22 orating with the sunrise. Tepes' camp along the waterfront with a casket being swum out to sea. The bittersweet triumph of a people that had lost too much in the gaining of their freedom. Years from now, people would still come and see the sculpture with the words, 'truly remarkable' on their lips.

The sculpting was becoming harder for Sechra. She assumed it was the lack of a decent diet; sleep deprivation, and the constant effort. And she would be right, but only partly. The layer of rock dust she was covered in was seeping through her skin, making it more chitinous. For example, she could no longer let go of her hammer. To think that she had become the hammer or the hammer had become her would be a creative solution, but wrong. Her hand had turned to stone.

Was Sechra driven to finish the work? Undoubtedly. Was she manic about it? Absolutely! Would she have torn the head off of anyone who tried to stop her? In a heartbeat. Was she crazy? Not even close. Sechra had never been so at peace with herself and the world, ever.

***

A week passed in the absence of Ahmed. Dracine was becoming comfortable on her own. She reduced the number of pipefuls she smoked during the day and night, although the first of the day was always the best. Normally she would chase that beast until sleep would overtake her, then, begin it again the next day. Typical junkie behavior. Dracine was making an attempt at balance, something she had never done before. Her duties as a magistrate became clear along with understanding the law. Sentences became opportunities for the criminal to learn. A man with no hands or feet only learns how to die. Dracine's past cruelties had been necessary, it would seem, to accomplish this. Her inhumane judgments on minor infractions and major were still fresh in everyone's memory.

To be honest, the week's work had been mundane, if not downright boring. Thusly her even-handedness went by practically unnoticed. Not completely, mind you. A little kindness goes a long way. Already the next week's docket was filling rapidly with peasants and businessmen hoping to get in on the wave of goodness, for surely it wouldn't last. The common man was already hip to the eccentricities of the ruling class.

While dealing with society's confusions, Dracine had been thinking about Ahmed's imminent return. 'Just be cool,' went her line of thinking. She would try to phase him out. If not, she would kill him. Killing men was something she was good at.

Dracine sat in a pile of pillows with her feet upon an ottoman, when there was a light but firm rap on the door. She knew Ahmed's knock. After checking the pouch at her side, to make sure it was ready and to give her confidence, Dracine waited for the second knock. It would have been out of character to answer on the first. When it came she felt the impatience behind it.

Laughing to herself she said, "Come in, Ahmed."

The door opened and when his head came through, he shot Dracine a hard look, as if she was blowing his cover.

"I am back, Ahmed. We will no longer be playing this charade. Come in. Was your journey uneventful?" Dracine was taking the fight to him, metaphorically.

"It was, my lord," he said, cautiously while closing the door.

The room reeked of freshly smoke opium and tobacco. Everything appeared in order as he scanned the quarters.

"Would you like me to open the windows and let some fresh air in?"

"Please, that would be nice. I was thinking about it, but just couldn't bring myself to the effort. It's been so difficult without you around," she drolled. "But leave the curtains closed, the light." So far so good.

Ahmed went around being a good servant before saying anything. When he was ready, "I shouldn't have to be leaving again for some time. I procured a sufficiently large quantity for you. At considerable personal risk, I might add."

"Thank you, Ahmed. But I fear your efforts have been wasted. I have found something new. Light a candle for me, will you?" Dracine untied the pouch and poured the works onto the table. There was a small hand-blown vial full of white powder with a stopper, large thimble, antique syringe or at least the oldest Karuna could find in the storage of the seaside estate, a lemon, and cottonball.

Dracine had practiced the ritual of mixing a dose over and over, so that when she did it before Ahmed she would be smooth, unselfconscious. A pro.

"Can you now squeeze my upper left arm, firmly?"

Ahmed did as he was asked. Dracine clenched her fist a few times before the veins stood up like tree roots protruding from the ground. With a slight shove, she slipped the needle through her skin, waiting for her blood to enter the glass syringe before pushing on the plunger.

"You can release me and go." He did, but took his time about leaving.

Dracine set the point down, laid back into the pillow and closed her eyes.

When Ahmed was sure Dracine was nodding heavily, he could tell by her breathing, he examined the articles on the low table. It was foreign to him. Ahmed's time in the future was limited to being the P.A. and bodyguard of his father. He had little opportunity to venture into reality and so knew very little about real life in the modern world.

The vial and syringe's method of manufacture could very well have been made in this time period. Glass blowing had already been popular for centuries. But where did it come from, who gave the stuff to Dracine? After searching the rooms for any other surprises and finding none, he went to interrogate the staff. Kill them if necessary, but he had to know.

Dracine opened her eyes after Ahmed departed. The dosage had been mild. What Jake would call a teeny weeny little speedball, basically enough to bring down a horse then send him racing the track for the rest of the day. The nod kicked in first, satisfying the first part of the plan. To instill the seed of doubt in Ahmed's mind. That there may be another waiting in line to take his place, who has something even more pleasurable to offer.

Ahmed was highly educated in the drug use of the time. It was obvious that what Dracine was putting in her arm was an opiate. But of a concentration that put his best to shame. What was it? In the meantime, he would be ever attentive and alert to her behavioral patterns. Something was changing. This was his world and he liked it the way it is. The thought of change made him vomit on the way to the servant's quarter.

Dracine knew she was walking a tightrope with the drug thing. Trying to be malleable, and in control at the same time, is a challenge for anyone. Some come to it naturally, others struggle, and most fail. Failure was not an option.

It never is.

She called and had the itinerary for the coming week brought in. While waiting, Dracine put the works away, reattaching the bag to her waist. She got up to pour a coffee and have a hit from the pipe before the servant arrived. She played the game for real now. There was too much on the line. 'The walls have eyes, ears, and noses,' she laughed, exhaling a halo of smoke about her head and absorbing the calming euphoria that came with it.

There was a light tap on the door. It was not Ahmed, nor any of the other servants, whose knock she knew by heart. A second, patient rap came thirty seconds after the first.

"Yes, come in," Dracine said placidly.

The tray came through the door first, bearing the scrolls of the itinerary. It was held by Atoli, the castle whore.

"The scrolls, Magistrate," Atoli said with her head bowed submissively.

"Please come in, Atoli. I have not had a chance to talk with you since taking you on." Dracine pointed to a table where Atoli could set the tray of documents down. She filled two glasses with coffee and brought them to a comfortable sitting area. Dracine set the coffee down and folded herself into a sitting position of royal ease.

"Relax, Atoli. I would like to consider us friends."

"I am a whore, dear sir."

"We are all whores, Atoli," Dracine laughed while patting the pillows beside her.

Atoli smiled at the small disclosure. She had the thought many times.

"Have you ever had the coffee?"

"No, but the smell of it being cooked in the kitchen is the aroma of the gods."

"Very true. How are your children?" Dracine smiled, taking a long slow drink, savoring.

Atoli followed. The warm brew brought a smile to her face while sating her tongue.

"They are very well, thank you. Your head cook was able to find suitable and meaningful work for them."

"She has been in my employ since she was a child. You can trust her."

"My one boy shows a talent for numbers and is being educated. There are no words for how this makes me feel." Atoli's eyes filled with moisture.

"Nor should there be. Some things can only be felt." Dracine reached over, taking Atoli's hand. A surge of lust both that of the body and blood coursed through Dracine. Never had both been so powerful, and at once! It took all of her will to slow things down, calm herself as sweat broke out on her forehead. NOT YET!

Atoli was drawn to Dracine as well. It was in her nature to read the signs of yearning and desire to assuage them. She scooted a little closer to Dracine and wrapped her in long arms that had a great deal of practice in these things. Atoli massaged the tense muscles in Dracine's neck, moving her hands slowly about her body, relaxing it. One hand paused, the briefest of pauses, as it caressed Dracine's breasts. There was no doubt in Atoli's mind. She had made love to women before.

"What can I do for you, master?"

"Number one, don't call me master in private. You can call me Dracine." Dracine knew she had been pinned out. "What I wish, I am sure has never been asked of you. I do not ask as your superior, but as a friend. And as a friend you have every right to say no without risk." Dracine gave Atoli some time to think about it.

Atoli wasted none of it. She knew what the term friend meant, but was only slightly confused about the vague quality of the proposition. Most men, and women, know exactly what they want and yet are afraid to express it. There was no fear sensed in Dracine's delivery, concern was more like it. Then again Dracine was not a man. "Anything."

"There will be no pain, only the smallest of scars. You will feel a little tired afterwards and must eat well to restore yourself. The cook will take care of that. There is one more thing." Dracine had never been this considerate to anyone before. What she wanted, she took, without hesitation or remorse. This was clearly out of character for her. She needed to trust Atoli without cutting her tongue out.

"Anything Dracine," repeated Atoli. "But there is something I must tell you." She waited for Dracine to signal to continue. When she did, "I come from the old country. The mountains. It wasn't until disaster struck that I moved to the city. I know a great deal of the dark matters that surround you. I saw it in you the first time we met. Then you went away. When I saw you just now at the doorway, I knew you had returned. I see your hunger and need. When you asked, there was no other answer I could give. It is my heritage. You could have taken it against my will and still I would not have spoken of it to anyone. Since you ask, it is my duty and honor."

Atoli unbuttoned the front of her frock, releasing her ample cleavage and laid back on the pillows. Dracine moved towards her. If there were anyone to see, it would appear the two were having a tender moment together. For that's what it was, an act of love and devotion.

Dracine placed her thumb firmly over the small bite on Atoli's neck until she was certain it had sealed. A damp cloth wiped away any excess blood. Dracine lay back on the pillows, absorbing the rush while Atoli dressed.

"Thank you, Atoli. You know I will ask again."

"Yes, and the answer will always be the same." Atoli rolled over on the cushion and gave Dracine a kiss on the forehead.

"Please tell the staff I do not wish to be disturbed."

"As you wish." Atoli left the room silently, not wishing to make any disturbance and went to bed.

Relief washed through Dracine, the pillows like clouds as the new blood coursed fresh in her system. The lifestyle she led had whitewashed, fogged and dissolved her actions within an opiated dream. A clean breeze lifted the billowing blindness from her eyes. For the first time in her life, Dracine was seeing clearly; 'a moment of clarity' as alcoholics refer to it. Gone was the wacko side of herself, the neurosis and psychosis of a twisted youth that had formed the psychopathic mindset that was Dracine's trademark.

Past, present and future merged into a never-ending panorama behind Dracine's closed eyes. Tears formed, creating rivulets down the sides of her face merging at the chin into a single drip that splashed silently on silk embroidered pillows. The tears were not for her, or the hundreds of faces she had disfigured in court, but for the whole of the peoples' plight across the country and her role in maintaining the status quo.

A knock at the door interrupted her reverie. Dracine sat up, downing the rest of her cold coffee and gathering her wits before responding to the second knock. It was Ahmed.

"Good afternoon, my lord. I see you have taken to spending time with the court's whore." Though said with great care, Dracine could not help but hear the condescension and sarcasm that was spit upon the breeze that blew gently through the window. Her own views on these and other things were changing. The last few days, culminating with a certain joi de vivre that came with the blood, was a dark epiphany. Normally she would have fallen in with Ahmed's charm and chagrin of the people, regardless of their public status. They degraded everyone equally, which abased and dishonored themselves and their position. Dracine now understood this.

She repeated what she had said to Atoli, but with a different emphasis. "We are all whores, Ahmed." She smiled at the phrase's cleverness. "I am sure your watchers have told you what went on while you were away. I wouldn't want to burden you with having to hear something twice. It was enjoyable to have a conversation with someone that doesn't want something from you. You should try it sometime."

"I have you, my lord," Ahmed responded warily.

"That's the catch. We need each other, Ahmed, and our talks are contaminated with it."

Ahmed felt like he was falling. Reality had just been pulled out from under his feet. He grasped for anything, anything to keep from vomiting as his knees went weak. "Perhaps we should smoke on this?"

Dracine, in the state of hyper-awareness that came with a fresh influx of blood, could 'see' Ahmed, struggling to cope. Was it their time together and circumstance that urged her to ease his torment? 'I will need him,' one part of her said. The other said, 'What for?'

Just because one is seeing clearly doesn't mean you get all the answers, too. Was she feeling compassion? Having never utilized such a thing before Dracine, herself, was as confused with the new reality as was Ahmed. How do you mete out compassion, apportion kindness?

Brutally, that's how, but you give them a chance.

This was the first time that Ahmed had shown confusion. He needed something to do, a mission that would get him out of Dracine's hair and give him a chance to collect himself. She was showing compassion in allowing him the time to bring his thoughts into collusion with hers. This was Ahmed's opportunity. If he continues to conspire against her, there will not be another. Dracine's judgment would then be quick and devastating.

"I think I will pass, thank you though. You know, Ahmed, technically Atoli ranks higher in the court's eye than you do. I recommend we treat all members of my staff with equal respect. Come sit, there is something I need to ask of you."

"I will, in the future, take heed of your exact words." 'Yes, I will treat her the same,' Ahmed murmured under his breath. 'The house staff was beaten to within an inch of their lives in order to get them to divulge what had happened in his absence. None of them broke under torture. Perhaps the whore will, as I treat her with an equal respect!' He sat stiffly within arm's reach of Dracine. 'I should kill her now!'

"All that would get you would be the edge of an ax," Dracine responded, reading Ahmed's mind. "You will never kill me." Dracine gave that mind something worth thinking about. "Now," Dracine deftly untied the pouch at her side, "what I would like you to do is to take a sample of what I have here and have your alchemists alter your opium to re-create it."

"My lord, the recent acquisition is the most powerful product they have yet to obtain from the poppy."

"I do not ask for excuses. I know it can be done and demand results. If you wish to continue with your belief that you control me, I suggest you comply."

"My lord Drache, I do no such thing!"

"Don't lie to me!" Dracine's hand whipped from the resting position on her lap to catch Ahmed's cheek with her fist. He tumbled over backwards from the blow onto the floor, his head knocking the stone floor solidly. He wallowed for a moment as the stars in his head flashed brilliantly before winking out. His thinking was awash with his angst. Ahmed wanted to lash out. He kept his hands by his side, listening to that little voice in the back of his head where blood oozed from a split in his skull. 'Shut the fuck up and get out!'

Ahmed picked up the sample vial. "As you wish."

His footsteps echoed loud in the empty halls of Castle Drache. Any of the staff that felt them would now hurry away in to a darkened alcove to avoid what had become a menace. Too many of them had the fresh scabs, missing teeth and purple welts of previous encounters as an unpleasant reminder.

Another set of steps merged with Ahmed's. At the intersection of a large hallway, the smaller Atoli sidestepped to avoid bumping into Ahmed. "Ah, dear Atoli. I hear you have been comforting the Magistrate?"

"It is what I am here for," she replied skeptically.

"Yes, indeed. Perhaps you can be of some assistance to me as well. I have fallen and wondered if you could come to my quarters and dress the wound."

Atoli walked around him, fingering the hair, matted by the drying blood. "It would be best if we cleaned this up promptly."

"I was hoping you would say that. Right this way." What Ahmed had in mind had nothing to do with mending an insignificant cut. He was certain in his twisted thinking that it was Atoli who was providing Dracine with her new drug and that the magistrate had taken the whore into her confidence. Ahmed was confident he could withdraw the information from Atoli, even if it killed her.

The door to the kitchen area was ajar. Eyes watched through the gap. Ears that could, filled the remaining open space. All were intent upon the encounter between Atoli and Ahmed. The staff liked Atoli. She was not like the others, and her children were well reared, respectful and always ready to help. The head cook did not want Ahmed to abuse Atoli like he had done to the rest of the staff. Since they were more or less invisible, or at very least not given the slightest countenance, no one noticed the bruises and damaged flesh delivered to them by the hand of Ahmed. She knew Atoli would be mistreated in ways that would not be seen by the magistrate; yet cause the whore a considerable agony equal to their own.

In her early years, the cook was considered quite a looker. That was before Ahmed took her to his bed. The first time she accepted it as part of her duty. After that, it was her fate. Several years of Ahmed's 'affections' left her the scared undesirable cook for the magistrate. Ahmed no longer took her away at night, yet would smile each time their eyes locked, mocking her decrepitude.

After Atoli and Ahmed left for his quarters, the cook sent her daughter to Dracine's to tell her what was going to happen. Years of practice made the dash to the magistrate's wing silent as well as fast. The knock was urgent.

Having a taste of what Atoli had to offer earlier in the day left Dracine in a high state of awareness. She was reaching for the door handle just as the door knocker stopped. The door swung open.

"What is it, my friend?" Dracine and the cook's daughter had been quiet friends since childhood, though the term friend was rarely used.

Dracine drew her into the room, into the light. "My God, what has happened to you?"

"It is not for me that I have come, but Atoli."

"She was fine when she left here. Why were you beaten?"

"It is Ahmed! And now he has taken her to his room. Mother says come quickly. He is going to hurt her!"

"Head back to the kitchen, have your mother ready." The servant gave Dracine a questioning look. "She will know. Go!"

Bare feet fled the room and disappeared down the hall. Dracine reached into the folds of her nightshirt, pulling the nine-millimeter. She jacked a round into the chamber, stuffed the gun within easy reach. Dracine did not run to Ahmed's room. An effort of extreme will caused her to 'be' at the door in question. Dracine stepped back a couple of paces, then took three giant strides to the door. A fourth was applied to the door itself, which splintered inward at the force of the kick. Dracine was right behind, gun aimed in the dimly lit room. Atoli was tied face down over a writing desk, a gag kept her screams muffled as Ahmed was working a pole viciously in her ass. The smashing in of the door barely broke his attention. The two slugs from the pistol, one into each knee, however garnered his full attention as he fell backwards against a wall. Dracine pistol-whipped him until he went unconscious.

She fell to Atoli, removing the gag.

"Get it out of me," she cried, tears rolling down her cheeks. Dracine carefully took hold of the short piece of rough wood and removed it as delicately as possible. Atoli whimpered but did not cry out.

By now, a gathering had formed at the broken door. Dracine called in the cook.

"Thank you for calling me. Your foresight will not be forgotten. Have some men dig a hole in the center of the yard before the courthouse entry. Then have them get the longest pole they have and sharpen one end of it. Once they begin the work, return here, you will have some wet work to attend to." To the daughter who ran so quickly, Dracine said, "Some salt and lye, my swift sparrow."

Ahmed began to rouse. Dracine kicked him solidly in the head; she wasn't ready to deal with him yet. Dracine wrapped Atoli in a sheet, then with all the care she could give, carried Atoli back to her quarters and gave the poor girl the medical attention she needed. The doctors of the current times were merely curious butchers. Dracine did all she could. It would be enough. Only after Atoli consumed a cup of tea in which a ball of opium had been mixed and was sleeping comfortably did Dracine return to the scene of the crime.

The cook stood menacingly over a cringing Ahmed who, if the fresh blood from pokes of the cook's knife were any clue, had tried to escape, failing.

"Excellent, excellent," Dracine commented as she entered the room.

"Lord Drache, my lord, help me," pleaded Ahmed. "You can not do this!" He now commanded.

"Shut up," Dracine said to Ahmed. To the head cook, "If he speaks again, cut his tongue out!"

"Our lord Drache is a woman!" Ahmed screamed this to the gathering of servants and guards. What he didn't know, as he only thought of himself, was that all her close attendants knew. More than that, they were loyal to Dracine and would voluntarily die before revealing the information.

The cook did not wait for permission. Her task was clear. Years of handling live animals and dead ones made the work look natural, and to Ahmed unnaturally fast. A strong hand, with equally powerful digits snatched his tongue as he said 'woman', pulling the tongue tight, stretching it out to the limit before it would tear. A flash of silver crossed Ahmed's eyes and suddenly the tension was relieved, only to be replaced with an iron tasting fluid filling his mouth. He tried to scream. He could not.

The cook smiled a toothless grin, tossed the tongue into the small fire that kept the chill at bay, and then wiped the blade on Ahmed's shirt. She did not want his filth on her. The cook stepped back, her duty done for the moment. Ahmed was in shock, from loss of blood. The cook's younger daughter, at a sign from her mother, went up to Ahmed and filled his mouth with salt, to help stop the bleeding.

The daughter was brushing the salt from her hands, stopping when Dracine came up to her. "Thank you. Now go and check on the men's work. Return when it is it finished."

"Yes, my lord."

"You may call me Dracine when we are alone." Dracine looked at all the faces in the room, her entire staff. "As can you all when we are amongst family." Dracine gestured to everyone. "Go girl!"

"Yes Dra... Dracine." Silent feet bolted from the room.

"All of you leave. There is to be no word spoken of this evening." Everyone nodded and turned to leave. "Except you, cook." When the room was empty of people, Dracine said, "Please close the door."

There was no reason to go into the drama of the cook's past with Ahmed. The atrocities were, unfortunately, common knowledge.

"Tie his feet and hands, to ensure your safety. When he wakes, shake the salt from his mouth, then cut off his genitals and stuff them in. When your daughter returns, have him taken to the courtyard."

"Yes, my lord."

Dracine looked at her queerly.

The cooked looked down. "You have been like a sister to my daughter. You will always be my lord."

"As you wish. I must tend to Atoli. There will be no need to notify me. I will know and be there presently." With a flourish of confidence, Dracine left the cook to her business, which she felt may have a cathartic effect on the cook.

Atoli slept peacefully, all things considered, while Dracine made herself a smoke. She had to maintain her composure, but tonight the eastern seaboard would learn not to piss off Dracine. She settled into a chair that overlooked the grounds where the people, far below, worked like ants. When Ahmed's body was dragged out to the courtyard, Dracine took one last hit and willed herself to the scene below, arriving in a billow of fog, scented with burnt almonds that dissipated quickly. She gave a mental push that she had been among them the whole time. The simple of mind fell for it, those wiser knew better and were rightfully afraid. The future could go either way. Cover your ass and keep your mouth shut was the word up of the day.

"Bring out a wine cask. An old and rotted one that will not be used again" Dracine inspected the hole for the pike while waiting for delivery. The wait was not long. "Place it there," she said, pointing. "And bring the pole."

It took four strong men to heft the pole and carry it to the barrel, setting the pointed end on it. Dracine walked up to the pole, feeling the freshly adzed surface. Without the flair normally associated with feats of strength, she picked it up with one hand. The men who carried it appeared shocked at her ability, so Dracine gave them something to do.

"This is a little trick my half brother is fond of. Hold him over that barrel, face down and don't let go!"

Seizing the pike like an over-sized javelin, Dracine took twenty paces behind Ahmed who was now pleading for his life through his balls. Lowering the pole to waist level, she began walking forward with a determined gait. Three steps before Ahmed, Dracine pulled the shaft backwards, then thrust it forward into Ahmed's ass, penetrating a good two feet. All this was done silently with an air of nobility and justice. There was no applause, a few gasps, but mostly there were nods of satisfaction. Those not pleased, were filled with fear and soon the air was thick with its odor.

Dracine stepped back; her hands surprisingly clean after the dirty work. She turned to the crowd. "My justice is swift and without fanfare. Do not cross the line with me. Now, place that pole in the hole," she commanded.

The four men who shaped the shaft finished the job. Ahmed was still alive, his eyes glazed over in agony and shame.

"Leave him there for all to see and remember."

"When should we take him down?" one of the workmen stammered.

Dracine considered it a fair question. Rather than have the inquirer defaced for the asking, she would answer him. "Never," she replied off-handedly.

A mental push by Dracine caused a commotion within the gathering. A child had begun to dance beneath Ahmed. All eyes went to the innocent one while Dracine willed herself back to Atoli's room. No one had seen her arrive or leave, adding to the mystery of their 'new' master.

Dracine fell onto a divan. Atoli, hearing her enter, roused herself to see what Dracine would need. What she desired, Atoli had plenty of. The magistrate was crying as the whore sat down next to her, folding Dracine in her arms and letting her head rest on her bosom. There were no words of comfort, only warm hands caressing Dracine's hair, while Atoli purred like a cat, lulling Dracine from her sadness. It was a role Atoli often played and she was good at it. And it sure beat working the streets having some drunken pig slobber on you while he tries to prove his manhood. When the monarch was asleep, two of the staff were called to carry her to bed. Atoli would sleep on the divan in Dracine's quarters, in case she was needed. She was.

Dracine had overestimated the amount of energy it took to travel by will. Along with a display of might and accuracy she slept until the small hours when she woke screaming. The physical effort was nothing compared to the mental blow of having brutally murdered a man. The fact that it was justified did little to appease her. The howl was already on her lips when her eyes opened. Ahmed had extracted himself from the impaling and now straddled her ready to do a little impaling of his own. Only the soothing sound of Atoli's voice and the firm hands that held Dracine kept the magistrate from flipping out, losing her mind, going insane, call it what you will. Madness suits best, I suppose.

***

D ino sat before the hot woodstove that heated the trailer with a cup of steaming coffee in his hands, smoking a cigarette. Sechra had to be in that blocked building. It was obvious Skender had tried to gain entry, for Dino had seen bent shovels and pry bars littered around the doorway. 'He had been a big strong biker and he couldn't get in. That's it! ... He was a biker! They think in c.c.'s.' Before heading into the cold, Dino ate a can of warmed beef stew, filled the thermos and loaded Sechra's gun. 'Whatever had those big feet could still be around.'

Using cubic liters of power, rather than cubic centimeters, he fired up his snowplow and headed to the building. There wasn't a lot of room to move around or get a good run at the door, but the tracks of the rig helped him pivot the machine to get pointed in the right direction. Dino put it in gear, ramming the doorway over and over again. Each crash against the doors came to a solid bone-jarring stop. "Son of a bitch!" Dino worked the kinks in his spine before trying again and again. 'There is no reason to destroy my way home when there are excavators in the yard,' he thought. Dino backed his rig out to the trailer and the work yard of heavy equipment. "What I need is a bigger hammer," Dino said to no one. He wasn't even sure Sechra was inside the structure. As far as he was concerned, the place was made of solid rock. With that in mind, he began looking over the array of road building vehicles parked about the yard in nice anal-retentive rows.

The road system that was meant to connect the mountains with the coast was started about twenty years ago. Work came to a halt less than a year later. It was just another failed government project as far as Dino was concerned. He had never thought much about why it stopped. Nevertheless, the place bugged him. Though he had not seen a soul, with the exception of Skender's soul wrapper, he got the feeling that he wasn't wanted here. It's not as if the trees were saying, 'hey man, get the fuck out of here.' It was the rock beneath his feet that emanated the feeling, coursing up his legs, making them want to run. Dino wondered if the road crews felt this. 'How could they not?' he thought, looking at a big excavator. With its extending, articulating, rock hammer, it should be able to punch a hole right through. The question was the same with all the equipment. It all had been sitting for nearly two decades. Would they run?

First came a generator. He needed power to run a compressor and charge batteries. The gas had turned to varnish, clogging the fuel lines, filters and all those teeny holes in the carburetor. Tearing the fuel system apart, then rebuilding it took half of the day. His rig held a sufficient supply of both diesel and gasoline. After topping off the tank, Dino set a pair of jumper cables from his rig to the generator, turned the key and pressed the start button. After several tries, she fired with a puff of black smoke so thick, he wondered if the pope had died. Nobody got the joke but Dino.

If the condition of the generator was indicative of all the machinery, he had his work cut out for him. Now which one? The excavator would take a couple of weeks to get ready. The man lift, on the other hand, wasn't that much different than the generator and he could have it operational by sundown or at the very most a few days. He checked his watch. 'If I could just get a look inside...'

Using the snowplow, he dragged the man lift into a work warehouse. Dino plugged the generator into the existing wiring. Instantly the generator roared as lights, compressor, and heaters came on line. Toolboxes lined one wall, all unlocked and fully stocked. He smiled. 'Too bad the project stopped. Somebody had their shit together.' It's impressive, in a manly sort of way, to see all the tools cared for and stored properly.

Well after sundown, Dino shut the generator off, shuffling back to the trailer. He was beat, needing food and sleep. He poured and drank a few shots of vodka before rekindling the fire. 'At least there is plenty of dried wood and food.' He gazed at the wall of canned goods. From sweet to savory, there was enough for months. Of course he had no intention of waiting anywhere near that long.

His choice for using the man lift was to gain access to the roof. The shingles were 50 millimeter slate slabs. Dino had seen the like before, when working construction as a kid. The contractor was into renovation, the ancient stuff. Most repairs to these roofs were the results of shifting foundations or earthquakes. The slate was heavy and quite durable as a roofing material, lasting centuries and more. It was also brittle. Dino was sure he could split one and remove it creating a window of opportunity. Drop a rope and pull her out. Simple, huh?

A couple of cans of something that looked and smelled like dog food was dinner. He chased the lingering aftertaste with shots until he fell asleep. The road had taken its toll on the mechanic. Even all the worry that bothered him could not stave the need for sleep. He had wanted to update his log on his computer, Dino was tracking the whole journey, yet he was lulled, not against his will but not exactly with it either, into the deepest sleep he ever experienced.

It was dark when he woke. He shook his head chasing a lingering buzz with cold coffee while starting a fresh pot. Dino figured it to be about four in the morning. 'Shit, I overslept!' With the second cup of coffee he went to the windows, still dark, so he flipped open his laptop. If there had been anyone to see the look on his face when he saw the date it would have been high comedy sublimed with dread. Dino had been asleep for three days.

"What the hell?" Dino spoke to the four walls that surrounded him. They had no reply. After an hour of updating his log and sufficiently charging his system with caffeine, he headed to the work shed, flashlight in one hand, shotgun in the other. A movement. Well, not really a movement, but there was a shadow ahead that seemed to shift away from the beam of light. Dino moved the beam, quickly catching the darkness that the light would not dissolve before it shifted again, to the edge of the illumination. Dino didn't wait. He saw the way it moved, raised the shotgun, firing three times. The muzzle flash kept whatever it was on the run. Dino chased it, left hand holding the flashlight and barrel, the right on the worn pistol grip. Each time he glimpsed the darkness, another salvo from the gun lit the night, exploding the silence. He knew he had to have hit it. Hit what was the question. What was it he was shooting at anyway, his imagination?

Dino's pursuit took him passed the oubliette, into the woods and over a hill. At the hillcrest he reloaded while panning the light across the slope.

There! Dino squeezed the trigger eleven times as fast as he could before bolting down the hill to where he last saw it. He had racked the speed loader en route, ready to ignite the night again as his light raked a wicked glare across the hill. When he found the dark spot, he fired a few times before stopping. It was gone but this was more of a feeling than knowledge. Finger on the trigger, he walked boldly to its last position. Nothing – except for black smelly drippings leading into a cave. Dino squatted looking closely at the 'blood.' It had the appearance and odor of diarrhea and rotted flesh, but he wasn't going to put his finger in it, that's for sure.

The entrance of the tunnel/cave had been hewn of solid rock, hundreds, possibly thousands, of years ago. As much as he wanted to, he wasn't about to hunt down a wounded animal in its own lair, not in the dark anyway. Dino headed back to the job site in the cold black silence of the late night. His footsteps crunching on the hoar frost did little to disturb the stillness. As he passed the building, he thought he could hear the tink, tink, tink of hammer blows from within the walls. Placing his hand on the rock surface, he was certain.

While maintaining the Dracul at the Cneajna seaside estate, he would spend time with the young Sechra, watching her chisel away at her hideous sculptures. No doubt the girl had incredible talent; it's just that the subject matter was, well, gross. But in those hours spent with her, he had learned the rythym of her work. There was a certain cadence to the way she worked her hammer. When she would pause in her symphony, Dino would anticipate the resumption, and usually got it right. For it was like music. He heard it now in the silence of the deep night, felt it through his hands and in his heart. He pressed his hand hard to the wall, resolving his determination before returning to his own work.

A pot of coffee and two bowls of oatmeal later, Dino was wrenching on the man lift under the lights. By dawn, whenever that would be, he would be ready. Whatever it was, it was not fond of light. 'Not much, but better than nothing.' The man lift was operational by sun up, but there were a few more things he needed to do before making a go of it; a length of rope, bag of food, and blankets, water, lots more ammunition, and plenty of lights. The sun was well toward its zenith by the time he was ready. At this time of day, the sunlight would illuminate the inside of the oubliette if he could remove a roof tile.

Dino had rotated the engine a few times by hand to free up the pistons and, well, see if she would turn over. After rebuilding the top end, the little engine fired with a minimum of effort, as he knew it would. Dino hopped into the basket without delay, leaned on the forward switch while he double checked the supplies that hung on the outside of the basket. The little machine crawled along at a snail's pace toward the oubliette as the hard rubber tires crunched the frosted ground, leaving Dino ample time to pour a cup of coffee and ponder the situation.

His thumb leaned on the 'up' toggle as the basket, with Dino in it, rose from the ground. As the basket lifted above the eve, a cold wind blasted over the roof swaying the arm dangerously about. Dino hit the down toggle to get out of the gust zone, leaving him at the edge of roof. Not the best place to work from, as he would now have to climb out of the basket, but better than tipping over from the wind with the twenty meter lifting arm fully extended.

Dino tied a safety line around his waist and attached the other end to the railing of the basket, just in case. Opening the little gate exit/ entry door, he got that sudden feeling of his stomach dropping away as he looked at the open space to the ground. Double checking the safety brought his senses back.

"So you fall, you just climb back up and start again." The words were cold comfort, but better than none at all. He stepped onto the steeply pitched roof. He climbed several courses of the roof tiles before driving a prybar under one of the pieces of slate. Once he had a good bite, he dropped his weight onto the bar popping the tile loose. The tile began to slide, taking Dino with it. Just before going over the edge he saw another tile slide into place as quickly as the other fell.

"What the hell! AHHHHH!" He screamed going over the edge. The safety line went tight snapping Dino into a folded position at the waist. Unfortunately, the knot had slid around from his back to his front side so when the line went taut he folded backwards, seeming to breaking his back.

***

Hammer blows and chisels scraped away at the cold, dark, silence within the oubliette. They were the only sounds with the exception of Sechra's breathing. Her chest no longer moved, yet the air would circulate as long as she was sufficiently motivated to take a breath. There were times when she no longer felt the urge or had the energy to breathe. But the work would suffer when she didn't. Her diaphragm moved like a stone. Not drawing a breath was far easier.

In fact, everything had become harder. The closer she came to finishing the sculpture the harder it was to continue, remain focused, and lift the hammer. The key for Sechra was not stopping, for starting again was becoming too difficult. The few times she would pause to slake her parched mouth or down a pot of coffee, she would find herself sitting afterwards, unable to move and the will to do so evaporating with every hollow breath. When this would happen she would begin to rock herself back and forth until the momentum would cause her to fall from the chair, fracturing the joints that had stiffened up while seated.

Sechra was now afraid to stop for fear of never starting again. As long as thehammer and chisel were moving, she knew she was alive. Sechra now worked on the final panel in the piece. For this relief, there was no history to call upon to shape the figures, for it was the future. Within its borders were being carved what could be the final chapter in Romania's history, or the beginning of a new one.

Out of Stone

PART THREE

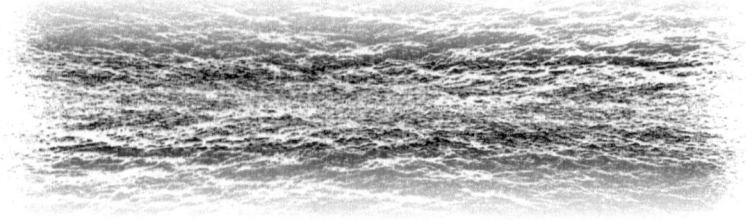

***

The cold penetrated his very being like an ice pick, sapping the warmth from his core. Blood cooling, thickening, becoming sluggish, as his heart slowed in its ability to push the viscous fluid. Breathing became virtually non-existent. When it seemed to stop, the air passage remained open, allowing a passive flow of ambient air to pass through. All movement stopped. He never felt the ravens, when they came to feast upon his ruined flesh, nor being dragged away, to be buried alive.

It was the blanket. The dimming spark of life in the man's core stabilized and began growing brighter with the help of insulation. His first breath was forced as the heavy wool did a near excellent job of suffocating as well as insulating. A second more urgent breath was forced through the fabric. A fourth and fifth before his eye opened and he realized the predicament he was in. The realization that you have been buried alive comes not without a certain amount of confusion.

The air was thick and going stale, Skender had to do something. Being rolled up like a glumki made it impossible to do anything but rock back and forth. A little bit one way then to the left. "AHHHHHHHHH," Skender screamed into the mound as the weight on his destroyed body brought him fully back to life. But it would take more than one roll on it to free himself.

It was winter and somewhere within Skender's reawakening mind he knew nobody would have dug a grave in the frozen ground. His screams echoed back on him until he rolled from the jumbled pile of gravestones.

In an agonizing effort, Skender pulled himself up and got to his feet. His mind had yet to come fully online, but he knew he had to get to the trailer or die out here. Draping the blanket around his shoulders, he stumbled into the work yard. He pushed on the door, falling into the still warm confines of the trailer. Pulling his coat off revealed the extent of his injuries. Medical school taught him much, but you didn't have to be a doctor to know that if he didn't get the bleeding stopped, he would die. But first, compresses on the heavy bleeders as the warming blood began to flow freely again. Bungees from one of the bike tie downs worked to stem the flow. Skender fell to the floor in exhaustion and pain. He felt like dying, part of him was, the other part knew that to survive certain things needed to be attended. Vodka, stoke the fire, coffee, food, and more vodka. After appeasing all of the above, there was still one more thing to be done. He slid a thin delicate looking blade from its sheath in his boot, thumbing it open. Skender knew the edge was keen. He didn't want to spend a whole lot of time thinking about what he was going to do. Skender brought the blade up, slicing through the remaining tendons and musculature before separating the dead finger at the first knuckle. When the appendage hit the ground so did Skender, almost. Next he had to remove the eye, which now hung loosely on the bridge of his check bone. With his bad arm, he was able to grasp the eye sack, pulling it free. With the length of the ganglia exposed, Skender sliced, close to the empty socket, separating the umbilical of vision. Sticking a wad of gauze in the cavity he fell, out cold from shock on so many levels.

Skender woke to the chirping of winter birds, busy scavenging whatever morsels the season had left them. With consciousness came the painful throbbing of his left arm, right eye and heaviness of chest. He was alive and had the nasty business of cleaning the wounds and dressing them ahead of him. But not before something to eat and coffee. Which, trying to do one-handed, was more of a challenge than he realized. A few spills later, he got something into his stomach, the rest went to the birds.

It was about this time that the mundane chores of living opened Skender's eye to more than his immediate needs. 'Someone was here,' he thought to himself. That was all it took. He shuffled into a shambles of clothing and was out the door, his arm forgotten, for the moment. A brightly colored emergency vehicle sat not twenty meters from the door of the trailer. 'Was it here before?'

"Hey, is there anybody here?" Skender listened but only the sounds of the forest replied.

"Shit," he pondered aloud.

Then, above the wind blowing through the branches he heard, "Help me," coming from the oubliette.

"Sechra," Skender screamed, making a clumsy dash across the work yard to the old building.

"What the fuck?" Skender looked up at the man dangling from the lift, arms thrashing but the legs strangely still.

"Don't stand there like a dumbass! Get me down!" yelled Dino.

Skender hurried to the rig, giving the controls a good look over before pulling on a lever. With a hiss, the arm of the man lift began to lower. He eased back on the control as Dino's body touched the ground.

Dino raised his hand to Skender without looking. "Boy, am I glad to see you. The name's Dino. I came here for Sechra Kcirb."

"What's wrong with your legs?"

"Think I broke my back," Dino replied looking up for the first time. "Son of a bitch! Get away from me," screamed the mechanic as he fumbled for his handgun.

"Wait, wait! My name is Skender!"

"I know! I buried you!"

"I was alive!"

"You what?!"

***

The windows looked out upon the broad expanse of shoreline. Lonely oil lights flickered from fishing boats preparing to sail upon the morning's tide. Otherwise all was dark in the hour before dawn. The entire view was but a stage set to capture the first rays of the sun as it would breach the horizon. But, these vistas, which had never been seen before by the current magistrate, were covered in thick black and crimson curtains. Only at night would they part to allow the ocean breezes to freshen the rooms and the stars and moon to illumine the comfortable surroundings. A cautious servant, silent as the shadows, moved through the darkness to close the window coverings before the black sky turned to deepest azure. But not this morning.

Dracine sat in the darkness. Her eyes, if you could see them, were intent upon a horizon that had yet to be revealed. Only the glow from a hookah kept Dracine from being the shadow, as she was framed in sanguine. She had woken an hour before, refreshed from a long night in the arms of Atoli. Only after the lightest of kisses to Atoli's forehead, did Dracine slip silently from the bed exiting the room and closing the door behind her.

Now this was out of character for the Dracine the world had come to know. Her whores were always killed before they had a chance to leave the quarters with the knowledge they had gained. None made it till dawn. But this morning, Dracine felt clear for the first time in her life. Her moment of clarity was stretching out, becoming part of her. Enjoying the moment, she opened all the curtains and filled the hookah with a mélange of Turkish tobacco and hashish with just a touch of Afghani opium to cancel the urge to cough. For some reason, she wanted to roll the tobacco into a paper tube and smoke it that way. Dracine laughed and lit the bowl. After a few hits she sat back and looked to the east with a thousand yard stare.

The slightest breeze disturbed the layers of smoke that slowly drifted out the open window. With the gentlest ruffling of fabric the view began to disappear. Dracine's hand moved invisibly through the space at her side until she was able to gently take hold of Moira's arm.

A terrified intake of breath by the girl almost broke the silence.

"Not this morning, child," whispered Dracine, who also used the mental push to calm Moira. Though the previous night had bonded the staff to Dracine with love instead of fear, a lifetime of knowing death is difficult to shake.

Moira nodded, understanding, and went to the next item on her routine. She bent at the waist picking up a long narrow sack, bowed to Dracine, and headed to the sleeping room.

"Moira," Dracine said close to inaudibly, and shook her head 'no' while waving the girl back. "Atoli is sleeping soundly, you need never bring the sack again."

Moira smiled in the darkness. "Look." She pointed out to sea. A single deep blue arc had just defined the horizon.

"Bring some coffee please, we will watch the sun rise together."

Moira's smile should have brightened even the darkest room, but she had no teeth. She rolled the body bag up and left the way she came, silently.

The two did not speak as night became morning, but rather watched it like it was the first time. In a way it was. Moira had never woken without fear clenching her gut and loosening her bowels. Nor had Dracine, with her own version of hatred and disgust at herself, ever seen the dawn with clear eyes.

With light came the activity and sounds of life. Dracine looked down into the courtyard where Ahmed's body was hung last night. A hushed gasp. Dracine suddenly felt the need to use the facilities. The pole remained upright, but Ahmed's body was gone.

Hidden behind hung tapestry, Dracine took care of nature's immediate need while trying to figure out where the body had gone. Ahmed was not dead when the pike was placed into the ground. No one had stolen him – that much was certain in Dracine's mind. 'He must have gone back to that place with the tiles.'

Dracine's moment of peace with the dawn wisped away like steam from a boiling pot as reality insinuated itself with the discovery.

***

Pain screamed from shattered kneecaps. His mouth tried to express this, but with his tongue cut out all that issued was a mangled ARRRRGHHH. Ahmed's mind was a whirl as his reality had become as wasted as his knees. Blood loss and shock left him catatonic. That is until he found himself held over an old barrel. He had witnessed Dracine's half brother, Vlad III, use this method of torture in the past, never thinking it would be him while he laughed at the poor unfortunates getting their due. Ahmed didn't have long to think about it. The pain in his knees was nothing to what came next...

He woke dying. Internal organs had been damaged by the impaling. Blood dripped from his nose and mouth while a cruel dark fluid dripped down the pole. A child danced twenty feet below him. With consciousness closing down, Ahmed had one chance to escape his predicament. He closed his eyes and began to imagine the seaside estate. His mind was racing, making it near impossible to control his thoughts. In time he was able to capture, vividly, the dining room of the estate, the coffee table next to the couch with a phone on it.

"This is the emergency hotline. Who are you and what is the problem?"
"Hel eee, ahhh, dy..." the phone fell from Ahmed's hand.

The 911 system displayed the location of the call. An ambulance was sent from Eforie Sud to the estate.

***

"I am alive," yelled Skender. "The blanket you wrapped me in must have warmed me."

"No way, man. I'm not in the habit of burying people, let alone alive. You were purple, no breath, no heartbeat and carrion were feeding on you. What else was I going to do?" Dino was perplexed. "I was warned about you people and your tricks."

"Yeah, you were warned," dripped Skender sarcastically. "For generations you have been warned not to trust the people in the mountains. What is it with you fucking city people? I don't care what your fear has done to you, but right now I need your help. And... it looks like you need mine. So you can either get over it or freeze to death out here. If you really wish to help Sechra Kcirb, I'd suggest the former."

Dino didn't like being lectured to by someone, let alone a gypsy, yet there was something in what Skender said and how he said it that caused Dino to put the pistol away. Besides, Skender was right about the freezing to death thing.

"Let me untie myself and why don't you get some gas? Don't look like you're in any shape to be carrying me."

Skender headed to the workshop while Dino pulled off his mittens to undo the knots. All the while he was cursing himself for the weather, his situation and now he had to trust someone he didn't know. 'Shit,' he said to himself.

"My sentiments exactly," said Skender struggling with the gas can.

"Hey I didn't mean..." Dino began.

"Yes you did. Now you're stuck up here with some hillbilly. Hell, I'd be concerned, too. I'll probably fuck you by midnight and eat you for breakfast."

"Now listen here!" Dino struggled with the imagery.

"No, you listen. You don't like they way I was raised or the history of my people. 'Watch out or we'll steal your babies,' right? Now drag yourself back into the lift and I'll set you down at the front door." Skender fired up the lift, waiting patiently as the engine warmed and for Dino to secure himself.

So here we have it in a nutshell. In fact, the troubles of all mankind could be summed up by the sentiments of these two men. If you were to take DNA samples from each, they would be nearly identical, separated only by a few generations and an unforgiving range of mountains. They could have been cousins, even brothers and probably were, if the lineage was tracked.

It was where they were raised and how, that made all the difference. Dino had been born in Bucharest, a city, with mills, offices, schools, commerce, banks, businesses, and people; lots of them, from all over the world. His father worked in one of the local factories as a millwright and his mother, a secretary at a law firm. Dino went to school at an early age and finished college with a degree in engineering without interruption. Now he owned and operated a high-end auto repair, servicing the upper crust that could afford him. There were many.

Underlying the culture of the west that now dominated Bucharest was a barrier to the past, thicker than asphalt and as hard as the mountains' basalt. The gypsy culture had been eradicated, squeezed out, pushed back and paved over. Those who would not or could not accept the culture of money and all that goes with it were forced back into the mountains from which all Romanians came, but few wanted anymore.

Centuries have passed since the split of a people. So long ago, no one really remembers. It was trade that drove the wedge into the family tree. The silk and spice routes used the Black Sea as a super highway to speed goods across a treacherous Persia. The ports along the eastern coast were the first to see the riches of the world. The people were sold in a heartbeat. Shiny, glittery, heavy things that they had never seen before and had no use for were now being fought for. Where money goes, greed is never far behind.

Where once a free society thrived on barter and service and need, it now devolved into a supply and demand economy. The clever ones became merchants, bankers and landowners. These, in turn, used the sweat and time of others to ensure that they would not have to toil. Yet people are like cattle. They settled into their new way of life regardless of their position in it. Wood cities turned to stone, mudded routes cobbled over, elaborate homes for the wealthy, hovels for the poor.

It was a pretty raw deal in the beginning. Life for the poor had little or no meaning and had become as cheap as the dirt they worked. Then religion came and made a fucked up situation even worse. All the while, the rich were getting richer and the poor breeding like rats to ensure there would always be a workforce. Sound familiar? It should. But a history lesson this isn't, commentary maybe. Over the centuries life got better, well not really better, just evolved.

All of this was happening along the coastal regions and major rivers such as the Danube. The trickle down effect of economy never really went past the fertile land below the mountains. And thus the split led along those lines. The mountains represented the other side of the people. And as far as the people in the cities were concerned, the dark side.

Civilization crept into the mountains like the roots of an insidious weed. But like the trees at the alpine level, it was stunted and deformed by the harsh habitat. This is not to say the mountains' people were not civilized. In fact, when compared to the cities below, it really makes you wonder just how civilized civilization is. Life in the mountains was no Shangri-La, but neither was it dog eat dog. That's not to say dog was not eaten, well, not regularly anyway. There would always be infighting within the family unit or between groups of families, yet they were tight, for they relied upon each other for survival.

In the cities, there was always another repair shop to go to or another schmuck to buy your shit. Not so in the mountains. Resources were rare, skills even more so and professionals did not exist. Everyone was a jack of all trades and it was easy to see which trades they were better at. Skender was about the closest thing to a doctor for more than a thousand square kilometers and he had never finished his second year. His internship consisted of tending to those who needed help. It was one of the reasons he had a motor vehicle. For the most part, the women would handle the bulk of the first aid. Cuts, breaks and midwifery were their stock and trade. If spirits were involved in the illness, as was often the case, some of the women would simply change hats and become a shaman, a spirit healer. Skender had more than once witnessed aged rituals, spoken in languages long forgotten, in the attempt to heal. Mostly they died, but a few would live on or at least come to some sort of peace within themselves as a result of the rites.

But there is little that the darker arts can do about an appendix that is about to burst, umbilical issues in a newborn requiring a Caesarian or repair torn muscles. Skender's skills filled in the blanks of a limited, desolate society. He also understood modern medicines. When they could get them, Skender could stop an outbreak of pneumonia, the plague, or syphilis. Rare indeed was the time you had what you needed when you needed it, so Skender kept his stash with him at all times in one of the cases tied to his bike. It wasn't much and hadn't been needed until now.

Skender shut down the man lift after unloading Dino. The quiet was deep in the forest and Skender used a few moments of it to breathe and calm himself before heading to the trailer. Stepping over Dino he opened the door, dragging the mechanic in after him. He set to stoking the fire and putting the place in order and making coffee, before approaching Dino with a couple of steaming cups.

"So, you a doctor? I looked through your wallet." Dino lifted himself on one elbow to get a better look at Skender.

"I pass for one, around these parts."

"What's that supposed to mean?"

"It means I'm all you got, so don't start being a dick. Somebody's going to have wipe your ass for a while. Now where does it hurt?" With that Skender bent over and lifted Dino into a sitting position.

"AHHHHHH God damnit! What the fuck are trying to do, kill me?" Dino screamed in pain, not realizing that the pain was a good thing. He crumpled to the floor, clenching his teeth.

"No," Skender said casually. "Undo your pants and roll on your stomach."

Skender inspected Dino's spine. Numerous vertebrae were twisted and cocked to one side but nothing appeared broken.

"Hmmmm. Okay, zip it up." Skender refilled his coffee cup.

"Well?" Dino asked.

"Well what? You'll walk, just not today," Skender dripped with sarcasm. "You have any sleeping gear or stuff you need?"

"There's a black pack in the rig..." Dino began.

Skender waved him off leaving the trailer. "I'll find it."

And wipe Dino's ass he did for the next three weeks. For Skender this was no different than doing a two meter tall baby. For Dino, it was not only embarrassing, but forced him to acquiesce humility, something he was not used to. But that's not all that was going on. The first week was spent 'fuck you'ing' each other while trying to follow Skender's first aid directions. Skender's arm needed to be set, his eye socket cleaned and cauterized with a hot iron and the crushed portion of his sternum needed to be sucked back out with a toilet plunger.

"I'm telling you, you were dead. No one could survive this!" Following Skender's directions, Dino cleaned and alcohol prepped the plunger, while Skender shaved his chest to help with the seal.

"We are gypsy, what can I say? Center it over the wound and press down, gently, to allow the air to escape. Check the edges for a good seal. When you think you have it, let me know."

Dino concentrated on placing the tool in position when he started to laugh.

"What's so fucking funny, Dino? Somebody always clean your toilets for you?"

"Fuck you! I was just remembering the last time I used one of these."

"Yeah, it figures you think of shit when dealing gypsies."

Without warning Dino yanked up on the seated plunger. This move created a vacuum, pulling Skender's crushed chest bones back into a nominally normal position. Skender screamed deafeningly within the confines of the trailer, but otherwise remained still. Moments passed in silent agony while Skender collected himself. His breathing became full and his heart no longer felt like it was in too small a box and was able to pump freely without pain.

Dino was just standing there, dumbstruck, with the plunger hanging from one hand. He had probably just saved Skender's life, but had no idea what to say. Engines don't talk back when you fix them. Before the moment got that uncomfortable feeling, Skender made one more request.

"See that poker sitting in the hot coals?" Skender chinned to the wood stove.

"Oh no! Unplug your toilet I got no problem with, but I'm not going to poke that thing in your eye!"

"You city people watch too many movies," Skender replied, disappointedly shaking his head."

"Well, what then?"

"You're willing?"

Dino nodded in agreement.

"That's half the battle. You're good with your hands, that's another half, the final half is do you have the balls?" Skender was reading Dino's mind a little and setting him up. There is nothing like an affront to one's ego to get them motivated.

"Fuck you. I am not a pussy! And right now I wouldn't mind poking you in the eye with that thing!"

"Good, then let's do it." Skender was close enough to the wood stove to grab the poker. The tip was bright orange white as he handed it to Dino. "I've done this before, so don't worry. If you want to kill me now is your chance. Sit behind me resting on your shins and hold my head between your knees to keep me from jumping around too much."

Dino got himself into position, his anger melting away with the heat of the orange tip. Once he had Skender's head secure...

"Well, what do I do? Just jam it in your eye and work it around a bit?"

"If you want to fry my brain and end up wiping my ass for the duration go ahead, but this is how it's done. Using one hand, peel back my eyelid and expose what's left. Take a couple breaths and when you are ready, bring the poker tip to the socket. You don't have to touch the eye socket. The heat will do it, making the remains boil and cauterize."

Dino raised the eyelid away, bringing the glowing tip to bear.

"Closer, closer, close, AAAAAAAHHHHHHHHHHHHHHHHH!"

A crisp popping boiling ensued, followed by a sizzling, not unlike a burger hitting a hot griddle. Dino held the head tight until he felt he had it, then threw the poker back into the stove. Skender was out cold as Dino went to the door for a handful of snow to pack the eye. In the rush, he failed to notice the fresh footprints at the doorway. After melting three snowballs in the socket, Dino dried the cavity, squirted a bunch of antibiotic in it and gauzed the burn over.

With Skender unconscious, Dino walked the trailer feeling empty and very alone. Of course the pain in his back didn't let him mull on the drama too long. The strain of performing the procedures aggravated the muscles and bruised discs. Couple that with the stress involved, he had a relapse. Dino crumpled to the floor in pain. He needed snow to make an ice pack to get the swelling down.

The snow on the stoop was hard packed from walking across it, but the footprints in it were now plainly visible to Dino. They were similar to the tracks that had come across the avalanche and the same as the ones left by the thing he chased weeks before. A cold shiver went down his spine that had nothing to do with the icy wind or his injury. He crawled back to his resting place with the bucket of snow, more afraid than he had ever been in his life. From then on, his imagination took over until he popped a couple pills Skender had given him. They were muscle relaxers, but back them with a couple shots of vodka and your imagination shuts down.

The morning was bleak, overcast, and frozen by a cold front that moved in over the night. With considerable effort Dino was able to kindle the fire, start coffee and take care of nature's call. He was pouring a cup when he heard Skender moving and poured a second before turning around.

Skender smiled and brought himself to sit. He reached towards Dino.

"Thank you, my friend." These were the first kind words passed between the men.

Skender shook the proffered hand. "You're welcome, brother."

"Thank you for hanging tough. I should not stand for a day or two, lest I damage your work and kill myself in the process. But I can and think we should get drunk, rest ourselves. Our work has just begun."

"We are all gypsy, I guess," Dino responded. "What work?" he asked while fetching a bottle of vodka and glasses.

"To Sechra!"

"To Sechra," added Dino with less surety than Skender.

"You know, Skender," Dino slurred, "we got a Yeti prowling around. Saw the footsteps when I went to go."

"I suppose it scared the shit out you," Skender drolled.

"Yeah it did!" Dino laughed until it hurt. "You stole my joke."

"Saw it coming a click away. That's no Yeti."

"I know, just trying to make light."

"You should. Make as much of it as you can 'cause we're going to need it. Luckily it is not after us. It has Sechra."

"What is it?" Dino poured another couple of shots. They mimed a toast and drank before continuing. This was the first time they were talking instead of goading each other. It was one of the reasons Skender wanted to get drunk. A good one will bond the participants. It was important they both be on the same page.

"A mistake. An accident of birth. An abortion that would not die. It is the dark side of our nature, personified. After it tore itself from its mother's womb, the people should have killed it while it was still possible, but they were afraid. So they put the thing in a cave and fed it. At first, it fed off the food that was given. Later it began to feed off their fears and hatreds. Now, that is all it eats."

"Geez and shit! What does it want with Sechra?"

Skender set the hook. "It wants to live among men. Sechra carves its form."

"But how?" began Dino.

"How is not important. Saving her, if we can, is."

"Lot of good we're going to be." Dino waved his hands at their plethora of injuries.

'When the time comes, it will be enough. Now we must heal, and that means not doing anything. Another shot, good sir, then we both need to practice."

"Practice what?" Dino was shitfaced and couldn't imagine doing any kind of practice.

"Doing nothing. Good night, Dino."

***

Weeks passed in peace at Castle Drache. Since the demise of Ahmed, Dracine was busy attending to matters of court and instituting the rule of a firm hand instead of a deadly one. The change in the peoples of Dracine's domain was almost immediate. Something that never existed before was taking place. It is called quality of life.

There was a surge in productivity that a whip could never produce. When the surge leveled off, there was no scourging to make them produce more. There was enough, with a little left over. There were smiles instead of the face of drudgery. Those who thought to take advantage of the good times were given a taste of greed, the old way.

One family, like Lenes, preferred a life of leisure. 'Our family has never worked,' said the head of the house. 'Nor shall you have to,' Dracine responded in court. Dracine did not force them into a labor camp or take away all that the family owned. Instead, that afternoon, an armed guard was sent to the estate in question. He was more like a repo man taking away all the servants and work force, leaving the family to fend on its own. Oh yes, he took one more thing, the youngest child.

A week went by before the guard returned to the estate. He had with him a large tray, so large it was towed behind on a wagon. A cloud of dust heralded his arrival and before he pulled up to the main house, the family was already gathered at the front. It was obvious they were out of sorts, some still had on the now filthy garments they had been wearing the week before. All looked hungry.

"Where have you been? Where is my staff! My God, man, we haven't eaten in days!"

"We sent a messenger several days ago inviting you and your family to the castle for a feast. When he arrived he knocked, but got no answer, so he left the invitation at your door. I believe that is it." The guard pointed to the invite pinned to the doorframe.

"You, you took my head servant, how were we supposed to know someone had come by?" he blustered. "We certainly would not have missed a feast at the castle. And a chance to honor Lord Drache," the head of the house added at the last moment.

"Yes, Lord Drache understands that you do not work, therefore he asked that the messenger be particularly persistent in trying to get you to come to the door. The young man said he made quite a ruckus."

"But there was no one to answer the door. Don't you see?" pleaded the lazy man.

"No, actually, I don't."

Already the hungry eyes we're spying the cart that emanated the smells of fresh bread and roast meat. The guard noticed and stretched the moment in silence, that is with the exception of growling stomachs and slapping wet lips. He smiled astride his horse looking down at the fools.

"Lord Drache had the cook create a feast for you since you were so unavoidably detained." He untied the cart from the horse without getting down. "Help yourselves."

Despite the pangs of hunger, verging on starvation, they did not move but rather twitched, unable to make up their minds. Even starving, they couldn't bring themselves to remove the tarp and set the table. The guard now got down off his horse and drew his sword. The family, as one, stepped back, away from the blade. He deftly cut the lashings and lifted the fabric away with the tip of his sword. Still they did not make a move. Again with the tip he raised the lid off of the platter and flung it to the ground. The smell of roasted meat now engulfed the immediate area. With the food exposed, the guard returned to his mount.

"You really should eat."

Now he watched as the group inched forward, surrounding the cart. Like an animal with many heads, the beast dove into the meal ripping away at the roast beast and cramming it into their mouths. He backed the steed away a few steps to give them more room. Twenty minutes went by in a gluttonous chewing and swilling of wine. Finally, fueled with food and spirits, the head of the house decided to open his mouth and say something stupid.

"If you would give me my servants back, you wouldn't have to keep bringing our food to us."

"You need not worry for me, good sir, we will not be coming again." The family looked stunned for a moment. With full bellies and head they did not hear what he really said and went back to eating. "Are you not concerned for your son?"

"My son? Oh yes how is the boy? I'm surprised the Magistrate has any food left trying to feed that one," laughed the head of the house nervously.

"You would know better than I." The guard turned his horse. "I am leaving, keep the cart. Have you a message you would like me to give Lord Drache?"

"Yes, tell him thank you for the piglet. The flesh was tender and moist."

"I'm sure it was and will pass along your message. One more thing." The guard untied a sack from the pommel of his saddle. He tossed the bag into the cart of food and left.

The family pounced on the bag, figuring it for after meal sweets. The women began screaming and the men retching. Inside the bag were the head, feet and hands of the child.

A few barbaric rulings every now and then, and then only to the most deserving, kept the remaining population alert and vigilant in their businesses. This, in turn, made for a thriving business atmosphere where one not need worry about being taken. Money began gravitating to the little port town. The town grew, people prospered and taxes were paid.

Once oppressed, the population began to grow into a thriving city. All knew better than to flaunt their newfound wealth. They were thankful, having learned the price of greed through the screams and public displays of torture of those who did not, or would not learn. Word spread and along with it came a trickle of immigration. Most just wanted a simple life without the tyranny of an overzealous magistrate or corrupt business climate.

Eventually, however, news of a good thing rings in the ears of those who would take it. Of course in seizing such a thing, they would ruin it in the process, but that is not the point. Vlad Tepes III had eyes and ears in all the municipalities under his control. Dracine's seaside demesne was part of it.

"Let it grow," was Vlad's first response upon hearing the 'good' news.

And it did. Nothing grows faster than an active port of trade and fishing hub. Dracine had set the wheels in motion. Now the beast, in the form of a thriving economy, was driving itself. It became less often that extreme forms of cruelty were necessary to keep the bourgeoning populace aware.

When Dracine would enter the markets to shop, a bubble of space was ever about her. No one need grovel anymore, but show any lack of proper respect and your smile would suffer for it. Without Ahmed around, she would haggle with merchants, testing their truth quotient. Never would she grind a salesman to agree to a sum less than the value of item X. She would, however, persuade them to come around to a decent price as if it were their own idea. Dracine looked at it as if she were teaching them to be fair without the barbaric price that used to come along with earning such knowledge.

Several years went by while the seed that was planted, sprouted and matured. At which point, Vlad said, "It is time."

His personal guard of one hundred men prepared for a journey to the coast. A battle contingent of one thousand would follow several days behind. Aboard a pitch black steed, Tepes left Tirgoviste in the early spring. "Excellent riding weather, don't you think?" he mentioned to one of the captains nearest him.

"Most excellent, Sire," he agreed. Captain Ignaski would have agreed if it was pouring rain and freezing. As it was he didn't have to lie. 'Men have been killed for a lesser meandering from the truth,' Ignaski thought to himself.

"So very true, my young captain. Mind your thoughts and you just might keep your head!" Vlad laughed heartily in a heartless manner.

Just then, a shout from the cook wagon called to Ignaski. "With your permission." Ignaski nodded to Tepes, wheeling his horse around and trotted away carefully so as not to kick up any mud on Vlad or his mount. He thought of nothing until reaching the wagon. The right wheel needed to be replaced. Luckily there was a spare. Ignaski was pleased with the timely breakdown to get him away from Tepes. 'Thank God,' he said to himself. Immediately, as if he were speaking to someone, the thought came into his head, loud and clear, 'your God had nothing to do with it, trust in me, Ignaski, Ahahahahaaha.' The laughter was wicked and cruel.

The road to the coast was clear and the trip uneventful. Not even the boldest of thieves would attempt an attack. Passing through a valley brought the first vision of the coast. Vlad paused with his guard there to remember a battle he once fought on this very shoreline. Wrinkles creased his forehead as a premonition overlaid itself on the déjà vu. His broad mustache pulled down at the ends as a scowl crossed his face. Without a word, he dug his razor sharp spurs deep into the flanks of his horse. Half a dozen cuts sprayed blood as Vlad bolted for the shoreline in a full gallop. His men were right behind.

A vanguard arrived days before to notify Dracine of her half-brother's imminent arrival. The town was cleaned, spring flowers cut and deep red banners bearing the Dracul insignia were hung for his arrival.

"Good morning, Lord Vlad," said Dracine as she rose from a shaded enclosure at the gates of the city.

"And to you, 'cousin,'" Vlad replied as piercing as his eyes did the folds of her tunic. With his first words, he implied his command of this knowledge and the tragic implications should Dracine not play according to his rules.

"Surely you thirst after the morning's ride." Dracine snapped her fingers and servants appeared out of nowhere to supply the request. A gilt cup was raised to the Voivode. Vlad slapped the offering away with disdain.

"From your hand, Lord Drache. You would not poison me."

"None of my people would try and harm you, Lord. As you wish." Dracine filled a goblet from her own service, approached the horse and raised the ice cold glass to Vlad, humbly. "It is fresh from the mountains."

Vlad downed the contents in one swill before smashing the glass into Dracine's face, carving a gash through the cheek and into the mouth.

"Your people! Since when did they become yours? You are mine, they are mine, it is all mine."

"A slip of the tongue, my Lord."

"A slip that could cost you yours, Lord Drache." This time the words came mocking, condescendingly. "And just how does the water arrive from the mountains?"

"Through an aqueduct system. We have been perfecting the design before offering it to you to use throughout the kingdom."

"That is very thoughtful, Drache, but I live in the mountains and have no need for such."

"Other, dryer parts of the country could benefit from a supply of fresh water to increase crop yields and your coffers by way of taxes."

"This I have discerned by reviewing your districts tax records. You have done quite well, Lord Drache. Perhaps better than even I am aware, yes?"

"Lord Dracul, our records are accurate and honest. Now may I please leave and have this cut addressed before lunch. Moira, our head servant, will show you your quarters where you may refresh yourselves." In a quiet tone to Vlad alone, "It is good to see you Vlad."

Dracine was working every angle, just as she knew Vlad would. She also realized her 'Shangri-La' was about to go to hell.

Worried less for herself than her people, she made for the kitchen and old Moira. The cook knew what had happened before Dracine's arrival and was thusly prepared. Stitches were out of the question due to the time period. However there was a natural repair that would keep the scaring to a minimum. Moira had never used this on a cut so severe, so she could only hope.

Dracine was lying on Moira's bed, next to the kitchen when the old woman entered with a basket of fresh eggs. After cleaning the wound and staunching the blood flow with sulfur powder, she cracked a half dozen eggs into a bowl and set the bowl aside. Carefully she peeled the inner skin from the eggshell halves. Once the edges of the cut were lined up, the 'skins' were laid flat across Dracine's check over the wounds. When applied, Moira fanned the moist area to get the skins to dry. The egg skin, after drying, adheres to the human skin, binding it together like a butterfly bandaid, minimizing scar tissue and accelerating healing. A fresh herb tea was brought in for Dracine to sip while the bandage cured. It also gave her time to think.

Dracine had known this day would come. The habits that come with greed rarely vary, and Vlad, a creature of habit, was not about to change. Dracine was not sure that even she would survive his visit. Unfortunately, she was not able to convey this to her people. They would just have to cope. With the old ways still fresh in their memories, the shift into a paranoid state shouldn't be all that difficult. That Dracine was struck a vicious blow upon the first encounter was actually a blessing and a warning. Within an hour everyone knew. Children and some women were spirited away into the forest to keep them from the harm that would surely come. The rest stayed to keep up appearances, die if need be, and protect Dracine if they could.

By afternoon, Vlad had taken up residence in what would be considered a throne room. It was normally used for celebrations, as Dracine was not want to sit there and be adored, the new Dracine that is. Instead of festive, the hall felt like the dead had entered and had no intention of leaving. Vlad sat on the throne, a goblet of wine in one hand and pointed dirk in the other that was busy destroying the ornately carved armrest.

At a knock, Vlad's guards opened the huge oaken entry doors. Dracine entered dressed in black and crimson, her hair tied back severely in direct opposition to the current style. It was more like a fifteenth-century version of a New Yorker's power lunch attire. She waited for Vlad's nod to enter. When it came, her stride forward was controlled, powerful, elegant and yet not arrogant. She knew Vlad well. If she wanted to survive, the fight would begin here and now.

Dracine bowed deeply. Upon returning to a full standing position she said, "Good afternoon, my cousin. I pray you found the arrangements to your liking."

"For a backwards people, I suppose." He eyed Dracine for any affront. There was none.

"We do the best we can with what we have. Thanks to your generosity and fair rule we have prospered, which is reflected in our increased payment of the taxes."

"Yes, yes. This pleases me, as not all territories are producing as well as you."

"We are lucky is all. The sea is plentiful and the farmland remains fertile."

"I see you say 'we'. Have you really become so close to 'them'?" Vlad snapped his fingers. Two guards brought the head servant Moira into the room. She was being pleasant with them; however, just behind her smile, fear was creeping into her eyes and voice. Something was going to happen!

Dracine saw the moment coming. There was nothing she could do.

"Moira is the finest head cook I have ever had. We have known each other since childhood."

"How touching." Vlad's voice dripped of sarcasm and cruelty. "Which will make our entertainment all the more interesting." Looking to the guards he said, "Rape her. Emilian take advantage of that toothless mouth. I know you like it that way."

The empty laugh of cruelty echoed in the hall. Moira's eyes blazed in fear of the very near future, while Dracine's wept in sorrow, frozen in her own fear and panic. Emilian pulled off his sword and tunic, casting them aside at Dracine's feet. The other forced Moira to her knees, yanking open her lower jaw. Emilian slapped her hard in the face before ripping her tunic off revealing the mature breasts. He jerked himself a few times before thrusting his hips into Moira's face. It was the last thing he ever did.

Dracine was still becoming used to her new self, diet and things she could do with it. Appearing and disappearing amidst the crowds that gathered for Ahmed's impaling was just one of the feats. Without thinking, the flight or fight instinct went into total fight mode. In a heartbeat, she dropped to her knees retrieving Emilian's sword, decapitating him in one smooth movement. Whirling like a dervish, the head of the second went flying while the sword went another way striking the third in the throat. The fourth charged Dracine, spear level and thrusting for the heart. There was no move she could make in time.

A movement, a whistle of air flew passed her cheek, just brushing the facial hairs, stabbing the last guard, burying the blade in the eye. The spear point pierced Dracine's skin between the ribs, almost hitting the heart before the assault stopped.

Moira sat on the ground, sprayed with blood that was not her own, staring at the hand that had just thrown the knife. Dracine pulled the point from her chest, dashing for the woman and held her in her arms.

Vlad clapped his hands in delight. "Huzza, huzza! Quite the display. Drache, you are full of surprises these days. Speed, might and the skill to use it. You remind me of... well... me!" noticing the chest wound stop bleeding so soon, added a, "Hmmmmm," to his vocalized thoughts. "Unfortunately for your handmaiden, I fear she did not satisfy Emilian, though her smile would say otherwise." A dark sardonic laugh followed. "His loss in more ways than one. As for Moira, I normally would not fault her, but for her quick hands and steel."

"She was protecting me as a loyal servant should. I would commend her."

"But I shall condemn her for murdering one of my guards."

"It will not happen, Vlad. These people rely on me and I them. If you wish to kill anyone while you are here, you will have to go through me first."

Vlad Tepes the III had never, and I mean never, been told what he could and could not do. He was not shocked or amazed or even angry. He was dumbfounded for a moment, but the wheels in his mind did not stop turning.

"Since you feel so strongly about this, you may take the girl and have her cleaned up. How sincere and earnest you appear, Dracine. You must teach me, for my old methods no longer serve me as they once did."

"My feelings are not an act, Vlad, and your methods never did serve your people, or you."

Vlad laughed loud at Dracine's twist of words. 'Very clever, very clever indeed, but she is now smarter, too. Someone, or something has taught her. Her movements and the lack of pain. There is something else going on here instead of a woman in drag playing it to the hilt. I will discover what it is before leaving. Even if it means killing all of them!' Vlad mused. The meeting was over.

Dracine returned, once again, to the kitchen. Moira was waiting with clean towels and fresh water, as she tended her daughter's mental and physical anguish. Moira had been raped before, but it is something you never get used to. Dracine began to explain the situation. The older Moira was good enough with numbers to handle the kitchen, but that is all. Her ability to put two and two together, however, was never an issue.

"Everything is going to change, my old friend, and not for the better. Vlad wants our success and is going to take it. How the mahjong tiles are going to fall I don't know."

"Are we going to have to leave?" Moira asked.

"If we are lucky. Slavery is the popular option. Pass the word, warn everyone, pack what you need. Our departure may be rather sudden."

While Moira digested the words, she inspected Dracine's cheek wound. "We will change the skins tomorrow. It does appear to be healing well. Thank you, Dracine, for everything."

It was the first time the cook called her by name. Things were definitely changing. Dracine went to her rooms to smoke a bowl and soothe her nerves. 'Had Vlad pinned her out?' He certainly knew something was going on. The old Dracine was clever but not smart, arrogant, vain and of course, a drug addict. Vlad was almost a carbon copy, with the exception of being controlled by drug abuse. He used opium, but did not let it use him. Of course he had found something much, much better.

Dracine watched Vlad move through the marketplace from her windows. He was alone. Well, not alone, but his guards kept a discreet distance so he may see the people at work without the disturbance a contingent of armed men always create. Vlad had removed his hat, which bore the insignia of Dracul, making him appear even more harmless. Just another rich dude. It had been years since his last visit and so at the beginning of his 'tour' he was treated as he seemed to be, with respect, smiles and eager, but not overeager, salesmanship. He even went so far as purchasing a few trinkets, testing the merchants. Now he was surprised. Here in the marketplace, he found an uncommon level of fair trade going without the groveling that usually came along with these things. They treated Vlad as an equal.

The longer he stayed there, the darker the atmosphere became. It was the older people who saw him first. The displays of cruelty meted out by this man were carved into their memories like they were cut in stone. The aged would do a double take glance, then blend into the background, passing the word as they disappeared. The shops Vlad passed started to close like a row of cards falling in slow motion. The owners and staff were evaporating like a drop of water.

Dracine saw what was happening and the shit was going to fly once Vlad caught on to it. Her hands gripped the windowsill until her knuckles went white. She began to chant in ancient Persian. Her voice was low, resonant and clear. Dracine repeated it over and over as fast moving black clouds formed over the sea. The wind picked up carrying the thunderheads along to the waterfront. Now all the markets were dropping canvas windows, shutting up to keep their wares from damage. Moments later a crack of thunder and lightening brought heavy rains pelting the beachfront. Everyone was running, but at least it wasn't for their lives or was it? When Dracine opened her eyes to view the storm, it was to find Vlad Tepes standing in the middle of the empty, rain drenched market staring right at her. The moment was intense as they stared each other down. Knowing a few tricks of his own, Vlad sent a bolt of pain that seared into Dracine's conscious mind. She wobbled before clasping her head in agony and fell from view.

Atoli was resting in Ahmed's old alcove when she heard the scream and fall. She was still weak from Dracine's feeding just prior to Vlad's arrival. But not so frail that a little will power couldn't cure her. She crouched next to the writhing Dracine, lifted her and put her to bed. There was little else she could do, besides making some opium tea in an effort to ease the pain.

Vlad returned to the throne room and sulked. Now he knew, without a doubt what his stepsister was. But how had she done it? How did she call to the darkness and make it her own as he had done? How did he not hear stories of another who lived off the blood of the people, not feel it? Dracine had no education, now she did. Nor did she have the skills to manage a successful district, yet she does. Then of course the big question, how do I kill it? There have been numerous unsuccessful assassination attempts since he had come to power after his tenure at the hands of Mehmed II. You name it, it was tried, all failed. As far as he was concerned, there was not room enough for two of them.

There was, however, a way. Far from the coast and the capitol at Tirgoviste was a district along the northern border with Carpathia. So remote, it was not even considered a place at the time. Only a few nomadic herdsmen and their families lived that far out and then only for the summer. The winter and lack of soil made the mountain region uninhabitable. The place was Borsa.

In present times, Borsa is a popular ski destination in winter and an alpine wonder in spring and summer. At that time though, it was hell on earth without the heat.

An hour passed before the throbbing in her head eased. In becoming aware again, Dracine also felt some serious déjà vu. This had definitely happened before and only to those of a similar dark nature. How she knew this she couldn't put her finger on, just like she knew that Vlad now knows what she is. Macabre scenarios played across her mindscape of what was going to happen. Would her people be slaughtered while she was forced to watch, or would she be debased, skinned and crucified? These were the only alternatives Dracine could think of, as these were the preferred methods of education for Tepes.

Atoli cleaned, dressed and coifed Dracine for dinner. The magistrate had completely forgotten. "I should wear some thing with the Dracul sigil on it, I suppose." Atoli laid out several outfits. "The more feminine would do. He knows."

Atoli gasped. "Yes, we grew up together, sort of. It was after his raping that I chose the garb of men."

"I am sorry, Dracine," consoled Atoli. "Was it you who caused the rain?"

"Yes, to save the people in the marketplace. They were becoming aware of just who walked among them. The pain I felt afterwards was his response. How do I look?"

"Dressed to kill."

"Then that's about right. Thank you, Atoli, for everything. For your own sake, stay hidden while he is here. He would kill you to know what you know."

"Thank you. I will abide, Dracine."

"There is one more thing..." Dracine began. Atoli began to unbutton her collar.

***

S kender opened the door to the trailer with a sigh of relief. It was overcast and the snow wasn't a brilliant blinding light. Then he inhaled. Since both men began living in the trailer, their injuries inhibited the ability to use the outhouse. Thus a few weeks of frozen piss and shit littered the front stoop. Not thinking about it too much he stepped over the mess and down the stairs in search of a shovel. Two wheelbarrows later it was safe to go back inside.

Dino was up, making coffee and reading an off-road magazine for the fifth time.

"Don't you get tired of that shit?" Skender said cheerily, despite his hangover.

"I was thinking the same about you, cuppa?"

"Yeah, real funny, sure man."

Skender smiled to himself. The last few weeks hadn't been a total waste. Tests, trials and saving each other had done what a conscious effort could not. They had bonded to a certain degree. It was something that would be key in the near future.

"How's the back this morning?"

"Grrrr, a little better every day," replied Dino.

"If you didn't say that, I was going to start to worry. You probably ruptured a disc. As the swelling goes down, the fibers in the disc will go back inside, eliminating some of the stenosis."

"God, I hope so. I could use some ice again." Skender had brought some in with him and set the bucket within Dino's reach.

After coffee came some vodka and a smoke. All three had the effect of getting Dino's bowel's moving. "Can you help me to my feet?"

Skender was there, helped him on with a coat and opened the door. "Just yell if you need a hand." He couldn't help the bad pun.

After taking care of a different 'call of the wild', Dino began to roam the aisles of dormant machinery. Under different circumstances, he would be tearing one apart to get it running and doze that building under. But they were dreams and he knew it. Hell, he could hardly wipe his ass, albeit under extreme duress.

The dream crumbled with reality rearing its ugly head, once again. No longer all that interesting, he pulled his eyes from the dead steel to look around the yard some more. Despite the fact that it was the dead of winter, the forest around him appeared as dead as the machinery. Something, the grayness of mortification, was instilled in the trees. He was looking in the direction of the oubliette. Turning around 180 degrees he saw the alpine as it should look; sparse, dormant, but alive. Even the needles on the pines were green when compared to those nearer the stone building. Dino turned again, leaning on the wheel of a truck for assistance. The tire was hard. Though it was cold, there should have been some resilience. And the color, a uniform grey instead of black.

Near the workshed, he found what he was looking for – a piece of re-bar about a foot long. Back at the truck, he took a swing at the rubber, as much as his back would allow, expecting a bounce when the rod recoiled. Instead it met with what felt like concrete, sending the force right down his spine, bringing Dino to his knees.

"SKENDER!" he yelled hitting the ground.

Two minutes ground on inexorably until Skender arrived, a roll of toilet paper in his hand. Skender had stopped at the toilet first, then following the fresh tracks that led him to Dino.

"What happened?" Skender was down on his knees trying to make the other comfortable when Dino spoke up, through the pain.

"Have you taken a look around lately?" Dino said through his teeth.

"Not really. Beyond getting snow for water and taking a dump, no," Skender replied straightforwardly.

"Take a whack at that tire, an easy one." Dino pointed at the re-bar.

Skender took a swing at the tread, chipping a piece off. "Son of a bitch."

"My sentiments exactly. Check out the look of the trees, that way, then the other."

Following orders, Skender focused, but it didn't take him long to figure it out. He walked to the green of a nearby pine and whipped the rebar at a branch. Nothing. Snow and ice broke loose from the needles and fell to the ground while the branch swayed, unaffected by the blow. He then walked in the direction of Sechra's prison.

Surrounded by grey stood a tree similar to the one he hit. The pine stood stock still and in a couple of seconds, Skender, would know why. The still air whistled before the steel connected with a resounding SMACK that shattered the branch, like rock. Which, of course, it was. Skender picked a few sticks and went to where Dino was lying.

"Everything has, or is turning to stone." Skender handed the rocks to Dino.

"Jesus Christ," Dino quickly did the sign of the cross. "What did this?"

"Must have something to do with Sechra's work."

"Her work! Hah! She is dead by now, Skender. No food, no water, no fire. Go figure."

"I have. Nevertheless, she is alive and working in there. I've heard her late at night."

"What could she possibly be making? In the dark, even." Dino remembered hearing the sounds of a hammer, too.

"Hopefully the only thing that could save us and Romania. Or... " Skender let his words trail off.

"Or what?" Dino demanded.

"A monster that will destroy us all. Now let's get you back inside."

Before leaving the out of doors, Skender pulled a rag from his pocket, blew his nose, then tied it to a tree that was at the border between death and life.

"This way..." Skender began.

"Yeah, I know I know."

Back in the warmth with coffee in one hand and shot of vodka in the other – this had become a morning ritual for the two in an effort to keep motivation at bay – they toasted to Sechra, each absorbed in their own thoughts about what they had seen.

"What will we do if that shit keeps encroaching?" Dino offered.

"Leave, I guess."

"Isn't there some spell you guys do when this stuff happens?" Dino's query was not intended as a sneer against the mountain peoples and gypsies in particular. It was far more beyond that, if you know what I mean. And Skender understood.

"My father was the man, but I fear even he couldn't do anything about this. Maybe earlier, but not now. Sechra and I passed many rituals on our way to getting here. The people are desperate and the spells, merely an effort to save themselves."

"Is there anything you can do with your voodoo?"

Skender smiled. "No. I think, however we are doing it."

"Yeah I get it, sort of. Pass me the bottle so I can get it a little more."

Skender poured, they both laughed until it became uneasy.

"What are we going to do?" Skender ran his hands through his hair, staring at the floor.

It was the first time since meeting Skender that Dino had ever seen him show anything but a window of opportunity. Of course, the options at this point were few and considering the situation, they were really fucked. And it was going to get worse. In an effort to get Skender back into the now, Dino got up off the ice and began to organize his gear and fill boxes with food from the stash.

"What are you doing?" Even Skender's ability to pick minds was failing him now, like the seers, he thought.

Rifling his pockets, Dino pulled the keys to his rig.

"I'm going to pull the truck around and we should load her up in case..." Dino tilted his head in the direction of the oubliette.

His rig started with little effort. After checking all the gauges, he scanned the back of the truck to see how much stuff could fit. It was then the little rag that Skender tied caught his eye out the rear window. It hung motionless in the breeze. He couldn't remember, damnit! Dino backed the truck to the stairs. Getting out he looked again at the little flag and walked up to it. He smacked it with his keys and viewed the reactions. Shards of thin rock broke further into smaller pieces as it hit the ground. Tentatively, he stuck one finger into the dead zone. Immediate cold. Stiffening as the skin began to turn grey, Dino pulled his finger out, heading immediately to the trailer, but not before noticing the trees next to it.

"Oh shit."

Inside he took the bottle and swallowed hard a few times. Skender was staring at him with a 'what the fuck' look on his face.

"Looks like you've seen a ghost," Skender pointed out.

"Yeah, ours!"

"What? What did you see?"

Dino stuck his forefinger out. The skin broke off like eggshells when he bent it before Skender's eyes. "Did you tie the rag to a green tree or rock?"

"Green, why?"

"It's rock now. The trees next to the trailer have been affected, too! We have to get out of here!"

They watched as the far side of the trailer turned that suspicious shade of death. It was where the food was. As quickly as they could Skender and Dino began throwing items to the exit door in an effort to salvage as much food as possible. Skender pulled on his jacket and reached into the zone to get the last few cases of vodka before the effect affected them. From then on it was a mad rush to load all the crap as fast as they could.

***

The oubliette was always in the shade regardless of the sun's position. It was as if the structure created its own: a moat of darkness surrounding the place of death. When Sechra began carving the final panel, the darkness began to extend itself. It was becoming an expanding circle of death, with the oubliette at its center. The thing, the evil within, was preparing to expose himself to the world. The sun would not do. His world, as it was now becoming, would be a place of shadow. The diameter of death would grow from its mere few hundred meters until all of Romania was within it. But it would not stop there. The dark foul thing grew. With growth came power. It would continue at an ever-quickening pace until the entire world was eclipsed. It was preparing to be unborn into a world of fear and desperation, 'just the way I like it.'

For the last six shits – it was Sechra's way of counting time – the thing had not gone back underground, but stayed within the confines of the place to die, as that was what the oubliette was. It was built ages ago, before even the Goths some say, to house the worst of society's criminals, prisoners of war and the inconvenient. The price one paid upon entering was your life. You would never leave. Instead with no food or water, the hapless souls would slowly starve to death, alone, surrounded by another hundred poor bastards sharing a similar fate. They were crammed in there like New York subway riders. What happened to the dead, you may ask? Nothing. The door was one way. Some were feasted upon, but most were rotting before they got there from wounds, thusly the bulk of its inhabitants were inedible. In the darkness, however, even the unthinkable happens. When the dead became too many and they were standing knee deep in a cold human body stew, their nightmares would really begin.

Those who lived long enough began to panic when the hatch in the floor began to screech as it tilted up. It was then that the screaming began in earnest. That which rose from the floor was not room service. The human cattle had nowhere to run with the confines of the all too small corral. Blood and severed limbs began flying as it tore through the group. Though none could see it, you could hear it rip the head from some lost soul and quaff from the fountain that exploded from the neck. One was not enough, never has been, never will be. As it waded through the men, the initial flight or fight response vanished, leaving them standing like sheep waiting their turn.

When the quiet returned and they heard the thing going back underground, someone would yell, "NOW, get the bodies in the hole before it closes." A mad clumsy rush ensued as men bent over to grab anything that was on the ground and dump it in. Fresh screams came from those not quite dead enough yet. Regardless of the pleas, they got dumped too. Then the screeching began. The men knew to finish up and get away. The last prisoner was shoving a body through the decreasing gap. He was a newbie and paid the price. Pushing as hard as he could the body would not go in. He spun around on the slick floor and pushed with his feet. He could not see the closing hatch. Had he, well, he was now screaming at the top of his lungs as the hatch had close over his legs just above the knee.

With room to move around, a few tentatively worked their way to the trapped man. There was nothing they could do. One consoled him. Another began asking a few pointed questions.

What are you in for? Treason. They beat you? No. So you are in good health? Other than a few bruises, yes. When did you arrive at Maison du Morte? A week ago, maybe?

Silently a small knife was slid from a boot. When the consoler was done consoling, the other man went to work. The blade was sharp. Drawing it quickly across the trapped man's throat brought him to rest, silently. Then the wet work began.

The reason this site was chosen for the oubliette was that it covered the opening where the gypsies, a millennia or so ago, had placed the abomination. As the thing grew, they could no longer keep up with its demands. A huge naturally round stone was rolled over the access hole to contain the horrid aberration. They wanted to believe that with no food or water, it would one day die. It seemed like a good idea at the time.

Sechra's role in this macabre affair was to create and birth the abomination. When it all started, seemingly ages ago to the sculptor, her fear of what she was creating overwhelmed her thoughts, leaving room for little else. Time passed, rock chips flew, and the dust coated everything. In the rythym of work came peace, eventually replacing the horror with a calm that comes from diligent effort.

So far she had been able to conceal the real images from her client. That she had fooled him, left a more than nagging thought surfacing in the cauldron of her mind. Sechra felt the carvings were of peace, struggle and a triumph of the soul and body. Yet when it would feel the rock, following her instructions, he could feels the cries of the damned through the eyes, cheeks, mouths, and body language the reliefs now brought to the surface. This, Sechra thought, was it seeing what she wanted it to see. So far it worked, but too well. She cursed herself. Not being able to see what she was doing created a schism of doubt through which more questions rose. Were the people depicted really happy, or was it like the rest of her work, morbid, debasing, punishing herself and her people? Feeling the stone now, she could barely discern the difference between joy and horror. The more she felt the worse it got, until it got the best of her. She had to sit, to think.

Sechra drained the last of the coffee, chasing it with the last of the vodka. 'What have I done?' she asked herself over and over again. The image of her grandfather appeared before her. He was at peace, working on a coppiced wall.

"What's the wall for grandpapa? How come it has all those spaces?"

"It is a fighting wall, little one. The soldiers can take protection behind this high spot and when they are ready to shoot they step in to the open, shoot and return to safety."

"Why do men shoot at each other?"

"Because they are fools."

"Then why make it so strong? Let the fools kill each other." Sechra had already in her young life seen more death and destruction at the hands of fools to make her question a normal one.

Dray looked at her smiling. "Because these fools are our Voivode. They fight to save us from certain destruction."

"But you are men. You can fight."

"We are farmers and masons, not soldiers, dear Sechra. The battle with the soil is our fight. We would be slaughtered by a real enemy and so rely on the Voivode and their guards for protection. For the most part, the system works quite well for all involved."

"Grandpapa?"

"Yes, Sechra?"

"What am I going to do?"

"Your best, always do your best and the rest will follow."

"What about that which you can't see?" The question did not throw the old man.

"Then you must follow your heart. Usually, when doing what you are supposed to be doing, the heart will lead, guiding your work. When you can't see clearly because your mind is getting in the way, close your eyes and work blind."

Sechra reached over to hug her Grandpapa, coming aware when the hug changed to a more full body kind of hug without the intimation of sex. When she opened her eyes, Jake was sitting next to her.

"Uncle Jake!"

"Looks like you got yourself in a little over your head, eh kiddo? You take after me that way. Got your nine with you?"

"Back at the trailer. I was just looking around when the door opened."

"And your curiosity got the best of you."

"Yep."

"I do that all the time. So what's the gig?"

Sechra explained the nutshell version.

"Well, Sechra, I'm a working man. When I commit to a job it means to the end, no matter what the cost. I gave my word." Jake began to fade. "Don't let the bastards grind you down!" He was gone.

She had dreamt! Damnit! That meant she slept. Sechra did not look forward to what comes next. She shifted her bulk to the left, then the right, until enough momentum was achieved to send her to the floor with the sound of falling rock as an accompaniment.

"OOOHHHhrrrrroooooooowoof," came the air as it expelled from her lungs.

By now she was as thoroughly a stone as the one she sculpted. No less than an exact copy of herself that she created. The final panel was rapidly becoming her most difficult. Her will to move was waning. She was slow, too slow. The dexterity and sense of feel were the last skills that remained intact. The rest had been lost in creation.

Sechra stumped back to the boulder. It was the boots. The climbing boots she had been given by Skender's son. Without them, she would not have been able to free climb the rock when the makeshift scaffolding failed her. The smallest nub of rock would catch the edge of the boot, carrying her full weight. She could work for hours, suspended so, before climbing to a new position. The boots had been invaluable. Without them, the carving could never have been completed. Sechra quietly thanked the boy, saying a small prayer for him that he might survive. She knew she would not. She gave her word, not to it, but to her people. It was the price.

Back at work, the tinking of hammer and chisel counted the hours, days, weeks, months, life. Time, like many other things, no longer mattered.

Her renderings were from the heart. There was no reason to doubt herself further. She worked on.

Off center of the last panel stood the oubliette. From there, the waves of goodness spread like ripples in a pond. Smiles, work, play, families and a road from deep in the mountains that meandered down touching on all the villages with connector arteries to major hubs before terminating in Constanta.

In time the hammering came to an end with the exception of minor alterations. Now was a coarse, grinding: shwoosh, shwoosh, shwoosh. The work was being polished. There were no tools in her bag to aid in this most laborious and tedious process, so she used her hands. They were not hard as rock... they were rocks. As mentioned before, her body was rapidly turning to stone. That particular process was now completed, indicating her work would be done soon. Sechra could keep this effort up, but for how long?

Her fingertips, palms, knuckles, and forearms did the abrasive work. Each digit would grind itself down to a stub by the time she would stop. Minutes later when she was ready to resume, the worn areas had rebuilt themselves exactly as they were before.

Deep relief and shallow would be ground and rubbed to a smooth satin finish. Soon, very soon, she hoped the sculpture would be finally done. Of course what happened then was really none of her concern. Her word was kept.

***

"Move it Skender! Move it." Their bags and personal gear was the last to get thrown in as the trailer became engulfed. Skender was in the driver's seat, revving the engine to hurry Skender. Skender tossed a load in.

"One more thing. The shotgun!"

"Fuck it, Skender!" Dino was talking to no one.

A minute passed. Then two. Dino was out the door. Skender had almost made it. He grabbed the grey hands and pulled for all he was worth. His back rebelled at every movement. He would not let it interfere, not now. "PULL!"

Dino snagged Skender's coat to the bumper, hopped in the driver's seat, hitting the gas until he had put a few hundred yards between the death and the rig. Skender was pulled along with the truck. It was only after he got Skender into the seat that Dino noticed he still had hold of the gun. There was no immediate compulsion to wake him and check for damage. What was done was done and there was nothing to be done about it now.

'Where to go? Where to go?' was the skipping record going round and round his head. Then it hit him, the cave. They needed protection from the cold. The truck would not be good enough. The entrance to the tunnel, that he now called Rue Dolores would do. The smell was not there nor the screaming walls. It was out of the wind and more than a kilometer from the road yard. He flipped on the GPS.

After carrying Skender in and half the supplies to the entrance, fire lit, he opened a bottle and took a long, deserved draw. At the truck, Dino pulled out a pair of binoculars, the really big kind, and focused on the road building camp. The perimeter of death continued to expand. How long they would safe here was a good question. Following the tunnel back up was not an option, nor was taking the route Skender and Sechra had used. The avalanche had sublimed, making a crossing impossible. They would have to wait until the first thaws of spring. Dino made a mental note as to the line of death, so he could remember the next time he looked.

Camp, just within the tunnel opening, was rustic. After getting Skender comfortable, he set to roping a tarp over the entrance. It was going to be cold. They had enough cold weather gear, but from now on there would be no heat. Skender looked like shit. A grey carapace of stone covered his face, neck and hands. His clothing, luckily, had turned to stone, saving the skin on his body. Dino would have to wait until Skender regained consciousness before attempting any medical stuff. Once the camp was in order, Dino sat in the darkness listening to the icy wind beat noisily against the tarp. 'At least it keeps the wind out,' Dino said drunkenly to no one. One more tip of the bottle and he climbed into his sleeping bag and dreamt of warmer climates.

With dawn came silence. The sound of it snapped Dino awake. He turned on a flashlight, panning his forearms until he was sure they were a skin color. The next order of the day was coffee. Whatever was going on outside could wait. He watched Skender's chest move regularly while waiting for the water to boil. With coffee in hand, Dino pulled back the tarp, wincing at the glare of the morning sun. The light of day helped make clear what had happened over the course of the evening.

He had forgotten to check on the encroaching grey death before sundown. Now, he stepped back doing a double take. The mortification surrounded them. Half the truck had turned to stone. A stark dividing line separated the living from the dead. For some reason it stopped just a few meters before the entrance. 'We're fucked,' he said to himself. The other part of Dino forgot to be thrilled he was alive!

Skender was moving around when he went back inside. He did not speak out or see through stone eyelids.

"Skender, can you hear me?" Skender nodded affirmatively, Dino continued. "First things first. The skin on your face and hands is like an eggshell of stone. I don't know what to do." Dino was rarely at a loss for an answer, so Skender gave him one.

Skender raised both hands, slapping himself viciously with a two handed blow to his face. Dino had surmised the condition of Skender's face correctly. And like the metaphor, Skender's skin on his face and hands shattered. As one would expect a fair number of shards, large and small, fell onto Skender's lap. The remainder hung on tenuously and would have to be removed by hand. He picked at the hardened eyelids first, peeling the pieces away with a wet sticky sound, just like a hard-boiled egg, with the exception of being raw dermis.

A sweat of blood wept onto the surface of the new skin. Next came the lips. The rock hard skin pulled off, but not without a certain amount of excruciating pain. Within moments the weeping of blood began. Instead of a perfectly formed mouth made from stone, it was now a bloody maw, slick, wet and glistening with agony. Through red stained teeth Skender was now able to lisp painfully.

"Pease get ma bagh." Skender pointed across the tunnel.

Dino hustled over in the dark to get the dirty white bag with a red cross on it. Skender shook his head.

"Odder won, back."

This time Dino returned with a worn black leather pack.

"Oven, emply."

Dino dumped the contents onto the foot of Skender's sleeping bag. There were a variety of syringes, sealed bottles and pill bottles. Skender pushed up his sleeve above the elbow and began to finger through the drugs until he found what he was looking for, dragging the items away from the rest.

"Hut away." Skender waved at the pile of meds then placed his hand over what he had taken.

Dino was back at his side in moments. "Now what?"

"Do ne." Skender pointed at the works. "Just lie da novies." Skender pantomimed shooting up.

Dino sort of knew the routine. Growing up had taken him around the block a few times. With the needle stabbed into the inverted bottle, Dino watched Skender as he filled it, stopping when the gruesome head nodded. Skender squeezed his upper arm until the veins stood proud. When Dino was finished, he relaxed his grip and let the meds go to work before trying to talk.

While Skender absorbed the bliss that comes with a mainlined full load of morphine, Dino started to clean himself up to some degree. Snow, a little soap and vigorous mechanical scrubbing cut the edge on the grime that crept deep into the skin. They weren't sterile, but they would do.

"Dino," Skender said more clearly now with lips that could move.

"Yeah, you ready?" Dino inquired, wiping his hands on his last clean t-shirt.

"Are you?"

"We all got to do what we got to do, so yes I am. By the way, where was the morphine when I couldn't walk?"

"I knew you'd live without it." Skender felt sorry now for holding out. "Listen Dino, I'm s..."

Dino interrupted him. "Don't worry about it, Skender. I can only imagine what losing your skin is like."

"That's no excuse."

"Right now we have more to be concerned with than your inability to prescribe. The circle expanded last night but somehow went around us."

"Like an ocean surrounds an island."

"It's a fair analogy. The problem is we don't have a boat. The front half of the truck now looks like a granite sculpture. I don't care about the rig. It's the fact that we are trapped that concerns me. Why did the death stop at our front door and go around us is what I would like to know?" Dino was quite serious and didn't like, one bit, the trapped part.

"Perhaps this tunnel will lead us out?"

"Been down this road, Skender. This is how I got here."

"Where does it go?"

"To a pass deep in the mountains. Take four or five, maybe six days to hike out. It would be near a week of pure hell to get where? There is nothing at the other end."

"Why do you say it would be hell?"

"Well, for one thing it stinks of rotting flesh. Then there is the masonry. Human bodies were used to grout the stones together."

"I've heard of this. Old tales passed down through the generations spoke of this place. Some time in the mid-1400s, Vlad Tepes III banished a people and their leader from the kingdom into these mountains. It is said they built this passage." Skender stopped.

"Yeah, a brass plague outside the opening mentioned him."

"It explains why the death did not enter here. This is a place of death. It's time to go to work, Dino. There should be some forceps in the med kit. Just peel me like an egg, but carefully."

"The sun is out. You think you can get outside? I'll make you a soft spot."

It was indeed an unusually bright day for the dead of winter. Dino would be able to see clearly, as far as he was concerned, maybe a little too clearly, for it gave an all too up close and personal view of the damage. The surgery took hours and required two more doses of morphine for Skender to withstand the procedure. Each piece, large or tiny, peeled off with a sticky, wet, tendrily release, leaving only the inner most layer of raw, pink porous, skin. As the sun dipped in the west, a cold, thick-skinned Dino carried Skender back inside. He slathered the near flayed areas with antibiotic goo, then took personal advantage of the private med kit. Caring for Skender aggravated his back injury, plus he could use a few hours of forgetfulness.

✳✳✳

The dining hall was set for two. Each place setting was at the end of a very long table. Dracine's place setting was, ironically, the same seat she had given Lenes so long ago. Candlelight was sparse, creating a foreboding atmosphere. Dracine had expected nothing less than a lavish meal with the wealthiest of the land, so that Vlad could mock her formally. The door opened to the dim, almost empty room. Vlad sat at one end of the table sipping wine when she entered.

"Good evening, Dracine. I see you have recovered. No doubt a little opium aided in your relief, ehh?" Dracine nodded as Vlad pointed to her seat.

"No appetizers?" Dracine broke the silence carefully.

"I no longer have the appetite I once had. I'm sure your diet has changed, too, since we last met."

"It has." Dracine was not going to lie, but neither was she going to volunteer information. If he wanted knowledge he would have to dig for it, and dig deep.

Picking up her thoughts Vlad said, "I considered digging you the deepest of graves, but know that one day you would dig your way out and be a perpetual pain in my ass. No, I am not here to pick your brain, to ask how, why and a million other pointless questions. The fact is you are what you are and there is little I can do about it now. There is however a solution for you. In our country we have a district that is sadly in arrears. After seeing what you have done here, I know you could help our extended family to the north. I will be sending you and 'your' people there very soon."

"How many of my people?"

"All of them," Vlad replied in a cocky manner. "You have created a little trading gold mine here and I do not need you to exploit it. After walking among 'your people' today I am sure they would rather be with you than live under my rule."

"Where is this place you speak of?"

"Borsa." Vlad smiled with deep satisfaction while Dracine tried to remain emotionless.

"There is not even a road to that place."

"You will build it with your people if you expect to get there. Do for me in Borsa what you did here and you shall be rewarded."

"Your rewards are a curse."

"This is true, but there can be only one of us in greater Romania and I am it. Surely you understand," Vlad said in mock consolation. Then in a more commanding voice, "Your people will be notified tomorrow and you will leave the day after. Death is the only other alternative. And a horrible one at that." Vlad laughed to himself, alone. Dracine left without permission.

There was no pomp for the three thousand people who had been notified of their very unique circumstance. Well, not all that unique. Banishing someone who had become inconvenient was all the rage in this day and age. But to do it to an entire city was what made it special. This type of relocation was usually left for the Jews.

There was no time to pack properly. It was a grab and go kind of deal. Vlad wanted everything left in place. Expediting the departure ensured this as well as the pointed spears of Vlad's guards. The one thousand soldiers that followed Vlad now entered the city to make sure there was no hoarding. As the groups of frightened citizens were rounded up, each person was inspected as they left the gates. The only items allowed out were clothes, food, cookware and tools. Most of the people did not take what they would need to survive the journey into the mountains. Instead they took their gold, jewelry, silks, fancy clothes and items they thought valuable. They were under the illusion that these things mattered. Where Dracine's people were headed, an ax and good shovel would be worth more than all the gold you could carry. C'est la vie.

Piles of gold and silks sat just inside the gates. Relieved of their precious burdens, thousands of people bemoaned their situation while waiting for Dracine to lead them.

Dressed practically with sturdy shoes, Dracine and her entourage were the last to leave. The inspection was cursory for them. One cart held the personal belongings of Dracine and castle staff. Two other carts were loaded with pots, pans, tools of all sorts, and heavy wool blankets instead of silk, ten horses, twenty mules, a small herd of cows and sheep, and a rolling chicken coop. Atoli, dressed as a hag, her children in rags, made it through the gate when the masses went through. Dracine wanted her kept safe, for surely Vlad would be watching when Dracine's entourage came through.

Vlad stepped from a tent with no walls as she approached. She halted her horse next to the piles of 'valuables,' hiding her disappointment as she dismounted.

"Good morning, Dracine." As he spoke rain began to fall from leaden skies. "No jewels or gold?"

"They would be useless where we are going," Dracine deadpanned.

"Apparently many of your people thought otherwise. A rather foolish choice don't you think, as they were not allowed to go back and refill their empty cases with useful things. They had their chance to decide. No doubt you thought they would have remembered and thus chosen wisely." Vlad enjoyed his bit of condescension and mockery. Dracine fumed behind steely eyes. "Yes, I would be angry, too. Many will die before the week is out and that is while you still have a road. The rest will die shortly thereafter while making a road to nowhere." Vlad laughed loud as the thunder that shattered the stillness of the morning, releasing a torrent of rain. Vlad looked up into the sky, smiling as the drops splashed on his face. "Rather auspicious for a dolorous journey such as this. Just so you won't be completely alone, a contingent of my men will follow you for inspiration, as well as keeping you headed in the right direction. Since you are family I could not kill you outright, though I rather think this will be better than death as it will surround you every day and night. A more fitting sentence I cannot imagine, a traveling oubliette. What, nothing to say, dear Dracine? This is the second time I have taken what I wanted from you..."

"There will not be a third. Your rule will last but a few more years before your own treachery brings you to your death. You banished the wrong relative." With that Dracine mounted her horse, adjusting her cape before shaking the reigns and leaving her half-brother standing in the rain, brooding over what she had said.

Once outside, the huge wooden gates closed with a grating slam! What Dracine encountered was worse that what she expected. Hundreds were standing in the pouring rain, near naked after their finery had been confiscated.

"Moira, blankets for the old, everyone else will just have to live with their choices." Moira and her daughter obeyed the command dutifully. Before distributing the warmth, the older Moira told the younger one to keep an eye on the blankets for there were only so many and to pick up the used ones when discarded. Discarded was a better way of putting it than saying, 'when they drop, pry the blankets from their cold dead hands.' Moira knew from her youth that when the temperature drops, you would rather have a dead guy's blanket than none at all.

In fact, all of the group were going to have to reacquaint themselves to survival. The talent had been lost, forgotten or unused for quite a long time while pursuing business endeavors. Business is about as far from survival as the equator is to the poles. In fact, it would be the polar opposite to coin a pun. Part of Dracine was like her people, clueless. The other half, however, understood what survival was from an intimate point of view. Each day, each hour, every moment required you to be in survival mode, ready to tear the face of anything that would keep you from keeping on.

But how do you do that for three thousand people? Vlad had been correct in his assumption that in the first week death would come knocking and often. Even she could see it coming after the first day. The old, infirm and helpless with no family or friends, fell behind. The only reason they kept moving were the points of motivation carried by Tepes' guard. Ten died the first day, twenty, the second, multiplying each day until the dying peaked at over two hundred on the seventh day. Late into the night, they dug shallow graves. After marching all day long, the men put their backs into the effort. Dracine was right alongside digging into the earth. Towards dawn the holes were being finished. As yet the bodies had not been laid to rest, when Dracine spied a shadow working through the rows of dead. It was not the priest. Was someone stealing from the corpses while the rest were sleeping or, like Dracine, still digging? This she would not tolerate. As long as she was alive the people would not devolve to this!

Silently, but with the speed of an arrow Dracine was at the looter's side, and had the left arm of a girl caught in a near bone-breaking grip. In a hushed, harsh voice Dracine said, "You are lucky you are not already one of them!" Dracine forced the girl to look closely in the dim light at the corpses. "Speak! The truth or you die here, now!"

"It, it, it is me, Moira," cried the daughter of the cook. Dracine's grip loosened, but not so much the girl noticed. The fact that Dracine knew mattered not at all. If she were guilty she would die, quickly, painlessly. With survival, there is very little room for compassion.

"Mother told me to collect the blankets from the dead. She said we will need them because there will not be any where we are going."

Dracine released Moira. "Let me help." Help was needed to pry the blankets free from rigor-mortised digits. "We will take any good shoes and clothing, too. After tonight you can get the older Atoli children to help you."

"You mean there will be more?" Moira asked through her tears.

"Yes. Until we get where we are going. There will be fewer, though. The old are having a very difficult time."

"Why did he make us leave?"

"Because of me, dear one." Dracine alone would bear the responsibility, quietly and without drama. "Now let's get all this back to the wagons. When we have time, you and the kids can wash them."

The clothes of the dead were an unpleasant reminder of the foolishness of their own packing. Young Moira was given charge of this duty. Her word, final. The items of the deceased were given to those in need, not those in want. There was never enough.

The first month was the hardest. After that it was merely brutal. Four weeks passed, while following a road built by the Romans during their reign. Now it was a rutted path used only by shepherds and their flocks. When that ended, the shovels and picks came out to forge a passable route. Mountain rock became as unforgiving as their destiny. Were it not for Tepes' guard and the vigilance of Dracine to muster the people, the herd would have disbanded or died long ago.

After several months of survival, wherein death was an everyday occurrence, the people, used to comfort and plenty, were hardening with less and being satisfied with it. Hunting parties now worked the trail ahead, stalking deer and fowl. The fresh meat was becoming as necessary as the air they breathed, as what few supplies there were, were rapidly being depleted. Dracine insisted they not touch the domesticated animals they brought along for food. They would be needed to develop herds once they got to Borsa. There were cows for milk and meat, sheep for wool and meat, chickens and geese for eggs, feathers and meat, and dogs to protect the meat from predators. Vegan they weren't. Vegetables alone would not provide the needed fat and protein to survive the winter. Aside from wildcrafting for the edible greens and roots of the forest, you need a garden and farm. The current situation obviously would not allow it. Not until they got where they were going. But by then, the dream of starting again in the mountains, the only hope that kept them going, would be crushed.

Their progress was horribly slow. Moving a few thousand people is a lot harder than moving a few thousand head of cattle. The mountains made it nearly impossible. For weeks at a time they would camp along the bare windblown slopes while a road, a wide path would be more exact, was cut into the mountainside. Until the road made it to another sizeable campground, they would wait. There were plusses and minuses to waiting. On the one hand, fewer died on the treacherous terrain. The lives that were saved in turn created a heavy impact on food consumption. As the alpine forest dwindled to scrub, too, so the wild animals they depended on for food became scarce. Soon, too soon, they would have to start eating the animals. Already chickens were disappearing from the coop and a guard was posted there 24/7.

Vlad's men, on the other hand, had nothing to worry about in the way of eating. A steady supply train arrived every week with food for them, and them alone. When the wind was right, the smells from cook fires drifted across the camp of the damned. Always a few would try to enter Tepes' camp for a handout, begging. They were spurned and given good reason never to come again. Of course if you were female... you could suck on a bone.

Winter bore down on them in the endless march of the seasons. Unless they could build shelters, they would all die. Dracine had begun to figure that this was the plan from the beginning. There was no relocation going on. Tepes meant for them to die enroute, damning Dracine for the upheaval of their lives. This was a migration to hell.

Eventually it came to a dead halt. The mountains rose before them on two sides, shear walls of volcanic basalt nearly vertical. On the third side was a cliff so steep the only way down was to jump to your death; more than a few would take the plunge when faced with the alternative. Behind them was Tepes' guard.

At the base of mountain, to the east of them, was what modern man would call a lava tube. The tunnel was formed eons ago when the region was volcanically active. How far it went or where to, no one knew, but they would find out.

Dracine was in the vanguard when they reached the end of the road. Part of her surmised the situation immediately. There were only two alternatives. Either they would be forced off the cliff, or allowed sanctuary within the cave. Dracine breathed deeply astride her horse. Surely death awaited them in a cruel twist of fate, regardless of what was chosen. 'The cliff would be quicker.'

"Oskar, make some torches. When you are through, send a runner to Tepes' guard and notify them of what had happened." She knew the runner would be beaten for arriving late. They needed time to inspect the cave.

Oskar had been alongside Dracine since the exodus. They bonded while digging graves and earned each other's respect at the end of a round tool. Dracine liked him for his imposing stature. Oskar was a big man. It was his honesty that drew her to him. After a lifetime of living around people who would inevitably plot against you, she admired the open eyes and clean smile, of which he had one for everyone.

When Dracine left Tepes in the dining hall, a lifetime ago it now seemed, she headed straight for her quarters. Rather than loading the pipe, seeking oblivion, as was her habit, Dracine opened the carpetbag with drugs from another time and ate something called 'quick clean.' Her people did not need a stoned out junkie to lead them to their death, but rather a leader who would do what was needed to ensure the safety and survival of the many.

One morning, before dawn, Dracine sat with Oskar away from the graves, tired from a long night digging them. Now they were being filled again. The work had been exhausting. Her guard was dropping, as she no longer had the will to keep it up. "Oskar, I need your help." The simple words came hard as she had never used them before.

"I know," he responded unbuttoning his jacket collar and opening his shirt.

'How could he know?' Dracine was thinking fast, but not fast enough.

"No one can work as hard as you and still maintain. You have not slept in four days. I have been watching."

"But how...?"

"Suffice to say I know. Know that your secret is safe with me. Now do what you must before the dawn light comes." Oskar pulled down his collar.

"No. I cannot." This was hard for her to say as his big heart pumped loudly in her ears. "It is not what I need from you."

"I know. I was just testing you." Dracine looked at him quizzically in the early light. "Whether you would think of yourself first, or them." Oskar waved his hand in the direction of the line of campfires behind them. "What is it you wish?"

"I need you to pick men and women that you know are decent people to help me. Be my captains, men at arms, eyes and ears. I cannot do it alone. The winter will be hard. Men with little to do and too much to worry about is a bad combination."

"We will be there when you need us. But please, do not single anyone out. Vocalize your thoughts. The words will reach the right ears. But what is it? What are you not telling me?"

"I do not think we will make it through the winter." Dracine whispered this, as if saying it aloud would cause it to be.

Oskar laughed loud as the sun broke the horizon, sparkling off his face. It was something Dracine had not seen in a long time, or was ever likely to see again. A man laughing.

"Oh, I know that," Oskar began as he quieted. Conspiratorially he added, "I think we should keep that to ourselves."

Soon the eyes, ears and hands of Dracine extended through the camp. Not only had Oskar been keeping an eye on her, but everyone was. For the first time, the people were seeing the finer traits of a Voivode coming through. None of them had actually seen one doing 'anything' before, besides condemning the poor that is, let alone give you the shirt off her back.

Oskar and Dracine began the habit of convening before the first meal of the day and after the last to discuss the day's events while prescribing for the next. Tonight Oskar was troubled. The moon played tricks with his eyes making him hard to look at.

"What is it, Oskar, you're freaking me out."

"We have trouble at the end of the line."

Soon after the forced march began, the people began dividing themselves into groups. Those of a common mind, kin and past friendships found themselves amongst each other as the road stretched on. The groups separated to within shouting distance for privacy and pace. The column of hell-bent travelers stretched for kilometers before encountering the wall of Tepes' men. To divide the groups into some sort of sensible order, it could loosely be described as follows. The folk in the rear still held some hope of redemption. By staying close to Tepes' guard they felt protected, certain, they would be spared, by showing respect to the powerful Voivode that upended their lives.

In the middle were the herdsmen, ever vigilant in protecting the animals from both the front and rear. They were neutral, always have been, always will be. The animals were their life, people a nuisance.

The lead consisted of those who would follow Dracine.

"Have you noticed some of the people falling to the rear ranks?"

"Yes, at breakfast, familiar faces gone."

"There is rumor that it is you that brought this upon us. Since we were never given an explanation..."

"The rumor is true, Oskar. Surely you knew that."

"I do, but you see I understand. They do not."

"Who would start such a thing? I told no one." Dracine strained at the thought she was being betrayed.

"Yes, you did. Children will be children. Moira traded secrets with the Atoli children. All of them are loyal to you, yet they were overheard.

You were betrayed by innocence. Since then, the flames of discontent are being fanned by Tepes' men."

"It would have happened anyway, men being what they are."

Oskar didn't wait for Dracine to show her confusion. "Do not worry. We have your back, for now."

"Thank you, Oskar."

"And now this," Dracine said to no one as she stared out at the vista. Somewhere out there was Borsa.

"The torches are ready." Oskar handed two to Dracine who nudged her mount in the direction of the cave. The opening was huge, about thirty meters in diameter with a relatively level floor. The walls were semi-smooth and rippled horizontally. Each ripple represented the level of lava that ran through it as it drained, leaving the empty tube. They rode and walked deeper into the cave. It went very far. Far enough to house the entire encampment through the winter if need be. Every now and then fissures in the rock released streams of fresh water. The enclosure was almost too ideal for their needs.

One by one the torches died. Only Oskar lit his second torch off the first. The one flame was weak resistance against the darkness. Spooked by the close emptiness, the others lit their torches from Oskar's. A common sigh of relief. Only Dracine sat in the darkness, seeing the nightmare to come.

Emerging from the cave, wincing while eyes adjusted to the light, they came face to face with Tepes' guard. Ignaski, Tepes' captain at arms, a flagitious man, sat scowling at them. "Why did you enter the cave without us?" he demanded.

Dracine held her ground, squaring off her shoulders and facing Ignaski. Her condescending glare didn't faze the gnarled features of Ignaski. She chose her words carefully, taking full responsibility.

"I was curious. It appears large enough to hold everyone, including your men. Look yourself, Ignaski."

"We will. Together. Master Tepes warned us about your trickery. Gather more torches! Enough for several days and food! Your journey, Voivode, has not come to an end. It has simply taken an undesirable turn."

For two days and more, a dozen guards and Ignaski followed Dracine down the sloping tube. It's not that Dracine knew the way, for she had only the chance to ride the very entrance. Ignaski used her to ride point without a torch. Dracine knew it was for his own protection. Should the floor give way or not be there at all, it would be Dracine to take the fall.

Surprisingly she found she could see quite well in the dark, perhaps better than with a torch. The ability was cold comfort when there was nowhere to run. There were no openings in the tube that would lead to somewhere else, just the ever-sloping passage. Towards the middle of what felt like the third day, Dracine's horse halted the endless clip-clopping over the rock floor.

"What is it? Why did you stop?" Ignaski always tried to talk down to her.

"Just ahead is caved in. The way is blocked."

"How can you know that? We cannot even see you! Do you think me a fool?"

"Yes Ignaski. Yes I do. Send one of your men. Surely you could risk one?"

"Razak! To the point!" There was a pause before a flare of another torch was lit, illuminating the group of men. The flame began to clip clop towards her.

"The way is blocked," barked Razak. "The rest can come forward."

More torches were ignited, fanning across the rubble of stone.

"As I told you, the end."

Ignaski's laugh was loud and ugly, echoing deafeningly off the walls of the tube. "I don't see an end. Do you, Razak?"

"Uh, no, no end in sight," he responded, unsure of himself, or the question.

"There you have it. No end in sight." Ignaski was smug.

"We must turn around. Surely there is another way to Borsa."

"Perhaps, but this is the way you will go, Voivode. We are not turning around. Your people have built roads where there were none. Found a way to survive away from the comforts of the coast. Surely they could move this little pile of rocks that gets in their way."

Dracine saw the immediate future. "But where does this go? Will it take us there?"

"To hell for all I know or care. You see, Voivode, I tire of this cattle drive, yet I gave my word to Lord Tepes I would see this thing through. So you see, my hands are tied. We must go on. Your only other option is over the cliff, which would be quicker and is my personal choice. But, since there is a way to make your suffering endure, we shall take it."

"I see," Dracine acknowledged.

"You, my dear Voivode, have not seen anything yet."

With that horse hooves began to clatter on the floor heading back the way they came.

***

A week went by while Skender's skin quit oozing and began to heal. Once again, more time was passing with Sechra still trapped in the oubliette. For whatever reason or why, they were being kept from accomplishing anything in the way of saving her. None of their goals had been met. Not that they had any, besides doing whatever it took. All Skender and Dino could do was survive and were doing a piss poor job of that.

Skender had been through many frigid and desperate winters during the course of his life on the mountains. Then it had been a simple matter of starving while trying to stay warm. A rather uneventful drama during which the only battles fought were within. Trying not to lose your mind was the big event during these times. Cooped up with a dozen other people along with their habits and smells for four or five months was enough to try any man's soul. If you didn't wind up killing each other, you'd make it through, or not.

But to be beaten and thwarted at every attempt to do anything was leaving them both crippled in more ways than one. Helplessness is not something that men get comfortable feeling. The funny/odd thing was that every injury was of their own making. The yeti thing that roamed the night had never once attacked or injured them directly. What it was or its purpose was still unknown, other than it seemed to be guarding the oubliette from intrusion.

Skender shot himself. Dino ruined his back, by himself. Skender dove back into the morphing trailer for the gun, ruining his skin. Each injury was one demoralizing setback after another. Stalling them. What Skender was beginning to realize was that these incidents were keeping them from doing anything. He remembered telling Dino when they first met about how doing nothing was the most important thing to do. Of course that sounds all well and good, but he knew that without the physical damage they would have done something. He was certain Dino would have been able to get one of the big rigs running, eventually bulldozing the structure back into the earth.

What they would have interrupted by doing such a thing was beyond his imagination. Sechra was still alive, or at least her consciousness was still functioning. This much Skender knew. How she could be alive after all this time was yet another mystery. Months had come and gone since the whole thing began. In another two, spring would be upon them. Then what? They could not leave their own version of an oubliette, surrounded as they were by three sides of death and one of hell.

A bucket was used for bodily waste. Each day Dino would take it out, tossing the contents from the safety of the entry into the stone death. As the shit flew across the line it changed to coprolite before hitting the ground. Dino hoped that one day it would just remain shit, but not today.

Four weeks into the forced relocation, food rationing began. There was less than either of them hoped for. In the rush to leave the trailer, much had been left behind. Water, they had plenty of. Neither man talked very much anymore. More often than not, the conversations consisted of 'uh huhs' and grunts. There simply wasn't anything to talk about that they hadn't already discussed in depth on previous occasions. Plus the conversations were always reduced to 'what we should've done.' It gets old. When they began accusing each other was when conversing stopped. It was the guilt of failing that ruined things. Now, living so close, they knew what the other was thinking.

It was eight weeks in when Skender pulled out the last of the vodka. "This is the last of it," Skender said solemnly.

"Of the Vodka? Bummer. What's for breakfast?"

"Of everything. We finished the food last night."

"Why didn't you tell me?" Dino was on his feet suddenly kicking through what little they had left. "There was more! I know there was more! What have you done with it?"

"Nothing, Dino, we stretched it as far as we could." Skender remained calm but it was going to get ugly.

Dino grabbed the first hard thing his hands could find in the dark. Grimy fingers wrapped around the cold steel barrel of the shotgun. "You lying fucking gypsy!"

Skender knew something was coming, just not what, when the butt of the gun slammed him hard in the temple. He tumbled from his mat into the small fire. Frayed fibers of his jacket caught flame instantly. Blood poured down his face into his eyes. He was slow to realize what was happening.

"That's right, mother fucker, burn! Burn in hell!"

"Wait, Dino. I haven't eaten in a week. I saved it for you," pleaded Skender.

"Liar." The gun came again, this time from the other direction, dealing Skender another vicious blow to the other side of his head. This knocked him out of the fire, smothering the burning jacket. Dino took the bottle and went outside. Skender lay unconscious, bleeding on the floor.

Hours, days later, Skender woke to the dark confines of the cave opening. He was alone. This he could sense before moving. His usual gift had failed him so often lately he was hesitant to rely on it. Skender moved one arm, carefully, then the other. When he felt ready, he pushed himself into a sitting position bracing for another hammer to the head. It didn't come, but nausea brought him to his knees as his head felt like it was spinning like a top. When the discomfort passed, Skender tried again to get vertical. This time he held it down.

The fire was out and ashes cold. Dino was nowhere to be seen. Skender stumbled to the tarp over the cave opening, pulling it aside. It had snowed over the last few days. Six inches of untrammeled fresh covered the ground and rear end of the truck. Beyond was a dark grey waste of stone. The fuscous monotone made it difficult to pick out different objects, as the grey seemed to camouflage everything.

Skender's head began to spin again seeing something off in the distance. "Oh God no!" he screamed running to edge of the safe limit. He dropped to his knees, tears running down his face and splashing off his pants. Twenty meters away was Dino with the bottle still in his hands. Skender fumbled with a scenario that was actually quite simple.

After hitting Skender the second time, Dino went out into the night and began drinking heavily. He was never a good drinker, having proved it many times with Skender in the trailer. He always drank too much too fast. More than once Skender had dragged him back into the trailer after he had passed out in his own frozen puke. Not this time. For a while the booze made Dino see what he had done to Skender all too clearly. Shortly thereafter guilt and shame rode his shoulders like a pack of monkeys. Unable to bear it, he found something else to blame and with bottle in one hand and shotgun in the other Dino chased after his demons.

Skender suddenly felt very alone. Looking about, his eye settled on the truck. He raised the back hatch to look inside, somehow hoping to find Dino inside ready to go. Crawling into the back, he began searching for anything he could use. A bag was stuffed under the back seat. It was food. Part of Dino's original supplies. Skender didn't care that it was stale and moldy, hell he would have eaten it if it were rotten. Cheese and a bottle of wine. The whole thing overwhelmed Skender. He stared out at the figurine he would have much rather shared it with. Skender sat there until the sun went down and the evening chill set in. It wasn't as cold as he had remembered. He took the remains of the feast and went back inside.

The weather held steady for the next two weeks. The food was gone except for one candy bar he was saving. Skender woke to the brilliance of the morning sun as a shaft of light entered the cave. The sun was moving north again. Spring was in the making. With it came a spark of hope that somehow everything would be okay. The spark did not catch flame. Stepping out of the opening in the sunshine slammed the painful reality, dousing the short-lived happiness. Skender could spot Dino clearly now and as far as he could see was nothing but the same dismal rock.

"Perhaps Dino had taken the wise way out," Skender said quietly, hoping he was wrong.

Skender was pulled in two directions. Half of him wanted to do something or at least try. The other said 'wait.' He thought of trying to hike out through the cave's tunnel. Sparing precious battery life, he made a foray into the tunnel. The walking wasn't bad but every step was a step up. After six hours he came to the landslide Dino had told him about. He panned the light over the mound of old bones that Dino had crashed through. Beneath the skeletons were shards of black volcanic glass. A few attempts at climbing the avalanche were rewarded with sliding down, cutting himself and his clothes to filthy ribbons and ending up amongst the many dead. Before leaving, he bound up the bleeders with pieces of shirt material.

'I had to try and do something,' he laughed morosely to himself on the way back to camp. His hands had taken the brunt of the fall. Once back in the sunshine, he examined the wounds. Nothing would need stitches, but he was utterly filthy and he needed to cleanse the cuts.

The cookstove gave him a couple gallons of lukewarm water before it died, too. Enough to bathe. The early afternoon sun was warm as he stripped. Looking down at himself he realized how much weight he had lost over the course of the winter. Twenty kilos and he looked like a scarecrow the blackbirds had attacked. 'Shit.'

The water felt good, and being clean even better. Once he taped himself up, there was clean underwear, socks and a tee. He felt like a new man, sort of. After washing some more clothes in the remaining water, he tossed the old into the forbidden zone. He turned, waiting for the sound of rocks to crash down. Instead there was a splash. Skender spun on heels, tossing the clean clothes over the line. The water fell wet onto the rock without turning to stone. Anxiousness crept up his spine, the urge to do something.

Instead he sat at the edge of the safe zone looking hard at the dividing line. Had it receded? Fresh sprouts of grass poked out along the border. Could it have? Using a small stick he stabbed in into the dirt at the edge to mark it. Skender did the same to the truck using a rock to scratch the paint where it met rock. There was nothing to do but wait.

Another week went by with no discernable change. Each day was a little warmer, a little brighter than the one before it. Skender remained in the cave, sleeping. His energy was sapped. Starving to death had something to do with it. He drank away his hunger, never once opening the candy bar for the relief it would bring. Something told him not to eat it yet. And he agreed. A few bites would not sate his hunger or end the malnutrition. It would, however, give him a boost should the need arise to actually do something.

The hunger insinuated itself into his dreams. There, he, Dino and Sechra sat a large table full with food. While the other two dove into the meat with a frenzy, Skender simply stared at the human thighbone on his plate. More bodies roasted at spits for the hungry trio while the chewed bones began to pile up on the floor. These were attacked by hordes of rats that bore their faces. Skender could look at the sight no longer. His jaws assaulted the leg before him. Soon he was screaming for more with bits of gristle and unctuous fats falling from his mouth.

Skender woke with the sound of his voice echoing in the confines of the cave. He stopped, shivering with the imagery of the dream. But the screaming did not stop. It came from outside the cave. He dashed to the opening tearing the curtain aside. Even though the sky was overcast, he winced painfully at the light he not seen for days before coming into focus. The stick. It now had a half-meter between it and the dead zone. The same with the scratch on the truck. It was moving back away from the cave.

The sound came from the direction of the oubliette. It was a scream unlike anything he had ever heard. It was as if the gates of hell opened, letting the cries of the damned come through. It became louder and soon Skender was clutching his hands over his ears to dampen the wailing.

He fell to the ground in agony as the pain ripped into his head. Blood leaked from his ears.

The earth itself was vibrating. It was the rock that was screaming. Then, with a terrifying screech, the cacophony crescendoed like two trains hitting one another and stopped, leaving Skender weeping in the dead silence.

Skender opened his eyes again. The sun shone brightly in an unblemished sky. Birds sang off in the distance as he watched in amazement. The rock was receding before his very eyes. Not quickly, mind you, but fast enough to see with the eye. He watched it for hours until starvation reasserted itself.

The next morning he was startled awake by more screaming. This time it was not his voice or that of the mountain. And it wasn't screaming but more laughing deliriously. It was Dino, lying on a field of fresh grass. Skender didn't think. He ran out to the mechanic, his hands searching his pockets as he went. Dino was aware of Skender's arrival and sat up. Skender, on the other hand, collapsed next to him. The effort of running tapped him. Adrenalin only buys you so much time.

Dino caught Skender on the way down and settled him into the grass. Dino's laugh dwindled along with his smile. Skender was almost dead. In the dying man's outstretched hand was a candy bar.

"I was saving it for you." Skender went unconscious.

Dino's smile returned. His time as part of the mountain changed him in ways he was just finding out. He took the bar and ripped the wrapper. One of the changes was he had been rejuvenated. He felt healthy and alive when he should be like Skender.

"Come on, Skender, open your mouth... yeah now here we go, bite this."

He cradled Skender while feeding him. At first the bites were small, barely nibbles. Minutes went by after the first couple of chews. He didn't have the strength to eat. By and by the sugar and chocolate, what little there was of it, went sparking through his system, flipping all kinds of switches. Five minutes later the sugar rush was on. Dino knew this surge of energy would be short lived. He pulled Skender to his feet, bent low, picking him up in the fireman's carry. Dino hefted Skender easily, carrying him back to the rig and dropped him in the passenger seat.

The mechanic did not look into the cave for supplies. There was nothing left. He hopped into the truck and turned the key. Once the glems were hot, he fired the diesel to life. Windows down, Dino put the truck in first gear and idled back to the trailer. Green, green, green, everywhere. When spring comes to the mountains it does so with a quiet fury of sorts. Sprouts burst from the earth after lying dormant the winter long. Everything that grew seemed in a rush to get the job done. In a week or two, the high mountain flowers would splash the scene with all the colors of the spectrum. But for now, green was enough.

Dino rolled quietly into camp. Only the clatter of the diesel's valves broke the silence. When they stopped it was the sound of birds instead. For the first time that Dino could remember he just stopped, listening to the sounds of the forest. "And I used to think the roar of a twelve cylinder Ferrari was sweet," he said to a marginally coherent Skender.

"Come on, my man, let's get you into the trailer and start some soup!"

For the next five days, all Skender did was sleep and eat. When Dino would go out, there was always something hot in the pot for Skender should he wake. It was after the second day that Dino felt comfortable enough to leave Skender for a while. He ambled about the parked vehicles before being drawn to the oubliette. He remembered the dismal grey sculptures of the rigs and surrounding forest. Now the parking lot was back to normal, sort of. Never had everything looked so distinct and beautiful, even the trucks glistened in the early light of dawn. The trail to the structure was almost manicured as it sparkled, alive and growing. Even the open area before the oubliette was groomed in a perfectly natural sort of way. The beauty was such that some time passed before he said to himself, 'what's wrong with this picture?'

The door to the oubliette was open. Dino sprinted to the opening. The object of the lesson was finally at hand. He froze at the threshold, steadying himself against the jamb. The full light of day was entering the doorway, illuminating the inside. It was not the smell that stopped him for there was none. Only the scent of fresh pine hung in the air. It was what he saw that froze him in his tracks. Inside was a giant ball of granite that was carved in deep and shallow relief. His eyes were captivated by its beauty and he had to pull his attention away to focus on Sechra. She sat before the sphere on the floor. Hard lines etched crow's feet at her eyes and smile lines cut deep across her cheeks. The shoulders were squared off, but relaxed. Her legs were crossed and her hands rested easily on her lap in what yogis would call the lotus position. Her hands appeared to be carefully holding something. Her eyes stared out benevolently with a slight smile upon her lips. She did not move. She was stone.

Dino dropped to the ground, stunned beyond belief. He simply stared into the oubliette unable to look away. He was not looking at Sechra, though tears still flowed from his eyes. It was the sphere that captured him. The stone almost glowed.

"It does," Skender said from behind him. "Sechra poured her life into it." Skender's voice did not jolt Dino out of his reverie, or rather meditation.

"Ya think?" Dino's response was calm.

"I know." Skender put out his hand to Dino and pulled him to his feet. "You go inside yet?"

"I got the feeling it was sacred ground and hesitated."

"Well then come on. We at least deserve to be the first to see it."

"You first."

Together they entered the place where no one exits. Dino took a cautious glance at the door, thinking they should chock it, then decided otherwise. 'Whatever it is, is over,' he thought.

"Or something is just beginning," Skender said circumnavigating the globe. After one loop around he continued. "Here, this is the beginning,"

"How do you know?"

"Just winging it, Dino, but I think I got it right. Son of a bitch!"

"What, what is it?"

"This is no less than a visual history of our people." Skender pulled a flashlight, "Let's read it."

And they did. The first of the eleven ellipses was the earliest, time wise, in the series. There were no actual written records of this time period. Sechra's time in the oubliette had opened up the ancestral memory to her conscious mind. She extracted pivotal moments and put them to stone.

The eye comfortably follows the images from one to the next in a flow of natural progression. Plus the carvings were easy to look at. The more you looked the more you saw.

The more you saw the more you looked.

There was a peculiar perspective at work on the sphere. It had an escheresque quality about it. When viewing from the left you perceived one aspect. Shift your juxtaposition to the right and you saw the same scene, yet it was not the same. Sechra captured a three dimensional effect in two dimensions. Computers do it, yet to have it done by hand and in stone was unique.

When looked at from above or below you were granted an even wilder explanation of imagery. Each perspective yielded another story or elaboration. In each there was pain and pleasure, sorrow and joy, failure and triumph. But mostly it captured the lives of the Romanian people. The images told a story in far more detail than words could ever hope to accomplish. The oubliette now felt more like a church than a place of the damned. Skender and Dino spoke not a word as they reverently inspected the art piece. Skender would point at different scenes with Dino acknowledging with grunts. There was no explanation necessary as the entire work was self-explanatory. You did not need to read and write. All you needed was sight. Failing that, the sense of touch would work just as well, since that was how she created it, blind. There was a twist in the tale told in stone that neither of the men could see nor imagine. In the years to come, as men came to study the sphere, they would not only see the emancipation of the Roma peoples, but they would also see the history of their own people carved into the rock. More than the story of one, it spoke for all of mankind.

Skender grew tired, not from the viewing, but from starvation. It would be several weeks before he felt back to normal.

"Come Dino, I have got to eat something and lie down for a while."

"But what about Sechra?" asked Dino.

"Say some small prayer of thanks for her. She gave her life so we might be free. We came to save her, instead she saved all of us."

"But we failed."

"No way, man. We did exactly what we were supposed to do."

"What – nothing?"

"Exactly. Now it is time for us to act. But first we eat."

Outside the open door, sitting innocuously in the grass were a pair of mountain climbing boots. The soles were worn flat and the leather dried, cracked, and worn through at the toes. A piece of paper stuck out of one boot. On the back was a note:

'Please return these to Skender Jr. and thank him for me. Thank you Skender and Dino. All my love, Sechra.'

The other side was a blank check, signed. In the memo spot was written, 'for the children's schooling.'

"She didn't forget," Skender said more to himself than Dino.

"Love never does," replied Dino, thinking the thought for the first time.

***

I t took weeks of preparation before the masses of people were finally herded into the lava tube. Guards were left at the entrance in case any of the townspeople decided to leave. More than a hundred torches lit the scene deep in the tunnel as the once spread-out group now crammed into the tube's confines. The smell of fear followed them deep into the bowels of the earth. Whips and chains kept the crowd moving. Those who fell in the darkness were left behind. Three days in, they came to the collapse of the ceiling.

Dracine sat with Oskar in the dark having their daily discussion.

"At least the dissent we have been going through has passed," intoned Oskar.

"No, Oskar, I fear not. They are just too afraid at the moment to cause any trouble. What do we do now?" Dracine was not above deferring to others when her knowledge failed.

"We will have to move it. I spoke with some masons earlier and they said we will need to reinforce the ceiling and walls or the tunnel will keep coming down."

"Can they do it?"

"They say yes. We have the manpower. It is just a matter of finding suitable packing to lock the stones together."

There was a disturbance nearby and both turned at the light, which was coming closer.

"Use this," came the ugly voice of Ignaski. A body was thrown at their feet, then another, and another. "They fall behind. At least now the wretches can be of use."

Oskar put his hand over Dracine's to stop her response, or at least slow it down.

"This appears to be an adequate resource," said Oskar sarcastically, "Can you get more?"

"As many as you need. Your people are dying like flies, but, should we run short, my men will make more available." Ignaski missed the sarcasm. What he lacked in humor was made up by the cruel nature of his being. "Start your vile work or die here where you stand. Cement is being made by the people in the rear. Begin!" He spurred his horse and rode back.

"We should, I suppose. Are your masons ready?"

"Standing nearby."

"Good. Then let them choose where to begin and clear the area of people. We should have enough hands for laborers."

"Fewer than you think, Dracine. They are weary from the road and hungry."

"We all are. Tell them the sooner we finish, the sooner we can get out of here."

"You should tell them. Many still follow you and will find the strength if they know you are with them."

"I am always with them. How could I not be?"

"The dark, Dracine. They cannot see you and we talk in whispers."

"Yes, yes. Thank you, Oskar."

"Always at your service."

"Why, Oskar?"

"Why what?"

"Why do you have faith in me? It is I that caused this, this nightmare."

"Why not? What you did for us on the coast has not been forgotten. You gave us life, a life we had only dreamed of. We prospered."

"I used and killed you for my own pleasure..."

"That was necessary for us to learn, strange as that may sound. The lure of gold and more would have turned us into a loathsome sort. Your cruelty broke the chains that bound us to that illusion. You earned the title Voivode as we earned our independence. We have all changed and for the better. We follow you because we would rather die free men than wear the yoke of the Draculs."

"I see. Where did you get your education, Oskar?"

"The Kcirbs, for most of us but me? University of Bucharest, class of 2222."

"What!" Dracine nearly shouted.

"I came before the revolution, saw it coming. I figured this was as good as anyplace to hide. After that life just kind of took over. I like it here."

"I didn't think anyone else knew how."

"You are not the only one who studied such things."

"Are there others?"

"A few perhaps, but they guard their secret. You should rally the people now and I will talk with the masons. They have been making a plan."

"One thing, Oskar," Dracine began, "How do you like it now?"

"Life takes its course, what are you going to do?" He shrugged lightly and turned to leave. Oskar was one of those people who made the best of everything.

With more torches lit, the crowd was pushed back away from the cave in. The able-bodied were brought to the forefront and work began. Unfortunately there were few with enough left in them to accomplish the task. Stones were moved and sorted according to size. Even with more torches, the lighting was awfully dim. Every scream that was not caused by the minions of Tepes was a crushed foot or mangled digits caused by mishandling the rocks in the dark. Soon they would be working by feel alone. Perhaps it was best this way for the masons and the greater horde.

Bodies, or parts of them, were placed between the courses of the stone walls and ceiling. A crude cement, using the blood and bodily juices of the damned to moisten the dust, was then applied before new rocks were set, crushing the bodies and locking the stones in place. In the darkness, it was sometimes impossible to tell the dead from the nearly dead. The screams of the human packing material would then echo through the length of the tube. More often than not, Dracine and Oskar were thankful for the lack of decent lighting. The people would have panicked and stampeded the entrance if they knew what they were creating, and then only to be cut down by a phalanx of Tepes' troupes.

Her logic was twisted by their situation. To fight back would mean certain death. These were farmers and merchants for the most part. Those who did work with their hands were tradesmen not soldiers. They would be slaughtered, and though Ignaski would rather expedite his mission this way, his fear of not following the dark lord's orders kept his personal desire at bay.

Only by going forward could they possibly hope to survive. 'If but a few make it, we will have won.' Dracine told herself this lie every day to keep from going insane, or back on the drugs. It would not be fitting that she drift away in dreams while her people died at her feet.

The work went slow, too slow. Piles of decomposing bodies were waiting for use. The bodies brought rats by the thousands, feasting on the moist, rotting flesh. When the workman would call it for the day, what few torches that were lit were doused to save them for the next day. This was the time Dracine and Oskar would go to work.

As mentioned, Dracine could see well in the blackness. She and Oskar would work during the sleep period setting stones while the workmen slept.

She learned the trade by watching the masons at work, at first, followed by a short but determined internship. They shared their knowledge freely with the Voivode, for they too remembered prospering under her rule, and had seen her working hard to save 'her people.' They respected Dracine for her actions, not her bloodline.

Long story, a little shorter, Dracine and Oskar set all the stones in the ceiling. This task would have been impossible for the masons without scaffolding. This high in the mountains, there was little wood suitable for such a thing and Ignaski would let no one leave to procure more back down the mountainside. "Use the dead," he told Dracine.

Instead Dracine used her will. Since entering the cave Dracine had not called on Atoli for her assistance. They were living at the edge as it was and surely should Atoli give of herself she would die. She would not become a victim of the trek, the damned, or of Dracine's dark desire.

At the end of another endless night setting stones, Dracine climbed down from the ceiling. "That's the last of it, Oskar. The workmen can finish it now." Dracine collapsed at Oskar's feet. Only when he picked her up did Oskar realize how wasted she was. The darkness had kept him from seeing her well, but the weight of her empty body told the stories his eyes could not.

Oskar carried Dracine to her encampment where Atoli, Moira and the rest of her personal staff waited. He laid her carefully on the soiled wool bed rest. The same that had given her comfort for endless dreaming now held her dying body. Atoli was the first, then one by one they all offered what they had to restore a person they loved.

"No," said Oskar. "She will not take what little we all have. If you wish to help gather the rats."

"God no," cried Atoli. "I give it freely."

"She would not, dear Atoli. This is the only way until we are free again."

No one argued, mostly because they were too weak for the effort. Then again they also understood.

The Moira's took to the task with uncommon ease. The younger rallied the Atoli children to capture as many rats as they could. Trapping the critters was not hard and anyone that saw the children would assume the magistrate's immediate circle was now consuming them to survive. A few laughed at the depths the Voivode had been reduced to. These, and there were more than a few, quietly packed their things and moved to the rear of the assembly to be closer to Tepes' guard.

In the darkness mother Moira would, one at a time, grab a rat and slice its throat and allow the dribbling blood to drain into the slack jaw of Dracine until the little death rattle shook the vermin. Unfortunately the life force of a rat is slim picking for one such Dracul. The weak crimson juice was merely staving off starvation for a later date.

Oskar picked up the slack. One thing they never lacked for was bodies for setting the rocks in place. Another was suffering. No, there was no lack of that either. The slow burn of starvation and privation was in full bloom.

During the trek to this damnable place, they at least had the outside, a sky above them and stunning vistas. Only the heart saw these things while they struggled to survive on the mountain slopes. It was enough to keep them going and give hope even as whips tore the skin from their backs in the relentless drive north. Now that was gone, the darkness penetrated the very souls, extinguishing the light that somehow burns within us all.

Oskar was the only bright spot amid the dying. He saw clearly what was happening. Only death awaited them. There would be no salvation. Ignaski showed his ugly face on a daily basis to reinforce this thought as well as to check on progress. In a few days, the work would be complete.

"Where is your Voivode now?" Ignaski sneered, looking down on Oskar from his saddle.

"She dies," Oskar said quietly.

"Yes, but she does not die, ehh, Oskar? I hear she eats rats now."

"Dracine would not take from her people what they need to survive."

"She is a fool. You will all die."

"Dracine knows. It is the principle of the matter."

"The dying always hold onto their principles, as if it would somehow change things. Now prepare your people to leave."

"The walls are not done."

"They are done enough. The masons can finish and follow behind. Tomorrow morning you move or die."

Oskar returned to the magistrate's group. Atoli sat in the darkness cradling Dracine's head in her lap. Moira was cutting strips of dried lamb to pass around. Young Moira and the Atoli kids had just returned from rat hunting. No one talked. The children eyed the lamb hungrily while Atoli stroked Dracine's hair. Moira paused in her cutting.

"What is it, Oskar? What did that bastard say to you?"

"Tomorrow we die."

***

Sechra gave her all in the unforgiving minute that was finishing the sphere. The polishing was done. All that remained was to wash the sculpture of unwanted dust and residue. There was no water. As Sechra felt over the work one last time, her tears began to flow, for her fingers saw distinctly the beauty of what had been created. From her eyes, her life flowed over the rock surface, rinsing away the dust and accumulated sweat, while imbuing the sphere with life, her life. Sechra caressed the rock once more and climbed down. Her work was done. There was however one or two more things.

As her feet touched the floor of the oubliette, a screeching of hinges was heard as the hatch in the floor began to tilt up. As it rose through the opening, Sechra sat in front of the sculpture facing the door and began to unlace her boots, ignoring its presence.

"I see you have finished. Let us take a look at what you have made of me."

Another set of hinges began screaming in futile resistance. Slowly, loudly, a crack of light speared into the oubliette. There was a garbled, rasping intake of breath. It was not Sechra. A faint "no, no," could be heard with the exhalation. As the door opened further and light filled the dark space the small "no's," became a growl that set the ground to shaking.

The growl turned to howl, "NOOOOOOOOOOOOOOOOOOO!"

As it screamed, all hell began to break loose. The earth rocked violently, snapping rocken trees, and sending boulders crashing down the mountainside. Outside, through the open door, Sechra could see the waves of power rippling across the landscape. She began to crawl towards the door and out, taking the boots with her. Just outside the doorway Sechra set the boots down and stuffed a piece of paper in them that she had written on long ago.

A large, clawed, black, hand reached out from the oubliette to grab hold of Sechra's head. It yanked her back into the four walls slamming her hard against the sculpture.

"What have you done?" it shrieked, threatening to blow the roof off.

"I have done as you asked, as we agreed. I have kept my word." Sechra resumed her seated position facing the door. Her palms were open upon her lap.

"This is not what we agreed upon. I wanted you to sculpt me!"

"I could not create what you imagine yourself to be. Have you never seen what you look like?"

The earth slowed in its violent upheaval, settling down as it began to understand.

"NO, NO, NO, no, no, no, no, no, no, no, no, no, no, no, no, no, no, no, no, no, help me."

It crawled into Sechra's open hands. Like a lotus blossom closing for the night, her hands wrapped gently around the thing.

"I will."

Sechra stared out the door of the oubliette. The distant landscape was turning green as was a single leaf on the tree nearest her. She smiled and the sculpture seemed to glow.

***

D racine opened her eyes to the sound of the women packing up what few items the entourage had left. Dracine's horse was saddled and waiting. The older Atoli boy held the reigns.

"It is time, Dracine. Can you stand?" Oskar reached out his hand to her supine form.

Dracine pushed herself into a sitting position, steadying herself for a moment as the dark world swirled around her. "Where is Ignaski?"

"Having a meeting with his captains. The rest of his men are in the rear, pushing the people towards us. They will be upon us in a very short while. I suggest we lead them on rather than be forced."

"You are right, Oskar." Dracine fought her way to her feet, declining Oskar's assistance. Gathering her wits, she quietly called her group to assemble.

"All of you have been my family for as long as I can remember. You remained loyal though you had no good reason to. You have shown me what it is like to truly live, and for that I will ever be in your debt. Thank you." Dracine's eyes filled with tears.

"We followed because we love you, Dracine. There was always a goodness in you, a thing so sadly lacking in of those in power. You are our Voivode." Though said by the older Moira, all concurred with nods and body language. Dracine took this moment, for her energy was passing quickly, to deeply hug each person of her group. She stayed with Atoli the longest.

"I fear all the love in the world will not get us through this day. I am sorry, Oskar. Will you help me mount?"

A row of bright torches could be seen coming around a corner that was far back in the tunnel. Suddenly the crowd was being pushed forward toward Dracine. Atoli, the Moira's and all the rest of Dracine's personal staff stepped forward as one into the blackness that beckoned their death.

No torches were given to light the way. Each step was a step into the unknown. Weeks before, Ignaski and some of his men had ridden past the construction zone to explore the depths of the tunnel. They returned less than a day later and fewer riders than when they started. No information was shared. The wicked laughter of Ignaski and his men as they rode through was enough to detail the events of the near future.

Three hours of walking and Dracine's horse halted whinnying. She could see the roadway ended, but not in another cave-in. Dracine hesitated but a moment before lightly tapping her mount with her heels. A second later she was gone. The road dropped away into a near shear cliff carpeted with volcanic glass. The rest of the group took hands with each other and stepped off, in silence.

The screaming began shortly after as the people began to pour over the cliff in one continuous mass. Dracine's followers were directly behind her. Their bodies shredded by the glass as they tumbled down the escarpment. More bodies and more and more and more. By the time her dissenters were driven over the drop off, they landed on a new carpet of fresh bodies, saving them from becoming randomly flayed. They survived. The last over were the masons. Once their dark work was complete they had nothing left to live for and thus no force was required for them to take the leap. They lived, too.

Dracine, too, had survived the fall. She was virtually unrecognizable, as much of her skin had been peeled away by the shards of black volcanic glass. It was her ring, her only real form of identification. The survivors left the tunnel to find themselves on a valley floor where an ancient gypsy encampment once stood. There also was the massive sphere that covered the access to the pits below that once held an abomination. It didn't take long for the mob to determine this was an unholy sight and that Dracine should be imprisoned there.

The masons were forced by mob pressure to build a structure over the sphere to house the damned. While building the impenetrable oubliette they realized there was a cave beneath the ball, but no way to move the ball. Instead they cut an access hole into the void below along with a massive hatch to recover the opening. No sooner than the hatch was finished, Dracine was dragged to the opening. Without ceremony she was thrown into the pit and the hatch dropped closed. The lifting eyes were then removed so it could never be opened again.

EPILOGUE

When the door to the oubliette opened, a veil was lifted from the eyes of men. The worldwide epidemic of madness subsided. Over night, the awe and amazement of Sechra's sculptures of the damned evaporated. The exhibit closed and the entire installation was returned to Romania C.O.D. The eleven pieces were then stored away in a warehouse and forgotten about.

Skender and Dino finished their meal. Though there was no longer an impending doom threatening them, there were still tasks to finish. Dino climbed to the top of the trailer and tuned on his cell phone. Four bars held solid as he speed dialed Riana's number.

"Riana, this is Dino."

"My God, where have you been?"

"Where I was needed." Dino was cold in emotion and was out of practice when it came to talking on a phone. "We need a chopper sent into the mountains where Skender and I are. I am texting the coordinates now."

"What's this all about?"

"Sechra. Get here as soon as you can. The passes are clear and snow all but gone." He hung up. Dino did not want to get involved in a conversation that he knew very little about. His phone lit up again moments later. Dino turned off the ringer. He just didn't have the words for it.

Skender was packing his motorcycle when Dino climbed down.

"Why don't you take Sechra's bike, Skender? She won't be riding it anymore."

"I guess not." Skender didn't take offense at Dino's blunt remark. Their experience had put them way beyond that.

"You've earned it, besides you have patients to care for. No doubt it will help."

The two men stood there staring at each other's emaciated bodies. It's a hard thing for men to express their love for one another. Without words that was exactly what they were doing.

When the message was complete, Dino broke the silence. "I'll transfer the fuel and will have her ready when you get back with the rest of your stuff."

The BMW G's 1200 was idling when Skender returned. Dino had tuned the bike, adjusted the suspension for Skender's bigger body and washed it.

The goodbye was short. A solid handshake.

"Thank you, Skender."

"Thank you, Dino.

With a slight rev of the engine the bike rolled away from oubliette and into the future.

Dino returned to the trailer. He would not be going anywhere. More was going to be done than building a few schools for the underprivileged. The road would be built joining the mountains with the coast. This location would be a destination for travelers and archaeologists for generations to come.

Riana arrived by helicopter two days later with an entourage of doctors, guns and lawyers. She was greeted by a haggard and wasted Dino. His face told the tale of the last few months.

"Get the doctor, quick!"

Dino waved the medic away. "Come with me," he said politely, "alone."

Riana hesitated, looking over her shoulder at the men in the chopper, before reassuring herself by patting her pocket. Inside was the nine-millimeter semi-auto Jake had given her years ago. She waved her people to stay.

Dino walked slowly. 'Apparently there is no rush,' she mused to herself. They wandered through the deserted work yard. The scene was self-explanatory. Only when they entered the trail to the oubliette did Riana express concern.

"Where are we going, Dino?"

"To see Sechra."

"What the hell is going on, Dino? You look like a speed freak. Are you on dope or something?"

"No and you will see. I will tell my story afterwards if you feel it is needed."

He kept on walking while Riana shook off the weirds. Before long, the trail opened up and the sky shone through. The oubliette, though dominating the area, almost seemed not to exist. Dino now took her hand and led Riana to the opening. Her gasp was small before she dropped to her knees. Not in reverence but to behold Sechra. Every detail was perfect including the teardrop that formed at her eye. Riana reached out to touch it. Tears of stone, yet her finger came away wet and salty.

It was then she felt a pounding on the floor. Dino was standing quietly in the grass giving Riana space. He was not tapping his foot.

"Dino come here. Can you feel this?" she pulled Dino's hands and put them on the floor.

"Someone is down there!" Riana pushed the panic button on the phone. Almost immediately her security guards were on them.

"Get some tools! We have to open this hatch…"

Just then rusted steel began to screech and a portion of the floor began to tilt up.

"Help me." The words came out of the darkness beneath the hatch.

Dino was first at it, jamming his fingers into the widening gap, pulling up with all he had to give. Then Riana and her guards added to the effort. A bloody hand escaped from the depths followed by a bloody everything else. The hatch closed with a resounding slam, leaving a woman in a growing pool of blood.

"Get her to the chopper! What was that, Dino?"

"I don't know, but then I've gotten used to the strange lately."

"What is this place?"

"An oubliette. A sort of death row where the inmates just get forgotten about."

"I've never seen one."

"Well now you have," Dino responded with less than what one would consider the right amount of respect.

Her hand was quick and would have left a red welt had it met with Dino's cheek. Instead one flayed hand caught it and another smacked Riana hard across the face, leaving a smear of red. Dracine grabbed Riana's hair and forced her to see the sphere.

"Have you really forgotten what is important, child?" Dracine scolded through shredded lips. Riana stared deeply into the relief carvings. "These are the people that voted you into office. The people you chose to serve. They are the backbone of this country, yet you are ashamed of them. Because they are poor, uneducated? These people bore the worst in order to survive, yet did not complain. Without them there would be no Voivode and those that held the title were and are not worthy of it. A few, however, were. It is up to you to choose the path of righteousness or follow the money."

By now Riana's guards were all over Dracine. At first she shrugged them like flies. After a few jolts from a stun gun, however, she found herself unable to stand and submitted. Riana missed the altercation, absorbed as she was with the sphere. The sculpture attracted her full attention, but without the morbid thoughts that came with Sechra's other works. It was a thing of great beauty. You did not so much want to reach out and touch it as the sculpture reached out to the viewer and touched you. Before long, tears rolled down Riana's cheeks.

While studying the stone, Riana received hints of just who it was that came from beneath the oubliette. The woman was seen during the dark ages of the third panel then again at the end. It was Karuna!

Riana spun around, dropping to her knees beside her mother. "Oh god, Karuna, what has happened? How did you..."

Dracine looked up through swollen eyes, her face lacerated to the bone leaving little to recognize, but Riana saw through it.

"Riana, Karuna no longer exists. She is me. I am her. We are Dracine."

"But how and what happened to you?"

"Stranger things by far have happened in this world as you should well know. Karuna came to me through the mosaics in order to help rectify the current events in your world. To do that, she melded with my consciousness and we became one."

"Can we separate you again?"

"No. We will die together and by the looks of things, that time is not far." Dracine scanned her shredded skin. Crimson, black blood flowed freely from every wound. "Oh my dear Riana, we have come a long way together, but I fear my journey with you is now at an end. I can only hope you still have the courage."

A long blood-filled hug ensued. "I love you, dear child." Dracine closed her eyes.

Dino paused long enough for Riana to get a grip.

"You should call whoever she was close to. She doesn't have long."

Riana's normal response would have been to slap him for the intrusion or at very least verbally rip him a new one. Instead, she nodded her head.

"Yes, yes, thank you Dino. There are still a few who remember." To the doctors she said, "Clean her up and make her as comfortable as possible. She has a DNR (Do Not Resuscitate) and is adamant about it. Please, now."

It was the nature of the request that got the med staff moving. Riana had been polite. They acted out of love, rather than fulfilling the demands of their employer. All the first-class hospitals that serviced the very rich could not have done a better job. To die in the shade cast by the oubliette is far better than to die in the darkness of its interior. Dracine slipped into what a doctor would call a coma. When in fact Dracine went into waiting mode, the heart slows, breathing all but stops, and the body shuts down; a form of temporary hibernation, and waited.

Riana was busy documenting the sculpture, Sechra, and the oubliette when Dino passed by.

"Dino, you have a minute?"

"Sure, Riana, 'sup?"

"What happened up here?"

Dino thought for moment before replying. "Nothing."

"Very Zen of you, Dino, but something must have happened?"

"Only when we acted did shit happen. Skender could probably explain it better than I. Once Sechra was inside, our job was to make sure nothing interrupted her work, and that meant doing nothing."

"How could you do nothing?" Riana's ire was itching to be worked up, but for reasons that to this day cannot be explained, she remained calm.

"That dear, Riana, was the rub. Sometimes doing nothing is harder than you think. Every time we conspired against the will of the universe, she kicked our asses."

Riana looked him over, then eyed the surroundings, seeing the evidence of failed efforts. "A small understatement. No doubt you conspired a lot."

"We were both a little slow on the uptake."

They both laughed lightly with Dino shrugging his shoulders and shaking his head.

***

So what happened to everyone else, you might ask? Well, I'll tell ya. In order as they come to mind.

Karuna now lives the dream of death. Jake and Johnny flew in from Baja. A chopper, flown by their old friend Yuri, took them into the mountains for another pickup before heading to the oubliette. An older Lacirot stepped in with his family. Within the silence, behooving a wake, there was a lot being said. The looks between the men were long, leaving the eyes moist, but no tears. Yuri, an ever-aware pilot, made the flight short and fast, giving the kids some bragging rights. All the men aboard the chopper were legends in their own time and the children knew the stories of their strength and heroism.

Jake played it up to the kids just a little. It was his way of lightening the load. So he played the good 'bad guy' letting eager eyes catch glimpses of the guns he wore, and being super cool with the eyebrows and chin. They held his hands departing the chopper that landed in the open area around the oubliette. Jake had bolstered their bravery, as they now did his. At a tent off to the side stood Riana, smoking a cigarette.

"I thought you quit these," Jake inquired giving her a hug without asking permission. "Got another?"

Riana fished out another, handing it to Jake before facing the faces in the dim light of the forest. "Thank you all for coming on such short notice..."

Jake interrupted, "Got a light?" Once it was lit he went on. "Come on, Riana, we're not the press corp. We are your friends, remember? I'm just glad you called. There was nothing coming in through the radar. You, Johnny?"

"Nah," Johnny was going to say something else, but glanced at the kids first. "Is there some place I can have a little privacy?"

Jake pantomimed someone shooting up while rolling his eyes. Riana was never slow on the uptake.

"My tent is over by the chopper." She smiled, stepped over to the tall Italian giving him a hug.

To Riana he replied, "Merci" and to the rest of us, "Ciao."

"Jake, you should go in first. We don't know how long she has."

"Yeah, but she probably does. It's her choice after all." Jake slid the zipper open and slipped inside.

Karuna lied unconscious on the cot as he pulled up a chair. Jake lifted the gauze that covered her face to keep the flies off. Her destroyed face did not repel him. Jake saw through the blood and bandages as he slipped his hands beneath hers. Within moments Karuna's eyes began to roll around under the lids. The eyes opened slowly like someone coming out of a deep mental fog. When recognition took place, a smile stretched stitches and tearing bandages.

Jake smiled back. There wasn't long now and he knew it with her touch.

"You want? I got," he said pulling a vial and syringe from his coat pocket. There was a touch of madness in the smile, just a touch.

"No, Jake, we've been there and done that."

"That we have. That we have. Is there anything you need me to finish up? Lawyers, your estate...?"

"Yeah right, you dealing with my lawyers. That would be something worth living to see." Karuna laughed before going quiet.

"I took care of everything when I left. Thank you though."

"So this is it, huh?"

"Yes, Jake, it is. Kind of anticlimactic, ya think?"

"Yeah. You know I love you."

"You have a long way to go, Jake, but just for now, hold my hand. You will be the last thing I see or feel." Karuna closed her eyes, a breath away from dying.

Jake leaned in close, inhaling her final breath and held it. Minutes went by before a strong exhalation followed by another intake. Some small part of his self hoped to be taken away on her final breath. It was not to be. Life goes on. Shit.

Johnny poked his head through the tent flap a moment after Jake's moment was getting that uncomfortable feeling. Jake looked up seeing his old friend with three loaded syringes.

'The guy has excellent timing,' thought Jake. "You're back quick." Jake had given Johnny an hour at least before he'd show again.

"Not quick enough. Made one special for her."

"She appreciates the thought. Got one for me?"

"Sure. Make it quick. We have no business here."

"What?"

"She has passed. There is no place for us during these important times of birth and death."

"I thought just this once the rules wouldn't apply."

"Yeah, me too, but it's not to be, so let's just leave quietly okay?"

Jake was finishing up his hit and thusly preoccupied for a moment. It's never a good idea to be distracted with a point in your arm.

"Okay?" Johnny repeated as he put the works away.

"Yeah, yeah, I'm good. Okay."

They both took a deep breath and stepped into reality.

"You guys really need to be more discreet." Riana waved her hand at the tent. Lit from the inside, the fuscous early evening made the tent perfect for shadow puppets.

"I suppose," Jake mumbled as he hugged her.

He and Johnny made the round of hugs before leaving the presence of men. Johnny left a note for Yuri, the chopper pilot. Jake and Johnny waited until the night was full on before leaping into the prevailing breeze to warmer climes. There were waves somewhere.

Riana returned to her life in politics. Something had changed in her heart. There was no longer a need for the hard line. A softer approach with communication and understanding would take the forefront. The appeals from the poor and needy all over the country rose to the top of the list. There were political and corporate battles to be fought against the new agenda. They would fail, but not through the use of an iron fist, but common sense and compassion. Romania will be the first such country to find a balance between want and need, becoming a blueprint for others who dream such radical thoughts.

Frederick Cezar bemoaned the loss of the Kcirb account. He was young as yet and had not been entirely foolish with his monies. There are other artists and he had a name in the biz now. Life would be good to Fred, for he never really did anything wrong.

Thora Wozniac, however, would spend eternity within the confines of the outhouse sculpture. Her own personal hell and it smelled like it. You know how after smelling something for a while you kind of get used to it? Not for Thora. Each moment was filled with the fresh foul odor of excrement and the terror of discovering where she was. Eternity was just beginning.

Skender found himself busier than he had ever been. A couple of hippie interns arrived in a van shortly after his return. Together, they had what it would take to service the people until better was available. Before leaving the deep mountains, he had talked with Dino about the blank check stuffed in the boot.

"What should I do with this?"

"Well don't make it out for some stupid small amount to be polite. Her estate would stagger you. No really, what I think she means is her estate is yours. That is why it is blank. It'll give you a hospital out here and schools. Real stuff, not the crap they dish out to the third world. And enough left over to pay the bills for the next hundred years. How's that sound?"

"Too good to be true."

"Maybe so, but get used to the idea. She is Kcirb after all."

"Yes she is, yes she is."

With more help, he was able to initiate and bankroll a beginning, while attending to the folk farthest off the maps. Sechra's bike was busy creating a legend of its own.

Dino stayed on in the deep mountains. He was convinced a roadway needed to be developed. Not only to this site. The site would be a hub with offshoots that would go deeper into the mountains. Not for development, mind you, no logging, strip malls, casinos, or industry, rather so the locals had better access to modern services that would otherwise be unavailable. It would be their choice whether to use it or not, but at least there was the choice. Having actually been part of the mountain, he now realized he had always been a part of her as were all the peoples of Romania and her neighbors. They only now were beginning to realize it. He would spend the rest of his life uniting the country with a system of highways and roads.

Ahmed brought himself to the present in a desperate attempt to save his life with modern medicine. Unfortunately the crude impaling had ruined too many vital organs in the process. With no identification, he was labeled a John Doe and buried in a mass grave for the poor.

And Sechra? She resides within the sculpted sphere, seated in the lotus position. In her hands she holds the balance between light and dark, good and evil, black and white. It gives her life and she it. Only time will tell how long this will last, but for now there is peace.

The early years of john g rees' life were spent in a funeral home in Indiana, his father, the mortician and his mother, the makeup artist. His parents also operated the local ambulance service. Fertile ground, huh?

Crossing the country and landing in Hawaii, he was happily employed in many different jobs that wreaked havoc with his body, enjoying them all thoroughly.

From contractor and painter to welder above and below water, rees' varied experiences lay full a vast storeroom for his vivid imagination. It all just simmered inside him, until too much death created the need for release. And he found it, suddenly, in writing.

john g rees lives on the Island of Hawaii, in the middle of nowhere. He hopes it stays that way.

You can check out his website at:
www.blackwaterbooks.com